1001 Dark Nights
Compilation 33

1001 Dark Nights Compilation 33

Four Novellas
By
Rebecca Zanetti
Laurelin Paige
Heather Graham
and
Kristen Ashley

1001 DARK NIGHTS
PRESS

1001 Dark Nights: Compilation 33
ISBN 978-1-970077-82-7

Published by Evil Eye Concepts, Incorporated

Sign up for the 1001 Dark Nights Newsletter
and be entered to win a Tiffany Key necklace.

There's a contest every month!

Go to www.1001DarkNights.com to subscribe.

As a bonus, all subscribers can download FIVE FREE exclusive books!

Table of Contents

One Thousand and One Dark Nights

Once upon a time, in the future…

I was a student fascinated with stories and learning. I studied philosophy, poetry, history, the occult, and the art and science of love and magic. I had a vast library at my father's home and collected thousands of volumes of fantastic tales.

I learned all about ancient races and bygone times. About myths and legends and dreams of all people through the millennium. And the more I read the stronger my imagination grew until I discovered that I was able to travel into the stories... to actually become part of them.

I wish I could say that I listened to my teacher and respected my gift, as I ought to have. If I had, I would not be telling you this tale now.
But I was foolhardy and confused, showing off with bravery.

One afternoon, curious about the myth of the Arabian Nights, I traveled back to ancient Persia to see for myself if it was true that every day Shahryar (Persian: شهریار, "king") married a new virgin, and then sent yesterday's wife to be beheaded. It was written and I had read, that by the time he met Scheherazade, the vizier's daughter, he'd killed one thousand women.

Something went wrong with my efforts. I arrived in the midst of the story and somehow exchanged places with Scheherazade – a phenomena that had never occurred before and that still to this day, I cannot explain.

Now I am trapped in that ancient past. I have taken on Scheherazade's life and the only way I can protect myself and stay alive is to do what she did to protect herself and stay alive.

Every night the King calls for me and listens as I spin tales. And when the evening ends and dawn breaks, I stop at a point that leaves him breathless and yearning for more. And so the King spares my life for one more day, so that he might hear the rest of my dark tale.

As soon as I finish a story... I begin a new one... like the one that you, dear reader, have before you now.

Vixen
A Dark Protectors/Rebels Novella
By Rebecca Zanetti

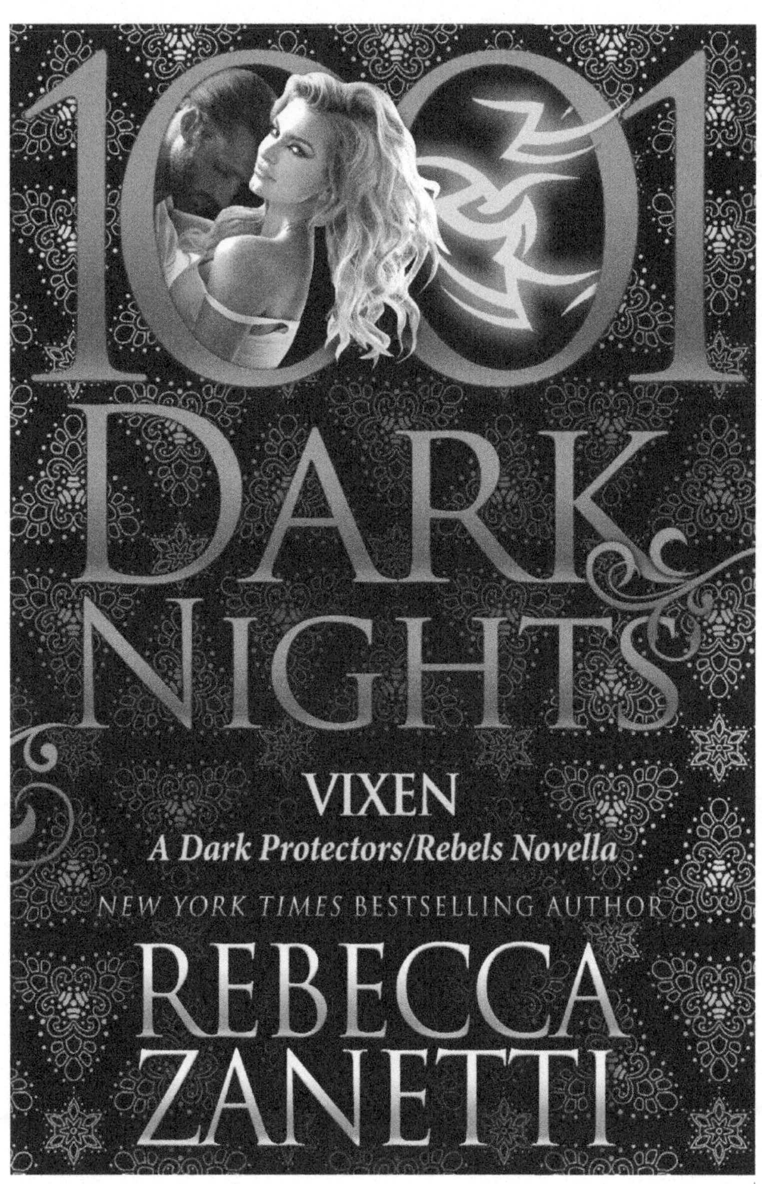

Acknowledgments from the Author

A huge thank you to Liz Berry, MJ Rose, and Jillian Stein for banding together this amazing group of authors who have become such good friends. It's nice to know that we're not alone with all of the voices and characters in our heads. 2020 hasn't been the year we all hoped it would be, across the world, but we've had each other to text, call, and Zoom, and I think that has made a difference for so many of us.

Thanks also to the entire 1001 Dark Night team: Kimberly Guidroz, Kasi Alexander, Asha Hossain, and Jenn Watson from Social Butterfly. Also thanks to Anissa Beatty and the entire FB Rebecca's Rebels Street Team for the support!

Finally, a huge thank you to my family, Big Tone, Gabe, and Karlina for the support and laughs. I love you three.

Chapter 1

Robbing a bank shouldn't take this much work.

Especially since said bank was in the middle of a podunk town in the middle of freaking nowhere. Tabitha Rusko stepped out of her souped-up BMW and into the darkness of night, having waited too many days for a cloudy evening. The moon over this part of the world was often over-bright, and it had taken forever for stormy weather to finally arrive.

As a demonness, she should be able to control the weather, darn it. Thunder growled across the sky as if in perfect agreement.

She tugged a black rope from the back seat and shut her door, winding the heavy nylon around her shoulder. Then she fetched the grappling hook from the trunk along with the compact drill.

This was ridiculous.

She took a deep breath and ran across the quiet street toward the silent building.

"Going somewhere?" a deep voice asked.

She jumped and bit back a yelp, swinging around to make out a figure leaning against a maple tree by the front door of the bank. Oh, crap. "Detective O'Connell," she breathed, her heartbeat ramming into a cadence that might kill her. "What are you doing here?" There was no way he'd followed her, because she'd driven all over the town to make sure she was clear. This was a bank robbery, for Pete's sake.

He pushed off from the tree, striding in the casual lope that screamed bad boy sexy—even for a human. "I had the oddest feeling you were up to something after seeing you drive by this bank so many times the last week, and considering you desperately want the recording I have secured inside, I went with my instincts." He reached her, and his unique scent of smoked honey wafted her way.

That smell had chased her through dreams until she could finally identify it. Why it was so blatantly masculine, she'd never understand. "You've been watching me? Stalking me?" When all else fails, attack.

"No. My office is just down the street," he said, his tone dry. He wore a dark T-shirt and faded jeans with a gun strapped to his thigh and a badge at his belt. He was about six-two with thick brown hair, matching beard, and blue eyes that seemed to see through her without much effort.

If she didn't know better, she'd think he was something beyond human. But he wasn't. Even now, she could sense the illness in him. One he thought he could hide. Yet another thing that had kept her up at night. "I'm not doing anything wrong."

He looked down at her rope, drill, and grappling hook. "Attempted robbery of a bank is a felony."

"I haven't attempted anything." She kept her feet on the sidewalk. "I'm not even on the bank's property." Yet. Of course, the cop knew that fact. Why had he stopped her before she'd at least trespassed? He seemed to rescue everyone, or rather, every woman around who needed help. "Do you keep a bunch of dogs and cats, too?" she blurted before she could help herself.

He cocked his head to the side. "Two dogs and no cats. Okay, one cat, but he just stops by when the weather is bad or he's really hungry." Evan stuck his hand in his jeans pocket. "Maybe two cats."

The guy was a natural rescuer. Also a pain in the butt. "If you're such a great guy, why won't you give me that recording you have of me?" She fluttered her eyelashes in an age-old move.

He sighed and took her arm, his grip firm. "I promise you'll get the video the second you graduate from anger management. You have to understand that you could've killed those guys, and while they probably deserved it for harassing you, I can't just let you off the hook. You do seem to have anger issues."

Oh, he had no idea. She'd been innocently minding her own business and the punks had accosted her, so she'd kicked their butts. It was too bad the whole situation had been caught on camera, and since one of the kids was the sheriff's son, she had been charged. Evan had helped her, though. She dug in her heels and stopped them both.

He stiffened and turned to face her. "How are you so strong?" Releasing her, he rubbed the back of his neck. "Or maybe I've just lost my strength." He sighed, his broad chest moving with the effort. "What was your plan tonight?" He sounded merely curious.

She couldn't tell him, and she really had to get a move on. "I'm really sorry about this," she whispered, setting her stance and turning more fully to face him.

He shook his head. "That isn't an answer."

"No, but this is." She lowered her chin and attacked his mind, sending enough power to knock him out and scramble his brain enough that he wouldn't remember the evening.

He cocked his head to the side. "What is?"

Her mouth dropped open. She'd sent enough pain his way that he should've dropped to the pavement instantly. Was there something wrong with her? All demons could attack minds—it was one of their strongest skills. While she was only twenty-five years old, she'd learned how in her early teens. She should be able to kill the guy with the right force.

Yet there he stood.

She tried again, this time holding nothing back.

His chin lowered. "What the hell are you doing?"

"Did you feel that?" she whispered. Tingles exploded throughout her abdomen.

He stepped closer. "Feel what?"

Oh, crap. Her powers were gone. How the heck had that happened? "This town is bad luck," she yelled, throwing her hands up and knocking him beneath the chin with the drill.

He snatched it from her hand. "Ouch."

"*That* hurt you?" she yelled, fury ripping through her with the force of a real demon mind attack. One that actually worked. "You should be slobbering all over the pavement right now."

The clouds parted, and the moon beamed down, highlighting the angles of his rugged face. His beyond blue eyes laser focused on her. "Are you all right? Maybe we should get you to a professional or something."

Yeah, she probably did sound like a lunatic.

Evan stiffened and then partially turned toward the street.

The air grew heavy, and Tabi sighed, her stomach dropping as a demon strolled their way from the shadows. "This day just couldn't get any worse," she muttered. "Evan? You might want to run now."

* * * *

Evan shifted his weight to put the blonde pain-in-the-ass behind him while he faced the threat. There was no doubt the man heading toward them, body relaxed, eyes intense…was a threat. He would've known that even if Tabitha hadn't just told him to run. "What kind of trouble are you in, darlin'?" he asked, resting his hand on the butt of his gun.

Her sigh stirred the air around them. "The kind you wouldn't understand. Please leave, and I'll handle this."

He almost grinned. The woman was frighteningly petite with long blonde hair and the deepest black eyes he'd ever seen. While she looked fragile, she moved with a power and confidence that had intrigued him from the first time he'd arrested her. Yet there was no way she could fight the guy headed their way. Although Evan wasn't at his best right now, either. If this current weakness in his limbs continued, he'd have to give notice at the department. But not tonight or until he solved the murder of the dirtbag Monte Loften. Tonight, he was helping Tabi.

The guy finally arrived and stopped walking a couple of feet away. "Hello, Tabitha."

So they did know each other. Evan cocked his head. "Care to introduce us?" His adrenaline flowed through his veins, and he sank into the sensation for the briefest of seconds. He missed feeling strong and healthy.

Tabi stepped to his side. "Detective O'Connell, this is Richard Goncharov. He is now leaving."

Had her voice trembled? Evan studied the newcomer as he was studied right back. Tall and broad, Evan wasn't accustomed to looking up at anybody. This guy was about six-foot-seven with dark eyes and thick blonde hair almost as light as Tabi's. Were they related? "Your brother?" Evan asked.

Richard smiled, revealing strong white teeth. "Her betrothed."

Betrothed? Oh, hell no. Evan snorted. "What century are you from?"

The smile widened. "You wouldn't believe me if I told you."

What was going on with these people? "Tabi?" Evan asked.

"It's a long story." She elbowed him in the ribs and settled her feet next to him. "But we haven't done anything wrong, so please let us be, Detective."

No way was Evan leaving her with this guy. While he might not understand what was going on, his instincts had never failed him. "Actually, you're both skulking near the bank, and I can take you in briefly for questioning." Which might be a good idea.

Richard stared down at Tabi. "Is this guy for real?"

She exhaled. "Yes."

Richard lifted his nose, sniffing the air. He paused and studied Evan with even more intensity. "You're dying."

Evan jolted and then regained control. How the hell did he know that? "Excuse me?"

"Leave him alone." Tabi pushed forward with the nylon rope still around her shoulder and a grappling hook in her left hand. "Let's go, Richard. We can fight about our future and leave the detective be. I won't allow him to be hurt."

"The mere fact that you don't want him harmed makes me want to harm him," Richard said slowly.

What the fuck? Evan shoved Tabi behind him again and tossed the drill to the ground. "That was a threat against a law enforcement officer." Well, kind of. Either way, he could get this guy away from Tabi and run a background check on him for crimes. "You're coming with me."

"I'm bored." Richard lowered his chin in the same way Tabi had earlier. "Say goodbye to your brain." He focused hard on Evan's face.

"That's it." Evan reached for the cuffs in his back pocket.

Richard stepped back. "What the hell?"

Tabi hopped back to Evan's side. "Oh, thank goodness. I thought it was me. I'm fine. You couldn't attack his mind, either?"

Okay. They were both nuts. "I think we should get you two some help." Evan set the cuffs back in place and reached for his phone. "We have a nice and secured area at the hospital where we can figure out what's going on." Was Tabi involved in some type of weird cult with this moron? It figured that a crazy blonde would make him wish he could live longer. The fact that she was nuts should diminish his desire for her. Nope. Maybe the shrink from anger management could help her.

"You really should leave," Tabi said, her gaze remaining on Richard. "I mean it, Richard. Don't hurt him."

Enough. Evan reached for his gun, stopping when Tabi cried out. Tears leaked from her eyes and her body shook. "Tabi?"

Her chin firmed and she snapped her head up. Her legs visibly trembled, and the air thickened around her. She coughed and then sucked in a breath. "You attacked me?" she all but growled at Richard.

He smiled. "Just wanted to make sure I still had it." Then he lowered his chin again, and his eyes gleamed in the darkness.

Fury lit her face. "Don't you ever—" She cried out again and dropped the grappling hook. It bounced near the discarded drill.

Evan instinctively reached for her arm. "Tabi?"

She jerked and then settled, taking a deep breath. Slowly, she turned her head to face him. "How did you do that?"

"Do what?" Evan didn't like how pale she'd become, so he gentled his grip on her. What the hell was going on here?

"You, um, stopped the mind attack," she breathed, her eyes wide.

Heat flowed through him. "Honey? I think you need help." How had the jackass in front of him convinced the woman that her mind could be attacked? "Let's get you to the hospital, and I'll take a complete report from you about whatever you're involved in. I am going to help you." While he'd sensed she was in some sort of trouble, he hadn't figured on anything this crazy. It'd be nice to take down a cult before he died, if that's what was going on.

His own headache was about to drop him to the ground, but he was used to that. In fact, if his head stopped hurting, he'd know he was close to death. Not that it wasn't coming for him, anyway.

Tabi slipped her hand in his. "Let's get out of here."

The sweetness of her gesture dug into his chest and took hold. "How about we all go to the station?"

Richard's lips thinned, and he stared at their joined hands. "I guess I can wait for your disease to kill you, human." His eyes sparked again. "Your deadline is Thursday, Tabitha. Take me, or take death. Your choice." He turned and strode away.

Evan stiffened and reached for his gun.

"No," Tabi said softly. "Let him go. You know he didn't break any laws."

True. Evan wouldn't be able to hold him for long. "What's going on?" he asked quietly.

She shook her head. "I don't really know, to be honest." Then she looked up at him, her gaze earnest. "I have to go home now. We can talk after the anger management class tomorrow. I'm sure you'll be there to make sure I go."

"Let me help you." He could just take her in, but at the moment, he didn't have enough to really hold her on. Part of that was his fault in that he'd stopped her before she could use the rope and hook. His time was limited, and saving her had become his focus two weeks ago.

He hadn't figured out why.

Yet.

Chapter 2

Tabitha paced in the kitchen of her rental bungalow—or what counted as a bungalow in this small town. Yeah, it was charming and she loved it, but there was no chance she'd be able to stay. If Richard had found her, the Popovs wouldn't be far behind. She looked at the clock, knowing it was way too late to call. Yet she picked up her phone and pressed speed dial.

"Somebody better be dead," a grumpy voice answered.

Then a soft female voice in the background. "Who would call this late in the night?"

Tabi winced. "I'm so sorry to bother you, Raine. I didn't realize you had company." The deadly vampire-demon hybrid could probably pick up a woman with a lift of his dark eyebrow. He was more vampire than demon by far. Hence the charm.

Blankets rustled, and Raine chuckled. "No worries. Did you manage to rob the bank?"

"No." Tabitha leaned against the counter, wondering at her sanity in calling the vampire. Sure, they were stuck in this town together, and he was one of the only immortals around, but they weren't exactly friends. Not that she had friends or family or pretty much anybody. "I didn't know who else to call."

A door shut and then the sound of water pouring into a kettle came over the line. "I can help you rob the bank tomorrow night, if you'd like."

She was a demonness, for goodness' sakes. One who shouldn't need anybody's help to rob a darn bank. "No. I, ah, have a couple of questions." While she'd only been alive a quarter of a century, Raine had lived at least three hundred years, if not four.

"Okay." His low voice rumbled through the line. "Fire away."

She pushed aside warning, having to trust somebody. "Have you heard of humans who can block a demon mind attack?"

Quiet came over the line. "Why? Did somebody block your attack?"

She bit her lip, not wanting to put Evan in Raine's cross-hairs any more than was necessary. "Can we just go on hypotheticals here?"

Raine sighed. "I'm not fond of playing games, demonness, but I'll go along with you for now. The answer is that there are some enhanced human females—a very few—who were known as demon destroyers because they could block attacks. In fact, I believe that Kane Kayrs mated one. Yes. That's right. He did."

Kane Kayrs? He was one of the Kayrs brothers who ruled the Realm, which was a coalition of immortal species. "You're not a member of the Realm, are you?" It'd be nice to talk to Kane's mate, but Tabi didn't know anybody in the Realm.

"Ha," Raine snorted. "No. The Maxwell clan out of Montana has never aligned with anybody. My brothers would cut off my head if I even thought about it, and I'd probably let them do it."

"What's wrong with the Realm?" Tabi asked.

"It's easier not being a part of any coalition," Raine said easily. "Your family isn't aligned with the Realm, if I remember right."

She sighed. "I'm the only one left in my family. Didn't you know that?"

He paused. "No. The Ruskos have a reputation of being secretive and, frankly, nuts. I hadn't realized you were the only one left. No family at all?"

She sighed. "No. My parents died in the last dustup between immortals, and I was left with a nanny, who raised me. A human nanny."

Raine sucked in air—loudly. "You were raised by a human?"

Tabi opened her fridge for a bottle of wine. "Yep. She was kind and I loved her. She also knew all about the immortal world, so I'm well versed in whatever she knew. But we stayed off the grid mainly." Until last year, when everything had gone to crap. Tabi didn't need to share that with Raine. She liked the guy, but even she knew not to trust the Maxwells from Montana.

"Interesting. Well, if you have found a demon destroyer, keep her identity to yourself, if you don't choose to kill her." A kettle whistled loudly. "Most demons are fine with killing anybody who poses a threat to them, which is probably why there are so few humans around these days who can block a demon mind attack. They've all died out."

Tabi poured a generous glass of Pinot Grigio into a long-stemmed wine glass. "Enhanced human females are distantly related to the witches, right?"

"That's the general consensus, but nobody really knows," Raine said. "They could be their own species."

In that case, why couldn't there be enhanced males, since witches were both male and female? Oh, vampires and their natural enemy, the Kurjans, were male only, and Tabi only knew of the enhanced females they'd mated. "Have you ever heard of a vampire mating an enhanced human *male*?"

"A long time ago, but I'm pretty sure the Kurjans took out all enhanced human males before this new campaign they're now waging to end all enhanced females. Why do you ask?" The sound of pouring water came over the line. "Where's my bourbon, damn it?"

Tabi swirled her wine in the glass, watching the liquid catch the light. "I just didn't learn any of this from my guardian."

"Uh-uh," Raine said.

So he didn't believe her. It wasn't like he was focused on her, so that was all right. "Why are you still here, Raine?" He'd shown up at the anger management class, obviously to keep an eye on a former member, who had left quickly. A member who'd been a vampire-demon hybrid, much like Raine, although Raine was much more vampire than demon. "You should've left after Ivar did."

"My job isn't done," Raine said, his voice losing the congenial tone.

"What's your job?" She had to ask, even though it was obvious he wouldn't tell her.

He took a big drink, apparently having found his bourbon. "None of your business, demonness. Don't think of getting in my way."

She wouldn't. "Don't get all assholish with me. It's not necessary."

"My apologies." He didn't sound sorry.

"Who's in your bed, anyway?" she snapped, not really caring.

He took another drink. "Nobody. Just a nice lady I picked up at the grocery store in the fruit aisle."

An unwilling smile tilted Tabi's lips. "Fruit aisle? I'll have to try that." It had been way too long since she'd had a date. Her mind wandered instantly to the tall and sexy cop who wanted, for some reason, to save her. She sighed.

Raine cleared his throat. "I'm heading back to my nice fruit lady, considering she's had an hour of sleep to rest up for round number four. If you've found a human male who can stop a demon mind attack, I'd keep that information to yourself. Otherwise, he'll have a bullseye on his back. It wouldn't be nice to do that to the kind cop who's trying to help you."

She gasped. "How did you know?"

"I'm not a moron." Raine clicked off the phone.

She swallowed. Her questions had led to an obvious answer. She took her wine glass and went to her living room, peering out at the cop car parked by her curb with Evan O'Connell keeping watch over her.

What was she going to do with him?

* * * *

The engine quiet after an hour of being parked, Evan settled back in his Jeep, a cup of coffee next to him and an empty bag of chips on the passenger seat. He'd lost his appetite about a year ago and figured that eating junk food wasn't going to kill him, considering he was already dying.

His cellphone buzzed, and he answered the call with a swipe of his finger.

"O'Connell?" came through, a little scratchy.

"Hey, Mabel," he said, turning up the sound. "Did you get a hit?"

The eighty-year-old sighed loudly over the line. "Nope. Nothing on a Tabitha Rusko, Richard Goncharov, or anybody named Popov. Sorry, buddy."

"No worries. I didn't figure to get anything. Why are you working so late? This could've waited until morning," he said.

"Oh, I'll sleep when I'm dead," she cackled. "Besides, I'd rather get my hours in when the dumbass sheriff isn't here."

Evan snorted. "That kind of talk will get you fired, my friend."

"I notice you didn't disagree," she chortled.

No. There was no disagreement. The sheriff was buddies with the mayor and was also related by marriage. It was one of the things Evan had hoped to change before he moved on, but time was getting too short. He looked down at his shaking left hand. The attacks were getting worse. "Regardless, make sure somebody walks you out to your car tonight," Evan said.

"I will, if you promise to run for sheriff next fall," she returned, ending the call before he could answer.

Yeah, he wasn't going to be around in the fall. It was probably time to turn in his notice, but he wanted to wait until Tabi and his other friend, Abby, finished their anger management course and then got out of town. He might not be able to do much these days, but he could at least make sure both women were safe before quitting his job.

His head pounded, and he leaned back. The pain was becoming an odd reassurance to him that he was still alive. How weird was that?

A knock sounded on his window, and he jumped, reaching for his gun. "What in the world?" Anger replaced weakness, and he shoved open his door, standing and looming over the tiny blonde. "Never sneak up on an armed man," he said, his teeth clenched.

Tabitha huffed out a breath. "It isn't my fault you're sleeping in your car. Speaking of which, why are you camped outside my house?" In the dim moonlight, her eyes glowed like the deepest coal, and in her dark leggings and loose-fitting top, she looked young and cute.

Cute slayed him. Always had. "I was making sure that wacko from earlier didn't bother you," he admitted.

She sighed, ducking her head to stare at her bare feet. "You can't save everyone, Evan," she whispered.

It was the first time she'd used his given name. Apparently sitting outside her home at night and trying to protect her had granted him some sort of a closeness. "I'm not trying to save everyone." The itch between his shoulder blades wouldn't abate. How had the interloper known of Evan's illness earlier? Was it becoming that obvious? "I can still help you, Rusko."

She looked up then, way up, her expression one that caused

intrigue. "What makes you think I need help?"

It was a good question. "It's my job," he answered, knowing it was a cop out.

She smiled. "Have you always had this desperate need to protect and defend?"

Ah. The motto on his police vehicle. He did love that Jeep. "I guess so." He scouted the quiet street and then gestured toward her bungalow. "You're safe tonight. Go on in and get some sleep." Her scent of mystery and unidentifiable flowers was going to drive him crazy, so he used his best official voice. The one most younger police officers jumped to obey.

The woman didn't so much as twitch. "I can't talk you into leaving?"

"No." It wasn't like he slept much these days, anyway.

"Then why don't you come inside, have some apple pie, and sleep on my sofa?" She clasped her hands together, looking like an innocent angel from times gone by.

Oh, he knew he had a thing for petite and fragile looking women, but this one had a strength to her that just plain and simply intrigued him. He needed to figure her out. But staying inside her house was a huge mistake, and he wouldn't make it. His radio buzzed before he could answer her.

"Evan? We have a nine-sixteen at 2827 East Beverly Street," Mabel said. "Again."

Damn it. He reached for the radio. "I'm en route." Then he nodded to Tabi. "Go inside and lock your doors. I have to go."

She lifted an eyebrow. "What's a nine-sixteen?"

He slid back into his seat. "It's a domestic violence call." He'd already been to the Baker house twice that month. Why the young bride wouldn't leave her husband, he didn't know. Maybe this time he could talk some sense into her.

Tabi frowned. "You're a detective. Shouldn't that call have gone to an officer?"

He nodded. "Yeah, but our two officers would've been called off by the sheriff. I won't be."

"Do you need help?"

He jolted. "No." Like the petite blonde could help him. "Just keep yourself safe tonight. I'll do a drive by later, but here's my cell number if you need help." He tugged a card out of his unused ashtray. "I mean it, Tabi. If you need help, call me."

She took the card, her expression bemused. "All right. Be careful." Then she turned and jogged back inside her house.

He sighed and started the engine, driving down the street.

"You know, you got a real hero complex, O'Connell," Mabel crackled through the radio. "What's the deal there?"

He rolled his eyes. "I'm just doing my job."

"Uh huh," she said. "Be careful at the Bakers' house. That moron is probably drunk again."

"Good," Evan said grimly. "Then I can arrest him this time." Although, considering the idiot was the sheriff's youngest son, the asshole wouldn't stay in jail long. "We've got to clean up this town, Mabel."

"Wouldn't that be nice?" she cackled, signing off.

Yeah. He'd think of something.

Chapter 3

Evan's eyes were scratchy and his left leg weak when he strode into the room used for the anger management class. After arresting Baker the night before, he'd parked down the street from Tabi's house to keep watch, and once daylight had arrived, he'd spent a shitty day at the office, avoiding the sheriff since he'd arrested the asshole's kid the night before.

The smell of coffee wafted his way, and he turned to make an instant beeline for the table set up beneath the wide window, considering he'd missed dinner.

Dr. Lopez looked up from sitting on a metal chair at the edge of a circle of vacant metal chairs. "Hi, Detective. We have donuts and fresh cookies this fine evening." The shrink had dressed in dark jeans and a silky-looking pink shirt with her dark hair in a bob around her pretty face. Her forehead wrinkled. "It's so nice, but I can't figure out why the leader of the gambling anonymous meetings keeps bringing us food. He only stole our room once."

Evan shrugged and reached for a peanut butter cookie. "Maybe he feels guilty. Who knows?" The guy had done a complete turnaround, and if Evan didn't know better, he'd think one of Lopez's group members had had a little discussion with him. But nothing had been reported, and he had enough to worry about.

She smiled, her brown eyes sparkling. "I've gotten used to you attending the meetings. Isn't it time you sat and actually participated?"

He paused with the treat halfway to his mouth. "I'm not here as a participant."

She tapped her tennis shoe on the old wooden floor. "You

might as well be, don't you think? I can tell that something is bothering you besides wanting to help Abby Miller, which I believe you already have. Why don't you participate?"

"Thanks, but no." If he was angry, it was because he was dying, and he didn't really need to share that fact with anybody. Abby Miller had been falsely accused of battery by her dirtbag ex, and the best deal Evan could get for her was probation so long as she attended these meetings. Of course, the ex was now dead. Thank goodness Abby had an airtight alibi for the murder.

As if reading his mind, Lopez frowned. "Are you here now because Abby's ex-husband was murdered?"

Evan shoved the cookie in his mouth and finished it before answering. "Don't you think it's odd that your group provided an alibi for each other?" The second they'd been questioned, the group claimed they'd all been having a pizza party when the murder had occurred. Abby should've been the prime suspect.

"No. They were all together. It's common for people in a group to try and make friends. I find it odd that you'd think that odd, considering they all just met a month ago. Why would any of them lie for near strangers?" She tilted her head.

"Good point," Evan admitted. Even so, something was weird with this group. With most of the members of the group.

Tabi swept inside, this evening wearing white slacks, a green blouse, and high heels with red bottoms. She whipped off what had to be designer sunglasses. "How did the domestic violence call go last night?"

"Fine." Evan's ribs still hurt from the bat, but he'd taken Baker down hard afterward, and that had felt good.

"Good." She poured herself a cup of coffee and strode over to sit by the shrink. "Good evening. How's the brain business, Mariana?" She sipped delicately.

The shrink smiled. "That's a tough question. If I say it's good, then people have problems. If I say bad, then I don't have patients, and I can't buy shoes like you're wearing. Those are stunning."

Tabi kicked out her leg and twirled her ankle. "Thanks. They give me four extra inches in height."

It was amazing she could be so graceful in the deadly things. Movement sounded near the door. Evan turned from staring at the sexy shoes to see Abby and her new friend, Noah Siosal, walk inside the room, holding hands. He wasn't one to judge, but meeting a guy in an anger management program probably wasn't the best move for Abby to make. Abby's ex had been an ass, and this guy was at least six-six and built hard. One punch, and he could kill a woman, without question. Plus, a sense of danger rolled off him.

She smiled at Evan, looking happy, her greenish-brown eyes sparkling.

Ah, damn it. Evan cut a harsh look at Noah, promising retribution if he hurt the brunette. Noah winked at him, his eyes as black as Tabi's but his hair a darker blond. In fact, they looked oddly alike, but Evan's background check on them hadn't pinpointed any relationship or past association at all.

Evan straightened. Besides a recent bar fight that had put Siosal into the group, he was clean. Yet something wasn't right.

The next person loping into the room set Evan's teeth even more on edge. Raine Maxwell, another muscled male that seemed out of place in the innocuous old school room. He had sharp green eyes, black hair, and a hoarse voice that was almost a low growl.

Evan knew a predator when he saw one. In fact, he'd once been one. A long time ago in the service.

Raine took a seat next to Tabi.

Fire lanced down Evan's spine. Why he felt so much for the blonde was a mystery he'd never have enough time to solve. Man, he really was losing it.

Then Johnny Baker walked in with his father, the sheriff, right behind him.

Evan went cold and then full hot. "I put you in a cell."

Johnny smiled and walked toward the circle. "Not for long." The punk was twenty years old with thick brown hair and beady brown eyes. He had his father's stocky build, but unlike the sheriff, he was muscled and his gut hadn't started to go to fat. Yet. His main hobby seemed to be beating up his bride.

The sheriff reached Evan's side. "We had an emergency hearing with the judge right after dinner, and Johnny was ordered to complete this anger management course, so the prosecutor agreed to drop all charges."

Evan's ears burned. "The judge, his uncle?" The sheriff's sister had married the local judge decades ago.

Sheriff Baker's jaw firmed. "There wasn't anything

underhanded. This was a first offense, and it was probably a mistake."

Even though the entire room was watching, Evan leaned down into the face of his boss, fury deepening his voice. "This was a first offense because once again, the female victim refused to make a report. But this time, your son hit a cop with a fucking bat. Me. That matters."

Hatred glowed in the sheriff's dull eyes for a moment before being banked. "I'd watch it, O'Connell. You might be a buddy of the governor, which got you this job, but you work for me."

Johnny sat next to Dr. Lopez and smiled, his eyes hard. "I can't have anything like that on my record if I want to be a police officer."

Evan straightened. "Excuse me?"

Johnny lowered his chin. "I take the police officer entry-level civil service exam in two weeks. Good thing there's an opening in the department, right? I hope I have a chance of making it." His chuckle held a shitload of derision.

All the moron needed was a high school degree, and he had that. "You have to pass a drug test and a psych evaluation," Evan shot back. Although the sheriff would make sure he passed those, probably.

Raine Maxwell cleared his throat. "It appears as if we have a problem."

The sheriff turned on him. "Mind your own business."

Tabi cleared her throat. "Well, hello, Johnny. How are your balls? I believe I kicked them nearly through the top of your head when you and your buddies tried to accost me."

It was the attack that had been caught on tape. Evan should give her that video. Definitely.

Johnny swirled to look at her, and he did pale the slightest amount. "Oh, you and I aren't done."

Evan stepped forward. "Watch it, kid."

The sheriff grabbed his arm. "Detective O'Connell? You're not needed here, and I suggest you get back to work. Don't you have a murder to solve?" He turned and stared at Abby Miller. "I believe the, ah, grieving widow is right over there." The condescension in his tone had Abby's head jerking up and Noah's eyes narrowing.

Dr. Lopez read the room accurately. "Actually, I've requested that the detective join the group, since we have some tension here.

Surely you're okay with that, Sheriff?" If that was the tone she used with her underage clients, she no doubt got definite results.

The sheriff paused and then smiled, his gaze running over the woman's form. "Of course. Anything for you, Dr. Lopez."

A low rumble sounded from Raine, barely audible.

Interesting. Evan pulled free from the sheriff before he could knock the guy out with one punch and lose his job. "Well, then. I guess I'll take a seat." He purposefully strode right over to sit next to Johnny. "You and I aren't done, either," he said, turning to face the shithead.

Tabi leaned back in her chair, watching him closely. "You're kind of fun when you're pissed off," she murmured, her dark eyes dancing.

"That's where you'd be wrong, darlin'," he returned, keeping everyone in the room in his sights. Threats were in every direction, and the feeling of missing something important wouldn't leave him.

Her small grin was nearly catlike and had the perverse result of turning him on. What was it with that woman?

The sheriff strutted toward the doorway. "O'Connell? Meet me at the station first thing tomorrow morning. I'd like an update on the case, and I have no doubt you'll be able to break the false alibi of the widow." He disappeared down the old hallway.

Abby sighed. "Detective? I'm so sorry to have gotten you into this mess. I did not kill my ex-husband." She'd been married to a lawyer, who'd been buddies with the sheriff and the judge, and there was no doubt she'd been railroaded in an arrest and then near conviction from a fake battery charge. Evan had used all his power to keep her out of jail and get her into probation and the anger management group before the ex had been murdered. "My alibi is solid."

Yeah. Her alibi was everyone in the room, except the shrink and Johnny. Something about a pizza party at Raine Maxwell's house, which just didn't set right. But it didn't make sense that these people, all from different walks of life, had conspired to kill a moron lawyer in a small Indiana town. "I hope so," Evan said, sitting back. "I do need to interview each of you soon, just so you know. We need follow-up information." Actually, he needed to compare their initial interviews with the second ones, just to see who was lying.

Although Monte Lofton had been an asshole, he'd been

murdered, and Evan couldn't allow vigilante justice in his town.

Abby smiled. "I'll gladly be interviewed again, Detective. Switching topics, why don't you run for county sheriff in the fall? You'd basically just deal with this city and the few outlining areas, and you'd do a much better job than that jackass."

"Hey," Johnny protested. "That's my dad."

Abby turned on him. "No kidding. The judge is your uncle, too. It's time this baloney stopped in this town."

Evan would love to run for sheriff. His right ankle started to tremble, heading up to his knee. He pressed a hand on his thigh to try and stop the movement while ignoring the pain. "I'm afraid that's not in the cards for me," he said, effectively cutting off all debate with a harsh tone.

Dr. Lopez jumped and then reached for manila files from the briefcase by her chair. "Johnny? Since you're new to the group, let's start with you today. You were arrested for battery of your wife and a police officer."

Johnny rolled his eyes. "I didn't hit Louise, and the cop came at me first." He looked at Lopez's breasts. "I wasn't angry, either."

"My eyes are up here, junior," Lopez said, her tone hard.

Johnny grinned and looked up at her face. "Your eyes aren't your best feature."

Faster than Evan would've thought possible, Raine Maxwell had the kid out of his seat and slammed against the wall, only knocking over one chair in the movement.

Evan reached them instantly, shoving Raine off the kid.

Raine stepped back, his face cold. "One more word like that, and you won't need anger management. You won't need anything," he said, his voice a bizarre growl.

Dr. Lopez clapped her hands, her voice rising. "I can see we have a lot to discuss. Everyone take your seats. Now."

Evan studied the furious man, his instincts humming. "Apparently I'm not the only one protective of the women here," he murmured as Raine turned his attention on him. "I think I'll interview you first about Monte Loften's murder, Mr. Maxwell." There was absolutely no doubt in Evan's mind that Raine could kill. He probably had.

Raine smiled. "Looking forward to it, Detective."

Chapter 4

"If you need an alibi taking that twerp out, just let me know," Tabi whispered to Raine as she strode out of the abandoned schoolhouse after the useless anger management class. Johnny Baker was a waste of space, as far as she was concerned.

"Thanks," Raine said, not smiling, the darkness surrounding him. The early spring breeze rustled through the night, chilly and unwelcoming. At least it wasn't raining.

She nodded and moved down the crumbling cement sidewalk toward her car as Raine turned and jogged across the street to his silver truck. Stopping at her car, she paused, not surprised to see the detective heading her way through the night. "You really have a hard-on for me, don't you?" she murmured.

"Yes." Both of his eyebrows rose. "You sure have a way with words."

She unlocked her vehicle, her body flaring to life at his honest response. "I was raised by a woman who called it like she saw it." Sometimes the pain at losing Janet still took Tabi by surprise. Why did humans have to die? "Unless you're going to give up my video, I suggest you head to work like your boss ordered you to do."

Evan opened her door, his sexy scent of smoked honey wafting around. "I'll give you the recording."

She jolted and turned to face him directly. "What did you say?"

His blue eyes seemed darker than usual, deep with what looked like pain. "I'll give you the recording. Come down to the station tomorrow morning for one more interview, and then I'll take you to the bank myself."

It was as if he knew she was going to blow town the second she got her hands on the video, even though her business was here. She bit her lip. If she got the footage, she could meet Abby at the factory and give her instructions before running. Man, she hated to run.

Evan smiled. "You're sure thinking hard. Why don't you tell me what's really going on? I can protect you."

Warmth flushed her. The man truly believed that. The only way he could come close would be if she—no. No way. She shouldn't even think of that. Was it even possible? Did she want a mate?

"Tabitha? What's barreling through your head?" As if unable to help himself, he reached out and smoothed a lock of hair away from her face.

Shocking electricity zapped beneath her skin.

His brows drew down. "Did you feel that?"

She nodded. "Why are you now willing to give me the recording?"

He sighed and looked across the vacant street. "I don't like that the sheriff's kid is in the anger-management group with you, considering you definitely injured his pride along with his body. Chances are, he'll come after you. Since you're planning to run, I thought to make it easy for you." His gaze scouted the area, something he seemed to do often.

"Do you miss the service?" she asked softly, wanting to know more about him. Abby had told her that he'd served in the navy a while back.

He blinked. "Yeah."

"Why did you leave?"

His gaze shuttered closed faster than a bank vault.

"I know you're ill," she said quietly.

He gripped his left hand with his right. "I hoped nobody had noticed the tremors." Retreating instantly, he backed away. "Go home. I'll follow to make sure that kid doesn't mess with you tonight, and I'll pick you up in the morning to take you to the station. After your interview, I'll give you the video."

Without waiting for an answer, he turned and strode down the sidewalk toward his Jeep.

Her face still tingled from his touch. Bemused, she slipped into her BMW and ignited the engine, driving down the quiet street. She'd been hidden most of her life, and it wasn't like she had any close friends. After a quick mental debate, she dialed Abby's number.

"Hi, Tabitha. Are we getting to work tomorrow?" Abby immediately answered, sounding happy. Very happy.

"Yes," Tabi said. "Let's meet at noon at the factory, okay?" She'd hired Abby as her assistant when the woman had needed a job, and Abby's organizational skills had turned out to be phenomenal.

Abby chuckled. "A job that starts at noon. I love working for you."

Tabi turned a corner, keeping track of Evan's headlights behind her. "Can I ask you a question? It's kind of personal."

"Sure," Abby said, her voice light. She'd once been an enhanced human, and her mating with Noah was still fresh. "Ask me anything."

All right. Tabi took the next corner a little fast and forced herself to slow down, since a police officer was tailing her. Evan would probably give her a ticket. "When you mated Noah, or when he mated you, did you change a lot? I mean, did your personality change? Are you even done changing yet?" There was so much she didn't know about matings, considering she'd been raised by a human.

Abby was quiet for a minute. "I'm not sure if I'm done changing, and I haven't tried to heal myself of an injury yet. Other than that, I don't think I've changed personalities or anything. Shouldn't you know all of this stuff?"

Tabi winced. "I should, but I don't."

"Aren't you like a couple hundred years old?" Abby whispered.

Tabi jerked upright, her foot pressing harder on the gas pedal. "No," she snapped, oddly affronted. "Do I look centuries old?"

Abby coughed. She'd better not be laughing. "No. You look like you're in your mid-twenties, but I wouldn't think my mate was more than thirty or so, and he's four hundred years old. I just assumed. How old are you? In years?"

Tabi rolled her eyes. "I'm twenty-five. In years." Geez. Like she didn't know what Abby meant.

"Seriously?" Noah's voice came clearly over the line. "You're really only twenty-five?"

"Yes, vampire," Tabi snapped. "Or demon. Or hybrid. That's my real age." For goodness' sakes.

Noah cleared his throat. "Shit, Tabi. Don't you have family?"

"No," she said, trying not to hurt at saying the word. "I don't have anybody, Noah. I was raised by a human who I loved, and humans die." Like Evan O'Connell. He was going to die and probably soon.

A sleek luxury car swerved out of a driveway blanketed by trees, skidding in front of her.

"I have to go." She clicked off, prepared to ram the vehicle and beat the crap out of Johnny Baker. Until she saw the light hair of the driver. Holy crap. It was Richard Goncharov. So much for giving her three more days. She almost slowed down, until she caught Evan's headlights.

Panic seized her lungs. She had to get him out of danger. Taking a deep breath and forcing those lungs to work, she slammed her foot on the accelerator and swerved around Richard's town car.

* * * *

Evan flipped on his siren and punched the gas as the black car did the same, both of them chasing the white BMW. He drew abreast of the black car, seeing that Richard asshole driving. He lifted his flashlight and made a motion for the man to pull over.

The guy smiled, tightened his hold on his steering wheel, and shot forward into the darkened night.

Damn it. Evan set the flashlight on the seat, his adrenaline flowing and his temper blowing. He lowered his head and sped up, a primitive power filling him as he gave chase. Protocol dictated he call for backup, but for once, he let his instincts rule. He'd figure out why later.

The tail lights of the BMW flashed as Tabi took a corner fast, whizzing around a set of trees and heading toward the more industrial part of town. Smart. There would be fewer people in that area, and she could get out of the way and let him handle this jerk.

He reached for his phone and pressed her number, having taken it off her the night he'd arrested her.

"I'm kinda busy right now, Evan," she said, her voice gritty and determined.

So much for reassuring her. He grinned. "Listen to me, darlin'. Drive two miles and take a fast right into the Mills Pond Industrial

Park."

"I don't need help here," she muttered, whipping around another corner like a Formula One driver.

Nice. The woman could drive. "Go to the farthest building—the one with the red metal roof. Then swing around it, and I'll take out this guy. Meet me at the station." He'd plow the luxury car right into the metal fence, once Tabitha had gotten safely out of the way.

"Um, this is weird for you, I'm sure. But I can handle my own problems." She slowed down and then zipped across a set of railroad tracks. "How about you go to the station?"

Was she joking? At a time like this? "Knock it off, Tabitha," he ordered. "Do what I said."

She drove right by the entrance to the Mills Pond Park, heading deeper into the darkness. "I've got this."

What the hell? She had this? "I mean it, Tabi," he snapped, driving faster toward Richard's car. If Evan couldn't get her cooperation, he'd have to come up with Plan B. "Turn into the next industrial complex."

"No." She drove right past it, with Richard right on her ass.

That was it. Evan punched the gas, swerved, and clipped the back of Richard's car. They both spun away from each other, correcting, and getting right back on track.

"Damn it, Evan," Tabi yelled, slowing down. "You don't understand any of this. Get out of here. Please." She flipped around and stopped.

Richard's tail lights flared as he skidded to a stop, facing the lights of the white BMW.

Evan slowed down. What the heck was going on? Some sort of weird game of chicken? Not on his watch. He slammed his foot on the pedal and lurched forward just as Richard did the same, both of them headed toward the BMW. Tightening his hold on the wheel, Evan jerked again, this time aiming for the left front of Richard's car. He spun them both into the metal fencing of another industrial complex.

His airbag exploded into his face, and he shook his head, jumping out of the vehicle while grabbing for his weapon.

The white BMW skidded to a halt next to him, and Tabi was out and running for him. "Evan!"

He grabbed her arm and pushed her behind him, trying to see

through the steam hissing from the front of his Jeep. "Stay down." Then he crept to the side, his gun at ready, pointed at the innocuous black car. "Put your hands outside the vehicle. Now!" he yelled.

Nothing.

He crept closer, looking for movement.

Tabi came up on his side. "He's gone."

Evan's ears rang, and he shook his head, leaning down to confirm that the car was vacant. He levered up, looking around the area. "Where did he go?" There wasn't even any sound.

"Heck if I know." She sighed, sounding more put out than frightened.

Evan turned to face her. "What the hell is going on?" He'd just wrecked an official vehicle, and he hadn't even called it in.

Tabi looked him over, her eye gleaming through the darkness. "Are you all right?"

No. His brain was fried. None of this made a lick of sense, and that included his own actions. "Tabi—" he started.

She ran for him, jumping and wrapping her arms and legs around him. "You tried to save me." Then her mouth was on his. Soft and sweet, her tongue slipping inside his mouth with the taste of strawberries.

He clamped his hands on her tight ass and took over the kiss, going deep with no thought. For the briefest of moments, there were no thoughts, no fears, no pain. He forced himself to reclaim reality and leaned back, when all he wanted to do was bend her over the car and take what she was offering. "I have to call this in," he said, his voice gruff.

She smiled and leaned in to nip his bottom lip. "You'll never find him, and who the heck cares? Don't you want to take whatever pleasure you can right now? Just one night? You and me?"

His left leg began to tremble, and he shifted his weight to keep her aloft. A year ago, he would've said no. Even a month ago would've been a different situation. Fuck it. If he was going to die, he was going to have this night. "My place or yours?"

The trill of sirens jerked him out of the fantasy he was already living. Lights came into view—red and blue and swirling. He let her slide to the ground.

She put her hands on her hips. "Somebody must've seen us speeding."

"Right," he said, turning and rubbing the back of his neck. Yeah, he was going to get fired for this. No question about it.

"You didn't have time to get to your radio. It all happened so fast," she said, facing the oncoming lights.

He glanced down at her calm face. Just who the hell was Tabitha Rusko?

Chapter 5

Tabi stormed out of the police station after giving her statement for the third time to a detective who didn't seem to understand English. Either he would arrest her or not, and she'd made enough of a threat about her lawyers that she'd probably bought herself some time. It was a good bluff, anyway. She could find lawyers if she needed them. Either way, she was clear that the car chase and wreck had been the blond stranger's fault and not Detective O'Connell's.

Hence her shock when she ran into him right outside the brick building, and he was holding a box of his possessions. "Oh, they did *not* fire you," she exploded.

Evan turned toward her, his eyes dark. "Yeah, the sheriff has been looking for a way to get rid of me for a while." He jerked his head toward her BMW in the lot. "Why don't you give me a ride home, and you can tell me what's going on and exactly who this Richard is."

Heat nearly blew steam out of her ears. "Why are you taking this so calmly? Get in there and fight, Evan." She could see he was a fighter—especially with the bruises now down his neck from the wreck.

He turned to walk to her car and waited for her to unlock it before shoving his box in the back seat and settling into the front.

She slipped into the driver's seat and turned toward him. "Evan?"

He rested his head back. "I would fight it, but there's no use. I'd have to quit soon, anyway."

She reached out and put her hand over his. That electricity from the one kiss arched between them and she marveled at the feeling.

Was it because he might be enhanced? Or maybe something was happening to her. Who knew. "Why?"

He opened his eyes, and the blue was fathomless. "I have Huntington's Disease. The tremors and limb weakness started about six months ago, and if I'm anything like my dad, I'll go downhill fast." His lower lip lifted in a wry smile. "I'd hoped to last long enough to get you and Abby out of probation and town, but it looks like I'll have to do so without my badge."

Man, she wanted to cold-cock that sheriff. "I've never met anybody like you," she admitted.

He grinned full-on this time, looking almost boyish. "A washed-up cop in a small town? We're a dime a dozen, beautiful." Now he sounded rueful.

She shook her head. "No. You try to save everybody, and you want to do the right thing. I bet you were a good soldier."

He sighed. "I did my job, and it wasn't pretty. I miss the teams, though. Got sick and had to leave."

The teams? He'd been a Navy SEAL? Figured. "So you got this job?"

He nodded. "I served with the governor way back when, and he did me a solid. I like it here. It would've been a good place to settle down and raise kids." He turned and pinned her with a look. "Now start driving and tell me what kind of trouble you're in. I can fix it before…"

Before he died.

She started the car, her mind spinning. A lot of immortals mated for political reasons. She'd never thought much about mating or love or forever before. What she did know was that Evan O'Connell was a good man who belonged on this planet a lot more than many immortals did. "I can save you," she whispered, turning and driving away from the station.

"Take the next left, and go for a while until Shavers Avenue turns into Fourth Street," he said quietly. "Nobody can save me, sweetheart."

She followed his directions, her hands shaking lightly on the wheel. Was she crazy to even think about this? "If you could live, possibly forever, what would you do?"

He rolled his neck. "Forever? I don't know. First, I'd run for sheriff and turn this county around. Clean out the bastards screwing everything up. Then I'd settle down and have some kids. Then, who knows. Forever is a long time, and there's probably a lot to do." He chuckled. "What about you?"

She'd never really thought about helping other people. "I'd, ah, try to survive, I guess. And I'd start a lucrative business." Which she'd already done, if she could just get the prototypes finished. Safety came from money, and she knew it. "You're a better person than I am." Than anybody she'd ever met.

He chuckled. "Honey, I'm not even close. I did things in the military that keep me up at night, but I'd do them again if I had to. You're meeting me at the end of my life and end of my illness. At full strength, I would've probably already beat the crap out of the sheriff and his son. The judge, too." He sighed. "I would've liked to have known you before all of this. Of course, you probably wouldn't have liked me. I wasn't so easygoing."

Right. Even now, he was being sweet. "Do you believe in, well, things you can't see?"

"Like germs?"

She coughed. "No. Like, I don't know, vampires?"

His chin dropped to his chest. "Oh, honey. I was afraid of that. The weird Richard guy who convinced you he could hurt your mind. Are you in some sort of cult?"

Cult? She sucked in air. "No. I'm not easy to manipulate." Wow. He had totally read her wrong. So he wasn't exactly open to a different reality. If she told him she was a demonness, he'd probably try to take her to the psych ward. Something told her there wasn't enough time for that. She tried a different tack. "If you had the chance to live forever, would you take it?" she asked.

"In a heartbeat," he said quietly, running his wide hands down his jeans. "So long as I kept my soul."

She swallowed, turning into the driveway of a small brick house set against a series of trees. "I hope you're sure about that." This was something she could do. If she mated him, then she was partially responsible for all the people he helped through eternity, right? That had to go in the plus column for her life. Heat flushed through her. Could she do this?

"It doesn't matter." He took her hand. "I think you should stay the night in my guest room, at least until we find that Richard who won't leave you alone. Once you give me the whole story, I'll call in some favors I'm owed, and we'll track him down. I promise."

She couldn't breathe. This was nuts.

He lifted her hand to his mouth. "Would you stay the night?"

She squared her shoulders, tingles wandering up her arm just from one kiss of his lips. Her palm flashed hot and painful against his touch. Holy immortal crackers. The mating mark pulsed on her palm—the one that appeared when a demon found their mate. Oh, there was something between them. That was for sure.

"I'm definitely staying," she whispered.

* * * *

Evan escorted Tabi into his small brick home, flipping on lights as they went. Having her in his space was making his clothes feel too constricting. Man, she was beautiful. There was something wild and untamed about her, especially after that car race, that made him shove his hands in his pockets to keep from reaching for her.

His dogs ran up, both panting. "This is Buck and Lewey." They were long-haired mutts, part black lab and part who knows what, and he adored them. "Outside, guys." They obediently ran for the back door, and he let them free. "Are you hungry?" He might have a waffle or two in the freezer.

"No." She looked at the freshly polished wooden floors and the hand-crafted fireplace mantle with self-placed river rock. "This place is lovely. Did you do all of this yourself?"

His ears heated. "Yeah. It's probably dumb, but I wanted to leave something complete behind. Something I'd created myself." Shaking himself out of it, he exited the living room and showed her down the wide hallway to the guest room, which held his grandmother's furniture that he'd refinished. He'd see her soon. Then he chuckled. He'd be okay after a good night's sleep and then could help Tabi out of this mess. Once he got her out of his space he could take some deep breaths. Alluring was too tame a word for her.

She stared at the cherrywood dresser. "What's Huntington Disease?"

He stilled. "Oh. It's a rare and progressive brain disorder that demolishes physical and mental abilities. Before you ask, it's genetic, and there is no cure. It's fatal, and my dad died from it." Sharing with her helped, somehow.

She tossed her purse onto the bed. "What about your mother?"

"Car wreck when I was nine. No other relatives." The blonde was a sweetheart in trying to connect. He didn't need connections, although she was a temptation, that was for sure. That mysterious and feminine scent of hers was heating his blood in a way that made him feel healthy again.

"What does your room look like?" She turned, those black eyes guileless.

"Oh." Of course, she wanted the tour, and he had redone the entire home. His chest puffed out just enough to make him feel like a moron. "I'll show you the rest of the house." If he got her anywhere near his bed, he might lose the control he was reaching for like a starving man.

She made appropriate noises at the rest of the house, until they reached his room. Then she gasped. "It's so…you."

He felt like shuffling his feet so he stood taller. "Thanks. I made the furniture in the garage, which I turned into a woodshop." The furnishings were oak with hand-carved designs of different angles of crests of his ancestors, who'd come over to the States from Scotland. He moved to flip off the light.

She stepped in front of him, looking up, a light pink flushing across the porcelain skin of her enticing face. "I want to stay in here tonight."

In another time, he would've already had her on the bed. But even he didn't need a pity fuck. "I appreciate it, sweetheart, but it's just not a good idea."

Her face cleared and her mouth opened slightly. "Oh. I see. You, um, can't?"

He coughed and then laughed full-on. When was the last time he'd felt humor? When he calmed, he tugged on a piece of her hair. "Yeah, I can. Parts of me still work just fine—at least for now." It was a sobering thought, and he didn't like it. "You've had an adrenaline-filled night, you must be scared of that wacko in the car, and I hit you with the fact that I'm dying. None of those are good reasons to make yourself vulnerable."

She tilted her head, studying him. "Do I look like I feel vulnerable to you?"

"No." She looked like temptation and innocent sin, which was a contradiction he'd never imagined. Until now.

She moved into him, sliding her hands from his abs up to his chest, humming in what sounded like appreciation. "Do I look scared or like I feel sorry for you?"

His cock pressed so hard against his zipper that he barely hid a wince. "I'm trying to do the right thing here."

She curled her fingers and her nails bit into his skin through his T-shirt. "So am I." With that illusive statement, she levered up on her toes and kissed him. Her lips were full and soft, and a temptation he'd never be able to deny, regardless of noble intentions.

He let her play for a moment and then slowly took control of the kiss, deepening it when she slid her hands beneath his shirt and across his abs. His stomach undulated, and he forced himself to slow down. While she was a siren, he was twice her size, and he had to be careful.

Her touch was hot. Very. He leaned back, desire clawing through him. "Are you sure?"

"Yes." She tugged on his shirt, and he ducked his head to let her yank it up and away.

Something caught his eye, and he grasped her right hand, turning it over to look at a tattoo on her palm. Winding vines surrounded the letter R, looking both ancient and delicate. It was beautiful work, whoever had drawn it. How had he not noticed it before? "R for Rusko?" he murmured.

"Yes."

"It looks fresh." Maybe he wasn't the only one trying to hold on to the past.

Her chuckle swam down his skin and landed in his balls. "You could say that. It's very new."

"It's stunning."

"I'm glad you think so," she said, her eyes nearly looking silver for the briefest of moments. Then she reached for the snap of his jeans.

Chapter 6

Tabitha saw the second Evan gave up the fight to protect her for her own good. His eyes shifted, and his shoulders went back. Smoothly, he lifted her and easily carried her to the bed. His strength gave her a slight pause. If he was this strong as a human, what would he be like immortal? Then he leaned over and kissed her, and she forgot all about reservations.

The cop could kiss.

He set her on her back, one knee next to her on the bed, his mouth working hers as if they had all the time in the world. His lips were firm, and he explored her, sliding his mouth away from hers and along her face, nipping where her jaw met her neck.

She shivered, her body lighting on fire.

Slowly, gently, he drew her blouse up along her ribcage with both hands, his fingertips caressing and teasing her rib cage. She reached for him, sliding her hands through his thick hair like she'd wanted to do for weeks. Then she tugged.

He paused, his palms warm against the sides of her breasts.

She smiled. "I don't need slow, and I'm not breakable."

His eyes burned the dark hue as dusk gave up the fight to night. "I'll go as slow as I want, and baby, I won't break you." Then he pulled her shirt over her head and looked down, male satisfaction curving his lips. "God, you're beautiful."

She wish she'd worn her fancy bra instead of the comfortable cotton one, so she reached for the front clasp and released it. "I'm okay," she murmured, having fun. She wasn't exactly well endowed, but by the flaring of his eyes, he didn't seem to mind.

He reached for her, palming both breasts, no longer holding

back. Electricity zipped through her skin and right to her core, and she arched against him, surprised at the intensity. Then he leaned down and kissed her again, taking control in the smoothest of ways.

Everything felt so good. *He* felt so good against her. She dug her fingers into the still hard planes of his chest, sliding her palms down to dig into each rippling muscle in his abs, need rioting through her so fast she could barely breathe.

He released the button of her pants and slid them down her legs, standing by the bed as he did so. "We're leaving the shoes on, baby." Watching her, seeing more of her than she'd like, he shoved his jeans down, revealing what she'd suspected. The cop was built. Like very nicely built.

Need and want coursed through her, powerful in the demand. Vulnerability hinted inside her for a second.

He must've caught her look, because he slid both hands up her thighs and placed a kiss right above her belly button. "I won't hurt you, Tabi. I promise."

She couldn't fool him. He was too important, and so was this. "I want to mate you. We'd be tied forever," she whispered, not even sure what that meant. But at least he'd be alive.

He paused. "Mate?"

Oh, crap. The guy was too grounded in his own reality. "Yes. Please say yes."

Confusion clouded through the desire in his expression. "Honey, I don't have long, and mating doesn't exist. Not like you said it." He brushed her hair away from her face, his touch infinitely gentle. "I'm not sure what you're caught up in, but I can help you." He started to draw back.

"No." She yanked him down and pushed his shoulder so he'd roll on his back. Levering with her knee, she slid atop him, straddling all of his smooth and strong body, her heels on the bed. "Don't stop. Forget I said anything. I'm not in a cult, and you're not taking advantage of me." She told him all she could, and he'd said he would want to live forever. If this actually worked, and he was pissed, they'd have eternity to work it out. If they stayed together. Nobody said they had to stay together. Not really.

He reached up, cupping her face while his cock pulsed against her core, obviously straining to get in. The feeling was too much, and the ache inside her intensified. "You understand I can't make any sort of claim here, right? I'm temporary, Tabitha."

Claim? The guy sounded like a vampire for a minute. "What if you weren't dying?" she whispered, unable to keep her body from rubbing against him. Pleasure burst through her with a promise of more. A lot more.

"Then I'd be inside you right now, making you say my name." As if going on instinct, he slipped his head to the nape of her neck, twisting his fingers in her hair and taking control. He tugged her head to the side and then drew her down. "I'm done fighting us both. Tell me now if you want this."

Oh, she wanted him. Whether she wanted what she was about to do, she wasn't sure. "I want you. Inside me and now," she said, going for honesty.

"Good enough." He kissed her then, putting everything into it this time. Power, male, strength.

She moaned, her hands curling into his shoulders.

He rolled them again, blanketing her, broad and long. So much bigger than her. He reached down, one finger gently sliding inside her. "Oh, Tabi. You're ready, baby."

She gasped, throwing her head back. Yeah, she was wet and ready for him. Fast. Really fast. She scraped her nails down his flank, over his hip, and touched his length. Full and pulsing, hard and long, he was ready, too. She chuckled, the sound hoarse. "Right back at you."

He chuckled, the sound pained. Then he licked along her jaw and headed between her breasts.

She grabbed his hair and pulled him back on. "I'm all for playing and foreplay, but I want you. Now." Everything hurt—she ached way too much for him. "We can go slow and play later."

His nostrils flared. "Hold on." He reached into the bedside drawer, pulling out a condom.

It would take too much time and maybe get him to stop if she explained that he didn't need that, so she let him roll the useless thing on himself. He smiled and kissed her nose, pausing at her entrance and seeking her eyes, as if making sure one more time that she wanted this.

To prove it, she reached around and clenched his very fine buttock.

His nostrils flared, and he entered her, going slowly and

allowing her body time to accept him.

The moment was intimate and the feeling delicious. Different than ever before in a way she couldn't quite grasp, and she shoved any indecision to the side. It was too late to worry about that.

He finally pushed all the way inside her, taking her.

Much too late.

* * * *

If Evan was going to die, this was a hell of a way to go. Tabi breathed out, her face flushed, her body warm beneath his. Those glorious black eyes looked silver again in the dim light, and her pretty pink lips pursed in an o. "Are you all right?" he rumbled, holding his weight off her with one elbow.

"Yes," she breathed, lifting her knees and giving him even more access to go deeper.

She was wet and tight around him, her internal walls gripping with a strength that made him want to start pounding inside her like a randy teenager. Instead, he pulled out and pushed back in, watching her carefully to make sure he didn't hurt her. She gasped and arched against him, her nails shredding the skin on his ass.

He did it again, holding on to control like always.

She did something inside her that gripped him even tighter, and he clenched his teeth. "Go, Evan. Now," she whispered, her voice the sexy hoarseness of a bombshell from days gone by.

Unable to stop himself, he plunged out of her and powered back in, setting up a strong rhythm that bounced her pretty breasts on her chest. Leaning down, he captured a nipple and lightly bit.

She cried out, wrapping her legs around his waist.

He leaned up. "I'm going to spend some serious time playing with those later tonight," he warned her, his body working on its own for that elusive release just out of his reach.

"Promises," she whispered, the cords in her neck straining as she met his thrusts with her own, stamping a claim on him he'd never felt before.

Right now, he was caught up in the moment and in the exquisite woman beneath him. Later he'd feel the remorse that they were so temporary and regret not meeting her earlier in his life. Right now, she was all heat, wildcat, and female. He slid his knees up and reached beneath her for the small of her back, lifting her up to meet his fierce pounding.

"Yes," she moaned, reaching almost desperately for his waist and digging in. "More. I need you. Here. More." She tried to pull him down.

Still powering inside her, he pushed his knees out and lay over her, overcome for the first time in his life. She was special, and there was no question about that. Possessiveness took him, shocking since it was impossible to keep her. He kissed her hard, his tongue diving inside her mouth.

She kissed him back, her hands frantic, her body tightening around him. Her right hand clamped on his hip, and her other manacled his hair, turning his head and kissing beneath his jaw.

Fire flashed along his hip, and a sharp pain ticked through his neck.

She cried out, arching against him, her body shaking so hard with her orgasm that his eyes nearly rolled back in his head. He kept up the pressure, sure to hit her clit, and let her ride out the waves.

With a soft sigh, she breathed out, licking his neck. Then, swear to God, she purred.

He lifted up, wanting to see her eyes. They looked all silver and only spurred him higher. He gripped her hip, pounding inside her, his entire being caught up in this moment.

She turned her head, revealing her smooth and vulnerable neck.

He pressed his lips to her jugular, electricity shooting down his spine so fast his entire back burned. His balls enlarged, and with absolutely no thought, he sank his teeth into her neck until he tasted blood. Then he exploded, his body shaking with an unreal force as an orgasm spiraled him nearly into darkness.

He stilled inside her, his dick still jerking with aftershocks. It took several moments, but he slowly came back into himself. There was blood on his lips. "Tabi. I bit you." He blinked, trying to concentrate. Then he leaned back to survey the damage to her delicate skin. Yep. He'd bitten her. He looked up to apologize, shocked.

Her sleepy grin stopped him short. "I bit you, too." Then she patted his chest. "You're very good in bed, Evan."

He couldn't find words, so he withdrew, almost smiling at her soft sound of protest. "Did I hurt you?" He'd never drawn blood with a woman before. Hell. He'd never bitten one, either.

"Nope. I'm good." She stretched like a satisfied cat. "But sleepy. Let's take a break."

A break? He wouldn't be able to go for a while. Instantly proving him wrong, he started to harden again. What was it about this woman? "Hold on." He slipped off the bed and moved to the adjacent bathroom to dispose of the condom, strode into the living room to let the dogs in, and then returned to her.

The woman was already asleep.

He let himself look his fill. Her light hair splayed out in every direction like sunshine, a perfect backdrop for her pale skin and firm body. Her breasts were small, with light pink nipples that matched her lips. He tried not to wish for things that could never be. Even now, after a truly spectacular time with her, his body ached. His hip hurt like he'd been burned, and his head was starting to pound.

He lifted her easily off the bed and pulled back the covers, setting her inside as gently as possible. Then he slid in beside her, turning to spoon his body around her. For as long as he was able, he'd protect her. Then he'd come up with a plan for when he was gone, which was going to be soon.

It already felt like he had a fever.

Chapter 7

God, she was hot. Burning hot. Tabi opened her eyes, blinking several times as memories rushed in. "Evan?" she whispered, turning to where the heat emanated from.

He lay on his stomach with the covers pushed down to the dip of his waist. Sweat dotted his entire back, which was flushed a deep red. The muscles bunched and tightened as she watched.

"Evan?" she repeated, rolling to place her hand between his shoulder blades. "Ouch." She jerked back, her palm slightly burned. Awareness swept through her, and she sat up, poking his sweating shoulder. "You have a fever. A way too high fever." When he didn't move, she prodded harder. "Wake up, Evan."

His face was turned away from her, so she scrambled over him, standing by the side of the bed and leaning down. More sweat rolled down his ruddy face, and his hair was sopping wet. She smoothed strands away from his forehead. "Please wake up." Then she leaned down and shut her eyes to listen.

He was breathing, but it was labored.

Oh, this was so bad. Had she been too late to save him? Still naked, she ran to the guest room and yanked her phone from her purse, dialing quickly.

"What?" Raine growled into the phone. "It's too early to call, demon."

"Who are you calling a demon? That just isn't nice," a sleepy female voice muttered. A different voice than from the one the other day.

Tabi's legs trembled. "I need help, Raine. I might've goofed up. Or maybe it's the illness. I don't know." Her voice rose as panic tried to take her.

"Okay. Slow down. Where are you?" Covers rustled softly as the vampire obviously got out of bed.

She quickly rattled off the address. "Come as soon as you can." She ended the call and ran back into Evan's bedroom, stopping short as a wave of power hit her. Whoa. What was that? Her hands shook, but she quickly put on her clothes from the day before. "Evan?"

He still didn't move.

All right. That fever couldn't be good for him. She hurried into the master bathroom and doused several towels in cold water, returning to gently place them on his back and behind his neck. Then she winced as she saw the clear outline of her bite right beneath his jaw.

Her fangs were small but sharp. Very rarely used.

She quickly braided her hair out of her face while watching Evan, her stomach cramping. What if she'd just sped up his death? Oh, she should've done more research before trying to mate him. What the hell did she know about the process?

A loud knock sounded on the outside door. She jumped and then ran through the house to yank it open.

Raine Maxwell stood in the dawn light, his hair mussed and his jeans wrinkled. A dark tee stretched tight his wide chest. "Are you all right?"

She gulped and nodded, pulling him inside. "I'm fine. Although I may have really screwed up."

Raine stepped inside and looked around, his green eyes blazing. "Where are we? This isn't your place."

"It's Evan's," she said, her breathing shallow.

Raine's eyebrow rose. "You killed the cop?"

"I don't know." She grabbed the vampire's arm again and yanked him. "This way."

Raine sighed and followed her through the house and down the hallway. "I thought he was on your side. Why would you kill him?"

They reached the master bedroom, and Tabi pointed inside. "I mated him."

Raine jerked to a halt, and his eyes widened. "You fucking did what?"

Tabi winced. "I mated him. He's a nice guy, and he should live forever."

Raine shook his head like she'd thrown water up his nose. "You mated a *human* male?"

She gulped. "Yeah. I think so. I mean, I've never done it before, but I bit him and I think I marked him." She held up her hand to show her family marking on her palm. When a demon found their mate, a marking appeared with the first letter of their surname, kind of like a family crest. The marking transferred during the mating.

"You think?" Raine snapped, stepping into the room. He stopped cold. "Wow. That's a bucket full of power coming from that bed."

The wooden floor was cold on her feet but solid. Very solid. "I know," she admitted.

Raine shook his head and continued forward, looking down at the burning-up male on the bed. With one finger, he slid the sheet down to reveal Evan's hip and the perfect branding of the Rusko marking. "Yep. You sure branded him."

Tabi's eyes widened as she studied the marking. It was far more delicate than the military tattoo on Evan's shoulder. "He bit me, too." Her neck still hurt, and she sent healing cells to the injury. "Does that usually happen when an immortal mates an enhanced human?"

"I don't think so," Raine said, tugging the sheet back into place. "But we don't know much about enhanced males, since there aren't supposed to be many, if any, still alive." He stepped away from the bed, leaned against the wall, and stared at the silent male still sweating profusely.

"What now?" Tabi asked, her legs weak again. What had she been thinking?

"Hell if I know," Raine admitted. "You're young to mate, and he's a human who was dying of some sort of disease that I could sense."

"Huntington's Disease," she confirmed. "But mating should cure him, right?" Although she wasn't as strong as she'd be one day, once she'd lived a century or two. Surely that couldn't hurt Evan. Or could it? Yeah, she should've done a lot more research, somehow, before she'd risked his life like this. She was so impulsive sometimes.

"Shit," Raine said. "You might've just created a monster. We really don't know much about enhanced males. There's even a theory that they're more related to dragon shifters than witches."

Tabi coughed. "There's no such thing as dragon shifters."

Raine crossed his arms. "Yeah, there is. I guess it's a big secret, but it's getting out these days. Secrets never stay for long, you know." He shook his head. "We need to find out more, just in case I have to put him down."

No way. Tabi shook her head. "You will not harm him."

"Might not have a choice," Raine said. "Either way, we have to make a call."

Tabi's eyes widened. "No. Please."

"Yeah. We're calling the queen." Raine reached for the phone in his pocket. "God help us."

* * * *

Evan burned from the inside out. So this was what dying felt like. It hurt.

He tried to open his eyes, but his eyelids stayed shut. Lights swirled behind his closed eyelids, white and bright, muted and colorful. Pain took him, head to toe, centering in his chest like a ball of fire. Memories assailed him. His childhood, his parents, even his football coach. He relived his time in the military, made friends, lost brothers, then got sick.

Finally, the night with Tabitha.

At the thought of the stunning woman, he growled.

"What the fuck was that?" a male voice snapped.

Everything inside Evan bunched and coiled. He opened his eyes and jumped out of the bed, looking for the interloper.

Raine Maxwell leaned against his bedroom wall, a phone in his hand, his eyes a piercing green.

The smell of woman caught Evan's attention, and he swung his gaze to Tabitha. *His.*

She stared at him, her eyes a wide black catching all the light in the room. "Evan?" she asked.

The rumble of her voice spurred the beast suddenly inside him, and he reached for her arm, jerking her behind him. She fell against the bed and sputtered, standing up. "What the heck?" she whispered.

Evan turned to face Raine, his chin going down. He clenched his fingers into fists and prepared to charge.

"You're naked," Raine said reasonably, slipping his phone into his front pocket. "I'm ready to go if you are, and it'd be a good fight, but you are buck-assed nude. If you want to grapple, that's fine, but I'd really appreciate it if you'd at least put on some jeans. Dude."

Evan looked down at his nude body. His very hot, sweaty, tingling body. The room began to spin around him, and he staggered. He growled. Really growled. What the holy hell was happening?

"You're okay." Tabi's voice cut through the cloud in his brain, and her soft touch on his arm eased the raging turmoil inside him. "Let's sit you on the bed before you fall down."

Evan looked toward the one threat in the room, appeased that Raine hadn't moved away from the wall.

"Here you go," Tabi said, her voice slightly higher than normal. Stress? Fear?

He reacted to her emotion and sat, pulling her onto his bare lap. The room smelled like sex…and sweat. She struggled against him, and he tightened his hold, forcing his gaze to focus again.

"Well," Raine drawled. "This is certainly interesting."

Evan swallowed, barely catching enough spit in his mouth to ease down his desert dry throat. "Why are you in my bedroom?"

Raine smiled, the sight not even close to being amused. "Tabitha? Want to field that curveball?"

She partially turned to face Evan, her butt nicely placed over his suddenly aching cock. "Well, now. I need you to keep an open mind."

Evan's gaze jerked from her face to Raine's.

The man chuckled and held up a hand. "No. Not that open. God."

Tabitha sighed and patted the side of Evan's face. "Concentrate, would you? It's like this. Well, I'm a demonness, and I mated you when we had sex."

Oh God. Evan deliberately, very gently, set her next to him and stood to face Raine. "You're a part of this cult?" What had he been thinking to sleep with her? His head pounded like he'd been punched repeatedly with a rock, but he'd deal with his illness later. Right now, he had to help the woman he apparently had just taken advantage of during the night. He'd known she was troubled. "Maxwell?"

Raine sighed. "Cult? What's he talking about?"

Tabi started to stand and then halted when Evan glowered at her. "It's a long story, but there's no cult. Honest, Evan. You're an enhanced male, maybe part dragon or witch or something, and I mated you." She frowned, peering closer. "Do you feel any better? Maybe stronger?"

Actually, he felt like his head was about to blow right off his neck from the pounding agony at his temples. "Okay. Here's what's going to happen." He needed to drink a glass of water to stop sounding like he'd been chewing soup cans all night. "Tabi? I'm going to take you to Dr. Lopez to get some help, while Mr. Maxwell and I go to the station. I think you're under arrest, Raine." He'd get the threat behind bars before making sure Tabi was cared for.

"You were fired," Tabi reminded him.

Raine's eyebrows rose. "Fired? What did you do?"

Oh yeah. Evan had forgotten. He eyed Raine. "Did you kill Monte Loften? As part of your cult or something? Is Siosal involved, and did he get Abby Miller to help?" It would make sense since they all had provided an alibi for each other. What had he gotten Abby and now Tabi involved in when he'd all but forced them into that anger management group? "Is the shrink part of the cult?"

Raine scratched his head. "Did the mating scramble his brain, do you think?"

"I don't know," Tabi said softly. "He has a pretty high fever. Maybe he's delirious."

"A fever?" Raine twisted his mouth, obviously thinking. "That's rare. I don't think Abby got a fever when Siosal mated her. I've never heard of that, but I guess it could be possible. We'll know soon enough."

Tabi stood, pausing when Evan instinctively turned to keep his body between the woman and Raine. "You did not text the queen," she whispered tersely.

"Queen?" Evan said, anger flushing through him hotter than his fever. "Your cult has a fucking queen?"

Raine rubbed the whiskers along his jawline. "Maybe you should show him the marking?"

Tabi gasped. "Maybe. Look at your hip, Evan."

Was this a trick? Evan looked at his left hip and then his right, seeing a perfect tattoo of the R that had been on Tabi's hand. It looked kind of small on his hip, set crooked and leading to his ass. He gingerly touched it, noting the slight pain. His eyebrows rose, and fury lanced his chest. Had they somehow knocked him out during the night? Had he been poisoned or drugged? He felt like it. "You *branded* me when I was asleep? With your fucking cult sign?"

Raine knocked his head back against the wall. "For God's sakes. He's too dumb to be immortal."

Tabi sighed and wrung her hands together. "You're just not getting this, Evan. Please pay attention this time."

He turned fully to face her, that weird growling sound emerging from his gut. The room wavered and then started to spin around him dizzily. They had drugged him.

It was his last thought before falling hard into unconsciousness.

Chapter 8

A pounding not inside his head jerked Evan awake again, and he bolted upright on his bed. His bedroom was empty. He lifted his head, smelling Tabi's alluring scent right before sensing threats. He shoved from the bed and yanked his jeans on, drawing his backup gun from his dresser and padding barefoot down the hallway toward the living room.

Raine and Tabi were at the door, and they let in a definite threat. The man had black hair, deep black eyes, and a wide chest. He was as tall as Raine and moved like he could fight. His expression was pissed off, without question. "Maxwell," he said, his slight brogue Scottish.

"Who the fuck are you?" Evan snapped, pointing the gun at the newcomer.

The guy looked his way. One very dark eyebrow rose. "He's got power."

Ah shit. Another cult member. Evan sidestepped into the room, keeping all three in his sights. "Tabitha? Behind me. Now."

She threw up her hands and strode toward him, letting him put his body nearer the men. "Evan. Listen to me."

"Against the wall. Both of you." Evan gestured with the gun, feeling in control for the first time that day, although his temples still thrummed. "What drug did you give me?"

The newcomer gave Raine a side-eye look. "You drugged him?"

"Of course not." Raine pulled the guy inside. "What the hell are you doing here, Adare?"

Adare kept his focus on Evan. "I was on my way to fetch my wayward mate when the king asked me to detour here and lock down a threat until he arrived."

Not another freaking cult member. "Do you guys have a size requirement, or what?" Evan muttered.

Raine paused and looked at Adare. "You're working with the Realm?"

"No, but I'm not working against them, and when the king asks for a favor, it seems prudent to grant it. For now." Adare's brogue deepened and he tilted his head to look at Tabi behind Evan. "Who's the demonness?"

Raine sighed. "Tabitha Rusko and Evan O'Connell, this is Adare O'Cearbhaill."

Adare jolted. "Rusko? I thought you'd all died out. Aren't you crazy?"

Tabi stamped her foot. "I am not crazy, and we did not die out. Well, I'm alive, anyway."

This was too bizarre. "Where are my dogs?" Evan asked.

"Outside," Tabi whispered.

Raine shrugged. "All righty then. I'm out of here." He began to move outside, into what looked like late afternoon.

Evan had slept all day? "Stop, Raine. I will shoot you," Evan growled.

"Listen, copper," Raine said, looking even more put out than he had earlier. "No offense, but the Maxwells like to stay off the Realm's radar, and they're about to descend on you like moss on a river rock."

Evan stiffened. "Are we in danger?"

Raine lifted a shoulder. "Probably."

Evan had to get Tabi out of there.

She pushed to his side. "You can't be leaving me with the Realm," she protested.

Raine smiled. "I sure can. Good luck, you two." He hustled away faster than Evan would've thought possible.

"Don't shoot him," Tabi said. "He didn't do anything wrong, except leaving me for the Realm, and I'll handle him later. Somehow."

The Realm must be the name of the cult. Evan focused on Adare. "You said something about your wayward mate." Was there a woman in danger from this guy? While Evan wasn't a cop any longer, he couldn't let this massive man harm a woman.

"Aye," Adare said, holding up his right palm to show a faint tattoo. "The brat has sat on my last nerve, and I've allowed her enough freedom." The tattoo was different from the one on Tabi's palm and now on Evan's ass. Why didn't they have the same tattoo? The Scottish guy looked Evan up and down. "How are you feeling?"

What the hell? "I told you to get against the wall." Evan aimed his weapon between Adare's eyes.

The guy actually rolled them. Seriously.

Tabi hovered next to Evan. "Have you ever seen an enhanced male human? Especially one who got mated?"

Adare slowly shook his head, watching Evan closely. "Nope. I thought the Kurjans killed them all—mainly because there was something off with the biology of enhanced human males."

Tabi audibly gulped. "Off? Like what?"

"Like when their chromosomal pairs grew to the immortal level, they became themselves times a hundred. Assholes became serious assholes, and so on." Adare smiled. "I hope this guy wasn't an asshole."

"He wasn't. I don't think," Tabi said.

"Enough with this cult bullshit," Evan barked. "I will shoot you."

Adare's eyebrows rose. "He seems like an asshole. I've also heard something about testosterone and strength in mated human males that's unreal and had other species wary, which is probably why they were killed off." Then he stiffened, lifting his head and glancing outside. "Well, now. I guess I didn't have time to do much here. Good. Truth be told, I'm not sure what should be done with you, human."

Oh, man. Did these people think they were aliens or something? Evan shook his head. "How big is your cult?" They kept coming out of the woodwork.

As if on cue, bodies poured inside through both the back and front doors, all huge and wearing black clothing outfitted with several weapons. Evan backed Tabi to the fireplace, his gun at the ready, keeping his body between her and any threat. As soon as the house was swept, the soldiers all exited, save one large bastard with messy brown hair and eyes hidden by dark sunglasses. He stood by the door and tapped his ear. "The house is clear."

Who the hell were these people?

Evan leaned to the side. "When I tell you to run, do it."

The mammoth by the door shook his head. "There's nowhere to run. We have the entire block blanketed."

Evan drew in a deep breath. All right. If this was his last stand, it wasn't a bad one. Then a woman walked through the doorway, and he kept his aim on the huge guy, careful not to point at her.

"Thank you, Max," she said softly, patting the big guy on the arm while carrying what looked like a doctor's bag in her free hand. She was about medium height with long black hair and stunning blue eyes, and she'd dressed in dark jeans and a light green sweater. Her smile was contagious, and those eyes really sparkled. "You must be Evan."

Tabi pushed him in the back and shoved her way to his side. "Um, hi. Your highness. I mean, Queen."

This was the queen? The woman looked like the girl next door.

"Emma," she said, her lips curving. "You demonnesses sure cause some trouble. I love that about you."

A man walked through the door, tension emanating from him. Was that charisma? Or something more? He eyed Evan and then moved to the queen's side. He was tall and broad with black hair, his eyes also shielded by glasses.

Tabi, swear to God, curtseyed. "King Dage Kayrs. I've seen pictures of you both."

King? Oh, holy crap. The woman was in deep. Evan switched his aim to this so-called king, and that Max fellow instantly growled and moved forward.

The king stopped him with a wave of his hand. "It's okay, Max. O'Connell isn't a shoot first kind of guy." He smiled, all charm. "I might've caught up on you and any records pertaining to you while we flew here. Nice job overseas, by the way." He then turned his attention to Tabi. "Tabitha Rusko. I was so sorry to learn of your guardian's passing."

Tabi gaped. "How did you know about me? About Janet?"

The king guy sighed, the sound long suffering.

Emma rolled her eyes. "He's the king. Sometimes people forget that." She turned and patted his arm. "I know you could blow up the entire world with your brain because you're so powerful and all of that, Dage, but let's stay on track here." She pressed her lips together. "So, Tabitha. You mated a human male? Fascinating." She turned and studied Evan, delight dancing across her face.

Evan had the strongest urge to step back.

Max, the massive soldier, pressed his lips together as if trying not to laugh.

Adare took in the scene from his position near door. "I'll leave you to it, then. You owe me, king." Then he smoothly walked outside and into the breezy day.

"Say hi to Grace for me," Emma called out, studying Tabi as strongly as she had Evan. "So. I was a geneticist before mating the king here, and I'm now the chief researcher for the Realm. Does anybody mind if I take a little blood?"

Evan snarled. "I have no idea what you're all into, but nobody is biting me." Did these wackos actually think they were vampires?

The queen frowned. "Biting? No. I brought syringes. Of course."

Evan calculated the odds, and they weren't good. There had been enough soldiers, fully armed, searching his house that it was possible the entire neighborhood really was covered.

Dage watched him. "Why is he so sketchy? If he agreed to mate, surely he understood the parameters."

Tabi rocked back on her heels. "Well, he might not have truly understood the situation."

Evan glanced at her, and her face turned a lovely pink. "You're wrong. I most certainly understand what's happening. You're all in some weird cult, you drugged me, and you branded my hip," he said.

The queen stood straighter. "Can I see?"

"No," Evan snapped.

Dage pursed his lips. "Let me get this straight. First, we have an enhanced male human mated by a young demonness, and second, he doesn't know about other species."

Max looked them over. "I'd say this is a clusterfuck."

Evan caught sight of the soldier's left hand. "Is that pink fingernail polish with sparkles?"

Max growled and shoved his hand in his pocket. "I lost at darts. Don't want to talk about it. Teenagers can be mean. Really, really, really mean."

Evan caught his breath. They were all crazy.

Dage shoved both of his hands in his pockets. "All right. Let's start small. Evan, I'd appreciate it if you didn't shoot me." He took off his glasses, and his eyes glowed an eerie silver.

"Nice contacts," Evan said.

Dage smiled, and fangs dropped down from his mouth.

Evan swallowed. He reacted instantly, going tense.

Dage snarled and backed away. "Jesus. That's some power. Everyone shield your minds."

Tabi nodded vigorously. "I forgot that part. He could shield before I mated him, and he even shielded me from a demon mind attack. It appears he can attack, too. The guy is talented, I'm telling you."

She actually sounded proud of him.

Evan's ears rang. "I didn't attack anybody's mind. For Pete's sakes, knock it off." How did Dage get the fake fangs? Probably some sort of movie prop.

Dage apprised him, and those fake fangs went back into his mouth. How did he do that?

Evan looked at the so-called queen. "I suppose you have wild eyes and fangs, too?"

She tapped her fingers on her doctor bag. "Of course not. I'm an enhanced human. No fangs." Her face lit and she jutted her head forward to stare at Tabi's neck. "Did he bite you, too?" She turned toward Dage. "That's interesting, right? Humans don't usually bite. We need to find more records of enhanced human males—there's so much we don't know. Even you didn't know there were any left."

Dage frowned. "I'm sure I never thought about it. Although, now remembering, I believe they could often be a threat. Something about human nature being compounded into an immortal with the male of the species."

Emma hummed. "Well, that might make sense. Enhanced females are probably more intelligent and adaptable than the male of the species. Any species." The woman didn't seem to be joking.

Dage stepped away from the queen. "It appears as if fangs and eyes aren't going to do it for you in this case, Evan O'Connell. I'm a rather busy guy at the moment, with possible wars breaking out and all of that, so let's get on with this. I guess you'd better shoot me. Aim for the shoulder or leg, would you?"

Max instantly stepped forward. "No. Shoot me."

Fuck, these folks were nuts. Evan looked at Emma, hoping for some sort of rationality.

She stepped away. "Don't shoot me. I mean, I heal as well, but I hate to get shot. It's such a pain."

Evan could feel the danger around him, but he'd never been a person who could shoot an unarmed man. He shook his head.

"For Pete's sakes." Tabi grabbed his gun, yanked it free, and shot Dage Kayrs three times in the left arm before Evan could stop her.

Chapter 9

Tabi's mouth gaped open. "I shot the king," she whispered. Who would've thought?

Dage gave her a look as blood poured from the three wounds. "Thanks for missing my head."

Evan launched into motion, grabbing a pillow from the sofa. "Press this against the wounds, and I'll call for an ambulance." His voice was low and controlled as he no doubt fell back on training.

Dage sighed and pushed the pillow away. "Watch the wounds."

"What?" Evan snapped, tension rolling from him.

"Watch," Dage said, looking down at the bleeding holes in his arm. He sucked in air, and three bullets instantly plopped out of his flesh to fall onto the wooden floor. Then the holes mended shut. He wiped his arm off, leaving streaks of blood. "All good. See?"

Evan took a step back. "But…no way. No. That was a trick."

"It was your gun, buddy." The king used the word buddy? He looked at Tabi. "You know him better than we do. If his human personality is amplified, is he dangerous?"

"No. Bossy, controlling, and protective, however," she murmured. And she'd mated the guy.

Emma smiled. "Sounds like a normal vampire to me. Now can I please take some blood? I've never studied blood from an enhanced human male or a demonness who'd just mated one. This is so exciting."

Dage lifted his chin. "I'd like him unconscious if you're near him."

Max stepped forward. "I'd be happy to knock him out."

Evan growled, low and hard. "Try it."

Desire, warm and fast, flowed through Tabi's body. That sound.

Her neck, right where he'd bitten her, pulsed as if in perfect tune. "Why don't you take my blood first?"

"No," Evan said, his back vibrating.

The queen sighed. "This is too much. Maybe they should accompany us to Realm headquarters, and we can make friends there?"

Dage crossed powerful arms, one still bloody. "I've heard worse ideas." He looked at Tabi. "How close are you to finishing with your prototypes at your factory?"

Her mouth gaped open and she quickly shut it. "How do you know—"

"The. King." Dage muttered. "I know shit. Just answer the question, please."

Very impressive. "I'm probably a couple of months out, and if those work, I can go into mass production within another couple of weeks." She tried not to sound too proud.

"Excellent," Dage said. "I hope you give the Realm the right of first refusal. We'd make it well worth your while."

She smiled. Most of her people, maybe all, really liked making money. It came in so handy for a demonness. "Of course."

Emma tilted her head. "What's your invention?"

"It's a spray that masks faces from all CCTV and other recording devices," Tabi said. "Since humans have caught up so quickly with technology, and since we potentially live for thousands of years, it's necessary."

Emma smiled. "That's brilliant. Good on you."

Tabi tried to gauge Evan's mood, but his face revealed nothing. His mind had to be spinning. "So I guess we should talk?" she asked.

He turned, disbelief still in his eyes. "I don't know what to say."

Vulnerability twittered through Tabi, and she turned toward the queen, who'd once been an enhanced human. "Was it difficult for you to accept that there were different species on the planet?"

Emma shrugged. "No, but I'm psychic and knew there was more out there than anybody else could imagine. It seems like your mate's ability is like a demon mind destroyer's. He probably didn't even realize he had an ability."

Evan shook his head wildly and then reached for his gun in Tabi's hands before placing it on the mantle. "I'm not saying I believe all of this, considering I might've been drugged last night, but if I did, are you telling me I'm about to turn into a demon?"

Max snorted. "No. Nobody turns into anything different than they started as. We're all different species. Stop watching late night television."

Evan lowered his chin in an intriguing and threatening move.

Tabi grinned. Man, he was sexy. Hopefully he wouldn't turn into an immortal jerk now that she'd forced his chromosomes to multiply. And if she believed in fate, which she might, the marking did appear on her hand after he'd kissed her. That mattered to her people. "Listen. When an immortal mates an enhanced human, the human becomes immortal and can't die except by beheading or being burned to dust. Also, mates share abilities, so that happens."

Emma nodded. "Most mates can communicate telepathically after a while, too."

Dage watched Evan closely. "Mating is forever. You touch another female, since you're mated to one, and you'll get an allergic reaction that is not funny."

Emma looked to her side at the king. "Well, mating doesn't have to be—"

"It is," Dage said, his jaw hard. "When both parties are alive, even a deadly virus won't negate the mating bond."

Emma shrugged. "That might be true." She smiled at Evan. "Welcome to immortality."

He turned and looked at Tabi. "Everyone needs to get out of my house. Except for you, Tabitha."

A shiver wound down her spine. Was it fear? No. She'd never be afraid of Evan. Maybe wary, though. Her nipples peaked.

Emma switched her bag to her other hand. "If you let me draw blood from you both, then I promise I'll take all of these soldiers out of Indiana and fly them far away. You have my word."

"I thought we were taking them to headquarters," Max interjected.

"No," Tabi said. "We have a lot going on here, but I'll contact you if we want to seek refuge." Heck. Once she told Evan everything, she might be the one needing a safe place to land. Then she placed her hand on Evan's arm and turned toward him. "Trust me. She just wants blood to study."

"Trust you?" he repeated, his gaze shuttered. "Are you insane?"

Max chuckled. "Most demons are crazy, and the Ruskos are legendary."

Tabi glowered at him.

Emma withdrew medical supplies from her bag, hopping with what looked like excitement. "Who wants to be first?"

* * * *

The atmosphere in his home did feel different after everyone had left. Evan tried to grapple with what he'd just learned and turned for his kitchen. He might as well see if he'd gone nuts.

"What are you doing?" Tabitha asked, following him.

He reached for a knife from the block. "Seeing if this is all bullshit." Taking a deep breath, he lifted the blade. It wasn't like he hadn't been cut before in a fight or two.

"Wait." She grabbed his wrist. "You probably don't have healing cells yet. Don't cut yourself."

How could he have missed an entire other world living around them? It just didn't make sense. He paused, his mind reeling.

She gently took the knife and set it on the counter. "Okay. This must seem really weird to you." For once, the woman looked unsure of herself. She sighed. "Fine." Faster than a human should be able to move, she recaptured the knife and plunged the blade through her wrist. Blood burst out of the punctured vein.

Adrenaline flooded his system so fast he leaped for the dishtowel and wrapped it around her wrist. "Tabitha," he gasped. "What the hell?"

She winced. "That really does hurt."

Blood welled through the thin material.

"Okay. Now watch." She pushed his hand away and wiped blood with the towel. The deep puncture slowly mended shut, a white scar formed, and then it disappeared into smooth skin. She twisted the faucet and washed the remaining blood off her now healed wrist.

Evan swallowed, his stomach lurching. It was all true. She was a demonness, and that didn't even mean what he'd thought it would. She was just a different species. There were different species? Fucking crazy. "I need to sit down." Before he could reach the barstool, his phone dinged from the counter, and he reached for it like a lifeline. "O'Connell."

"Detective? It's Noah Siosal, and I just returned from the store. Abby was arrested when I was gone—do you know anything about it?" The man sounded like he'd just eaten glass.

Evan straightened. "I was fired, so no doubt the sheriff is taking matters into his own hands, and he was very good friends with Abby's ex." Abby's very dead ex-husband, that was. "Do you really have lawyers outside of town?" He went into cop mode and strode through the living room for his bedroom, reaching to yank on a T-shirt and searching for his socks.

"I just called in a couple from Indianapolis, and they'll be here in about an hour," Noah said tersely. "Why were you fired?"

"Doesn't matter. Does Abby know to ask for a lawyer? I made sure the two interrogation rooms have video surveillance, so she should be okay until one arrives." Evan sat and tugged on his socks, reaching for his boots by the dresser. "I still have a couple of friends in the department and will head down there right now to make sure she's okay." He didn't put it past the sheriff to intimidate her and try for a confession.

"I'm right outside of the station. That turd threatened to arrest me if I didn't leave the premises. Get here now." Noah ended the call.

"Tabi, let the dogs inside." Evan tossed the phone on the bed and dashed into the bathroom to brush his teeth and take care of business. When he returned, Tabi was already dressed with her hair in a ponytail. He paused. Wait a minute. "Is Noah—"

She nodded. "Yep. Part vampire, part demon. He mated Abby." Tabi's black eyes lit. "Hey. You can talk to her about all the changes. Maybe you are going through the same things." She rubbed her nose. "We didn't get a chance to talk, but you have to know, if you can't get Abby out, Noah will just storm the building and damn the consequences."

Evan shoved his hair into some sort of shape. "Wait a minute. Noah and Raine are hybrids, and you're a demon? What the hell are you doing in my town and in a stupid anger-management course? You're all immortal."

Tabi blew out air. "Well, let's see. Noah was forced into it to help that Ivar dude who's gone, and then I think he stayed because of an interest in Abby. Raine was there to maybe kill that Ivar guy, and I'm not sure why he's still around. He must have a reason. And I was there because you got me on video and wouldn't give it to me until I'd successfully completed the course."

Evan shook his head. "Immortals are crazy. Batshit nuts."

"That's just not nice," she countered.

He looked at her—really looked at her. Sexy, beautiful, and something else. Yeah. He could see it. A heat spiraled through him, landing hard in his chest and expanding out. *His*. "Before I was sick, when I was me, I was a possessive and way over-protective jackass," he rumbled.

Her eyebrows rose. "Why tell me that?"

"Fair warning," he said, a newfound power filling his body. He didn't have time to figure this new reality out right now, but whatever was going on, it started and ended with the miniature blonde looking warily at him right now.

"Hmm. Well, bottom line is that I saved your life." She tugged her wrinkled shirt into place. "We can be friends, we can be sometimes lovers, but I'm a free spirit. Don't ever forget that."

She was cute, too. He let his teeth show. "Don't think for a second that I've forgotten about Richard. Is he a demon, too?"

"Yes. You can tell by the light hair and really dark eyes. And mangled vocal cords." Her eyes flared. "I can take care of myself, Evan." A stubbornness tightened her jaw, and an impressive power flowed from her, easy to discern now that he knew more about her.

"Well now, I wasn't going to let you deal with him by yourself before I knew he was a demon." Evan strode through the living room, reclaiming his gun to tuck at the back of his waist. "You should've gotten to know me a little bit better before mating us together for eternity." The whole idea was blowing his mind, but the more he settled into it, the more he felt like himself again.

He would've never let the woman take on a powerful adversary on her own. Immortality or not.

Chapter 10

Tabi didn't mind hiding from enemies, and she enjoyed having a good fight once in a while. However, what she hated was feeling off balance. Evan had made her feel that way from the beginning, and now that she'd mated him, that sensation increased tenfold. "I really think we should talk about us and what we expect from each other," she said as he drove through town. The man had insisted on driving, and damn if she hadn't let him.

"That's fine, but right now I want to know who Richard Goncharov and the Popovs are." He turned a corner, his gaze scouting both sides of the car.

She'd forgotten he'd heard the threat from Richard. "You don't need to worry about them."

"Tabitha." One word, steel in the sound.

She rolled her eyes. "Fine. I was business partners with the Popov brothers for a while, and we didn't get along. We amicably split up our business interests. Then my developers created the spray that's going to make me billions, and the Popov brothers are pissed and out for blood."

Evan pulled into the lot of the police station. "And Richard?"

"He's very wealthy and owns a few islands. He's offered to mate me and protect me from the Popovs." Not that she needed protection, as soon as she made her own billions from the masking spray. "I'm a purebred demon, without any family, and that matters to him."

Evan frowned. "Does it matter to you?"

"No. I'm not going to mate him, and I'll handle the Popovs." She released her seatbelt.

"Oh, I don't think so." Evan cut the engine. "As I see it, you've made all the decisions so far. It's my turn."

She didn't like that at all. Her chin rose. "Now wait a—"

He was already out of the car and striding toward Noah, who waited near the front stairs of the station, looking for all the world as if he was about to storm the building.

Tabi scrambled out of the car and ran behind him, catching up just as the two males stared at each other. Why hadn't she realized how broad Evan was before?

Noah cocked his head and took them both in. "You did not."

Tabi kicked a pebble out of her way. "I did."

Evan watched him. "How can you tell?"

Noah, his eyes a blazing black, shook his head. "I can smell the change in you. In you both." He focused on Tabi. "How did you even know he was enhanced? I didn't sense anything. Didn't even know there were enhanced males around."

She swallowed. "I couldn't attack his mind, and he protected me from another attack."

"So you just went and mated him?" Noah lowered his voice. "Are you nuts? There's a reason we let enhanced human males die out." He shifted his gaze to Evan. "No offense."

"None taken." Evan turned and started climbing the steps. "You two stay out here."

Oh, she was not starting this matehood by taking orders. Tabi hustled after him. "Abby is not only my friend but my employee, and I am going to help her." Even if she had to melt the minds of everyone inside.

Evan opened the door and leaned down, his gaze hot. "Don't even think of attacking anybody. I will handle this. Got it?"

Man, he was bossy. She swept by him without answering, for the first time wondering what she'd gotten herself into. This time. "Hello." She put every ounce of charm she owned into her smile at the lone uniformed officer behind the reception desk.

The man had to be in his early twenties with wiry blond hair and a smattering of freckles that went from his forehead down his scrawny neck. He gulped. "Hi. Um, hi. Can I, um, help you?" He sat straighter in his chair and put his narrow shoulders back.

She reached the desk and leaned over, tapping her nails on the wood. "Oh, I'm sure you can, Officer…Thomas." She read his name and then focused on his eyes. "My friend was brought in here."

He swallowed loudly. "Your friend?" The man sounded like he'd really like to be her friend, too.

"Yes," she purred. "Abby Miller. Could I see her?"

The man turned red and breathed in. "Um, Abby Miller. Let me see. Um, I probably have a file here."

Evan reached her side. "Jesus. Give the kid a break, would you?" He frowned at the officer. "Barry? The sheriff arrested somebody with a solid alibi, and her name is Abby Miller. I don't want you to get in trouble, so sit here and talk to my girlfriend. I'll be right back."

Tabi's head jerked. *Girlfriend?* He'd said the word with more than a hint of possessive warning to the officer. "I'm not the girlfriend type," she retorted. She was a demon, for Pete's sake.

Evan turned, pinning her with that unreal blue gaze. Was the blue rim around his iris darker than it had been before? His chest seemed broader, too. Although he'd been pretty damn muscled before the mating. "Oh, we'll find the right term for you later, Tabitha. Right now, stay here."

A threat and an order. She'd created a monster. So she smiled, lowering her chin, and gave him a full shot of charm. "No problem." Then she winked at the furiously blushing cop. "Barry and I will just have a nice chat."

Evan's nostrils flared and he turned to stride past the desk to a wide wooden door, which he easily opened. Then he was gone.

Tabi lost the smile. Oh, that male had another think coming if he thought he was calling the shots. "Bye, Barry," she said, turning toward the outside door.

"Wait," Barry protested. "Evan said you should stay here and talk to me."

She pushed open the door, smiling over her shoulder. "Evan should learn not to give orders." Then she left the station and her new mate behind.

Jackass.

* * * *

Evan nodded at the few folks he liked and strode into the sheriff's office, slamming the door with enough force to knock a framed painting of the sheriff and his pompous family off the wall. It fell to perch on one corner of the metal frame, teetering by a scratched file cabinet. Silence reigned outside the office, and it was telling that nobody tried to intervene. "I don't think anybody likes you," he observed, staring at the sheriff across his shiny desk.

The sheriff's pudgy nostrils flared. "What the hell are you doing here? I fired you." He stood, broad and beefy, with the window open to the quiet trees outside.

"You have one second to tell me where Abby Miller is before I call the press, Baker," Evan said, leaning back against the door. "Not just the local press, either. Those big city reporters love a small town corruption story, now don't they?" The place smelled like mothballs. Why hadn't he noticed that before? "Where is she?"

Baker's face turned a motley red color. "She's cooling it in a cell right now before I question her."

"Probable cause?" Evan barked.

"Murder. I know she murdered Monte, and I'm going to prove it. Maybe she paid those criminals in anger management to cover for her. Maybe she fucked them all. I don't know, but I will find out." Baker's eyes swirled a furious hue.

Anger settled like a cold punch in Evan's gut. "You don't have probable cause, and you know it. Not only have you harassed an innocent woman, one your buddy beat the crap out of for a year, but you've opened the county up to a lawsuit now. You're not fit for the job."

"You think you can challenge me for the job? I fired you, and doesn't that look just great?" Baker smiled, showing tobacco stained teeth. "Besides, we both know you ain't gonna be around for much longer. I've seen you shake and tremble. I saw when your leg gave out and you fell into your chair, just a couple of weeks ago. Even if you live through whatever is happening to you, you can't do this job."

"A doorknob could do this job better than you have," Evan growled, his limbs feeling like his own for the first time in years. Could he run for sheriff? Had this whole mating thing cured him, or was this just temporary? He needed to get answers from Tabitha before making any plans. Hope tried to rise in him, and he ruthlessly shoved it down. For now, he had a job to do. "Let Abby Miller out right now. Her lawyers are going to be here any minute, and from the sound of it, they'll already be planning the lawsuit." Well, probably.

Baker shifted his belt over his big belly, his eyes darting around. "I'm not out of line here."

"Wrong." Evan was done. He grabbed the keys off the hook by the door. "I'm letting her out. If you try to stop me, I will beat the absolute shit out of you in front of the other cops here. The whole town and no doubt county will hear about it, I'm sure. Yeah, I'll take a battery charge, but it'll be a first offense, and it'll hit all the papers. You know what? That might be a decent launch to a campaign for sheriff."

Baker sputtered, even his ears turning red.

Evan opened the door and strode through the bullpen to the back hallway leading to the cells. Quick movements had him at the farthest cell, unlocking the door.

Abby looked up from sitting on a blanketless cot, her greenish-brown eyes wide. She looked small and defenseless in the claustrophobia-inducing cell. "Detective O'Connell." She stood, looking over his shoulder.

"Noah is outside," Evan said, gesturing her toward him, his temper fraying. How dare the sheriff scare her like this?

Relief smoothed her features as she hurried out of the cell. "Thank goodness. I thought for sure he'd come in ripping off heads and everything." She stopped cold. "I meant that figuratively."

"Right." Evan clasped her arm and started down the hall. They probably didn't have much time before Baker found his balls and tried to stop them.

Pain ticked through Evan's palm, and he jerked away, looking at the rash on his skin. "Oh."

Abby kept walking. "Maybe you're allergic to my laundry detergent."

He opened the hallway door for her. "Or it's the mating allergy," he muttered.

She swung toward him, her jaw slack. "What did you say?"

"Later." He pointed toward the end of the bullpen, careful not to touch her again. The rash was already abating. It had appeared so quickly. Was it because they were both newly mated? Man, he couldn't believe any of this was real. "Let's get out of here."

"Good plan." She smiled serenely and nodded at the other

officers, picking up her pace until she reached the door to the reception area.

The sheriff stood in his office doorway, his hands at his sides. "I'll let you go for now, Mrs. Loften. But we're not done."

Abby paused by the doorway and turned to face him fully.

Evan stopped and then waited.

"It's Ms. Miller now." She smiled. "You're a corrupt moron, Sheriff Baker. I know it, you know it, and I suspect most of the people who work for you know it. Falsely arrest me again, and I'll sue you for everything you have." She looked around at the silent officers at their desks, confidence in her gaze and her shoulders back—so much different from the woman Evan had rescued just a month before. "One of you should think about running for sheriff—if Detective O'Connell doesn't want to do so. I'll start a campaign fund right away." Then she turned and opened the door, her head held high as she exited.

Evan banked a grin and followed her through the reception area and outside, where she ran full bore into Noah Siosal's arms.

Noah grabbed her up, lifting her, inhaling her scent. "You're okay?"

She nodded. "I'm fine." When he let her down, she snuggled into his side.

Evan looked around the quiet sidewalk. "Where's Tabi?"

Noah shrugged. "She came out a while ago and drove off like hell in the BMW."

Evan's jaw set. His nostrils flared. His chest heated and his ears began to ring. "I told her to wait for me, and I believe she agreed." Oh, she had. They were about to have a serious discussion, once he found her. For now, he focused on Noah. "So. Rumor has it you're a vampire-demon hybrid."

Chapter 11

Rain started to fall as Tabi drove sedately home from her factory where the techs would work late. She was so close to mass production, and she was going to make a fortune. She glanced at her phone, which she'd left in the car all afternoon. Yep. Several calls from Evan. Too bad. He shouldn't have ordered her around earlier that day. The sooner he figured out she was her own person, the easier this transition would be for him. Hopefully Noah had given him a ride home from the station.

She shouldn't feel guilty about ditching him, so she didn't. Yet she bit her lip. The poor guy was probably really confused by this new world, and maybe she should help him out a little, considering she'd yanked him into immortality. Maybe she'd look him up in the morning.

Turning into her driveway, she stilled at seeing him leaning against her one-car garage, a badass motorcycle to the side of him.

Her panties turned wet. Plain and simple.

She swallowed and turned off the car. Okay. She could handle this. Keeping her posture ramrod straight, she stepped out of the car, grateful for the four-inch heels on her boots.

He crossed his arms, his gaze a burning blue through the dusk. "Where have you been?"

Irritation prickled up her back while heat flowed down her front. She blinked from the contrary sensations. "I was working at my factory." Not that he'd know which one was hers—there were many outside of the mainly industrial town, and she'd purchased it using several dummy corporations. "Also, you don't have the right to question me. You're no longer a detective."

"I wasn't asking as a detective," he rumbled, the rain dancing lightly over his hair.

Why was he giving her the arrogant immortal act? "You're human," she blurted out.

"I'm male," he countered, the statement firm. "Maybe human, maybe not. I don't know. What I do know is that I told you to wait for me at the police station hours ago."

She couldn't breathe. There had always been something about him, this steel hard core covered by protective instincts and kindness. "I don't take orders from you," she said, stopping a couple of feet away from him.

He cocked his head, studying her.

Tingles exploded across her skin, zipping through her body. She set her stance to hide her reaction to him. This was not going according to plan. At all.

"I had quite a nice talk with Noah today. All about vampires, demons, and the rest. All about mating and the rioting feelings that arise." His voice was low…silky. "You know what I think, Tabitha?"

Her mouth went dry. "I have no idea."

"I think you mated a human on purpose. Ambitious and independent twenty-five-year-old demonness obviously running from danger finds herself a nice human male to lead around by the nose. Have some fun and then move on, safely mated but with all the freedom in the world."

There was enough truth in the statement that her hackles rose fast. "I saved your life."

"That remains to be seen, although I have stopped shaking and feel like I could handle anything." His arms dropped to his sides. "Including you."

"That's doubtful, human." She tossed her purse back into the car and slammed the door. While only a quarter of a century old, she'd trained to fight almost from birth. If she had to beat the crap out of her new mate and show them both how this was going to go down, she'd do it. "Your stance is the wrong one. Change it." Her voice trembled just enough to piss her off even more.

He blinked. Once and slowly.

Never in her life would she have thought a blink could be threatening. Yet this was. Those blue eyes burned through the dusk, and that rim around his iris had darkened. She was sure of it. "You've lived in my world for one day, Evan. Don't think for a second you understand it," she said.

"I've lived in this world, our world, about a decade longer than you have, sweetheart. I've seen war, and I've done things for God and country that you can't even imagine." He moved then, headed her way.

For the first time in her entire life, Tabitha Rusko had to fight the urge to back *away* from danger. It was true that she'd only met the mellow detective who had thought he was at the end of his too-short life. Apparently she'd never met the soldier or the male who'd been strong enough to survive an immortal mating even while ill. He was no longer ill. What he was, she didn't know.

He reached her, standing a mere foot away. "The marking on a demon's hand only appears when their mate is near. Yours appeared when I kissed you the first time."

"Yes," she admitted. "But I don't believe in fate and all of that." Yeah, she sounded defensive and unsure.

"I do," he said, his chin down, studying her like he'd never really looked at her before. Like she was now in *his* world, and he was trying to decide what exactly to do with her.

She threw up her hands, going for a good offense. "You seemed like a laconic cop who just wanted to help people. Even though we had this obvious attraction for each other, you stayed distant. Like I plan to do." She couldn't just drop everything and trust somebody right now. Not until she set herself up with enough money and power to keep safe. Maybe to keep him safe.

"I was dying," he said, that focus becoming unnerving. "Now I'm not. Probably."

"You're not," she snapped. "Mating makes you immortal. While our blood can't cure diseases in humans, a mating does." Although he could use some doubt in his mind, apparently. She spoke too soon. Maybe she should try to reason with him, but as far as she'd heard, that rarely worked with mated immortal males. "I'm kind of on my own mission right now."

"World domination?" he drawled.

She grinned. "No. Just security and safety, which comes from money."

"I think safety now comes from me, baby." This close, power already cascaded off him—strong and sure.

Oh, crap.

* * * *

Evan hadn't felt this strong in two years. His body felt like his own again, and he studied the female in front of him intently. Interest and a barely banked vulnerability glimmered in those eyes that had haunted his dreams, and he should probably back off and let her come to terms with what they'd voluntarily done. While he had no clue what forever meant, right now, they had to come up with a plan together. The bottom line was that even though she was the immortal being, he did have years and experience on her. "You're naïve if you think money brings safety." Even he knew that.

She lifted her chin, the challenging sight stirring his desire for her even higher. "It sure doesn't hurt."

"True." The skin along his nape prickled, and he turned instinctively to see Richard Goncharov stride along the house from the backyard. Had he been waiting? Evan's chest filled and his blood flowed faster through his veins, sparking almost painfully. What was happening?

Richard, his face hard, reached the other side of the vehicle. "I've waited long enough. The Popovs are coming, and you need to leave with me now." His focus remained on Tabi, and he ignored Evan as if he wasn't there.

Evan crossed in front of the BMW, coming within a foot of the demon. "She's mated, friend. You've lost—leave town." The sense of possessiveness taking him held a life of its own—strong and brutal. He forced his hands to relax and not form fists. Whatever was happening, he would handle it like he had every other challenge in his life. "Goodbye."

Richard turned his body to face him fully, his extra inches of height making him crane his neck. "You're human."

"So I've heard," Evan said evenly.

Richard's nostrils flared in his pale face, and his eyes widened. "I smell her on you." He turned so suddenly the air cracked. "You mated a *human*?"

"Yes," Tabi said, meeting his gaze over the sports car. "It's complete and a done deal, so there's no reason for you to remain in town. I believe my mate told you to leave."

Evan settled—slightly. Hearing her claim him as her mate

calmed some of the fire raging inside him. "Go."

Richard's lips peeled back and his fangs dropped. "The Popovs will kill you both. At least sell me your business—you'll have enough funds to get somewhere safe." Then he named a price that had Evan's eyebrows lifting. These people worked in millions and not thousands.

Tabi scoffed. "The business is worth billions—possibly trillions. I'll never let it go."

Evan stepped closer to the demon, not liking the fangs out. "She's safe now and will remain so." Even as a human, he would've protected her.

"You're not." Richard attacked faster than a whisper, grabbing Evan's arms and slashing sharp fangs down his neck.

Pain exploded near Evan's ear, and he shoved the demon off him.

"No!" Tabi leaped for Richard, sliding on her knees across the BMW hood, her nails scoring down his face.

The demon roared and backhanded her. The sound of his hand impacting her cheek echoed through the rain, and she cried out, tumbling backward and off the side of the car.

Anger exploded inside Evan, and he dodged forward, grabbing Richard by the neck and yanking him away from the hood with one hand, punching with the other. Richard fought back, his punches holding more strength than any human's ever had. They dropped to the ground, hitting and grappling for position.

Richard nailed Evan in the nose, and his entire skull clamored. His vision blurred.

"Stop it." Tabi jumped back into the fray, punching Richard in the neck and trying to protect Evan from the blows.

"Damn it." Evan grasped her arm to pull her out of the way.

Richard jumped to his feet and kicked Evan in the gut. Agony ripped throughout Evan's rib cage. He shoved himself to his feet, pulling Tabi up and shoving her behind him.

She pushed to his side and kicked up, nailing Richard beneath the jaw.

The demon's head snapped back, and he quickly recomposed himself, his fangs dropping even lower and his eyes swirling to a lighter gray. His reach was long enough that he swung out, smashing her right in the temple with his large fist.

She smashed into Evan's side, crying out.

Fury swelled and heated inside Evan, and he moved without thinking, punching with all his strength toward Richard's neck. His fist kept going through flesh, cartilage and bone, snapping a vertebra at the back. Growling, beyond rational thought, he swept his arm right and then left, decapitating the threat.

Richard's head dropped to the ground, rolling under the car. His body fell forward, landing on the wet pavement, his legs kicking out. Blood poured from the neck and covered the pavement.

Tabitha held her cheek and backed away, her wide eyes staring at the decapitated corpse. "You punched through his neck."

Evan stepped away, the demon's blood on his hand burning. He shook it and released the cartilage sticking to his palm. "Yeah." He came back into himself, his breath fast.

Tabi looked at him, her mouth open and shock freezing her features. "You really punched his head off."

Evan looked down at his fist. "I guess I did. I must've gotten stronger with the mating?"

She lowered her hand, revealing two large and mottled bruises forming. "You don't understand. You can't just punch through an immortal's neck. I mean, you…can't."

Evan frowned. "I did." He winced at the sight of the decapitated body. "Do demons have weak necks?"

"No." Tabi's voice trembled.

He looked at her, a cold pit settling in his gut. "Maybe Richard had some sort of neck disease?"

She slowly shook her head, watching him like *he'd* become the threat.

Huh. Evan held his hand out to let the light rain wash off the burning blood. "You've never heard of that happening?"

"Maybe during battle or in extreme duress, but only when an enemy is already on the ground," she whispered. "Nobody should be able to do what you just did. I mean, we take heads, but we usually use a sword or boot or blade. Not just a punch."

Evan sighed. "So I'm not normal."

She took another step away from him, slicing his heart in two. "No. Which means you're in more danger than we thought. We have to get rid of this body. Now."

Chapter 12

The buzzing of her cell phone awoke Tabi from a deep sleep. She reached for it before remembering where she was. A glance to the side, and she confirmed she was in Evan's bed next to the ex-cop and his incredibly hard body. Two snoring dogs sprawled out on the floor. "Hello?" she answered, trying to center herself.

"Hi, Tabi. It's Emma. I'm sorry to have awakened you," the queen said, sounding distracted.

Tabi sat up, her breath catching. "That's all right. What's going on?"

"Nothing. I just finished the blood tests, and your blood is reacting like any new mate's would. Evan's is different, but I think it's just because he's the only enhanced human male I've ever tested. The cells are wild, really. How is he doing?"

"Great," Tabi said. "How is his blood different?"

Evan turned on his side, his blue eyes clear as he watched her.

"His blood is changing much faster than I've ever seen a mate's blood change, which might be unique to him, rather than all human males. The cells are amping up like they've been shot full of adrenaline, and the chromosomal pair advancement is almost already done. I just don't know. He might be stronger than most immortals as well, but we'll see. I assume he'll be like most mates and gain your skills, but his might be enhanced on their own, which would be something new. I'd like to conduct more tests on him."

Tabi swallowed. "We'll definitely keep it in mind."

"Is he showing any unusual signs? Anything that has caught your attention?" the queen asked.

"Well, he's being a bossy and overbearing butthead," Tabi said, remembering the night before when he hadn't really given her a choice in where she was staying the night. "I'd even say controlling."

Emma laughed. "That's not out of the ordinary for a mate. I meant something more or that doesn't seem right."

Like the fact that Evan had punched right through a demon soldier's throat the night before and then had calmly dug a grave in the middle of nowhere that would never be found? "No, I haven't noticed anything," Tabi lied. "If I do, I'll call you right away. For now, we have some adjusting to do."

"I understand. It's not an easy time for a new mate, even one who's a demonness. Take it from somebody who's been there. Life is a lot easier if you work together on it, and being protected and safe is a pretty nice way to live—especially once you have kids." The queen signed off.

Kids? Who said anything about kids? Tabi was at least a century away from wanting kids, and if Evan was this overbearing now, he'd be impossible once they had kids. If they had kids. If they stayed together to have kids someday in the far away future, which was something she had not agreed to yet.

She looked over at her mate. After disposing of the body the night before, Evan had insisted she stay the night at his bungalow, and she'd basically passed out from exhaustion and what was probably shock.

In the early dawn light, he watched her in that way he had—one he'd used even as a human. Now it held even more power.

Her body short-circuited in response, one more thing out of her control suddenly. Rain splattered against the window, with the storm having strengthened throughout the night, and her blood started to pump in tune with the wild weather. "Your tests show you might have a very rare extraordinary strength," she murmured.

"No kidding." He continued to watch her.

She met his gaze, refusing to back down. "If you have something to say, say it."

"If I'd met you when I was healthy, I would've handled you differently," he said, his voice a low rumble in the morning.

She partially turned to face him, comfortable that the borrowed shirt covered her completely. "Handled me? I don't think so, Detective."

He leaned up on his powerful arm, and the muscles rippled

across his chest. "I was trying to save you from the hypocrisy in this town, in this county, so you could leave before I died."

She forced a smile, hoping it looked somewhat bored. Or sarcastic. "You're done trying to save me now?"

One of his dark eyebrows rose. "Oh, I'm definitely going to save you from whoever these Popovs are, and we're going to have a nice long talk about them later today. I want to know everything, and if there's a way to reason with them without killing, I'll find it."

"And if not?" she whispered.

His gaze didn't waver. "Then I'll take off their heads." He looked down at his other fist. "Apparently I don't need any other weapon to do so."

Just because he'd been able to decapitate one demon that way didn't mean he could do it again. Maybe this bizarre strength was temporary as his body completed the mating to become immortal. "Listen, Evan. I'm not sure what's happening to you and how you're changing, but I think we need to set a couple of parameters here."

Was that amusement in his eyes? "Interesting. Tell me how I'm changing."

She'd wanted to talk about parameters, but maybe they should discuss this. "I don't really know, but it seems like new 'immortal pain-in-the-ass' testosterone, or whatever male demons or vampires have, is flooding you and changing you a bit. I'm sure it will abate." She hoped. Forget the fact that it was sexy and intriguing. She'd better set him straight now.

"Hmm." He ran his free hand down her arm, the touch electrifying. And possessive. "Different theory. The illness I had as a human changed me, and now that I'm getting healthy, and believe me, I feel healthy again, maybe I'm going back to my default setting. This is the real me, Tabitha."

"I'm not certain what that means," she admitted, acutely aware of the strength he now possessed as well as the fact that they were in bed together. Intimacy wound around them, through her. She swallowed, trying to hide the sudden sense of vulnerability.

"You never have to fear me. I promise." He tugged her down and rolled on top of her, heat and male pressing her to the mattress and stealing her breath. "I understand that we're both in new worlds all of a sudden, and we can navigate it all together. But you need to understand, I'm not relenting on this one fact. We are a team, and that's how we'll proceed forward."

"A team has a leader," she said, her gaze dropping to his mouth.

"We can divide the tasks," he said, grinning. "I remember the early days before my mom passed away, and my parents created a plan together. She handled school and he handled sports. She handled health and church, and he dealt with the money. They worked well together."

She blinked. "That sounds like a good family. I'm sorry you lost them."

His face softened. "You are a sweetheart sometimes. You don't have family?"

The idea hurt. "No. There's nobody."

"Wrong. There's me. You and me." He kissed her forehead, his lips heated. "Are you mine, Tabi?"

Whoa. Wow. "Um." A jolt of awareness and want took her by surprise. His? Her thighs softened. "This isn't turning out like I thought." Yeah, her voice went hoarse and needy, and her core started to ache. For him. Only for Evan O'Connell, a male it appeared she couldn't control.

His grin held steel. "I figured. Why don't you tell me what you'd planned?"

That was the problem. She never planned—or hardly ever. "Well, I guess I thought you'd be grateful I'd saved your life and then I'd kind of protect you from afar and do my thing." It was difficult to concentrate with his hard body over her.

He shifted his weight, settling his rigid cock between her legs. Only the thin material of her panties separated them. She bit back a moan.

By the flaring of his eyes, he felt it against his chest. "Is that how things usually go with immortals?"

She snorted. "No. Not at all. Didn't you notice that either Dage or Max could've taken both of us out if either of us had threatened Emma? I'm sure the queen can fight, and I'm also sure the queen has never needed to fight." She paused. "But—"

"No but. I've had more fighting experience than you have, and it appears I'm stronger." He frowned, for the first time losing the arrogant glint in his eyes. "We're going to have to watch that and make sure I can control it. I'd never want to hurt you. Or anybody else, really."

Relief swamped her. Evan was back. The one she knew. "I agree, and I'm willing to stay here until you feel comfortable with your new powers. We'll work on it until you're sure you've got it under control."

"Tell me about the Popovs so I can handle them," he said.

Damn it. The Evan she'd known was *so* not back. "I'll handle them."

He brushed his nose across hers, both hands sliding her camisole up her ribcage. "If I haven't been clear, I apologize. You are no longer handling anything by yourself."

The thrill that took her was because of his warm hands and not the thought that she wasn't alone. That this big, strong, badass of a gentle giant was now being a bossy asshat should not turn her on or make her happy.

Yet the warmth in her center wouldn't leave. "Evan—"

"You haven't answered my question, so I'll lead you there." He removed her top, settling his bare chest over hers and groaning softly. "Are we mated?"

She rolled her eyes, her hands working on their own to caress down his flanks. Her nipples hardened against him. "Yes."

"Is mating forever?"

"Apparently so," she said, scratching down his heated back, still sure she could turn this around. "You're welcome for my bringing you into this world."

"Hmm." He kissed her then—finally. Deep and sure with more than a hint of power. Oh, it had been there before, but he'd held back. Now he gave it all, giving her no choice but to take it. Then he released her, leaning back as if time had no meaning. "I was already in this world but hadn't realized how big it was. Now you're with me in it, demonness. I'm being as gentle as I can be with you, but you're going to come to grips with it and soon."

How had she missed this in him? "What the hell does that mean?" Why was he turning her on and pissing her off at the same time? It was too hard to concentrate.

"You mated me knowing full well what mating meant. I'm just taking you up on the offer." His phone buzzed and he stiffened, reaching for it on his dresser. "It's the king."

She stiffened. "The king has your cell number?"

"Yeah. I called in a favor before he left the other day." Evan sounded so damn casual about the freaking king of the entire Realm.

Who was this male she'd mated? What had she done? "What favor?"

"I let his woman take my blood and yours." Evan lifted the phone. "Morning, Dage. What do you have?" His voice was all business, and then he listened, his gaze remaining on Tabi's eyes. "When?" Those blue eyes narrowed. "Thanks for arranging the meeting." He ended the call, his jaw hardening.

"What?" Tabi whispered.

The phone shattered in his hand. He looked at it, his brows rising. "Shit."

She shivered, taken aback. Maybe he was more dangerous than even she'd realized. "We need to work on that strength."

He tossed the useless pieces toward the floor and looked back at her. "*We*. I like that. Now you're learning."

Irritation mixed with the desperate desire flooding her. This entire situation had gotten away from her, and it seemed Evan had the control now. Oh, she had to do something about that but couldn't think of the right move. "What did the king say?" she asked.

"The Popovs flew to Indiana yesterday. They're here now." He rolled off her to stand.

She sat up, grabbing the covers. Wait a second. They had been getting naked and working out this dynamic between them. Hopefully an orgasm or two would get them on the same track. "What the heck are you doing?"

"I'm going to take care of them. One way or the other. You stay here." He reached for his discarded jeans.

She jumped out of bed, not caring she was only wearing light green panties. "Oh, hell no."

Chapter 13

The Popovs weren't what Evan expected. He sat across from them at Jimmy's diner in the middle of town, their table at the rear of the local landmark. They were brothers, and they looked like it. What they didn't look like were demons.

Allen seemed to be the leader of the two, and his black hair was longer than his brother's and reached his shoulders. He also looked to be an inch or two taller. Both males had reflective topaz colored eyes and a lot of facial hair that wasn't exactly groomed. Did some demons look like hicks?

Tabi sat next to him, her expression serene but her eyes lively. "Heard you two had some trouble down in Argentina with your factories."

The younger brother, Lance, leaned forward. "That was you?"

She waved her delicate hand through the air. "Of course not. You know that's not my style. Although I wouldn't be surprised if it had been Richard Goncharov in an attempt to woo me."

Allen snorted. "I heard about that. Apparently you didn't take him up on the offer, and yet I'll track him down about those factories. Thanks for the tip."

"He's dead," Evan said smoothly.

Lance looked at Tabi. "You?"

"No," Evan said. "Me."

The two males turned to study him, although they'd been unobtrusively doing so since Evan and Tabi had sat in the still busy café.

"You're not a vampire or demon," Lance said quietly.

"Neither are you," Evan said.

Tabi jumped. "Didn't I tell you? Sorry. They're wolf shifters."

Wolf fucking shifters? People who actually turned into animals? That only happened on television. How many other species were in the world, anyway? Evan kept his face stoic and his questions at bay. So many questions. "My mate forgets to fill in details sometimes."

Tabi stiffened. "I've been busy."

Allen's eyebrows lifted. "Stealing from other people instead of just us these days, have you?"

Evan kept the male's gaze. "Tabi? Did you steal from these folks?"

"No." She hopped on her chair, irritation wafting from her that ticked up his spine. Interesting, his body reacted to her emotions, and his hand closed into a fist. "We ended our arrangement before my techs discovered the best prototype," she finished.

Oh, there was no doubt the female had ended the partnership at an opportune time, but as far as Evan was concerned, that was business. "Well, then. What is it you gentlemen want?"

Lance tilted his head. "Not a shifter or witch. I've got it. You're a fairy."

Fairy? Evan frowned.

"Yep. He's Fae," Tabi agreed. "Most people can't sense it. Nice job, Lance."

Fae? Yet another freaking species? What was that about witches? Man, Evan needed to get caught up on this world. Why had Tabi lied? Apparently it was less dangerous for him to be thought of as a Fae than an enhanced human male. Was he really that deadly? Maybe it wasn't safe to be around him, but he'd always had skills, and he'd tempered them. Could he do so now? "All right," he muttered. "Let's get to it, then."

Allen gazed at him. "I heard your people can no longer travel between worlds. That must suck."

Worlds? What worlds? Evan's patience was rapidly shredding. Being in the dark was never a good position. Apparently he needed to sit his smart-ass mate down and get more answers about pretty much everything. "Let's keep to the subject. What. Do. You. Want?"

Allen blinked. "Half ownership of any company with a stake in the new masking spray. I know you're close, Tabitha."

"No," she said smoothly.

"We won't take anything less," Lance said. "Make the agreement, or you'll be looking over your shoulder for the rest of your probable short life." His eyes swirled, looking nothing close to human. "It'd be a pity for you to lose your new mate so quickly,

Tabitha."

Evan leaned forward. "The only thing that saves you from a quick death is that you threatened me and not her." He'd never fought a shifter before. "Asking for half of the business is ridiculous, and you know it." He looked to his mate at his side. "Is there any agreement you'll reach?" If she said no, then they might as well forget lunch. He took a drink of his coffee, letting her think it out. This was her business and her decision.

She sat back, calculation crossing her features that was probably the sexiest thing he'd ever seen. Smart girls had always knocked him out, and this one was brilliant and cunning—and a little reckless. He could temper the last one so she didn't get hurt. She twirled her coffee cup. "Well, I suppose we could reach a new deal."

Allen sat back, distrust darkening his eyes. "Go on."

"In order to mass produce the spray, I'm going to need several more facilities in the form of production and distribution. You have an excellent pipeline throughout most of the world. You pay me ten billion dollars so I can create the production facilities, and we use your distribution channels."

"Sure," Lance said. "For sixty percent of the company."

"Twenty," Tabi said, sipping calmly.

God, she was magnificent. Evan sat back to just watch her work, his chest expanding. From day one, she'd fascinated him. The first time he'd kissed her, he'd sank into home. Every new facet of her was fascinating…and his.

Allen laughed. "Not a chance, demonness. We'll give you no money up front but use our production and distribution systems for half the company. Forever."

"No," she said, finishing her drink. "My production facilities, because I don't trust you not to steal the invention. In my position, you wouldn't, either. Ten billion up front, and you get a thirty percent interest in the company. That's my final offer, and you have until tomorrow morning to decide. After that, I go another avenue." She pushed back her chair and stood.

Evan followed suit, leaving money on the table for all of the coffee. "Thank you, gentlemen." He pressed a hand to the small of his mate's back and escorted her from the restaurant, acutely aware of the different atmosphere from the shifters. Hot and angry.

Furious.

* * * *

Tabi held her head up high as she slipped into the passenger side of her own car. "I don't see why you have to drive."

He sat and looked at her, starting the engine. "You drive too fast. Way too fast."

"I like speed," she protested.

"Yeah, well this is a peaceful place with kids who don't look both ways before chasing a ball across a street," he countered, driving out into the quiet main drag.

There was the small town cop she'd crushed on from day one. Thinking of kids chasing baseballs. How was he the same guy who'd dug a grave the night before? "Are you okay about last night?"

He slowed down to let two elderly ladies cross the street toward the Eagles' Lodge. "Yes."

"I'm talking about killing someone and then burying his body—outside of the law." Had she ruined him?

He stopped at the one stop sign in the town, turning to look at her. Full on, blue stare. "He threatened what's mine. He threatened you. I'm absolutely fine with him no longer being a threat."

Whoa. Oh boy. Okay. "Is this a new thing, since we mated?" Maybe she should call the queen.

"I was a sniper for a SEAL Team before becoming a detective here as I prepared to die, sweetheart. I don't like killing, but I will protect my country and now you, with whatever means are necessary." His broad hands were more than capable on the steering wheel, and the muscles in his forearms flexed nicely. At least he hadn't broken the car yet.

She studied him. Strong and capable. He was dressed in a dark T-shirt with faded jeans, filling out both with ripped muscles. His body was impressive, and there was no doubt he was intelligent. But his heart, the protective way he had of caring for the people in the town, was what had caught her eye. Even though she'd been in trouble after beating the crap out of those boys who'd tried to mess with her, he'd been sweet and had helped her through the court system.

Her heart warmed.

He took another turn, heading back to his house. "Since we're talking billions here, how much is enough? Why not go into business with these guys?"

"They're jerks, and you can never have enough. It's the only way to stay safe," she countered.

"You mated me. That's your way to stay safe," he said, his voice way too calm.

She couldn't think. He was sounding more like an immortal than ever, and now what was she going to do? "Money is good, too."

"Maybe. You hungry? We didn't get breakfast."

There he was again, making sure she was all right. It was decent that he'd changed the subject, too. She jumped on it. "Yeah. I don't suppose you can cook."

His grin flashed quick and smooth. "You haven't lived until you've had my blueberry pancakes. I'm about to make you very happy."

The promise went deeper than that, and she could almost touch it. So she backed away. "I'm not one for sharing."

"You'll learn."

She blinked. "What I'm trying to say—"

"I know what you're trying to say," he said, pulling into his driveway. "You've been alone for a long time and you've never relied on anyone. Especially a man. I'll give you time to work through it, Tabi. But I won't let you run, so get that out of your head right away." Even with the threat, his voice remained soft and kind—with absolutely no give.

"If I ran, you wouldn't find me," she challenged.

"Want to bet?" he asked.

Definitely. Oh, she couldn't run right now with her factory, but someday, they were going to play that game. It hit her then. She had started planning with him. How had he done that? Her mind spinning, she stepped out of the car and didn't feel the threat until it was too late.

A multitude of darts impacted her side, shooting down her legs. "Evan," she whispered, trying to turn and see him.

His roar of raw fury sounded more animalistic than anything she'd ever heard. So many darts showed on his face and down his torso that she couldn't count them all. The blue of his gaze, primal and desperate, was the last thing she saw before the darkness pulled her down.

It swirled around her, while nausea rippled through her stomach. The ground was hard and the rain soft. Grunting, she flipped all the way to her back, letting the cool droplets plaster her face and along her body. She couldn't move her hands or feet. The hum of her vehicle, still running, competed with the rustling wind and strengthening rain.

Good. The stronger the storm, the better.

The drugs from the darts coursed through her body, rendering her limbs useless and her mind fuzzy. Darkness swam in from the edges of her brain, and she fought hard to remain semi-conscious.

Her temples pounded like she'd been punched as her body tried to diffuse the drugs.

Where was Evan? She could only hear the BMW and the rain storm. Finally, she could wriggle her fingers. Then her toes. Preparing for the pain, she blinked open her eyes.

Even though the day was cloudy, the light pierced right to her brain in sharp agony. She moaned and rolled to her side, gagging several times but keeping the coffee down. How long had she lain there? Slowly, painfully, she pushed to sit, accidentally knocking her head against the passenger side door. "Evan?" she called.

Only the rain and the engine echoed back. She pulled the darts out to drop on the ground.

Heaving, her stomach rolling, she curled her hands over the tire and pulled herself to stand. She staggered around the front of the car, balancing herself by holding on to the hood. She reached the other side and found rainy cement. No Evan.

She shook her head, trying to focus. It took three times for her to be able to open the driver's door, and she flopped into the seat, twisting the ignition off.

A note was stuck to the steering wheel. Taking a deep breath, she slowly unfolded it, her hands shaking. As she read, she forced bile back down her throat. Tears filled her eyes—either from pain or fear, she wasn't sure. The note was short and to the point.

The Popovs had Evan, and they'd cut off his head within sixty minutes if she didn't bring the prototype to them. She looked at the clock.

The note had been left more than an hour ago.

Chapter 14

Evan awoke face down on a dirt floor. He turned his head and coughed out dust before sitting up.

"Hello, Sleeping Beauty," came a low voice.

Evan shook his head, trying to remember where he was. Back in Afghanistan? He couldn't concentrate. His stomach lurched, and he rolled to the side, coming up to his knees and then his feet. He swayed but remained standing in a perfectly square metal cell—the box kind that's moveable. He wiped dirt out of his eyes and focused to see Lance Popov on the other side. "Where's Tabitha?"

"We took you and not her," Lance replied.

So he was bait. Good to know. "Why the dirt in this metal cell?" he muttered, his teeth crunching dirt he must've inhaled.

Lance sat on a folded chair in what appeared to be a vacant warehouse. "It has molecules of planekite in it, just in case. I didn't think you were a witch, but it never hurts to be sure."

"Planekite?" he asked before his brain kicked back in. Crap. He probably should know what that was. Grunting, he pulled out the darts to flick toward the shifter.

Lance rolled his eyes. "I know there are several names for the mineral, but we call it planekite. You know what I'm talking about." He cocked his head. "Or don't you? I guess if you're Fae, you have probably been off world for a long time? Until recently, anyway."

What the hell did 'off world' mean? Evan moved to the bars of the cell. "Right. Off world. So—planekite?" He couldn't quite manage full sentences yet.

"It's a mineral that weakens and ultimately kills witches," Lance said. "Guess you're not a witch."

"Guess not." However, hadn't somebody said that enhanced humans were related to the witches? Nobody had sounded sure. He was feeling weak and his blood was flowing sluggishly, but he'd also been darted pretty heavily. "What was in those darts?" They'd pierced his skin easily enough.

Lance chuckled, the sound echoing around the empty room. There were two large doors and bays, so this was probably storage for vehicles or maybe boats? "Those darts held enough sedative to take down a cadre of vampires. You should still be out and in lala land. I guess you crazy fairies have some gifts I hadn't heard about."

"Guess so." Hopefully enhanced human males had even more gifts. Evan planted his hands on the bars to test their strength. Solid. Pretty solid. "What's your play here?"

Lance tugged a knife with a jagged edge out of the sheath in his right boot. "Your mate is bringing the prototype here to trade for your life. It's pretty simple."

"Is it?" Evan drawled, his faculties slowly returning.

Lance grinned. "Well, maybe not. Your mate is a lying bitch, even for a demonness, so we're going to get the prototype and kill you both once she arrives. If she arrives. Think she'll come for you?"

Evan tightened his grip around one of the bars. "I think it's interesting your brother isn't here." Tension rolled through him followed by a healthy dose of anger. "Where is he?"

"You're not as dumb as you look," Lance observed. A phone trilled, and he tugged one from his front pocket with his free hand. "Lance." Then his eyebrows lifted and he looked at Evan. "No shit. Guess you won that bet. See you soon." He ended the call. "The bitch is on her way here. Guess she does have a feeling or two for you."

"That's the last time you call her a bitch, Lance," Evan growled, the energy beginning to run through his veins again. "Where is your brother?"

Lance twisted the knife, staring as it reflected light around the room. "He followed her to the factory. We couldn't find it, you know. The female is a master at using dummy corporations." He flipped the knife up and caught the handle on the way down. "I have wanted to cut her for so long."

Evan snarled, his chest widening. He stood taller. Her image flashed through his mind, giving him more strength. Tabi. His Tabi. He should've told her how he felt about her, even though it didn't make a lick of sense that it had happened so quickly. Instead, he'd just bossed her around. Not that she didn't need a little bit of protection and sense. "You're not going to touch her."

"Oh, but I am," Lance said, twirling the knife again. "Who knew that she'd lose this game over a mate? I didn't think she had it in her to care."

"So you darted us and then your brother followed her to find the factory—just in case she didn't come for me." As a plan, it didn't suck. Tabi was smart. She had to know she was walking into a trap. "She won't come for me. Your brother is mistaken."

The door opened and Tabi strode inside, holding a medium-sized light blue box. "Wrong." Her blonde hair was long down her back, and she wore black jeans with those deadly heels giving her additional height. She looked at him, her black eyes glittering. "You okay?"

Allen walked in behind her, a green gun in his hand and a wary light in his eyes. "This was too easy."

Evan pulled on the bar, his hand slipping off. "What the hell are you doing here?"

She shrugged. "I couldn't just let them kill you." One of her light eyebrows arched.

He subtly shook his head. So far, the bar hadn't moved. Either his super strength was gone, or the bars were fortified even against such power.

She sighed. "Well. This is unfortunate."

Man, she was cool under pressure. Or maybe she didn't realize that their situation actually sucked. "What's in the box, Tabitha?" Evan asked quietly.

Her grin was catlike. She tugged out a black remote control.

Allen pointed the gun at her. "What is that?"

She pressed a button, and an explosion rocked the entire county.

Evan dropped his head. "Please tell me you didn't just blow up your factory."

"There was nobody inside, Evan. Give me some credit." She threw the box toward Lance. "I went inside to make sure the place was clear. See how you're influencing me already?"

Influencing her? Considering he was in a cell and she was outside of it with two maniacal shifters, he wasn't getting through to her. "I'd really appreciate it if you wouldn't walk into danger like this."

Allen fired the green gun toward the high roof. Green lasers zipped out and apparently turned into metal when hitting the interior metal of the roof. Shards rained down, all around him, and he didn't so much as flinch. He then pointed the weapon at Tabitha. "Where is the formula?"

She tapped her head. "Right here, jackass. It's the only place, you know. I created it."

Lance stood to face her. "So we need your head and not your mate's. Okay."

"Nope," she said, widening her stance. "I'm a demonness. You can't torture me for information. He goes, and I go, and we'll make an agreement. I'll give you half of the company in exchange for your distribution channels. The labs remain mine."

Evan reared up. "You are not giving in to blackmail."

She waved a hand. "This is normal business practice in my world."

Great. Just freaking great. "I don't think kidnapping me should earn them fifty percent of your business, honey. It's rewarding bad behavior," Evan drawled, looking for a way out of the cell.

Surprise flashed in her eyes. "I thought I'd find you a little more freaked out. Maybe your time in the military prepared you better than I'd thought."

At least she was finally seeing him. "Why are you here? Why come yourself?" He had to know.

She sighed. "Fine. I like you. Have since the beginning. You're hot and strong and kind. Maybe a little bossy. Definitely sexy."

"Just like me? Only like?" he asked, releasing his hold on the bars.

Allen cleared his throat. "Do you two mind? We're in the middle of something here."

"Right." Tabi lowered her head. "I guess I'll just fry your brains." Power shot from her, nearly visible.

Allen immediately yelled in pain, blood spurting from his ears.

Lance leaped between them, taking the hit. He screamed.

Allen dropped to the floor, using his brother as a shield. He leaned around his writhing brother and fired several times toward Tabi.

Evan bellowed a warning.

Bullets hit her and she went down, her eyes wide as blood spurted from her torso. Agony darkened her expression. "Well, shit," she muttered.

* * * *

Pain blew through Tabi's chest and she cried out, trying to breathe. She might've overestimated her ability to take on both shifters with her mind. As her body rushed to heal itself, her brain slowed down with the demon mind attack. She'd been so intent on saving Evan that she hadn't thought of the consequences. Not at all.

Whimpering, she shot out another mind attack, trying to remain conscious.

Allen stood and fired again. Blood burst from her leg a second before the pain jolted her system.

A savage roar bellowed from the cage, the sound so primal that everyone froze. She gasped and turned to see Evan grab above the bars and swing his legs, kicking two bars out. Then another two. They shot across the empty warehouse, dropping to the concrete and bouncing away with loud tings.

He moved faster than a blur, right at Allen, who pivoted and fired several lasers at Evan.

Tabi cried out and tried to sit, sending healing cells where she could. Blood continued to pour from her.

Evan impacted Allen, taking him down to the concrete. Blood and dirt coated the way he'd traveled. The gun spun away, smashing into the broken cell.

Tabitha scrambled toward it along with Lance, both of them fighting to reach the weapon.

Allen shrieked, the high decibels reaching every corner of the warehouse. Tabi paused, shaking, turning to see Evan lift the shifter's head up and throw it into the cell. Allen's hair caught on the broken bars, and his head hung there, swinging back and forth.

Lance swung his entire body around and kicked the gun to fly yards away. Yelling, he lowered his head.

Tabi leaned up. "Run, Evan! He's going to shift. Now!" The

percussions sent out might kill them both.

Evan stood and turned, blood coating his chest.

Lance's arms and legs stretched out, and fur emerged all over his face.

Evan leaped over him, landing next to Tabi, and rolled her across the floor. Ripples spread around them and a crash echoed. Evan stopped them yards away, planting his body over hers and covering her head to toe.

The air exploded, sucking in and then out. The force pulled Evan off her, and he fought to cover her, tucking his head over her neck.

Then silence.

She gasped and looked over to see a fully formed wolf.

Evan shoved to his feet, positioning himself between Tabi and the animal. "Holy shit, he's big," he muttered. "Bigger than any wolf."

The animal snarled, saliva dripping from its razor sharp canines.

Tabi planted one bloody hand on the cement and forced herself to stand. She wobbled. "He's much stronger in this form."

Evan's back was covered in blood, too. Had the bullets gone all the way through? He sucked in air, pain cascading off him. "Get out of the way, Tabitha." He staggered forward, pushing her behind him with one dirty hand still dripping with Allen's blood.

Tabi elbowed him in the side. "I've got this." She lowered her chin, but before she could send out an attack, the wolf leaped through the air.

The animal hit them both, sending them sprawling across the cement floor. Tabi smashed her head on the wall, and lights flashed behind her eyes just as the bone in her wrist snapped in two. She yelped.

The wolf growled and jumped for her.

Evan careened off the floor and wrapped both arms around the wolf's body, tackling the beast to the cement. They landed hard, both scrambling for purchase. The wolf raked sharp claws down Evan's arm, and he bellowed, punching rapidly toward the animal's throat.

Grunting, swearing, Evan scissored his legs around the wolf, trapping it. Then he punched the animal between the eyes, his fists too fast to track.

The wolf snarled and snapped its teeth, aiming for Evan's neck.

Evan swore and grabbed the wolf's jaw with both hands, yanking in the opposing directions. The bone dislocated with a loud snap, and the animal yipped. Evan kept going, tearing the head in two. The body shuddered, furry and bloody, into death.

Holy crap. Tabi turned and coughed, trying not to throw up.

Evan hitched toward her, leaning down. "Like me? You only like me?"

She tried to answer, but everything hurt. "We need to heal ourselves." She pulled him to sit next to her while also sending healing cells to her wrist. The bone popped back into place, and she jumped.

His eyebrows rose. "Okay."

She took a deep breath. "Imagine your injuries and send healing cells to them. Close your eyes. You can do it."

He followed her orders. "We're not done talking, mate." Then the cut on his forehead healed much faster than any new mate's should.

It figured.

Chapter 15

The storm continued outside while Evan finished showering, letting the heated water get rid of all the blood and dirt. He looked at his chest. Oh, the scars from his time in the military were still there, but no recent bullet holes. Not a one. He should feel good about that.

Right now, something was driving him. Something deep and uncomfortable. He didn't regret killing the Popovs, because those two would've never stopped coming for Tabi and her company. While he didn't give two fucks about the company, she did, so that mattered. More importantly, she mattered.

He flipped off the water and stepped out of the steam, drying off. Power sang through him, even more so after the fight. Was that normal? Maybe it was just normal for him. He'd have to figure this whole immortal thing out and deal with this bizarre strength, but that was second.

First was waiting for him in his living room because he'd told her to wait there. After her shower.

He stalked into his room, not surprised to see both dogs on his bed. He gave them a look and drew up clean jeans, not bothering to button them. Then he padded barefoot into the living room and finger combed his hair as he went.

Tabi sat on the sofa, dressed in his faded Metallica T-shirt with a blanket over her knees. "Feel better?"

"No." He paused, looking at her. God, she was beautiful. Strong and smart and fragile and spunky. An entire package, and she'd only lived a sliver of her long life. What would she be like in a hundred years? A thousand? Everything inside him wanted to know. Wanted to be there. But there had to *be* a there. "You will never walk into danger like that again." The words were out, and he let them hang in the air.

She paused in her perusal of his healed chest. "They had you in a cell."

"I got out of the cell," he countered.

She plucked a string on the blanket. "How did I know you could get out of a cell?"

"Again, that doesn't matter. What you know or don't know—don't ever walk into a trap like that. You're smart, Tabitha. You knew it was a trap." More importantly, she had to learn to trust him. He could take care of himself, even in this new world. "Yet you came—with a fucking light blue box from a jewelry store."

"It was an extra box," she said, all sass.

"Watch it, baby," he warned, wanting to go gentle since it had been a shitty night. "I like your sass usually. Not so much right now."

Her eyes flared and warmed. Yeah, she liked it when he called her *baby*. She equally didn't like being told what to do. He knew both facts about her, because her feelings all but danced across her pretty face. "Please. I knew one of them wanted to follow me to and from my factory to find it. Yet I figured I could get you free. Didn't know you could break bars," she muttered.

"You blew up your factory for me." The idea warmed him, while the sight of her bloody on the ground chilled him at the same time.

She shrugged. "Yeah. You're more important than a factory."

Now she was trying to charm him? It was working. "How far behind does this put you?"

Her body visibly relaxed as they turned to business talk. "Only a month or two. I know the recipe, and the techs are mine, so we just need to get another production facility up and running. And buy the ingredients, of course."

"Good. Have you ever seen shifters do that before?"

She nodded. "Sure."

He licked his bottom lip. "So you knew about the percussion wave created when one of them shifted near you?"

She moved uneasily on the sofa, sliding to stand. "Well, kind of."

"Tabi?" His voice softened, and she was smart enough to catch it. "What happens to a demon mind attack when a shifter turns into a wolf?"

She swallowed. "I don't think that's really—"

"Tabi." He waited. Not so patiently.

"Fine. When a shifter turns to the animal form, most often, a demon mind attack no longer, er, works." Then she rolled her eyes.

Mistake. Big one.

* * * *

Nerves jumped inside Tabi's belly. So she rolled her eyes.

He came at her then. Full on, right for her. She was a second late in identifying the vibe in the room as scary, pissed-off immortal. She swallowed and sidled around the coffee table.

He stopped. One eyebrow rose.

She moved a little more, edging toward the kitchen.

"Where are you going?" he asked, his voice gravelly and low.

"Thirsty?" If she could just get some air, she could figure this out.

"No." He clocked her progress, looking big and bad and pretty damn sexy. "You done trying to make a run for it?"

It was one of her skills. "You're in a mood." One that was having the interesting result of heating her abdomen and softening her thighs. What was it about him?

"Good of you to notice." He tracked her then, sure and strong steps.

She backed away, her heart thundering, her body healed. "What are you doing?"

"Settling things." He reached her, his scent of smoke and honey wafting along her skin.

She took another step back, caught between the wall and his body. If she could just slide to the right, she could reach the kitchen. Although the broad spanse of his ripped chest all but begged for her mouth.

As if reading her mind, he planted a hand on the wall by her head, caging her. Easily. "I'd like to give you another chance to respond to my statement that you do not just breezily walk into danger that *does not* include you rolling your eyes." While his voice was soft, his eyes were intense, and his body vibrating.

She couldn't have rolled her eyes if her life depended on it. Plus, breezily hadn't exactly described her actions. "I guess I could agree to those conditions." Her lungs seemed to be fighting her.

"No more danger, Tabitha."

She shivered from the heat in his eyes. Human, her ass. He was all immortal badass. "Danger isn't my thing." She tried to sound agreeable.

He traced his free hand along her jaw and down her front, between her breasts. "Right. You go into business with shifters, and you double-cross them."

She gasped.

Now he rolled his eyes. "Please."

Okay. Her grin even felt sassy. "No more business arrangements with shifters."

"Good. No more beating up humans, either." His fingers were gentle as he lifted the shirt over her head, baring her to him.

She shrugged. "Whatever. I don't have to beat people up." Although, those boys had certainly deserved it. She caressed over his chest and down his abdomen, tucking the pads of her fingers into each hard ridge. She purred.

He tangled his fingers in her hair and twisted, forcing her to meet his gaze. "No more casually walking into traps. In fact, no more traps. If there's a trap, you find a way to *not* be in the middle of it."

Well, he'd probably need some time to really figure out the immortal world. Half the fun of traps was springing them. She leaned up and licked along his too firm bottom lip.

His hands—both hands—manacled her hips and lifted her. Fast. Way faster than she could move. He pressed her back to the wall and leaned in, his nose touching hers. Those eyes, blue and dangerous and slightly amused. Yeah, he knew her. Somehow. Maybe this had been his trap all along. "Panties off," he ordered, kissing her before she could respond.

Heck, yeah. She shoved them down, tucking her hands in his jeans and pushing. "Now."

He pushed inside her, going slow, easily holding her, his body warm and strong. "You merely like me?"

Pleasure rippled through her, so much and so strong. She laughed, enjoying everything about him. He was more than she could've ever wanted—and she gave herself over. Finally. "All right. I love you. Happy now?"

"Oh, I'm just getting started." He moved then, driving inside her, taking everything she was. "I think you knew exactly who I'd be. Who I am."

Maybe. Although admitting that to herself hadn't been easy. She'd been alone for so long, and now she'd found somebody who'd never let her go. Yeah, it was a dream she'd always held but hadn't thought would work out. So much for handling him. "Harder."

He went harder, his hands digging into her butt. The ripples were fast, the tide strong. She broke, the room flashing hot, the orgasm stealing her thoughts.

Dropping his head to her neck, he shuddered with his own release. "I love you, too." Then he lifted his head, his gaze bright. "That's fast, right?"

She laughed, happy and not alone. Not even close. "That's immortality, Detective." The faded mark on her palm tingled. "Or maybe it's fate. Does it matter?"

"No." He kissed her deep. "So long as it's forever."

Chapter 16

Epilogue

Tabi snuggled into Evan's side as Dr. Mariana Lopez handed out cake. She took a piece and then handed one to her mate. Her stubborn, sexy, more than she could've ever imagined, mate.

"You took the one that has more frosting," he said, his lips at her ear.

She laughed. He'd given her video to her earlier, and they'd smashed it together. She smiled at Abby sitting next to Noah, trying to steal a frosting flower from him. Cocking her head, she watched Raine Maxwell refuse a piece of cake, his gaze on the shrink.

Mariana sat and smiled. "You've all graduated, and I'm so proud of you."

Tabi took another bite of cake. "You're a good counselor."

"Thanks, but I'm heading back to working with kids. No offense, but adults are too much work." Mariana took a sip of the punch and then frowned. "Who spiked this?"

"I did," Raine said. "Thought we could use something fun." His gaze heated on the woman.

Tabi looked around. "The sheriff's moronic kid hasn't been back in weeks. He doesn't graduate, does he?"

"No," Mariana said, crossing her legs. "I already let the court know, but we'll see what happens."

Evan set his cake aside and reached for the punch. Obviously the alcohol interested him.

Tabi finished her extra frosting, her heart warm. "Evan's running for sheriff. We need a committee, if you're interested."

Raine's eyebrows rose. "You're staying in town?"

"For a while," Tabi confirmed. At least fifty years, but then they'd have to go. "We're rebuilding my factory that somehow caught on fire, and Evan wants to clean up the town. So we're here for now. You?"

"I have a mission and am leaving tonight," Raine affirmed.

Well. So much for Raine and the shrink. The woman was enhanced, somehow, but Tabi didn't know with what. Probably empathy since she had become a psychiatrist. She could've sworn Raine had seemed interested. Too bad.

Mariana looked up at Raine, her expression inscrutable. "There's still an open homicide case, and I think all the witnesses, meaning everyone in this room, has to stay available."

He smiled then, and the sight looked like a warning. "Oh, I'll be back, Mariana. Probably sooner than you'd like."

Tabi swallowed. All righty, then.

Noah finally gave his frosted flower to Abby. "We're staying a while as well. Abby wants to help rebuild the factory, and she likes working with Tabi." He grinned. "If you become sheriff, you'll need a deputy. I'd like to help clean up this town, too. I guess doing it by running for office isn't a bad way."

Tabi smiled. No doubt, Noah had just planned to rip off the sheriff's head, since he'd threatened Abby. This was a better way to go. Two immortals in small town law enforcement. Life was weird. "That's true."

Evan nodded. "I'd like that." He leaned down and kissed her cheek. "See? That's a good plan."

Yeah, probably better than what she'd had in mind for the sheriff. "All right, handsome. We'll try it your way." She leaned up and kissed him, sighing when he took over. So long as they were together.

He leaned back and smiled. "Forever."

* * * *

Also from 1001 Dark Nights and Rebecca Zanetti, discover Vengeance, Blaze Erupting, Tangled, Teased, Tricked, A Vampire's Kiss.

Discover More Rebecca Zanetti

A Vampire's Kiss
A Dark Protectors/Rebels Novella
Coming May 3, 2022

From *New York Times* and *USA Today* bestselling author Rebecca Zanetti comes a new story in her Dark Protectors/Rebels series…

* * * *

Vampire
A Dark Protectors/Rebels Novella

Dr. Mariana Lopez has finally stopped bailing friends out of difficult situations. Well, except for substituting as the leader for another anger management group, pitching in as a campaign strategist for a prospective sheriff, and babysitting three dogs. Even with such a full life, she can feel the danger around her—a sense that something isn't right. Nightmares harass her, until the real thing comes to life, and only the dark and sexy male sitting in her group can save her. However, with safety comes a price she might not be willing to pay.

Raine Maxwell is one of the Maxwells out of Montana, which means he's not only one of the most deadly vampires alive, but his path is set and his mate has been chosen for him. To save him—to continue his line. Unfortunately, his mate is an enhanced human female who has no idea of her abilities, of his species, or of her future. He'd like to lead her gently into this new world, but his people aren't the only ones who've found her, which puts her into more danger than she can imagine. Plus, in order to follow his laws, he only has one week to convince her that immortality with him is what she wants—and needs.

* * * *

Vengeance
A Dark Protectors/Rebels Novella

Vengeance and revenge are the only forces driving vampire soldier Noah Siosal since losing his brother to an enemy he's been unable to find. He's searched every corner of the globe, going through adversaries and piling up bodies until finally getting a lead. The last place he wants to be is in a ridiculous anger management group with people expressing feelings instead of taking action. Until one fragile human, a green-eyed sweetheart being stalked by danger, catches his eye. One touch, and he realizes vengeance can't be anywhere near her.

Anger and self-preservation are the only motivations Abby Miller needs or wants right now. Falsely accused of attacking the man who's terrorized her for years, she's forced as a plea bargain to attend an anger management counseling group with people with some serious rage issues, while learning true self defense on the side. Yet a man, one more primal than any she's ever met, draws her in a way and into a world deadlier than she's ever imagined. He offers her protection, but she finds the fight is really for his heart, and she's ready to battle.

* * * *

Blaze Erupting
Scorpius Syndrome/A Brigade Novella

Hugh Johnson is nobody's hero, and the idea of being in the limelight makes him want to growl. He takes care of his brothers, does his job, and enjoys a mellow evening hanging with his hound dog and watching the sports channel. So when sweet and sexy Ellie Smithers from his college chemistry class asks him to save millions of people from a nuclear meltdown, he doggedly steps forward while telling himself that the world hasn't changed and he can go back to his relaxing life. One look at Ellie and excitement doesn't seem so bad.

Eleanor Smithers knows that the Scorpius bacteria has and will change life as we know it, but that's a concern for another day. She's been hand-picked as the computer guru for The Brigade, which is the USA's first line of defense against all things Scorpius, including homegrown terrorists who've just been waiting for a chance to strike. Their target is a nuclear power plant in the east, and the only person who can help her is Hugh, the sexy, laconic, dangerous man she had a crush on so long ago.

* * * *

Tangled

A Dark Protectors—Reece Family Novella

Now that her mask has finally slipped…

Ginny O'Toole has spent a lifetime repaying her family's debt, and she's finally at the end of her servitude with one last job. Of course, it couldn't be easy. After stealing the computer files that will free her once and for all, she finds herself on the run from a pissed off vampire who has never fallen for her helpless act. A deadly predator too sexy for his own good. If he doesn't knock it off, he's going to see just how powerful she can really be.

He won't be satisfied until she's completely bare.

Theo Reese had been more than irritated at the beautiful yet helpless witch he'd known a century ago, thinking she was just useless fluff who enjoyed messing with men's heads. The second he discovers she's a ruthless thief determined to bring down his family, his blood burns and his interest peaks, sending his true nature into hunting mode. When he finds her, and he will, she'll understand the real meaning of helpless.

* * * *

Tricked

A Dark Protectors—Reese Family Novella

He Might Save Her

Former police psychologist Ronni Alexander had it all before a poison attacked her heart and gave her a death sentence. Now, on her last leg, she has an opportunity to live if she mates a vampire. A real vampire. One night of sex and a good bite, and she'd live forever with no more weaknesses. Well, except for the vampire whose dominance is over the top, and who has no clue how to deal with a modern woman who can take care of herself.

She Might Kill Him

Jared Reese, who has no intention of ever mating for anything other than convenience, agrees to help out his new sister in law by saving her friend's life with a quick tussle in bed. The plan seems so simple. They'd mate, and he move on with his life and take risks as a modern pirate should. Except after one night with Ronni, one moment of her sighing his name, and he wants more than a mating of convenience. Now all he has to do is convince Ronni she wants the same thing. Good thing he's up for a good battle.

* * * *

Teased

A Dark Protectors—Reece Family Novella

The Hunter

For almost a century, the Realm's most deadly assassin, Chalton Reese, has left war and death in the past, turning instead to strategy, reason, and technology. His fingers, still stained with blood, now protect with a keyboard instead of a weapon. Until the vampire king sends him on one more mission; to hunt down a human female with the knowledge to destroy the Realm. A woman with eyes like emeralds, a brain to match his own, and a passion that might destroy them both—if the enemy on their heels doesn't do so first.

The Hunted

Olivia Roberts has foregone relationships with wimpy metro-sexuals in favor of pursuing a good story, bound and determined to uncover the truth, any truth. When her instincts start humming about missing proprietary information, she has no idea her search for a story will lead her to a ripped, sexy, and dangerous male beyond any human man. Setting aside the unbelievable fact that he's a vampire and she's his prey, she discovers that trusting him is the only chance they have to survive the danger stalking them both.

About Rebecca Zanetti

New York Times and *USA Today bestselling* author Rebecca Zanetti has published more than fifty novels, which have been translated into several languages, with millions of copies sold world-wide. Her books have received Publisher's Weekly starred reviews, won RT Reviewer Choice awards, and have been featured in Entertainment Weekly, Woman's World, and Women's Day Magazines. Her novels have also been included in Amazon best books of the year and have been favorably reviewed in both the Washington Post and the New York Times Book Reviews. Rebecca has ridden in a locked Chevy trunk, has asked the unfortunate UPS guy to release her from a set of handcuffs, and has discovered the best silver mine shafts in which to bury a body…all in the name of research. Honest. Find Rebecca at: www.RebeccaZanetti.com

Also From Rebecca Zanetti

DARK PROTECTORS
Fated
Claimed
Tempted
Hunted
Consumed
Provoked
Twisted
Shadowed
Tamed
Marked
Teased
Tricked
Tangled
Talen
Vampire's Faith
Demon's Mercy
Alpha's Promise
Hero's Haven
Guardian's Grace

THE ANNA ALBERTINI FILES
Disorderly Conduct
Bailed Out

DEEP OPS
Hidden
Taken
Fallen
Shaken
Broken

REALM ENFORCERS
Wicked Ride
Wicked Edge

Wicked Burn
Wicked Kiss
Wicked Bite

SCORPIUS SYNDROME SERIES
Scorpius Rising
Blaze Erupting
Mercury Striking
Shadow Falling
Justice Ascending
Storm Gathering
Winter Igniting
Knight Awakening

SIN BROTHERS
Forgotten Sins
Sweet Revenge
Blind Faith
Total Surrender

BLOOD BROTHERS
Deadly Silence
Lethal Lies
Twisted Truths

MAVERICK MONTANA SERIES
Against the Wall
Under the Covers
Rising Assets
Over the Top

Slash

A Slay Series Novella

By Laurelin Paige

Acknowledgments from the Author

To my family—Thank you for the best albums of memories. I'm lucky to have shelves and shelves stacked with your love.

To Liz Berry, Jillian Stein, and MJ Rose—I'm inspired by you and so honored to be in your family. And to you, Liz, especially for trusting my telling of this story. It was what I needed to write, and you let it grow into what it needed to be.

To my tribe: Rebecca Friedman, Candi Kane, Melissa Gaston, Roxie Madar, Kayti McGee, Melanie Harlow, Lauren Blakely, C.D. Reiss, Amy "Vox" Libris – You've made a crazy, terrible time feel so much more bearable. I wouldn't survive a pandemicalypse without you.

To my readers—Thank you for letting me explore this ugly, broken, beautiful world with you. I'm eternally grateful you've come along for this ride.

To my God—Help me to remember to always wonder and love. Thank you for being patient all the times that I've forgotten.

Introduction

Foreground: The area of an image—usually a photograph, drawing, or painting—that appears closest to the viewer. - *MoMA Glossary of Art Terms*

There's no way to see an entire life in a single photograph. It takes a portfolio, an expansive collection to understand the nuances of character and experience and circumstance.

Still, there can be a complete story in a snapshot. A good photographer knows how to find that narrative, knows which moments are worth capturing and which aren't. A good photographer can adjust the lens just right, so the background becomes hazy and unimportant and undistracting. A good photographer knows when the foreground is enough to tell the story that needs to be told. A good photographer focuses in and snaps at just the right time.

That's what the snobbiest of professional photographers say—that the perfect shots are planned and executed with precision. I've said it myself on several occasions, when my work has been acclaimed, when I'm feeling prideful about my compositions.

If I'm being honest, I don't know that there's much reason to boast about any of the photos that have earned me attention. Most of the time, I just got lucky.

Chapter One

Cropping: Editing, typically by removing the outer edges of the image. - *MoMA Glossary of Art Terms*

You've got to be kidding me.

The thought races through my mind repeatedly as I shuffle through the registration papers in front of me, as if I might have the wrong stack, as if I might see something different when I return to the sheet with the names of all my students.

Of course nothing changes when my eyes return to the enrollment form. There are still thirteen names arranged in alphabetical order. There are still more women than men by a three to one ratio. And Hendrix Reid is still the last male name on the list.

It can't be a coincidence. It's bloody unlikely there are many Hendrixes in the photography world, less unlikely more than one of them has the surname Reid.

Despite the unlikelihood, I hold on to the slim thread of doubt, mainly because I have no other choice. I have no time to prepare mentally for the alternative since class is set to begin in, oh, four and a half minutes. A good majority of the thirteen students are already sitting at the three tables squaring the room in front of me, and since none of them are recognizable, it isn't impossible that the Hendrix Reid enrolled is not *my* Hendrix Reid.

Not that I have a Hendrix Reid. He was never actually mine. Even for the one night we spent together, we remained strangers. Sure, we took our clothing off and engaged in wicked behavior, but the lights were out so it was more anonymous than not, despite having exchanged names, which I try to never do. Technically, I hadn't then either. The conference we'd attended had taken care of that, listing both our names and our bios with headshots in the event directory, without any regard to the fact that some of us became photographers because we preferred to remain on the other side of the lens.

Which is neither here nor there.

I would have told him my name anyway and with no regrets. The conversation that had led to the tryst in his hotel room had been rather remarkable, and a lot of it had centered around the fact that we were both notable photographers, so anonymity wasn't ever going to apply between us.

And why would famed wildlife photographer Hendrix Reid be registered for a portrait course, in London, of all places? He'd told me he was wintering in the savannahs, and while spring is definitely upon us now, there is not much in the way of wildlife here beyond the hedgehogs and kestrels at Regent's Park. Certainly nothing to attract him. The idea it's the same man is ludicrous.

Except, hadn't he said he was sure that we would see each other again one day?

I bite the inside of my lip so that I won't audibly groan.

I was stupid not to go through the enrollment form earlier. Strike that, I was cowardly. I'd been nervous about the prospect of teaching the class in the first place. Almost immediately after agreeing to lead the advanced course, I'd wanted to back out. It had been my brother who had convinced me it was a good idea, for reasons I can no longer remember, and why am I listening to his advice about how I live my life these days when he's practically settled in New York with his new wife and child? It's not like he knows what I need now any more than any of the other times we've been apart over the course of our lives, and he's halfheartedly tried to parent me from afar.

I listened to him, though, because while I am well into adulthood and a single mother/career woman who doesn't need governing, I also sort of do.

"Do you actually live your life?" he'd asked, and how dare he, but also maybe thank goodness he dared because I didn't have a good answer to the question, and though I very much objected to his right to know, it was probably something my therapist would want me to

consider. Just. There was a reason I didn't see her anymore, and it wasn't because I'd achieved mental clarity.

Rather, like in all things that scared me, I was the type to lower my head, as I had with Hendrix. As I had with this class.

One and a half minutes to go.

One minute.

I watch the seconds tick by on the analog clock hanging on the wall, one of those old-fashioned kinds that dictated time in every class I'd attended through secondary school.

Forty-five seconds.

Thirty seconds and there are now twelve students bowed down over their mobiles. None of them are Hendrix, and my confidence bolsters. He chickened out. He registered as a joke. He registered by accident. Whatever the reason, he's not here, and I'm calmer by the second.

And then the big hand is on the twelve, the little hand perfectly pointed to the ten, and it's time to begin this ludicrous teaching experiment.

With a deep breath, I gather my stack of papers and approach the podium. "Good morning, fellow photographers. As you likely already know, I'm Camilla Fasbender, art director of Accelecom Media, which is a rather fancy title to say I get final approval of the company's branding materials while other more talented artists do all the work and get none of the credit so thank goodness this course isn't meant to instruct in that arena because, really, I know nothing."

The students chuckle—is that an appropriate word for adult learners? It seems so odd when at least three of the faces I'm looking at appear older than me, reminding me how unqualified I feel to be standing before them.

Which is silly. Because I am qualified. *"Find the proof,"* Dr. Joseph used to say, and the proof is that, while it isn't my day job, my portrait photography is revered in some circles, and I do have things that I can share. A whole lesson plan, in fact. I'd managed to pull my head out of the sand long enough to put one together, fortunately, and it wasn't as hard as it might have been because I do know what I'm talking about.

But just as I'm about to confidently plummet on, the door swings open and a tall, muscular figure slinks in, taking the last available chair and sending my heart up to my throat even before his eyes meet mine, and I'm locked in the gaze of Hendrix Reid. *My* Hendrix Reid.

Bloody hell.

That four and a half minutes did nothing to prepare me. Even if I'd spent it actually believing I might come face-to-face with my one-night stand, I still would have been breathless from the shock of seeing him. His sun-tanned face and light brown eyes are quite breathtaking all on their own. Add to that his broad shoulders and sculpted jaw and a muscular frame that somehow moves lithely despite its bulk, and seriously, how can anyone be expected to bother with oxygen when looking in his direction? He's the kind of man who is beautiful enough to model and yet too spectacular to photograph. The light hits him too evenly. There aren't nearly enough shadows to tell a story that isn't about how perfect he is to look at, and stories about perfection become boring really fast so I avoid using my lens to tell them like the plague.

I can't imagine ever getting bored gazing at that face without a lens between us, though. His perfection is captivating in a way that can't be captured. There's something about his features that reflect what they see, but it's only interesting in real life, when the elements around him are present. He doesn't work cropped down to just him. He's meant to be seen in context.

I, on the other hand, prefer to not be seen at all.

Which is why I'm mortified that he's here. It would be one thing if there were a one-way glass between us, where I could look and look until I'd had my fill—if I'd ever have my fill. It's quite another when he's here with nothing between us but this podium, and my looking is met with his looking back.

Obviously, I lose my train of thought.

I have notes, but all the words seem to blur together, and I can't make meaning out of any of the pen strokes. My pulse takes off like it's a locomotive without a destination, my hands are clammy, and thirteen pairs of eyes are staring at me, waiting for me to say something worthwhile. Imagining them all naked is not helpful when I actually know what one of them looks like in the buff.

Well, my hands know, anyway. I did mention the lights had been off.

"Enough about me," I say, as though I've said anything about me at all. "I want to hear about you. What made you decide to enroll? What do you hope to learn? Let's start over here, shall we?" I look at the chair farthest from Hendrix and his perfect everything. "Tell us about yourself."

"Kaila Morrison" seems glad to take the baton. She gives us all a spiel about her photographic aspirations and her career ambitions as well as providing us with a not-so-brief resume. It is an advanced course, after all. No one was allowed to enroll without submitting a portfolio, all screened by the London Academy of Art, thankfully, or not so thankfully since I would have been able to avoid the Hendrix disaster had I been involved with curating submissions.

What would I have done if I'd come across his registration form? Would I have tossed it out immediately or reached out to him or...what? I dwell on that when I should be more attentive to Kaila.

Then, instead of listening to the next student as he speaks, I berate myself for my preoccupation which doesn't get any better by the time the third student is introducing herself.

Needless to say, by the time we've reached Hendrix, I've learned very little about the people I'm meant to be teaching, and, worse, I'm no better prepared to actually teach them.

When he speaks, though, I'm completely present. Time slows down and the room is suddenly quieter as it disappears into background, and all there is to capture my focus is him.

"I thought it was time to widen my scope of the art," he says, and it feels like he's talking only to me. "I know how to capture an animal as it moves stealthily in its habitat. I know how to adjust my camera for all versions of natural light. I don't have a single clue where to begin when it comes to photographing a person in a studio."

I haven't commented on anyone's introduction thus far, and yet I'm compelled to pry now. "And you've suddenly been met with an abundance of requests to shoot portraits? Don't tell me National Geographic isn't giving you work anymore."

"Uh, no," he laughs. "National Geographic and I are fine." His smile fades from his lips, but it lingers in his eyes. "There's more to life than just the job, though. This whole life of mine began for me with snapping pictures of things I liked to look at. Then it became something else, and I love it. I do. But it's been a long time since there's been any passion."

"And you think that you'll find that here?" My tone verges on hostile, but it is what it is. The words are already out, and there's nothing I can do to flower the message after the fact.

"Yes," he says, and my next breath comes easier for some unknown reason. "Yes, I think I will."

I go through the rest of the class in a daze. I manage to stick to my talking points, for the most part, besides the random time I sidetrack to recommend Nightsky, my favorite bar that happens to be in the vicinity of the Academy campus with decent priced top-shelf drinks and live music and an ambiance that draws me in no matter how terrible the cover bands are. How I got talking about London nightlife is beyond me except that I'm sure it has to do with Hendrix and memories of that dive of a bar that we ended up in that evening last September in France, both of us content because of the company despite the dreadful service.

Somehow I find my way back to the planned topic after that meandering, and somehow I manage to teach something, though I'm only sure that I make sense because of the nods of understanding coming from my pupils. Twelve of them, anyway. Twelve rapt students who give me their full attention, which I'm certain I don't deserve.

I can't bring myself to give Hendrix any attention. It's easier to stumble on, pretending that he's not in the picture.

Ignoring him physically doesn't work to draw my mind from him, however. As I lecture about the basics of portraiture and the art of creating concepts, I'm thinking about him and why he's here and what he said and what it could mean. We did have a passionate night together. Not just in the bedroom, but definitely in the bedroom, where he made me feel for one glorious encounter like my body wasn't a hindrance or a prison for my soul but instead that it was *part* of my soul. There, in the dark, with his mouth at my ear and his hands on my skin, he made *me* feel like the story that needed to be told.

But it was a one-night stand. Silly to think of it as anything more. Even if I were someone who was in the market for something real or long-lasting, it would be ridiculous to hedge any bets after just one encounter.

Hendrix didn't strike me as ridiculous. Or impulsive. Or silly.

Why on earth, then, would he believe that there could be something worth seeking out with me? If that's what he meant at all.

Which...he did, didn't he?

It's confusing, and confusion makes me hide, on the whole. But since I can't hide because I'm the fucking teacher in this class—seriously, how did this happen?—and for some reason the educator is expected to stay present, I find my confusion turning to anger. It works itself through me until the beauty of our night together is cropped out of my memory and what's left is trite and fleeting. His presence feels nothing like flattery—which it did feel flattering, admittedly, for a half second there in the midst of everything else. Now, though, it just feels invasive and unprofessional and mean.

Perhaps I'd confront him about it, if I were a different sort of person, one who isn't afraid to stand up to a challenge. One who isn't afraid to live her life.

But I'm not that sort of person, so after I give out the assignments and send the students on their way, I plan to gather my things and get on my way as soon as possible, so fond of hiding that I am. I was stupid enough to believe—or perhaps hopeful is the better term—that Hendrix would let me do that, as he'd let me leave that night in Paris, not that I'd given him a choice.

He doesn't, though, of course. *Of course.* He approaches me, his leather camera bag slung over his shoulder, a man satchel underneath.

"Camilla," he says in that American accent that makes me both cringe and swoon all at once, and for the briefest of moments I find myself considering something different for a change. I consider staying.

But underneath my long sleeve polo neck, my skin throbs with an intensity that equals the blaring of a car alarm, and I think of Fred waiting for me at home to take him out for ice cream and the dead husband who hurt me as much as he loved me and the ugliness that marks me inside and out. And in the chaos of those thoughts, there is no option to stay.

"You being here is in bad taste," I say before he has a chance to say anything else. "Don't do this to me."

I brush past him then, and with the heat of that brief contact following me in radiating waves, I rush outside to disappear among the Saturday-morning Londoners who are out enjoying the early signs of spring.

Chapter Two

Color: The perceived hue of an object, produced by the manner in which it reflects or emits light into the eye. - *MoMA Glossary of Art Terms*

I stare at my empty glass, wondering if I should order a second negroni. Wondering if that will be enough to douse the thoughts of Hendrix. I refuse to look at them, but he's there at the edges of my mind, stirring like the late embers of a fire, or perhaps they're early embers.

I don't want them to be. God help me if this is just the beginning of this spiral.

It's cause to consider that second drink.

But when the bartender passes by, I don't flag him. Not yet. I will, eventually, because I always do. A trip to the bar is never just a one-drink sort of experience. I suppose that some might say I'm an alcoholic, and maybe I am, though I don't tend to crave booze in any form, and I can easily go weeks without a drop.

I have other vices that are much more tempting.

And when those temptations become more vivid, when they transform into foes that have me in a wrestling match, pinned to the mat and about to give in, that's when I find myself sitting in front of some sort of cocktail. It's not the healthiest distraction, but it tends to work. And when it doesn't, sex is another useful diversion.

I hate to think of what impression I might give to a stranger who spent a significant amount of time observing these habits of mine. What would be said of me? What conclusions would be drawn? Does my behavior tonight color the rest of my actions? Would I be slapped with one of those derogatory labels that tend to say as much about the person labeling as the one being labeled?

Lush.

Slut.

Poor excuse for a mother.

No, I won't entertain that last one. I'm a good mother. I'd give my life for my son. If Frank hadn't died, I would have left him for Freddie's sake. No questions asked. I never would have considered leaving before getting pregnant. Back then, I took what I was given. I didn't even run, and hiding always did more harm than good.

That was more than six years ago, that little voice says in the back of my head. It's a nasty nag of a voice, one that tends to love to bully and belittle and is especially loud on the days that I find myself sitting in a crowded bar.

I know how to speak to her, though. *Where's the proof?*

I fiddle with the orange peel dressing the edge of my glass as I count the motherly actions I've performed in the past week. I worked. I earned an income. I got out of bed.

That last one is sometimes frighteningly the hardest.

And though I've left him with the weekend nanny, who arrives at nine AM Saturday morning and doesn't leave until nine AM the next day, I always, always, always spend all of Sunday with him. I deserve this one night to myself. How I use this time bears no reflection on the kind of mother I am. Bears no reflection on the kind of human I am.

Say it enough times, maybe I'll believe it.

The volume of the environment drops significantly as the band quits for a break. The quiet amplifies the noise in my head, but also makes me more aware of my surroundings. I feel the figure sidle up beside me before I see him, and when I look, it's only a quick glance out my periphery, noting the strong forearm protruding from a rolled-up sleeve leaning on the bar at my side.

"Negroni, stirred, on the rocks," he says, and then I have to look more closely, even though I already recognize him. If his thick American accent hadn't given him away, the order surely would have.

I forget to breathe before I lift my eyes, which is a mistake, because as always, the wind is knocked out of me at the sight of him. He's dressed himself up since class this morning. The same jeans maybe—hard to tell without standing back and fully ogling him—

but now he's exchanged his T-shirt for a crisp white dress shirt and a waistcoat that shows off his trim build. His face had been smoothly shaved earlier. Now stubble peppers his jaw and I'm slammed with a haptic memory of the burn of his rough jaw against the sensitive skin of my inner thighs.

I blink the thought away and raise my eyes to his.

"Make that two," he says to the bartender, his gaze locked with mine.

I like being the focal point of his gaze. Whatever he sees when looking at me reflects back, and it's like he's turned on a light in this dark section of the bar. It's like that light is me.

But I didn't come here to be light. I didn't come here to be seen.

Once again, rage courses through my veins. He's already infiltrated my professional life, registering for my class like he did. Now he's trying to steal my recreational life as well?

He can't have it. He can't have any more of me than he already has. I won't let him.

It's only the intensity of my need to protect this one sacred space that gives me the energy for an outburst. "No," I say clearly. Firmly.

Not helpful, really, since I've put the word out there without any context.

I try again. "Did you follow me here? Are you stalking me? I'll get the authorities involved if need be. This is highly unprofessional. What on earth are you after? You can't just invade my life like this. Don't you get it? I don't want you here."

A little more aggressive than needed, perhaps, but I'm not practiced in handling conflict constructively. Dr. Joseph would be impressed I attempted to handle it at all.

Hendrix's brow furrows. "I, uh. Didn't know you'd be here, honestly."

Which has to be a load of bullshit because obviously. "You expect me to believe out of all the bars you could find yourself at in this city you end up at the one I'm at?"

His lip works itself up into a smile, and I have to remind myself not to be charmed. "Well. You did recommend Nightsky in class today."

My momentary courage deflates like Fred's inflatable plastic microphone, the one I bought him on a whim the last time we were perusing the shops in Covent Garden thinking he'd like to use it to play rap star as he's been fond of playing recently. He loved it instantly, but it only took two days before the sharp edge of a Lego poked a hole in the material and leaked all the air out.

That's me, right now. My confidence seeping out as I realize he's exactly right.

And in case I am about to try to save myself with a rant about how, just because I recommended the place doesn't mean he should go—I mean, who does that? Who actually takes someone else's unsolicited advice, on the very day the advice was given no less?—he nods his chin toward something behind him. "A few of them thought it would be fun to check it out. Get to know each other in the process. They convinced me to tag along."

My face feels hot as I turn to look, my stomach sinking as I suspect I know what I'll find. Sure enough, there's six of them, sitting round a large table on the other side of the room. Including Hendrix, that's over half the class that came out to Nightsky tonight, simply because I said I loved the place. In another situation, I'd be startled by the power of my words.

At this particular moment, however, I'm nothing short of mortified.

I turn back to the bar and press my hands to my face. They're cool against my hot skin and smell like orange since I still have the peel tucked under my thumb, out of Hendrix's sight. I'm already humiliated. He doesn't need to realize what I was drinking as well.

"Yes, right," I say because I surely need to say something. "Of course." Of course he isn't here for me. How self-centered to think otherwise. How narcissistic.

Though, he did come to this spot at the bar to order. And as the bartender sets down two negronis on the counter, my embarrassment lessens. "You came to London," I accuse. "You took my class."

"I did." He doesn't offer more. Just that twinkle in his eye and that half smile. He nods again to the table of his classmates. "Care to join us?"

I'm hit with a vivid memory of that night in Paris, the two of us sneaking away from the crowd of fellow conference-goers to debate about the best wide-angle lens, which quickly led to a discourse on the purpose of art and an instruction on how to react to a tiger in the wild. He introduced me to negronis and we'd thrown back more than a couple when he leaned in and whispered, *"My recipe is better. Come to my room, and I'll show you?"*

He never did make me that drink.

"I shouldn't," I say, declining his invitation. Even if there's a part of me that longs to sit among the bunch of them, drinking and laughing with ease, I can't begin to imagine how it would work. I wouldn't know how to *be* around them. I barely know how to be around myself.

"Shouldn't doesn't mean no." He's as much a tease now as he was then.

"But I'm saying no." It's with regret, knowing that my response will mean he leaves, and while I don't want him to stay, I don't want him to go either.

"Okay, then."

He pays the bartender, and, against my better judgement, just when he's about to grab his drink, I ask, "What happened to wildflowers in the countryside?"

It's probably telling that I remember his agenda. *Winter in the savannahs, spring wildflowers, Iceland in July.*

He turns toward me, leaning his elbow on the bar. "I had a better option."

My chest feels tight and my eyes prick suddenly. I pick up my glass and throw back the remains, which is just melted ice now. His better option is me, right? That's surely what he's saying. I'm not obtuse.

But, if he means me or if he doesn't, I don't know what to make of the statement. I don't know what to make of him. Or men in general, if I'm honest. It's why I stick to string-free sex and random hook-ups rather than relationships.

Speaking of string-free sex…

Dylan, the Thrashheads' bassist, steps up to the end of the bar and flags down the server.

"The usual?" the bartender asks, already filling up a pitcher of beer from the tap.

"The usual." Dylan notices me, and since our gaze catches, he has to acknowledge me. "Camilla," he says with that awkward sort of grin that ex-lovers share.

Could we be called lovers? "Shaggers" seems a more appropriate term to describe the quick, sordid romps we had in the back room, neither of us ever taking off more clothing than necessary, each of us rushing to orgasm like it was a race.

It's silly for him to be uncomfortable around me. We were never awkward between encounters before. Does he feel guilty for falling in love with a woman half his age and getting married, putting an end to our trysts? He shouldn't. Good for him. I hadn't expected he and I were going to turn into anything. That was the whole reason I shagged him on more than one occasion.

"You sound good tonight," I say, hoping that will ease whatever tension he's feeling.

"That's a relief. I barely can think straight with the lack of sleep."

Well, that was your fault for having twins, I want to say. But I'm polite, and so all I say is, "I'll bet."

Despite the casual air of the interaction, I'm still well aware of Hendrix and his invitations and his declarations of better options.

I'm definitely aware when he's suddenly closer, his voice low. "Are you together? Are you the cause of his lack of sleep?"

"What? No." I'm so taken aback that I'm honest without thinking. "No. Definitely not."

"But you have fucked him."

I twist my head to pin him with a scowl. "That's none of your—"

He doesn't let me finish. "I'm jealous."

I have to take a deep breath to settle the racing of my heart. To let the little lift it gives subside. To swallow the smile that very nearly surfaces, unbidden, at the thought that Hendrix is thinking about sex and me right now. What does he want from me? Am I capable of giving it? Do I want it too?

Dylan and I had a good arrangement, both of us understanding it was just sex. Could it be possible to have that with Hendrix? The bathrooms here are singles with doors that shut. We could sneak in and be out before the band started their next set. Get it out of our system, whatever this is. Would that be enough to get him to forget me and take off in search of wildflowers?

Before I can make a decision about how to respond, there's another body between us, tugging at Hendrix in a way that has spikes shooting from my skin.

"We need you, Hendrix," she says. "I have no chance at getting the history trivia without you."

She picks up the extra negroni, the one that I was sure had been ordered for me, and takes a sip. "You're right! It is good."

It's only then that she really looks at me. "Oh, it's you! I didn't realize. Of course you'd be here, since you're the one who recommended it. Still, always strange to see your teacher out in the real world."

"Just as strange to see your students," I say, though strange is a mild way of characterizing my current emotions. "Kaila, was it?"

She nods.

I only remember because of the unusual spelling of her name. She'd made sure everyone knew in her introduction. "*Kaila with an i,*" an odd bit of trivia to share, in my opinion, since if I hadn't seen it on the enrollment form, I'm pretty sure I would have wondered where exactly the i was supposed to go.

It's a fitting name, I have to admit. Creative and bubbly like she is. Based on her looks, her actions, and her resume, she's the youngest in the class. She's already working in the business, but I'm guessing she went straight from high school to an internship. She climbed the ranks quickly at the international fashion blog she works for, and I can't help being petty and wondering if she's really got talent or if she had nepotism behind her.

Hypocritical, since I only have my cushy job because of my brother. Takes one to know one, I suppose. I might not even hate her if she wasn't so obnoxiously pawing at Hendrix.

Or maybe I hate her because he ordered the negroni for her.

Or maybe I hate him for it.

Or maybe the only one I hate is me.

She takes another swallow of the bloody drink—I swear she's bragging about it—then fans herself with a flat hand. "I don't know how you're wearing a sweater. It's hot as Hades in here."

Self-consciously I tug at the cuff of my black sleeve. It's been years since I've worn anything shorter than a full-length sleeve, and I've grown used to always feeling like I'm being roasted, but I am ever aware that my outfits come across as odd at certain times of year and in certain situations.

"My temperature runs cold," I say, practiced in the excuse.

"God, I wish. I'm always a sweaty Betty. My makeup has probably melted into a mess of goo under my eyes." She glances at Hendrix, as if inviting him to say otherwise.

When he doesn't, I pick up the cue. "You look fine." I don't manage to sound very convincing. Granted, I don't really try.

It's a good enough attempt for Kaila with an i. "You should come sit with us," she offers. Her eyes are hooded, though, and as dark as her skin, and I know the only one she wants to be sitting with is Hendrix.

Yes, I've been there. And of course, the one who is jealous now is me.

"Actually, I'm leaving." I dig into my purse and find a ten pound note that I leave on the counter. It's a tip. I rarely keep a tab open, paying out after every order. I tend not to like things that keep me anchored to a place, and I avoid them at every turn.

"Oh, then." To her credit, she sounds disappointed. "We'll see you in class."

The "we" feels barbed, and I hate that I wonder about it. Wonder if Hendrix is as keen for that "we" as she is. Wonder if it's a standard routine for him to charm female photographers with negronis and his American dialect. I wonder if he'll strip her from her sleeveless romper later, if he'll bury his face between her thighs, if he'll say she tastes like tangerines, and if she'll swear it's from all the citrus drinks.

And when he moves above her in a slow, languid dance that surely mimics the stealth it takes to capture a leopard in the wild, I wonder if she'll let him keep the lights on.

"Camilla..." he says, some sort of apology in his tone, and with that single word, I'm sure he knows the color of my thoughts.

It's a relief, almost. Worrying so long about remaining hidden, to be on the brink of being seen. It's like standing at the edge of a cliff, so fearful that you'll fall that you consider just taking a step and getting it over with.

It felt like that last time with Hendrix, too.

I take a breath, and the air clears.

"See you next week," I say, blatantly shutting down whatever point he meant to make. Then I push past them both, relinquishing the space that had always been mine.

Relinquishing the man who was never mine at all.

Chapter Three

Angular: An object, outline, or shape having sharp corners, or angles.- *MoMA Glossary of Art Terms*

I dump a package of pasta in the boiling water and make a mental note to take it off the burner in ten minutes. Vegetables are strewn over the cutting board, but I haven't yet got to the chopping, which means the pasta will definitely be done before the sauce. And if Freddie continues to need to show me every single one of his robot drawings with an expectation of a full art critique, there's no way I'll be getting to a salad.

Of course that's when my mobile begins to ring. A glance at the screen shows it's my brother, Edward, and God I'm tempted to let it go to voicemail.

It's not always this hard.

Or I tell myself it isn't always this hard. I'm spoiled, to be truthful. I was born into privilege and have spent most of my life basking in its advantages, but I also spent several years of my youth in a foster home where my guardians lived very much payday to payday. It was a household as short on love as it was on money, and the suffocating awfulness of those poverties is not only vivid in my memory but also branded on my skin.

So I recognize what I have is luxury. A cook and a nanny on the weekdays. Another nanny who does the cooking on Saturdays. But employees take holidays and Anwar certainly didn't plan to get sick, which is why I'm stuck both caring for my child and cooking on a Wednesday. When you add the burdens of my job and preparation for a photography course I shouldn't be teaching and the distraction of a too handsome, too charming man from my past, the tasks start to become overwhelming.

I should have ordered take away.

But I'd planned the menu when I'd given the cook the week off. I'd been very domestic about the whole thing, making sure I had the right ingredients and that each meal was well-rounded with a variety of food groups the way that responsible caretakers do all the time, all over the world, imagining Freddie's delight that I prepared something myself instead of from a ready meal, and the idea of abandoning that plan tonight made me feel inadequate. So I set out the vegetables, and I boiled the water because I *am* a good mother. I *am* a responsible caretaker.

It's being alone that's the hardest. Being the only parent. The one person who is ultimately in charge of not fucking up the most important being in my life. The task of it all would be less crushing if there was just another person to lean on every now and then. Someone to tell me I'm doing it okay. Someone to commiserate with when I've done it wrong. I don't have parents of my own to turn to since mine died when I was very young. And not only has Edward extended his time in the States, but he's also taken both his adult children with him.

I literally have no one.

Which is probably why I've spent every night this week fantasizing about Hendrix as I've fallen asleep. And it's definitely why I don't send Edward's call to voicemail, why I pick up the mobile and balance it on my shoulder with my cheek so I can have both hands free to chop the onion. Because I'm desperate to have this connection, small as it is, even in the midst of my chaos.

"The internet branding," Edward says instead of hello. Snaps, rather, and I already regret answering.

"I know, I know," I say before he goes on.

"It was due today."

"By the end of the day your time, though, right?" I glance at the clock which reminds me of the pasta, which is now boiling over. "That gives me five more hours." I drop the knife, wipe my eye with the back of my hand—onions never fail to make me cry—then rush to lift the pan of pasta from the burner.

"No, not end of day *my* time. End of day *your* time. I specifically gave that deadline so that I was sure I'd have the materials for my meeting this afternoon."

"It would have been helpful if you'd specified as such." I curse as a splash of hot water scalds the back of my hand.

"I don't usually need to specify. It's usually in my hands the day before, but you said you needed the extra time."

I had needed the extra time yesterday because a fuse had gone out on my floor at the office, and it was hours before I could even get the files loaded to examine. When I'd finally looked at them around six pm, I'd found a mistake and had to send the art back to the designer. I'd meant to go over the files as soon as I got them today.

But then Anwar got sick, and I had to leave to pick up Fred from school, and then he'd begged for the park and there was the tussle with the neighbor's rottweiler and the incident with the ice lolly and suddenly it was time to start dinner, and I hadn't opened my laptop at all.

Seeing that the water is settled, I set the pan back on the burner and leave the kitchen to grab my briefcase from where I dropped it by the front door. "I had something come up," I say as I walk, not wanting to make excuses.

"Of course. These things happen." He's not even trying to pretend he means it. Sarcasm is dripping from every syllable. "I'll just tell that to Hudson Pierce and Nathan Murphy when I sit down with them today. 'Well, I meant to have the branding graphics for the launch taking place tomorrow but, sorry. My sister said something came up.'"

He's really on a tear tonight. A man doesn't become the successful head of one of the largest media companies on the continent without having a slim intolerance for slack, and I get that. I don't expect any favors as his sister. It was favor enough that he took me in when I needed it, when he gave me the job that I certainly hadn't earned. If I have to endure his wrath for my tardiness, so be it.

Doesn't mean his words don't wake up the nag in my head. *Just like you to drop the ball. Did you expect anything different? You always fuck it up.*

My usual weapon of defense isn't helpful at the moment. *Where's the proof?* Well, the proof is that I forgot about an important deadline. That's the fucking proof.

But I have my laptop in hand now. I awkwardly open the computer as I head back to the kitchen, well aware that the pasta could boil over again if I don't keep an eye on it. "Give me half a second," I say, the mobile again propped up with my cheek. "I just need to get online and look it over. It should be a quick approval."

Unless it isn't. There's been more than one occasion that I've had to send creative back twice.

Please God don't let this be one of those times. I drop the laptop on the kitchen work top and study the image now on the screen. It's good. I mean, it's fine. It has all the elements I asked for, and the mistake from yesterday is gone.

I also suddenly have a flash of an idea, a different design altogether. More curved, less angular, a friendlier message for the alliance of three powerful companies.

It's too late to pursue the vision now. What could be has to be left at what could have been. On too many occasions, it seems. Never enough time. Never enough energy. Never enough bandwidth.

A more talented artist would have seen it earlier.

I ignore the nag and forward the file to Edward. "I sent it. You should have it shortly." Then I'm cursing again as I abandon the laptop to rescue the pasta. This time I turn down the flame when I return it to the burner.

"Got it," Edward exclaims. He becomes more compassionate with his relief. "Is everything okay over there? It's not like you to miss a deadline. Is there anything I should be concerned about?"

It's a loaded question, isn't it? Whether he means to or not, he's reminding me of all the times he's had to be concerned in the past. How often has he had to rescue me? He's been a better knight than I could ever ask for, which is another privilege, really. Especially considering that I never would ask that of him if he ever gave me the option.

There's the other reminder there too, of the time he didn't know to be concerned. How different would things be if I'd told him earlier about Frank? If I'd told my brother about the beatings and the gaslighting and the verbal abuse years before, my escape might have come at less of a cost.

But I'm not faced with a foe now as I had been then. What is there in my privileged life to concern my brother about? I can imagine how the conversation would go.

"Parenting's hard."

"Then get more help."

"It's not as easy as that."

"Should I send money?"

"That's not the support I need."

"Have you heard of an app called Tindr?"

The weight of depression is immeasurable outside of its confines. It's indescribable. There are never words to express the burden of being underneath.

It's a waste of time and energy to even discuss.

So I answer the question on the surface instead of the one he's really asking. "Just a lot going on. Shelly's on holiday, and Anwar called off sick, and Fred's a handful." I immediately feel guilty for even that. His baby is only two months old. How hard is it to run a billion dollar corporation when you never get a full night's sleep? "You know how it is."

"I do." He hesitates. I can feel him warring with himself, wondering if he should pry. "Camilla…?"

I think of Hendrix on Saturday night, the way my name sounded hanging on his tongue. I'd wanted to say more then, too. I'd wanted to say more than I'd ever said, wanted to unburden everything on him. Wanted him to hold me and tell me I was okay.

But then I'd hid, like I always do. I don't think I know any other way.

"I'm fine," I say to Edward. "Really. But if I don't get off the phone, my pasta is going to be overcooked."

He laughs, likely because the man doesn't have the slightest idea of what it takes to cook even simple spaghetti. "I'm here though. If you need anything."

"I know. Goodbye."

I throw the mobile down and resume the chopping, determined to see this meal through. I get through the rest of the onions and move to the tomatoes. The work is hypnotic—the slice of the knife through the peel and guts, the sound as it hits the board underneath. There's a satisfaction in each cut. There's permanence. A mark made that can't be undone. The most addictive form of art.

Tempting. So very tempting.

When Freddie runs in, I'm shaken from an adrenaline-filled daze. The sleeve of my long-sleeved shirt is rolled up, and I'm staring at the knife in my hand.

I blink. Horrified, I toss the utensil in the sink, as eager to have it out of my hands as I would be if it were a hot coal.

"Look at this one, Mummy. I made this one dynamite."

I laugh aloud before I take the robot drawing from him, startling us both. I turn off the burner, wipe my hands, and pick up my mobile. "Hold on one minute. Let me order dinner. Tandori sound good?"

"Extra na'an," he says. He's not disappointed in me in the least.

Chapter Four

Framing: The method by which information is included or excluded from a photograph, film, or video. A photographer or filmmaker frames an image when he or she points a camera at a subject. - *MoMA Glossary of Art Terms*

I'm quite an idiot.

I realize it when I stand in front of the class the following Saturday. Looking around, I notice most of them in jeans or relaxed wear, an appropriate choice for a weekend course, while I'm dressed in a long-sleeve trouser suit that would be better suited for the office. I can excuse my choice of attire as wanting to be professional, which is true, but the decision to apply heavier makeup and—God help me—curl my hair makes my look stand out.

It says I'm trying too hard.

And I am.

Hopefully, they believe I'm trying for them, to present myself as a suitable teacher, which again, is true, but the reality is I spent the extra time getting ready with only one student in mind. A student who I have forbidden myself from caring about.

Obviously that's going swimmingly.

It's not fair that Hendrix looks absolutely scrumptious in a pair of light khakis and a dark blue Henley. He hasn't even shaved in a couple of days, and somehow that lack of effort makes him all the more delicious.

It's quite the opposite from how he appeared in Paris. There he was clean-shaven and freshly cut, the kind of look that generally catches my eye. Paired with the slim-fit suit he'd worn for his presentation, and I was a goner.

It strikes me now that I might not have even given him a second glance if he were relaxed as he is now, yet this look is more fitting. This is who he is—rough-edged and indifferent with just a hint of wild in his eyes, despite the laid-back posture.

I memorize him in this moment, a photo snapped in my mind, framed without Kaila beside him—wasn't she a dear for saving him a seat?—so that I can study it later and fully appreciate his rugged beauty without all the noise surrounding him.

Then I put him out of my head and turn my attention fully to the class agenda.

"Every photograph should tell a story, even a portrait," I begin, and all eyes laser in on me. It's weird being the most fascinating thing in the room. Unsettling. Especially when I feel the bob of my stupid curls at each turn of my head. I feel like a performer rather than a field expert. Like I'm pretending to have something worthy to share.

It's easier when I really get into the lecture. The words flow when I'm talking about something I know, something I'm passionate about, and this particular subject is one I could spend all day on. Unfortunately, I've only allotted myself twenty minutes so I have to stick to the bare essentials, only having time to show them examples using my own work when there are so many other artists I'd love to discuss with them.

But this is a workshop, not a lecture study. I've done the math—thirteen students, a three-hour class. After I speak, that leaves them twenty minutes to get started on the activity. Then I'll have ten minutes to coach each of them individually as the rest continue to work.

I watch the clock and wrap up quickly when my limit is up. "Now it's your turn," I say, hoping I've given them enough scraps of information to make something meaningful. I divide them in three groups of three, one group of four, and send them to the hallway to take turns taking portraits of their team members.

"Why the hallway instead of in here?" one asks. Arthur who goes by the too-appropriate nickname of Arty.

My immediate reaction is to assume I've made a mistake, and I briefly question my decision along with him. The classroom is set up with backdrops and flash kits, and surely the students expect to be given time to use the equipment.

But I want to teach them photography skills that transcend the studio, and the hall outside the classroom is both quiet and magnificently lit with natural light coming through the floor-to-ceiling windows. I hadn't realized how perfect the setting was last Saturday because it had been slightly overcast when I'd come in. This morning, though, the sun was streaming in rays of gold, and I'd had to stop to catch my breath imagining the photos that could be caught there.

I'm thinking of a fancy way to explain myself, trying to figure out how to address anyone who might believe the class should be more focused on studio work when Hendrix answers simply for me. "Because of the light," he says simply. "You'll see."

Of course he's the one who understands. While everyone who registered had to have a background in art, Hendrix is the only one who had real camera experience. It's a photographer's habit to notice the light. Always measuring the luminance with the mind, at least, if not an actual photometer. It's impossible not to. Light is the basic element of photography, as necessary to the art as air and water are to the human body, and just as a person would notice when a room lacks oxygen, a photographer notices when a room lacks light.

I find I'm seeking it constantly, anchoring myself in it when it's found like a cat curling up in a bright patch of sun. Hoping one day that the light will penetrate past the layers of clothing and my mutilated skin and warm up the person inside me.

And so maybe it's the light that draws me out to the hallway with them when I'd planned to send them to work on their own while I read at my desk until it was time to meet with them one-on-one. I'd almost believe it myself if my attention was spent equally across the groups as they pose and adjust and click, click, click.

But it's hard to watch anything other than Hendrix, his expression intent as he measures angles with his eyes. I cringe imagining sitting for him, which isn't quite fair because I'd cringe sitting for anyone. But for him, especially.

I don't think about the fact that I'll have to coach him soon.

That's a lie.

I *try* not to think about it, but it's very present, like a fly trapped in the car, buzzing and buzzing as it searches the vehicle for escape, slow to take the one presented when a window is inevitably rolled down.

I'm annoyed with the buzz of Hendrix. More so than with a fly because it's my own mind that's trapped him. My own mind that refuses to shoo him out of any one of the hundred windows I've opened up to let him out.

Although I wouldn't be obsessed with him if he hadn't enrolled in my class. There. It's not my fault alone, it's his fault too. It's his fault first.

But it's my fault when he catches me watching him. And it's my fault again when I don't look away. He's too captivating, the way he studies me. His face illuminates and if I had my own camera, if I snapped right now, anyone who looked at it later would see the story. *Brutally handsome man pleased by what he sees.*

I shiver when I remember that what he sees is me.

Oh, look at that. It's time to mentor.

"All right, who's ready to discuss their work so far?" Immediately, I regret giving them the choice to step up—what if Hendrix is the first to volunteer? I can't start with him. Can't, can't, can't.

Fortunately, Salima is bouncing eagerly like Freddie when he's waited too long for the loo, and I happily attend to her first, pulling her aside in the hallway so the others in her group can continue practicing while I talk with her.

And now it's easy again. Honestly, I'm meant for one-on-one, as long as the conversation isn't centered around me. It's especially easy when there is a particular focal point for discussion and even more so when I have something worthy of saying. In this case, I have lots. Soon I've slid into the role of art critic, my tone brusque and honest with Salima and then Arty and then Karen and on down the line.

"These aren't stories, they're headshots," I say, clicking through one student's series of takes. "I feel as though I'm a casting agent. All shots looking directly at the camera, their smile fake and plastered on."

"It's not my fault Sara doesn't know how to pose."

I'm grateful I've pulled him away so that Sara doesn't hear Charlie's complaint. It's not really about her anyway. It's about him and he's being defensive.

I remind myself it's hard to accept criticism, no matter how well-meaning the critic, and take a deep breath before I speak again, more gently this time. "You have to ask for what you need if you're not getting it in the moment. It's not the job of the subject to create the art."

And so it goes, one student after another, and I discover that a few of them have a natural eye and that others are bloody awful and that most are wobbly as toddlers, still trying to adapt to the medium, but all of them are willing to learn. I see when my notes resonate, and I pivot when they don't, and each of them is quick to adjust when I watch them take a few more pics after our chat.

But now there's only one group left—three students, one of them the one I've been avoiding, and as much as I didn't want him to be first, I equally don't want to leave him for last.

I watch the three shuffle and work together, one sitting for the other two who dance around each other with their cameras. They've had more time to get shots in, and there will be a lot for me to look through, so I shouldn't delay.

Gathering myself, I call him out. "Hendrix."

He takes a second to respond, tearing himself from his hyper-focus in stages. First, he lowers his camera. Then he takes a step back. Finally, he pulls his head from Marie and looks at me. "I'm up?"

"You're up," I confirm, surprised my voice sounds as giddy as it does. Surprised that it's genuine enthusiasm.

Because I'm eager to see his work, of course. No other reason.

But when he's standing next to me, hovering over my shoulder as I flip through the pictures on his Sony A7R IV, a camera too new and too specific to portrait work to be his usual camera, I find it rather difficult to really see anything at all. My sight is overwhelmed by my other senses—the musky scent of man, the steady sound of his breaths, the heat radiating from his body that's oh, so close in proximity.

I've passed by at least a dozen shots without seeing them before I manage to force myself to blink and focus.

And now I've something new to distract me, because I've gone so far back that I've missed all the photos he took of Marie, a cheery gray-haired plump woman that one can't help but adore, and am now seeing the shots he took of Kaila. Frame after frame she fills the digital screen, and, really, she's flawless. Her skin, her coloring. The stupid little quirk of her lips.

Has he kissed those lips? Has he parted them with his tongue? Has he explored her fully with his own mouth?

I can't know from what I'm looking at, and it hurts to wonder, but it hurts even more to hope that he hasn't so I lean into the pain and accept that he probably has. And why wouldn't her lips quirk up at the attention of her lover? Why wouldn't she look radiant in his presence?

Except that's not her, I realize when I study further. That's the photographer making her glow. That's Hendrix's ability to capture the light.

Once I see his talent, I'm able to see past the subject. I knew he was good before, of course. I've pored over many of his nature shoots online late at night since our tryst in the autumn, enough to understand his style, and I'm sure I could correctly identify his work out of dozens of others.

I see that style here in the framing and the angles and the concept. But beyond the technique, there is something missing, something I can't identify.

"What's the story?" If he can't articulate it, that will be the reason I can't find it.

"A bright, young ambitious girl nervous under the scrutiny of someone she admires."

I frown at his answer, unwittingly. I'm both impressed and annoyed that he's that aware of his subject. "Yes, I suppose it would make her nervous to be photographed by the man she's crushing on."

Is my envy evident? It's nonsense jealousy, wanting his attention and not wanting it all-at-once. I'm sure I confuse him. I'm confused myself.

"I was talking about her teacher."

Now I'm confused by him. I look up questioningly, prompting an explanation.

"She knew you were watching. Of course she was preoccupied wondering what you were thinking. What you observed."

I actually laugh. The man is not as self-aware as I thought. "She's preoccupied with you, not me. Trust a woman to know."

"Well, then," he says with a shrug, "I guess I was confusing her story with mine."

A strange spiraling emotion takes me over, tightening my chest as it wraps around me, leaving me warm as it slithers down. I'm embarrassed and thrown. What's his motive? He can't be speaking from a place of sincerity. And also, dammit, he saw me watching, and now I suddenly want to bury my head in a hole.

I throw my gaze back to the screen so he doesn't see the flush in my face and take the moment to regroup. "It's the right story," I say, as though he hadn't just shot an arrow to my heart. "It doesn't matter exactly who it was who had her flustered. The fact remains that she is pleasantly uneasy. I can see that clearly." It's most evident in the series of shots, which is not a lesson I have planned to teach for another couple of weeks. Leave it to Hendrix to tackle assignments in advance.

I stop at a particularly well-composed frame. Technically, it's perfect, but it's not right. I mean, it's head and shoulders above anyone else I've critiqued today, which is what makes it all the more frustrating to not be able to put a finger on the flaw. There is agony in the "almost." More so than when a mark is missed entirely. I'd rather the miss any day. To be so close to the goal and miss it by a hair? That's a kind of torment that haunts.

It makes me all the more eager to figure out the fix, not just because it's Hendrix who is facing this potential torment. I would be equally motivated if it were any of my students, but also, admittedly, this torment will also haunt me if not resolved *because* it is Hendrix.

I twist my lips, studying, thinking. I flip through the last images. I flip back. "I need to see something," I say. Without waiting for his response, I march through the classroom door—propped open since it's the kind that automatically locks when shut—to the computer at my desk. I wiggle the mouse to wake it up, type the title of the photo I'm looking for in the browser search bar, and hit enter.

It isn't until the image is full on the screen and he leans in to look with me that I realize that he followed me in here. That I realize that we're practically alone. That I realize that I've made an awesome mistake.

My heart quickens its pace.

"Leopard, sleeping," he says, repeating the name of the photo before us. "That one won me the BWPA. Almost four years ago now. Flattered you knew it by name."

Sure, he's flattered. I'm...well, I'm a bit embarrassed, of course, but not as badly as I would have imagined I'd be. I'd forgotten that about him, that he has a way of easing me like a fragrant balm against sliced skin.

"It's worthy of the award, though not my favorite." I'm not sure why I'm being so honest. Probably because I've gone completely nutters and have lost all control.

"And which one is that? Your favorite." He's closer now, his head lowered so that I can feel his exhale at the side of my cheek.

"Elephant playing in black and white," I admit.

"That one is a favorite of mine as well."

As it should be. I'd be beside myself cocky if I'd taken that shot or anything near it. It's complete magic how he captured the animal spouting water from its trunk at its companion, the droplets of water catching the sun like diamonds. It's playful and charming and poignant, capturing a kinship between two animals that is rarely caught among humans. Or perhaps it's that I have been so rarely playful myself.

I've spent endless hours with it, and still, every time I see it something blooms inside me.

But I didn't rush in here to fawn over his art.

I nod toward the screen. "This is nearly identical to that photo of Kaila."

"I'm not sure she'd appreciate being compared to a wild animal, but go on."

"Not the leopard itself," I sigh. "The composition. The angle, the way you've framed it, the direction of the light. Do you see it?" It's his style epitomized in both shots.

"Are you worried I plagiarized myself? I promise I'm not going to issue a complaint."

I shoot him a look that says *would you please understand me*? Sometimes I find that works as well as explaining myself, if not better.

This time it seems to do the trick. "All right, I see what you're seeing," he says. "This shot is much better than any on that camera you're holding though."

Exactly my point. "So what's the difference?" I've had mentors ask me similar questions. I always assumed they knew the answer when they asked and just wanted me to find it for myself, but now I wonder if they just realized the only person who can really say what's missing from a piece when it's that near perfection is the person who sees it best of all, the person who saw it from scratch before it was a moment or a story or art. When it was raw and living.

Hendrix straightens, and I follow like I'm tied to him with an invisible string because I know he knows the answer, and I'm eager to have the mystery solved.

"Easy," he says. "My subject today wasn't the most fascinating thing in the vicinity."

It's a loaded statement, one that has me rejoicing and melting and panicking all at the same time. It's a relief that he doesn't like that twit, which isn't a fair thing to call her at all since she has not demonstrated any reason to be labeled as such except to exist. And it's exactly what was missing from the photo. It's a breakthrough when a person can identify the flaw so succinctly, and always deserves to be acknowledged as such. Which makes me want to give him a high five or a fist bump or whatever it is that's the current way to express congratulations. Makes me feel almost playful enough to do so.

But his answer was also pointed, and while I'm quick to self-doubt, I'm perceptive enough to know what he's saying, and now I can no longer cling to any confusion about why he took this class. He's here for me. He took this class for me.

"Camilla…" It's the same way he said my name the other night at the bar, an invitation and a warning that whatever follows will be hard for me to hear. A pause to let me decide if I can bear it.

Frankly, I'm not sure that I can. It's a lot to process. And the clock is ticking in the back of my head. Two more students to get through. No time to acknowledge this. No desire to deal.

"I have to get back to the others," I say dismissively. I hand him his camera and, like I did at Nightsky, I head for the door.

He follows this time, though. Because that's where he's supposed to go, not because he's chasing after me, yet it feels like being chased, and while I wanted to get away from him that night, I don't feel that desperation today. Turns out I sort of like the feeling of being chased, a surprise to me since I dreaded anytime Frank came after me. Different circumstances, of course. Frank rewarded me with beatings when I was caught, convincing me I deserved it because how dare I run? It would be understandable if I had permanent PTSD from it. I definitely did for quite some time. Perhaps that's why I'm always running from lovers who I am absolutely sure will not follow.

Hendrix, though.

Is it possible I like that he's come for me? Is it possible that I could enjoy what would be waiting if he caught me? Is it possible that I could try?

I'm not sure. There's a hopeful buoyancy in my limbs, though, as I conference with the last two, and a smile dresses my face as I wrap up the class and give the homework for the week. I'm nervous for the class to end, knowing Hendrix will surely approach me, but I'm excited too.

Which is why I'm crushed when he doesn't stay after to talk. He lingers to gather his things, letting everyone else leave ahead of him, but then he slings his camera bag over his shoulder and starts for the door, a door that will lock as soon as it swings shut behind him, and he won't be able to come back in, and I'm so scared by that metaphor that I call out after him. "Hendrix!"

He turns without hesitation, his brown eyes warm like melted chocolate. "Yes?" he says, and he doesn't sound at all annoyed. Rather he sounds as desperate and anxious as I am, and the pressure to say the right thing is there, pressing against my trachea as if to block the possibility of words in case they are the wrong ones.

"I…" God, what are the right ones? I know how to seduce a man, but I don't know what this is, and I sure as hell don't know how to do it.

But Hendrix does, and like I coached the class today, he coaches me. "Say it, Camilla. Say what you want, whatever it is. Big or small."

I close one eye, like I do when I'm behind the camera, and zero in on the shot, barely breathing in case I lose it. Then I shoot. "I find you the most fascinating thing in the vicinity too."

He smiles and nods, as though he already knew, before I even did, and maybe he really did because I said it, and I mean it, and he isn't surprised. His smile fades now, and he grows somber, and I brace myself for the seriousness of what he's about to say. "Dinner tonight?"

I laugh, the tension relieved by his simple request. Or not so simple since it's not the easiest thing for me to agree to on most occasions, but it's so much easier than whatever else I thought he might say, which is silly because what could he say that would be so frightening?

Actually, a lot.

But all he's asked for is this, and wanting to live my life, I tell him yes.

Chapter Five

Concentric: Two or more things having a common center. - *MoMA Glossary of Art Terms*

The perfect photo creates a memory.

It's the same the other way around. The most important moments, the ones that feel crafted and composed and perfect, those are the ones that stick with you. A lifetime is a collection of those moments, collected like snapshots in the scrapbook of your mind.

There are a lot of photos in my past that I don't like to look at, entire albums of memories that I've stored away on shelves. They're dusty and faded now, and even when I do pull them out to look at, I'm not sure anymore that what I'm looking at is accurate. They're too yellowed, like photos from the past, the kind taken on Kodak paper that wasn't meant to endure through time.

The evening with Hendrix, seven incredible hours, fills a memory book all on its own. Like so many others, I try not to look at that one very often. I sneak it out on occasion, usually in the dark when Freddie's asleep and the house is quiet, when the presence of the album flashes like a neon sign in the dark. I regret it every time, tucking it back on its shelf in the morning, promising not to touch it again. Sometimes that promise lasts a week or two. Sometimes I don't make it more than a day.

The problem with looking at this particular album is how happy it makes me feel. Sunshine peeking through the trees on Tarr Steps kind of happy, which, in my opinion, is the ultimate pinnacle of happiness. That's what the night was like last autumn.

It's funny how sometimes joy can hurt as much as pain. Because it's fleeting, perhaps. Because even when you're in the middle of it, you're aware that it won't last. It's a bubble of a feeling, buoyant and light and free. The kind of feeling you want to chase after, even knowing that once it's caught it will pop.

And, oh, that pop is always such a surprise. Where once there was something and now it's completely gone.

In the space of time between class and my date with Hendrix—no, not date, I refuse to call it that when it's merely a meal we'll be sharing—before I get fussy over my attempt to get ready, I allow myself to take the album out and look at it in the daylight. It's heavier than I remember, divided into four distinct series, each containing their own arc, and each individual photo memory is as vivid and bright as the day it was taken.

I wear a smirk as I study the first series. I'd been part of the final conference event of the evening, a panel discussing the current trends of photography in the corporate field. I'd been nervous about the whole thing and needed a drink when it was all over, but in the end I'd been pleased with my contributions, pleased enough to accept the invitation to go to a local restaurant with the other panelists and a group of conference attendees.

I'm not sure how Hendrix got in the mix. He'd known one of the speakers or had nothing better to do with his night and had popped into the panel out of curiosity. However it happened, I found myself seated next to him at one of the several tables our group occupied, and with the buzz of the event being over and a job well done, along with a dirty martini already in my system, somehow idle conversation among many turned into a heated discussion between just the two of us.

"Of course branding should be considered art!" My exclamation came in response to his suggestion that graphic design didn't have a place in the community. "There is just as much sweat, blood, and tears invested in the pieces that come across my desk as there are on any of the prints hanging in the Foam. More so even, considering what's on the line for the designs if they don't do the right job."

"But that's just the thing," he protested. "They have different goals. Branding is meant to get people to spend. Art is for people to enlighten and enjoy."

"As if you aren't looking for a payday when you're trekking through the wilderness. There's a reason they call it a money shot."

"Of course I'm hoping to get paid, but the shot is the end

product for the consumer. It's not a bridge to something else."

"Isn't it?" I fired back, enjoying the debate. "When National Geographic uses one of your photos, they're expecting it to draw people into the accompanying article. Exactly what branding is meant to do, except that branding is honest about it. And more practical. It should be rewarded."

"It *is* rewarded. With a paycheck."

"It should be rewarded in the galleries too, as far as I'm concerned. It's an outdated notion that a creation is either profitable or it's art. I promise you, it can be both."

He paused then, studying me before a grin appeared, the first full grin I'd seen from him, and it was electrifying. Literally. I still remember the shock that jolted through me at the sight of it. "It can be both," he repeated, as though testing out the idea.

"It most definitely can." I smiled back, and yes, I was flirting. The conversation had moved from a discussion about something I found interesting with a stranger to a discussion about something with a stranger I found interesting. That didn't happen very often for me. I found a man I was attracted to easily enough, but I was never interested beyond the endgame. The conversation was the branded design leading to the eventual fuck.

With Hendrix, though, I was interested in being in the moment. I was interested in more than what he had hidden under his clothes. I was also interested in what he had hidden in his brain. He was engaging and arresting, and I was undeniably charmed.

He was too, it seemed. It was in his eyes, in the tilt of his head. In the words that came next from his mouth. "Want to discuss it over a drink in the lounge where it's quieter?"

Maybe I hemmed and hawed about it a bit before saying yes, but it was already decided in my mind. I knew that I would spend every last second of the night with him, whatever it took, even if it meant only the drinks and the banter. Even if it meant accompanying him to his room. I remember knowing that. I don't remember the details of actually moving from this sequence to the next, but I do remember knowing I was all in for the night.

Mostly, I remember the warm glow of happiness. He made me smile.

The next series of memories picks up in a dark corner of the lounge, the rest of our group abandoned along with my dirty martinis. Instead, he'd ordered negronis for us both, and I was instantly in love. With the drink, not the man.

Well. The man too.

It seems naïve to say that I could use such a bold word to describe my enamorment so quickly and be certain that it was accurate, but I am certain. I'm not romantic about it. I don't pretend to believe that he would feel the same or that I would want him to feel the same or that it would ever be more than just that one evening together. I only know that sometime between the first sip of the Italian cocktail and when Hendrix paid the tab, I fell in love.

It might have been when he confessed that he still carried a film camera with him on location along with his digital or when he thoughtfully traced across the back of the hand I'd rested on my lap like he was painting it into being with his thumb. I'd definitely realized it by the time he was describing what it was like to burrow in a forest and hide for hours at a time waiting to capture a shot of an elusive lynx.

"It's a constant adjustment of position," he said. "Always subtle so as not to disturb the environment. Just enough to wake up the limb that's fallen asleep in the previous position."

"That sounds like it takes tenacity." I'd been in awe. I wasn't a big fidgeter, but I certainly wasn't great at being still. Except, perhaps, when he spoke.

"Patience is probably one of my strengths." His cheeks might have got red at that. It was hard to tell in the dim light of our corner, but he was humble enough about it that I imagined the heat in his face at the self-recognition. "It's worth it though. Waiting and waiting and waiting and sure you're going to be disappointed and then suddenly, there it is—a creature wild and uninhibited and free. And that specific animal has likely never been seen by another human. It's deeply profound and quite personal. I don't usually talk about it, to be honest."

My first impulse was to say he didn't need to talk about it with me then—it's the instinct I've learned, to detach myself from another's possible regret. But he and I were already past that, and I wanted to linger in the intimacy of his sharing. The feeling I got when I realized I'd been in his confidence. "That sounds beautiful," I said, my voice hushed as though I were in the forest with him.

"It's the most I feel alive. When I'm face-to-face with

something fierce and feral. Not that everything I photograph is dangerous by any means. In fact, most animals I shoot aren't. I photograph a lot of owls, for example—they're so expressive, I can't help myself. But the fierce ones have the most impact. The lions. The tigers on the prowl. The bear defending its cub. The hippos—any encounter with a hippo is memorable. The wolves."

"What's your favorite of them all?" I asked, my gaze darting to his lips.

"Of all the wild animals I've encountered?" His tone said I'd asked him an impossible question, and yet he didn't hesitate after my nod. "You."

I left for the lavatory then, and he followed after me, which I had hoped he would do. This series of memories is filthy and frenetic—my trousers pooled on the floor around my ankles, my hands braced on the sink, the rip of the condom packaging, the slapping of his thighs against mine as his cock pounded rhythmically into me.

The end of this sequence would normally be where I walked away. There hadn't been a man since Frank that hadn't received a goodnight from me seconds after the disposal of the condom.

That wasn't the case with Hendrix. When he finished zipping up his slacks, he turned me around and pressed his forehead against mine. "This can't be all I have of you," he pleaded, as though he suspected my usual habit to run. "Please, please let me have more."

I wondered if that was his prayer in the rainforest, when after waiting for most of the day for something incredible to show itself, a jaguar crept into view only to immediately turn and flee at an accidental sound made by Hendrix in his excitement to capture the animal on camera.

It wasn't because he sounded so desperate that I agreed. It was because I echoed his prayer. I not only wanted more of him, I wanted more of me. The witty, confident me that I was with him. The me that he saw me to be. Were they one and the same? I wasn't sure, but I wanted them to be. And he was the reason I'd seen the possibility.

I wanted them to be so much that I didn't think about what I was agreeing to, not as we walked hand-in-hand to his hotel, not as I followed him up the narrow staircase, not as he slid the key into the lock—one of those old-fashioned kinds, not the plastic keycard sort—not as he pulled me past the threshold and into his arms.

My lips shifted against his easily that time. The first kiss back in the restaurant lav had been awkward with its greediness, our teeth clacking and our tongues in the way. In his room, the kiss was like slow dancing, languid and in sync, and though I was not often very big on kissing, I could have stayed in that embrace, our mouths locked, for hours.

But of course there'd be more than kissing, and it wasn't until we were on his bed and his hands reached for the buttons of my long-sleeve blouse that I began to panic.

I put a hand up to stop him, and before he could ask for an explanation, I cupped my palm over the thick bulge in his crotch, which turned out to be an effective distraction for all of about five minutes. Soon enough, he was fumbling with the buttons once more.

This time putting up a hand wasn't enough. "Could we…" I'd never stumbled on this request before. I didn't know why it was so hard to voice it this time. "Do you mind if we keep most of our clothes on?"

He let go of my shirttail and cupped my face, pulling me in for a searing kiss. "Whatever you need," he said, and I knew he meant it. He had the patience of a wildlife photographer, after all. "Just, you should know how badly I want to touch you."

I could have let it go at that. Skin-to-skin during sex is a beautiful thing, definitely heightens the intimacy, but since beautiful and intimate are not ever my objective, I am apt to not care about the absence.

Most men don't care either once they've got their cock inside me. It's helpful in this that they tend to have a one-track mind.

But there with Hendrix, pressed up against him with my clothes on and still feeling miles away from satisfaction, it was harder to ignore his desires. His desires were my desires, deep and desperate and greedy.

I glanced across the room at the windows, covered with blackout curtains. The lamps around the room were already all turned off save the one on the nightstand. An excited sort of anxiety tightened around my chest, gripping tighter as the urge to speak increased, like a failsafe my body had set up in case of stupid decisions like this one, a warning that it would shut down my ability to breathe before it let me proceed.

But Hendrix made me feel brave. Because I was in love with him. Because I was in love with the person he saw when he looked at me. Because in that moment, I was happy.

"Turn off the light?" It was a question because I was uncertain about what I was doing, but he answered like it was meant for him to answer.

"I can do that if you prefer."

I didn't know what I preferred. I knew what was necessary because now that the idea was in my head, I needed to be naked against him as surely as I needed to not be seen. So I said, "Yes. Please."

It was torture just to lose his presence long enough for him to roll over and reach for the lamp. He flipped the switch, and we were pitched into the security of darkness. Pretty solid darkness, too. Those blackout curtains earned their name.

It was more eagerness than nerves that had me fumbling with the buttons of my shirt. Then I was fumbling with his buttons, and quickly we were both bare, top to bottom, wearing nothing but the dark.

And God, had touch always felt that magnificent? Like a favorite blanket fresh from the dryer, I wanted every part of my skin wrapped with his. I can still feel that want with an embarrassing degree of lust. Can still feel the desire to explore every inch of his nudity with the tips of my fingers.

I didn't indulge, of course. Those kinds of liberties are expected to be exchanged in kind in those situations, and I couldn't endure much in return. I did allow him to fondle my breasts, let him tease my nipples to sharp peaks. Allowed my own palms to sweep up and down the sculptured landscape of his chest.

When it seemed the touching might progress to more wandering, I distracted him yet again. "I have a condom in my purse." It was going to be hard to find in the darkness, but I was up for the challenge.

"I have one. Grabbed it from my wallet before my pants came off."

What a gorgeous man. Sincerely. Perfection.

Also a mite alarming that he'd had more than one condom stashed away, but I wasn't about to get hung up on his possible sexual habits when I was the benefactor, and who was I to judge anyway?

The series of photo memories that play out from here aren't necessarily my favorite of the album, but they are the ones I look at the most often. Usually with my eyes shut tight and my hand buried between my legs. It's an absolutely wicked arc of a story they tell, provocative and obscene with the way he drilled into me, the way he ground his hips against mine. The delicious drag of his cock moving in and out and in and out. It was slower than the frenetic pace from the bathroom earlier, but still a tempo that had us soon sweating.

The sticky feel of his body pressed to mine may have been the trigger for my first orgasm. Bless the man, I had three total. Three earth-shattering Os that each wrecked me in its own beautiful way.

I'm not sure I would have had any of them at all if I hadn't been able to relax with him as I did. I tend to be overly tense with my clothes off, even in the darkness, but the fear that Hendrix's hands might roam while we fucked was quickly eliminated when he drew my arms over my head and threaded his fingers through mine.

Strange how connected to a person you can feel just by having your hands laced.

His cock inside me, too, but our hands...maybe because it was exactly what I needed at the moment, I'm not sure. Whatever the reason, it's our locked hands that I focus on the most whenever I look back.

The series ends with his collapse on the bed next to me, my cheek pressed against his chest as his breathing evened out and grew deeper, his arm wrapped loosely around my waist. I don't ever look at the sequence of events that followed—the part where he fell asleep, the part where I swallowed back a sob, the part where I stealthily rolled from his arms and groped around in the dark to find my clothes and then dress and then leave that me—*his* me—behind with him. There's a story in those memories too, but I've done my best to forget them. And today when I'd do best to remember why I snuck out, why I couldn't possibly stay, why there is no way on God's green earth that it could happen again, I still can't bring myself to acknowledge them.

Maybe I avoid that story because it's too hard to bear.

More likely I avoid it because it's so easy for me to see it ending another way.

Chapter Six

Juxtaposition: An act of placing things close together or side by side for comparison or contrast. - *MoMA Glossary of Art Terms*

It was a moment of weakness to agree to dinner, but at least I had sense enough to insist that I'd meet Hendrix at the restaurant instead of letting him pick me up. It makes it easier to lie to myself about what this is, why I said yes. It's a fact-finding mission. That's all. Not a date. Not an encounter with expectations beyond the meal. Not an opportunity to spend time with someone I am really, really fond of.

He picked well for the location, too. It's more pub than restaurant, which keeps it casual and helps enforce my lie. Since it's not one of those fancy places with rules about only complete parties being seated, he's already at our table when I arrive. He sees me when I'm still across the room, watches as I approach with keen eyes and barely any movement. I know in my gut that this is exactly the way he looks when he sits in wait for his elusive wild creatures to appear.

It makes my breath catch, the awareness that he's waiting for me with that depth of perseverance.

He stands when I reach him, but he's wise enough not to try to greet me with any physical connection. I find that both admirable and disappointing.

"You're ravishing," he says after his gaze takes in my gray ruffle blouse (long-sleeve, of course) and my black cigarette pants. His voice is reverent, as though he's awed by the sight of me. As though he still sees me as that woman I became with him.

Talk like that will be my undoing.

"This is not a date," I say, an attempt to plant myself on firm ground.

His lip twitches like it's fighting a smile. "Of course not."

I'm not reassured. But I sit anyway. He follows suit.

So. This is really happening.

"I'm not late," I say, more of a statement than a question. I know I've arrived right on time. I planned it so, but as much as I despise small talk, I need something to say and it's the first thing that comes to mind.

"No. I'm early." He's still looking at me with that expression of wonder that has me feeling all sorts of wrecked inside, and fuck it, I can't sit here if he's going to keep this up.

"Stop." I can't even look in his direction. His gaze is like a studio lamp, too bright to look directly at. "Stop looking at me that way."

"What way?"

I'm annoyed by his feigned innocence. "Like you're amazed by my presence." I feel uncomfortable as soon as I've called him out. Then it occurs to me that maybe his awe is in the fact that I showed up. "You didn't honestly think I might ghost, did you?"

He gives a half-shrug. "It crossed my mind."

My chest loosens. That's a much more tolerable reason for awe than the alternative. "Please. I said I'd be here, and so I am. I'm not scared of you."

"Yes, you are."

And just like that, I'm tight and tense again. It's not fair that he knows that. It's hard enough being the one afraid.

As though he senses my alarm, he adds, "If it makes you feel any better, I'm scared of you too."

"Bollocks. As if I'm to believe that after all the adventures you've been on. It's unlikely you're scared of anything."

He folds his arms and leans them on the table between us, pitching him forward. "Now that is awfully presumptuous. Just because I'm out facing the fear doesn't mean I don't feel it. Believe me, I feel it quite intensely."

"Then why do what you do?"

"Maybe I like being scared." His tone doesn't sound like he's trying to be a tease, rather that he's trying to figure it out for himself.

"Maybe it makes me feel alive. Maybe it's because the truly scary things tend to bring the biggest reward."

Well, then. We're far from the shallow now, aren't we? Is it too late to run?

Fortunately, Hendrix decides I need a reprieve. "How about I go order? Do you know what you want?"

I'm so eager for him to be gone, for me to have a moment to regroup that I don't even bother with the menu. "Fish and chips are fine." Greasier than I usually go for, but it's an item I'm sure they'll have.

"And to drink?"

"You choose." It instantly feels too personal for some reason, but it's been said and even the "Whatever" I add doesn't diminish the intimacy.

But it's enough to send him on his way, and with him gone, I can breathe. In, out. In, out.

And now that I can think again, I miss him.

I contain multitudes. Not just contradicting myself from day-to-day but from minute-to-minute. I don't want to be here, in this situation, feeling this unmoored. And, also, there's nowhere else I'd rather be.

It's better when he returns. Like his absence has reset the conversation, and we start again, on surer footing when he asks my opinion on the Gupta exhibition at the TPG. We quickly slip into that familiar banter I remember. It's easy to discuss art and philosophy while we sip contessas, a variation on the classic negroni, I learn, when Hendrix explains all of his favorite varieties of the Italian cocktail.

I learn other things too. Silly, trivial things. That his favorite movie is Kurosawa's Ikiru. That Hendrix is a family name and not a tribute to the famed guitarist. The evening is reminiscent of the first series from our first night together—engaging dialogue, passionate opinions. Nothing too personal. Nothing too hard. And all underscored by that happy glow of feeling at home with someone. If I'd wondered at all that our ability to connect had been a one-time thing, I now know definitively that it was not. Hendrix Reid fits me tonight as well as he did last autumn. Like tailor-made trousers. Like a memory card in my Nikon D6. Like the key in the lock of his hotel room in Paris.

While it's both of us directing the turns of conversation equally, I avoid the questions that I have told myself are my reason for being here. Not because I suddenly don't want the answers but because I suspect those will be harder subjects to negotiate. For me, anyway. Perhaps for him too.

It's not until we're on our third drink and I'm pushing away the scraps of my meal that the shift occurs. It's my fault because I bring up Freddie. Nothing major, just an anecdote that relates to our discussion on conceptual inspiration, but speaking his name at all opens a door to more personal topics, and exactly as contradictory as I was earlier, I'm not sure if I want to cross that threshold or not.

Hendrix makes his own decision and steps in before me. "Are you interested in more children?"

"No," I say quickly. Too quickly so it reads as untrue, and it is, which feels very unscrupulous. I might not be forthright when it comes to this man, but I haven't been outright dishonest. I don't like the taste of the dishonesty now.

I take a sip of my drink, and I amend. "Well. I did."

"What made you change your mind?"

I almost laugh. Isn't it obvious? "I'm too old now."

"No. You're not."

I circle my neck, stretching the tendons that have tightened there. "I might be," I say, and that's honest. For some reason it's easier to just assume that I am. The possibility that the season hasn't passed is way too fragile of a thing to hold in my head. "Biologically, I might be done. Once a woman hits thirty-five...it's harder."

He nods in acceptance, as though my answer has anything to do with him. "Then you adopt," he offers.

I've actually considered it. Especially when Fred was younger, and I dreamed of having another for him to play with. And also I've considered it recently. Now that he's six and the age difference between him and a new sibling would be the same as the age difference between me and Edward.

There's only one thing that stops me. "I don't want to do it alone again. I can afford it, I know. I could hire the help. I believe, I think, that a parent doesn't need to be omnipresent to do a good job. But it's lonely. To not have someone invested as much as you are. To have to wonder and worry and dream all on your own. I hadn't planned to parent alone the first time. I don't think I can do it willingly."

"Then don't do it alone."

Now I do laugh. "Just poof a partner into being? It takes time to do the whole dating thing. Then the engagement. The marriage. There's an order to it. Even if I found the right man today, it would take probably more time than I have, especially since I won't be giving my heart out easily this time."

He does that arms on the table lean, bringing him centimeters closer to me. "Fuck the traditional order. Do it however you want. Find the guy, decide to be parents together, take your time to see if it turns into more."

Even fucking the order, there are still flaws in his idea. Finding a guy who wants to partner in parenting, finding a guy at all.

Unless he's offering to be the guy.

And I'm suddenly hopeful and terrified that he is. The bubble is on the verge of popping and I'm not ready.

Oh, God. What am I doing?

"Why did you come here?" I blurt it out, out of nowhere. Because it's time. Because I need to know. "Why did you enroll in my class, out of all the classes you could take in the world? And don't give me some bullshit about wanting to broaden your skills because that doesn't answer why me. And after seven months with no word between us, why now?"

"You were the one who snuck out without leaving any way to contact you."

"That's the universal code for this is only a one-night stand."

"Which is why it took me seven and a half months to show up."

He's intense when he's serious. Intense and vulnerably accurate. I'd held back adding the half to our months apart because I didn't want to give away that I've counted the time, but he's put it out there for me to see it of him. Even if he's scared, he's so much braver than I. I'm too scared even to respond.

Boldly, he reaches across the table to stroke my hand with his thumb, the way he did that other night. I should pull it away. This series cannot lead to the same series now as it did then.

But he's pinned me in place with the simple power of his touch, and like an animal frightened by a possible predator, I remain in place.

While I stare at the path his thumb takes, I can feel him staring at me. "I was trying to honor your choice," he says softly, a whisper really. "I really was, Camilla, but I couldn't do it anymore. I couldn't keep pretending that there was anything in the world that interested me besides you."

Oh my.

To be wanted. To be wanted enough to be pursued. I haven't entertained those possibilities in a very long time. Haven't even entertained the fantasy. It's too ludicrous when I feel so unworthy of that kind of wanting.

But I'm trying to look at the proof, and the proof is in his words. The proof is that he's here. And for a handful of seconds I consider what could become of that.

The considering doesn't go too far before I remember that the vulnerability he's offering has to be met in kind for it to work.

And I can't be that naked, in any sense of the word. Not for Hendrix. Not for anyone.

I pull my hand away abruptly. "I'm sorry, I don't feel the same." The bitter taste of deceit returns. Before I'm tempted to wash it down with truth, I stand. "I think it would be best that we call it a night."

I'm heading out the door before he can stop me, confident that he won't follow. He knows there's no use chasing after the animal he's after. He knows it's best to lie in wait.

Outside, I pull up the Uber app as soon as I realize that catching a taxi in this part of town on a Saturday night is not happening. Car ordered, I lean against the stone exterior of the pub and will myself not to cry.

Next thing I know, Hendrix is standing next to me. Because I'm not an animal, I'm a woman, and why would he stay in the pub when the bill was already paid and I'd left?

And if he was the type of man to follow me to London, he certainly wouldn't be the type of man to leave me brooding in peace.

I sigh when I see him, a big, desperate, anguished sigh. "I can't," I say. Because I can't. I can't anything with him. I can't even with myself.

"I know," he says calmly. "So let me." With his hands in his pockets, he steps in, so close that I can't look in his eyes. So close that we're almost touching. It feels like we're touching, even though there's not a part of me in contact with him. "I know you don't mean what you said in there. I know that you feel something. And I know that, for whatever reason, you aren't able to let that keep you from walking away right now."

His tone is patient. His words, given as a gift, not to persuade but to soothe. And the electricity bouncing between us...would it send mixed messages if I let him take me in the alley for a quickie?

It's sad that that's where my mind goes, when sex is already part of my routine and what he's offering is something so much more uncommon in my life. Happiness. Not the daily small joys I have naturally with Freddie, but the kind that come from being chosen. Is that why I run from it? Because it's too foreign? Too unknown?

Probably that, and also it's hard to trust something so intangible. Sex is easy in comparison. It's concrete. It has a clear objective. It has a clear end.

Of course, with what he's said, with the declaration of his interest, sex can't just be sex anymore. It will forever after be more.

So I bite my lip so I don't suggest it. I breathe in his scent, a mix of sandalwood and musk. I take a snapshot for my memory book. I don't lean forward to press my forehead against his chin. When he speaks again, I listen.

"I need you to know that I'm here," he says. "Afraid because of how much I want you. Willing to wait for any scrap of you that you're able to give. If this is all I get, if this is all I *ever* get, it will still have been worth it."

He goes then, walking in the direction of the tube, without so much as the barest brush of his body against mine.

I watch him leave, my heart heavy and full, the camera behind my eyes click, click, clicking until he's just a blur disappearing in the distance.

Chapter Seven

Proportion: Refers to the harmonious relation of parts to each other or to the whole. - *MoMA Glossary of Art Terms*

"You said we'd go swimming." Fred tugs at my arm as he attempts to pull me in the direction he believes goes to his uncle's house.

"We will go swimming," I promise. Edward has a pool on his ground level, and though he's still in the States, we often slip over to use it. I'll only don a costume if we're alone, and Freddie's much too young to be swimming without someone ready to jump in after him if need be so my brother's mansion across from Regent's has become our swim spot. I've even taken to leaving our costumes there to make the journey less of a hassle.

Though I do intend to keep the Sunday plans I made with my son, there's another thing on my agenda as well. "Remember I said we were going to the park first?"

"But this is the boring part of the park." He kicks at the walk with the toe of his shoe. I'm lucky this is his version of a tantrum, he's such a well-behaved kid. "Do we have to look at weird art again?"

That was my bad. The last event I dragged him to at this park was the Frieze art fair. I learned too late that he'd been maybe a little too young to fully appreciate it. I'm hoping today's art will be of more interest to him. "It's a little weird," I confess. "I think it will be fun too."

He frowns as he kicks the walk again. "But will it be as fun as swimming?"

Swimming, for him, involves splashing half the water out of the pool, shrieking in glee, and heaving toys to and fro until he's exhausted. This won't involve any of those things. I consider lying, but I've committed to a parenting style that embraces honesty as much as possible, so I toss the idea aside and settle for the truth. "Probably not quite as fun. We won't stay long, okay?"

He heaves a sigh that seems awfully large for his little body. "Okay."

I survey the horizon, pinpointing my destination. With a twinge of guilt, I tow him toward the performers ahead of us. I haven't been completely transparent, hiding my motives for this part of our trek. What am I supposed to tell a six-year-old boy, though, when I can't fully explain my reasons even to myself?

I should take that as a sign that this particular adventure is better avoided, but here we are, my child and me with my multitudes standing in front of the living statue competition against all better reasoning.

Fortunately, Fred is mesmerized. "Are they…?" He's hesitant to make his guess out loud, understandably since the performers are that good. "Are those real people?"

"They are. Isn't it incredible?" Together we walk closer toward one of the "statues," a man covered head to toe in bronze seated on a park bench and frozen in a pose. He's so still, it takes me a minute to discern he's actually breathing.

Fred clings next to me, suddenly intimidated. "He doesn't get to move at all?"

"Well, he won't stay like that forever, but he'll certainly stay for long enough that it grows uncomfortable. Can you imagine sitting that still?"

There's a part of me that can imagine it. The part of me that finds discomfort so familiar it's become a friend. I can imagine the tingle of a limb beginning to fall asleep, the buzz of nerves turning into spikes of pain before finally, finally, there's the welcome numb.

It's worth the ache, in my opinion, to reach that finish line. A reward few can understand.

I'm sure Fred does not have that goal in mind when he says, "I bet I could do it!"

"You think you could?" He couldn't sit still for even half a minute, but I'm a mother who encourages even the boldest of dreams. "Maybe we should paint you up and let you try it?"

"I'll try it now." His trepidation gone, he runs to the empty seat next to the bronze man and attempts to replicate his pose. His little face alternates between imitating the bronze man's seriousness and a pleased smile with himself.

I bite back a laugh, wishing I'd brought my camera. I try not to take it out with us too often on our days together. This time is for him, and it's hard to stay present in that when my mind is consumed with the business of making art.

Right now, though, I want to capture the image for the moment, not the craft. Remembering my mobile, I dig it from my purse and snap a pic on the rarely used camera app, impressed that Freddie has managed to hold the position this long.

"He's a natural," a familiar voice says at my side and like a pleasant breeze on a humid day, I feel a sudden relief.

Trying not to smile too widely, I peer over at Hendrix. "I suppose he is. It's come as a surprise."

Just then, Freddie begins to fidget. Just wrinkling his nose, twice, three times, as though it needs to be itched. "Perhaps I spoke too soon."

Hendrix chuckles, the camera slung across his chest bouncing with the movement. "He seems to really be struggling there. Poor guy."

"You're doing great, Fred! Bravo!"

My encouragement draws a grin on my son's face, wide and toothy. "Told you I could do it!" Then he's up and running toward one of the other living statues. He clearly considers himself their newest coworker and I could watch this all day.

As I follow after him, without discussion, Hendrix does too, matching my stride.

I curse myself for being as thrilled as I am for his company. "Fancy seeing you here," I say when I can't think of anything else and the need to speak to him feels like a butterfly cupped in my hands, its wings beating desperately to escape.

"Yes. Quite a coincidence."

I roll my eyes. At him. At me. No coincidence at all, actually, since the assignment I gave class the day before was to get some shots of the competition today. The statues are perfect models, their stillness removes variables and allows the photographer to focus on other elements—the light, the angle, the story. Also, the performers already expect to be photographed so there isn't the ethics issue of taking pictures without permission, a debate many of my peers have had about snapping pics of people in the park.

"The exhibit goes on all day," I protest. "I could have missed you." It is honestly a stroke of luck that we happen to be here at the same time as he is. I'd tried to be, of course, but I had little hope that it would actually occur.

If I believed in that sort of thing, I might think the universe is trying to tell me something.

"You wouldn't have missed me," he says, and suddenly I know he's been looking for me. That he likely arrived just as the event opened and planned to stay until it closed for just the shot at an encounter.

That patience of his. It unravels me.

Why am I here, why am I here, why am I here? When I told him this isn't what I want. When I insisted to myself that this isn't what I need. Maybe my truest addiction all along was to feeling the happiness he draws out in our talks.

I dragged my child into this tangled mess. How fucked up am I?

Though my selfish reasons for being here seem to be an accidental score because Fred is having a "dynamite" time running from statue to statue, posing next to them. He pretends to raise a gun with the green army men. At the group of golden cowboys, he adopts a tilt to his posture that allows him to fit right in. When he gets to the woman made up to look like a bronze replication of the queen, he bows deeply before her, his small legs teetering in the position.

He's so funny and so fast flitting from one scene to the next that I hardly have time to recover. At one point, I have to bend over to contain the fit of laughter.

When I'm able to stand again, I wipe tears from my eyes and catch Hendrix beaming at me. He's been laughing along with me, and it felt so natural, I forgot that it's not. Forgot that few people ever see me like this, loose and uninhibited.

It makes me feel captured, in a way. I resent him for it, for witnessing this part of me.

But also it makes me want him to see more.

Fred runs back to me, his eyes wild with excitement. "Mummy!

Did you see the mermaid?"

I glance around until I spot the woman dressed and painted in green sitting on top of a rock, her mermaid tail dangling down the side. "I see her now. Is she your favorite?"

"So far!" He abruptly settles his elation when he spots Hendrix at my side. "Hello," he says, not the least withdrawn like I am. "I'm Fred. You can call me Freddie."

Hendrix looks to me, and I nod. "What a very adult introduction. Better than what I could have offered myself. I'm Hendrix. You can call me whatever you like, I'll probably answer."

"He talks funny," Fred whispers loudly.

"He does, doesn't he? American dialects are the silliest."

My child beams like we've shared a joke, then addresses Hendrix once again. "Are you Mummy's friend?"

God, the rippling of my insides makes me feel like I'm on the Eye instead of feet flat on the ground. It feels so big, this introduction. A monumental moment between the three of us. And inappropriate since I have no intentions of keeping Hendrix in my life. Irresponsible too. What kind of mixed messages am I giving the man? What kind of mixed message am I giving my son?

But if I were to keep Hendrix…

I don't even know how to fantasize that without an understanding of how he'd fit into my full life when the biggest portion of my life is Fred.

Again the man looks at me. I don't venture an answer, intrigued with what he'll say on his own.

"I'm a student in her class," Hendrix says, a safe answer that I should let stand.

But I'm an idiot of a creature so I amend. "He's in my class, but yes, Fred. Hendrix is a friend."

Hendrix's eyes light and his lips curl up as though he's won a grand prize.

Has he?

No, he hasn't. It's just a fact. We knew each other before he enrolled in my class. He's not just a student.

If we're actually accounting for facts, of course, he's not just a friend, either.

"I don't know many of Mummy's friends," Fred says thoughtfully. "Do you have a kid too?"

It's the natural assumption. Most of the people he has met as "Mummy's friends" were really arranged playdates with mothers who had children Fred's age.

Hendrix squats down so he's eye-to-eye with my son. "I don't. Sort of unfortunate because I always wanted kids."

"Why don't you have one then?"

The questions of children.

It reminds me of the encouragement Hendrix gave the night before, suggesting that it wasn't too late for me to have more. Had I imagined that he was suggesting the possibility of fathering them?

Hendrix shrugs. "Good question. I'll get on that."

Fred nods his head like it's a done deal. "You can pretend I'm your kid for today," he suggests.

Hendrix looks up at me. "I'm not sure how your mother would feel about that."

My chest tightens and releases. Tightens again, and I'm not sure if it's a good feeling or a bad one. Not sure if it's okay to let my child play out this whim or if it'll do long-term damage.

But oh, what a delicious whim it is. A fantasy I'll play over and over, having a partner in loving my son. Someone to share the wonder and joy of watching this little miracle discover the world. A partner who loves me just as devotedly. Who wants to discover the world with me.

I don't have to respond, thankfully, because Fred shrugs it off like it's no big deal, and then is instantly distracted by a wizard statue in the distance.

"Stay within sight," I shout as he runs off ahead of us.

"I'm sorry about that," Hendrix says. "I hope it didn't make you too uncomfortable."

I shake my head, trying to adopt the same nonchalance as Fred. "Not your fault. He's just starting to realize he doesn't have a dad, and I think it fascinates him that there are men who might want to be one." I barely let a beat go by before adding, "And don't ask about his father, please. He passed away before Fred was born, and that's all I like to say about that."

"Understood." He's quiet now as we walk. I've ruined the mood. Which is probably for the best since I'm not trying to form any attachments between us.

Any more attachments between us.

Still, I can't help being sour over it. I'm so busy brooding, in fact, that it's Hendrix who has to point it out. "Look," he says. His face says that he's charmed by something. I know that because I've seen him look at me in the same way.

I follow his gaze and see Freddie standing in front of the gray-stone colored wizard, his expression full of wonder.

Quickly and with stealth, Hendrix approaches them, taking the lens off his camera and bringing it to his eye as he does. I creep behind him with equal excitement, hoping he caught the picture I'm seeing in my own head.

"Let me see," I say eagerly when he pauses his clicking to look at the screen. He hands over the camera willingly.

The photos are good. They're really good. Much better than the shots he took in class yesterday. These aren't missing what those lacked.

Still.

"May I?"

He understands me immediately, taking the sling off his shoulder so I can use the camera. Slowly, hoping that Freddie stays exactly as he is, I crouch down and manually adjust the focus. I only click three times, but when I stand up again, I have exactly the shot I envisioned—Freddie looking up at the wizard with awe, taken from his height so that the wizard appears as looming to the observer as he does to the child.

"That's it," Hendrix says as he peers over my shoulder. "That's the shot."

It's twenty-two degrees, and I'm warm under my long-sleeve floral wrap dress, but I shiver at his words. Just like I've never had a partner parent, I've never had a partner in my other aspects of creation.

I hadn't ever imagined how much I might want them.

"Look at the witch!" Freddie is off again, running toward a bronze woman with snakes for hair.

"She's Medusa," I correct, handing back the camera to its owner. I start in the direction Freddie headed, then stop with a frown.

Hendrix stops with me, slinging the camera over his shoulder. "What's—?" He catches sight of what caught my eye, or rather *who* caught my eye. "I didn't come with her," he says, seeming to know how much I want to hear it.

He probably didn't. Kaila with an i had the same assignment that Hendrix did. Of course there was every chance she'd be here, too.

I force a smile and wave at my other student, grateful that she's too consumed with her photography to do anything more than wave back.

It doesn't do anything to lighten the lead in my stomach.

Hendrix is deeply in tune with my displeasure. "It's the first time I've seen her all day. Swear."

It shouldn't matter. It *doesn't.* He can do what he pleases. He has no need to give me excuses.

Yes, my jealousy is irrational, but it's as real and spectacular as the humans pretending to be stone. "Why would I think otherwise?" I say cattily. "Because she's here at the exact same time you are. Because she partnered up with you in class. Because you bought her a negroni while she hung on you at Nightsky."

It's amazing how Hendrix tolerates my petty behavior. "She said to get whatever I was getting," he says simply. "And she was the one doing all the hanging."

"You went with her to the bar in the first place. She arranged it, I'm guessing?"

"She did," he admits. "Remember there was a group of us."

"But she's the one who asked you."

He steps closer to me, his body almost brushing against my arms crossed over my chest, and though I'm acutely aware what we might look like to Kaila, to any other student observing us, I don't move away. "And I said yes," he says quietly, "because I was already planning to go as soon as you told the class you liked to go there too."

I glance up at him, needing to hear what I so shouldn't hear. "Why?"

"Because I wanted to see you. And so I went to where I thought it was most likely that would happen."

The photographer-in-wait. Staking out the subject's known habitat.

"Some women file restraining orders over such behavior." I say it like a dare, though I don't know what I'm daring him to do.

"Tell me to stop, and I'll stop."

Was that what I wanted him to say? Because how easy. It's one simple word that will magically put all this to an end.

But I can't make the word form on my lips. I can't even think it in my mind. Because as much as I say I don't want this, as much as I pretend I don't want him, we both know it's a lie.

So if not stop, what now? Do we follow each other around? Do we continue to do this, whatever this is, every time we "bump into each other"?

How long is he going to stay interested in that?

But more importantly, what happens to my happiness if I don't let him in?

I drop my arms and step away, needing space, but I only end up angling one side of my body from him because I can't bear to be any farther away. "Why do you care? Was it the sex?"

"No." He looks disgusted that I even asked. "Don't get me wrong. It was fucking amazing sex. Mind-blowing sex. Out-of-this world sex. Both times. I've honestly never felt more at home than I did inside you, Camilla. But do not ever think to degrade this to just sex." He waggles a finger from him to me on the word "this," indicating the crazy attraction that exists between us.

He feels it too.

It makes me want to cry, and I'm not certain if they'd be happy tears or sad. Sometimes they feel the same. Bubbles. "You shouldn't say such things to me, Hendrix. I left last night when you started talking like this, remember."

He lets his hand brush against mine purposefully. His pinkie strokes up and down mine, letting me know how purposeful the move is. "The only thing I regret last night is not kissing you."

My breathing becomes heavy. I thought about that too, all night as I lay in the dark. I repeated the entire dinner over and over, the kiss we didn't have ending each replay.

I almost say it too.

But that's too honest. Too naked.

I pretend he didn't say it and double down on my previous statement. "You should find another tactic. The heart-on-your-sleeve method isn't working."

"I don't know. It seems my tactic is working just fine."

"Really?"

He wraps his pinkie around mine and electricity shoots up my arm like the light going on when the plug is locked in place. "You're here, aren't you?"

I blink up at him, then have to immediately lower my gaze because it's too hard to look at him and feel all the things I feel at the same time. "I don't know what I'm doing," I say, my voice trembling with the confession.

"I know," he says, and it isn't at all patronizing. "We'll go slow. We'll figure it out together."

I can't speak except to say, "I have to go."

And when I get Freddie and head us in the direction of Edward's for our swim, I haven't the least idea if I'm walking away or toward.

Chapter Eight

Tension: The state of being stretched or strained. - *MoMA Glossary of Art Terms*

Three minutes until class, and I'm as nervous as I was on day one.

This time, instead of worrying that the Hendrix Reid listed on my class sheet is the same one that I met in the autumn, I'm flustered because I'm sure that it is.

Excited too.

There's a quote that comes to mind from a famous musical when Little Red Riding Hood has first met the wolf, the fear she has at seeing his teeth bared is equally balanced with excitement.

I feel that way about Hendrix, not that I believe he's a wolf per se. But he *could* be. He could be any kind of man. He could be secretly cruel. He could lash out when he drinks too much. He could use his fists when he doesn't get his way.

Or he could be the gentlest man on the face of the planet.

That last possibility might actually scare me the most. I've found the other sorts of men so typical in my life that I feel unfortunately experienced. I'm not sure what to do with kindness. Not sure how to take love that doesn't feel like a wound except from Edward and Freddie.

It's a wonder that the past six days away from him hasn't given me time to rethink and reform. Going to the park, letting him meet my son—those were risks I should never have taken. And though I left that day with a light step and an uncharacteristically pleasant outlook, I had fully expected it wouldn't last long outside his presence.

But strangely, it has. The time in between made room for doubts, yes, but it also allowed hope to settle. Allowed excitement to burrow into me. By mid-week, my yearning was stronger than my fear, and all I could think about was being close to him again, no matter what the cost.

God, why does he make me wait? Is he not as anxious to see me again too? Has he changed his mind? What if he's given up and doesn't show at all? Each second that passes, the room feels darker and smaller, too dark and small to hold the growing mass of anticipation within me. My heart is pounding. I'm practically in a sweat. I'm about to spin from the winding tension.

It *is* an addiction.

Then, thirty seconds to start time, as my hope leans toward turmoil, he walks in the door, bringing a beam of sunlight with him and a stream of fresh air.

Our eyes meet instantly. His lips twitch. His gaze is warm. He's so obviously happy to see me that even I can't find a way to twist the proof into something other than what it is.

I have to clamp down the kind of grin I want to give him. I present a smile more suitable for the entire class instead and launch into the day's lesson. "Studio portraits. Where light is your best friend and your worst foe. Let's take it on, shall we?"

The half hour spent on lecture goes well enough, despite the split in my attention. I have to force myself not to rush. Each word spoken brings me closer to the breakout sessions when the students will be let loose to work, and I'll walk around to counsel them.

This time, I will not leave Hendrix for the end.

It's still another thirty minutes after I'm done teaching that I actually get to him. Working in the studio is a foreign experience for many of them and much help is needed setting up backdrops and softbox and umbrella lights before the first shoot can begin. Eventually, though, there's a student on a stool and another with her camera focused on her. The others are lined up to take a turn as photographer, and I'm free.

I somehow manage not to run straight to him, stopping to go over the weekend's assignment with Charlie and then Salima before I wander over to Hendrix. The anticipation is delicious, even the smallest buildup of time echoing vastly inside me.

"May I?" I say, reaching for his camera. Our fingers brush as I take it, and it's not an accident.

I bend my head over the screen, slowly flipping through images that barely register as they pass by. I'm focused on the perception I'm giving to the others who might be watching rather than his work. I'm focused on how near he's standing. On the rise and fall of his breaths. On the sprout of happiness inside that's grown from the seed he planted.

"I can't stop thinking about you." My words are quiet, and we're nestled near a corner in the back, but I glance around the room casually just in case.

"You don't know how happy I am to hear that." His voice isn't quite as low, probably not necessary since what he's said is more innocuous. He could be happy that I like his composition. He could be happy that I think the sun will stay out all day. He could be happy that I liked the sushi bar he recommended.

It's a little bit of a game, I realize, pretending in front of the others. A thrilling bit of taboo.

I look up at him, eager to connect with his gaze. "You had me wrecked when you didn't show up until the last minute for class. Kept me on pins and needles waiting for you."

I'm surprised I'm being so forthright. It's almost as if I have no choice. The feelings have been so bottled up inside me, they spill out like a shaken-up fizzy pop once the top comes off.

He rewards my honesty with a smirk. "Now you know how I feel."

My ribs tighten and the smile flickers on my lips as I try to decide if I'm bothered by being called out. Trying to decide if I'm supposed to feel guilty.

"I'm used to that feeling from waiting in the field," he says, reading my apprehension correctly, and this time his voice is nearly a whisper. "I'm comfortable with feeling it. No pressure, Camilla. I'm okay."

I nod, air moving through my lungs as my chest loosens. "Was your motive payback then?" I ask playfully.

"Nope. I'm just very bad with time." He pauses for my chuckle. As though he expected one. As though I give them easily. Only with him. "To be honest, I got here much too early, so early the door wasn't unlocked yet. Then, when I saw you approaching, I suddenly worried I was being too presumptuous or too, I don't know. Eager. So I slipped off to take some pics for a while. Got caught up in that and forgot to watch when to come back."

I've been there. Many a time. The inner world of the artist is awfully large. It's easy to get lost in it.

But that's not the part of what he's said that requires commentary. "You came early?"

He nods, a shy grin forming. "I couldn't wait to see you."

"I couldn't wait to see you either."

I'm not sure if the words feel better in or out at first, but after they hang for a few seconds, crackling the air around us, I decide I like them there. I like him knowing. I want to share that happy sprout with him instead of keeping it hidden.

A shuffle in the background as the student posing switches off with one in line draws my attention back to our surroundings. My skin feels itchy all of a sudden. "You're a student," I say, forcing my eyes back to his camera. "I keep wondering if this is inappropriate."

"Do I need to point out that nothing inappropriate has happened?"

"The kinds of thoughts I keep having feel very different." There I am again being candid.

"Well." He moves a step closer, and the closure of the distance between us combined with the throatiness of that single syllable has my thighs clenching. "Considering that all of your students are adults and that this isn't the type of school where you give a grade or wield power in another way over us, I think you could probably fuck each and every one of them and no one would bat an eye."

"Fuck the lot of them then?" My cheeks feel warm, and I'm very near giggling. I hardly recognize who I am with him.

He's abruptly serious when he answers. "Please don't do that."

"Not any of them?"

"Maybe just one."

I'm so risk aversive that I'd all but forgotten the sweet misery in being dangerous, in saying dangerous things.

And these are dangerous words. Because there's still a bit of the forbidden, no matter what he says, but mostly because there's an underlying challenge to this exchange. An admission that we've been thinking about each other in the naughtiest of ways. An invitation to make those naughty ways come to life.

I want him. I do. I've never stopped wanting him.

But the suggestion reminds me of the last time, of how I moved naked against him in the dark. Pursuing this with him will mean more of the same, good and bad. What are the chances that his flat has blackout curtains as well?

Instinctively, I tug at the cuff of my sleeve while my stomach ties itself in knots. "There might not be grades given, but there was money put forth. I should at least appear to be giving you all equal attention."

With that, I turn my head back to the camera screen and try to nudge my focus to the images before me and away from the gnawing tension in my gut. It's impossible, of course. How did I end up here, standing on the edge of this precipice? I've been so drawn by the view that I forgot how sharp the cliff was.

The photos pass in a blur as I scroll through. Vaguely I'm aware of the scenery changing, of the series moving from the living statues competition to another familiar setting—the walkway outside the school. I freeze on the image of someone that I know entirely too well, one that I have argued with and gone to war with. One I have tried to reason with, tried to love, tried to hate just as much.

It's exquisitely composed. The proportion is spot on, my body filling exactly as much of the image as it should to be compelling. The angle is remarkable and unique, the lighting superb the way it hits my face as I lift my chin to the sky. The story is quite clear—a woman who has found the sun before it disappears behind the clouds. I would see it perfectly even if I wasn't the subject, even if I hadn't lived it.

Seeing myself on his screen like this, in this context, a shot taken without my knowledge, without even knowing I was being watched—it makes me feel all sorts of twisted, like I'm tangled up in barbed wire. He had no right to take this without my permission. He has no right to see me this clearly. He has no right to make me feel this exposed.

He had no right to take the first image of that other me. She should have been mine.

The emotions would be best stored and sorted through later, but my words seem to always come out untethered around Hendrix. "How dare you?" I ask, not careful about my volume. "You were watching me when I arrived? How dare you?"

He gapes, shocked by my outburst.

He's not the only one watching. I feel the eyes of all my students on me like needles, and I still can't pin my mouth shut. "You can't just take pictures of people without their consent. It's unethical. It's wrong. It's not fucking nice."

I'm shaking with anger and something else. Something I'm so unused to I have trouble naming it. Vulnerability? It makes me feel stripped down and smothered all at once, and I *know*. I know the feeling only partly stems from the stolen photograph, that I'm being ridiculous, and that the bulk of my ire is rooted in this cyclone of a situation that I'm in with Hendrix. It's defense against the possibility that this happiness is false. I've moved from the calm of the eye into the overwhelming winds of the storm, but that knowledge does nothing to leash my temper.

"Camilla," Hendrix says, naturally taken aback. "I didn't know. I'm sorry."

Tears sting at my eyes, and I can't look at him. Turning away means facing everyone else—twelve faces wearing identical shocked expressions.

"That goes for all of you. No photos without consent. Ever. Not in my classroom. I won't accept it." It's not a believable cover. It's not enforceable. It's not even practical.

I can't deal with those details at the moment. I'm dizzy and unsettled and embarrassed and there's no way I can stay here like this, bare and on display.

"Take this." Without looking at him, I hand Hendrix his camera. "Continue on, please," I say to everyone else.

Then, heading to the door with even steps, I run.

Chapter Nine

Expression: The means by which an artist communicates ideas and emotions. - *MoMA Glossary of Art Terms*

I was sixteen the first time I picked up a camera. One of those early therapists Edward hired had suggested it. It wasn't the first activity I'd been prescribed. The Four Ps, that doctor had called his recommendations—painting, piano, poetry, and photography. Four Ps for therapy. I'd been an utter failure with the first three, so I was less than thrilled when he'd informed my brother it was time to try the last.

"Less than thrilled" is a kind way of describing how I'd felt, actually. I broke the first camera I'd been given—a Kodak DCS that had cost over ten thousand. Digital was still new and this one was cutting edge, which was why Edward had selected it. Inaccurate as the feeling may have been, I had a sense that the gift had been an attempt to buy my forgiveness for the time after foster care that I'd been enrolled in private school. It was no secret that I harbored resentment. I made it known whenever possible, including when I'd opened that box, seen the expensive contraption, and proceeded to throw it across the room.

I have a different view of that time now that I'm an adult. It was hard enough to become a parent in my thirties. I can't imagine what it must have been like to have to parent a sister at the age of eighteen, especially a sister with as much baggage as I'd had. Have. Some of that baggage I share with Edward. Our well-to-do household fell apart when our mother died. My father, distraught by her loss, chose her over us and ended his life to be with her in the grave. Thanks to a swindling relative, the fortune he'd left us was soon gone, and both Edward and I ended up being separated in the foster care system until he was old enough to assume guardianship over me. Luckily, he'd inherited our father's ambition and quickly built his own wealth, which is helpful but didn't fix anything. All the money in the world couldn't erase the damage done. As a teen, I made sure I let him know it often.

Edward did the best that he could, I know. I did the best that I could too, and, unfortunately, while he had his own issues to work through, he fared much better than I did.

It's part of the reason I've kept that secret hope of a sibling for Freddie in my heart. It would be another chance at the relationship Edward and I were robbed of when our parents died.

Thankfully, Edward was always a patient man, particularly when it comes to what he believes in, and he believed in me. Yes, he admonished me for the outburst, but he also bought me another, this time allowing me to choose the camera for myself.

Instead of going for a fancy digital model, I selected a Nikon 35mm. I was drawn to the process of developing film. Truly, that was the only thing that excited me about the idea of photography—the hours I'd get to spend tucked away in the dark.

It was quite a surprise when I discovered the real joy was behind the camera, with one eye pressed to the viewfinder, the other closed tightly so that my whole world narrowed into what was in front of me. And that world was completely shaped by me. No one else.

It was life-changing. I was able to take the emotions I had bottled up inside and place them outside of myself. I could look at them from a different angle. I could detach.

I'm not sure if it achieved the goal that my therapist had intended since I soon moved on to another. But even through the long string of specialists that followed, I clung to my photography. It was an art that became a fast friend. An only friend sometimes. In the darkest days with Frank, taking pictures was most often my only form of escape. No matter how much he bruised and mangled my body, he had no power over what I chose to express. He didn't get to be the author of the stories I told.

I learned to tell those stories in other ways over the years, more destructive ways. Sex has become another favorite method of expression as long as I am the initiator, because though it involves a participant, I get to choose it. After all the men in my life that chose what happened to my body for me, fucking at my whim is a powerful reminder that I'm the one who has control now.

It's a false reminder, though. I might be able to direct how and when and what happens physically during the act, but I still can't control the things that happen inside me. It's the same across all forms of expression, whether it be with my pussy or my camera or a knife, I can only control the external, and not even much of that.

The reality is I am still powerless.

I am still subject to my emotions.

I am still shaped by the actions of people outside of me.

I am still very much human.

* * * *

It only takes a quick trip to the restroom to pull myself together. I'm still flushed with humiliation when I walk in the door, partly because I didn't take my key and had to knock to be let in, but it's not so bad I can't show my face.

Dr. Joseph would count that as growth.

I'm more reluctant to name it so until I discover what I do in the future. The important reactions aren't always immediate, I've found, but rather what happens later, usually in the dark, when I'm alone and free to really express myself.

For now, I'm composed enough to be attentive to the students, mentoring them through the rest of the day's activity.

Not all the students, of course. I stay clear of Hendrix, unable or unwilling to even glance at him. I'm not sure if I'm too angry or too embarrassed or if I'm simply too scared to see how he might look at me now. To see if the reflection of me he wears in his expression has changed.

It's a tension that I carry throughout the rest of the class, as I count down the time remaining before this exhausting session is through. Half an hour. A quarter of an hour. Ten minutes. Now five.

Finally, I give this week's assignment and dismiss them.

I turn my back to them immediately, not watching as they leave. There is much to clean up today since we worked in the studio.

Lights that need to be unplugged, backdrops that need to be rolled and stowed. I'll get to all of it soon enough. Right now all I can do is lean my palms on one of the work tables and try not to think. Try to breathe. Try not to wonder if Hendrix will be there when I turn around.

I tell myself that if he is or if he isn't, that will be my answer.

Not entirely sure what the question is. Maybe having the answer will help me figure it out.

I wait until I hear the door click. It's shut now. If he's on the other side of the door, he's not coming back without me letting him in. I slowly count to ten. The room is silent. Too quiet for company. I'm certain I'm alone by the time I'm brave enough to pivot.

I'm relieved to find my "certainty" is flawed. He's here, hands shoved in his pockets, camera bag hanging from his shoulders.

And God, his eyes. The way they look at me. What he sees hasn't changed at all.

"Camilla…" I can't blame him for not knowing what to say. He tries again. "I didn't mean to—"

I don't give him a chance to finish before I'm advancing across the room, my palms itching until they're wrapped in his collar, jerking his face toward mine.

His mouth is tentative against mine at first. Questioning. No man has ever shown me I'm the one with the power like this before. It's intoxicating, even though we're almost barely doing this. He tries to pull away once, but it's a halfhearted attempt, and when he gives in, he gives in entirely. His lips part, inviting in my tongue. He drops his bag on the floor—gently enough to do no damage, but not nearly as gentle as I'm sure he normally handles his camera—and his arms wrap around my waist. I'm tugged flush to him so I feel the whole of him against me. I feel his heat merge with mine. Feel the hardening bulge at my abdomen.

I've never kissed someone so urgently. Never clawed at a man's trousers like they hid my only source of survival. Never got out of my own pants so quickly that I tripped during their removal.

And I've been frantic to fuck before. Hendrix and I were frenzied that first time in France, but this feeling is even more fraught. There's an added desperation that I can't quite name. I'm not secretly praying that he'll know what he's doing or for a decent-sized cock like I was back then. I already know that he does and that makes these seconds of anticipation all the more intense.

He's just as manic as I, fumbling for a condom, tossing his wallet behind him before ripping the package open with his teeth. I'm more hindrance when I attempt to help him roll it on, but I can't help myself. I need to touch his cock. I need to be part of the action required to get him inside of me.

Finally it's on, and with a grunt, Hendrix hoists me up. I hook my ankles around his waist while he notches his cock at my entrance. It proves difficult in this position, and instead of trying to work it out where we stand, the man is smart enough to carry me to the worktable. My bare ass meets the wood, and with my legs still around him, the angle is just right for him to push inside.

I cry out on the first thrust. It's always a delicious sort of torment, as my body stretches to accommodate girth, as the empty place inside me is filled. There's an added satisfaction of discovering that the memories of my night with Hendrix were not a trick of the mind. We really do fit perfectly. The happy hum, under everything. He really does make me momentarily feel whole.

I'm tempted to make him slow down so I can draw out the ecstasy, though I'm unsure either of us could hold back right now. The tempo seems to be driving us rather than the other way around, as though the force that compels us toward each other is in charge here. As though our fucking has been orchestrated by a higher power.

It's nearly unbearable being this out-of-control.

And it's euphoric all at the same time.

I cling to him, not just with my legs, but my arms too, wrapped tight around his neck, holding on to him like an anchor. When that's not enough, I press my forehead against his. Together we peer down between us where his cock disappears repeatedly inside my pussy, and without looking at his eyes, I'm sure he's as mesmerized by the erotic sight.

It looks like being chased, the way his cock returns again and again to nest inside me. I'm wrecked with pleasure and absent of much coherent thought, but I wonder fleetingly if being caught by him for real would feel as good as it does when he's buried to the hilt.

It's so terrifyingly thrilling of an idea that it sends me into orgasm, and the thought is lost in the whirlwind of bliss that spins me, unwrapping me until every good thing inside is unleashed at once. I'm dizzy from the ecstasy, limp and spent and dazed.

His release follows right after, his accompanying moan ragged and relieved, as though he'd been waiting for me and the wait had been hard. The head start to recovery should be to my benefit, but I'm still having trouble with my breath when he grips my chin and places his mouth over my own.

Has kissing always been this monumental? Was there always so much communicated between lips and tongues moving together like ours are now?

I'm not sure I have the strength for what's being said.

I break away first, letting it happen in stages. A slowing of my tongue. The closing of my lips. The arching away of my spine.

He's not ready to let me go. I can tell with the way he pulls me back to place a kiss on my cheek, then on my eyebrow. Now on my hair.

I set my hands on my thighs and note the contrast of the bare skin against my sleeve-covered arms. It's as much as I can give. I cannot give any more.

"I shouldn't have assumed," he says, his cheek pressed against my forehead. "I know you aren't at all like the creatures I shoot in the field, but I'm not used to considering consent."

I shake my head against him. I gave consent, albeit silently. For my body. It's my heart I'm protecting now. "You did nothing wrong. It's me."

It's always me.

I nudge him away and jump down from the table. I keep my back to him until I'm put back together, which goes smoother than the undressing. When I've turned around again, the condom's been taken care of, and his cock's put away, and now it's time to put us away as well.

"This is the end of this," I tell him. "It's out of our system, and it can't happen again."

I think I hope that he'll leave now. Or maybe I hope that he'll stay, which he does.

"Why?" he asks, and it's not like he's angry, he just wants to know.

What a complicated question, though. With complicated answers.

Or perhaps they're really simple.

"I'm your teacher," I say, which is the truth and also a lie.

"That's not why. What's the real why?"

"It's as much why as I need to give you." I fold my arms over my chest, like I'm closing a door.

He studies me for long seconds. "When the class is over, what then?"

Fuck, I didn't bloody think this through.

And now I'm worried I might cry.

"Is it really what you want, Camilla? For this to never happen again?"

I swallow hard. *Yes*, I mean to say. Instead what comes out is, "No."

Before he can take that admission and run with it, I say more. "But also yes. It's what I need. And that's more important than what I want right now."

He studies me some more. He considers. He swears under his breath. "I shouldn't have let this happen. I knew that sex needed to stay out of this because you would find a way to make that an ending. I knew this was a bad idea."

He's right, and yet I'm hurt. "It's my fault then. If you were so all-knowing, why didn't you try harder to push me away?"

"Because I fucking want you, Camilla." It's the sharpest he's ever been with me, and it's still softer than Frank ever was. How can I let this in, knowing there's any possibility of it ending? "Because I want your skin and your mouth and your brain. And your pain."

The last word closes me up tighter. "I don't know what you're inferring. I'm fine."

Isn't that what people say when they're exactly the opposite of fine?

He takes a step toward me. "You can tell me. I'll listen. I'm not going to judge."

I'm trembling with rage. Or fear. It's all muddled up. All I know is that he needs to stop. "You don't know what you're talking about."

I turn toward the equipment that needs to be put away, an excuse to be done with this conversation.

"I felt you, Camilla," he says to my back. "I felt your body that night. I felt your skin."

A bolt of terror strikes like lightning through me. "Don't."

"Did someone do it to you?" He pauses. "Or did you do it to yourself?"

Pins and needles spike every inch of my skin. I whirl around to face him. "You need to leave."

"Camilla…"

"Leave! Now!"

He knows he's crossed the line. He's been around enough wild animals to know when they've turned dangerous.

He picks up his camera bag on his way out and opens the door before he pauses with a sigh. His head turns toward me. "Leave forever? Or just leave for today?"

Forever.

Or not at all.

The bubble floats between us.

What answer should I give?

I give him the truth. "I don't know."

Chapter Ten

Background: The area of an artwork that appears farthest away from the viewer; also, the area against which a figure or scene is placed. - *MoMA Glossary of Art Terms*

After class, I'm too distracted to spend my free day as I usually do. There's a new exhibit at The Gallery and a farmer's market I'd meant to visit.

I come home, instead. With Sylvia here to nanny, I can tuck myself away in my room, pull the covers over my head and sleep through the rest of the day if I want to. I do want to.

But my mind's too buzzy for sleep.

I find myself lying on the floor in the playroom with Freddie while Sylvia fixes him lunch. Silly if I thought this would help. It's often a difficult task to be completely in the moment with a six-year-old, especially when there are pressing items to give attention to. The work to do sitting in my inbox. The discrepancy in the electric bill that needs to be sorted. The manicure that's well past due. The opportunities that could be taken with my camera and the late afternoon light.

Typically, I can lose myself in the simple pleasures of watching my son. He'll never know the childhood I had. His occasional loneliness will never touch how alone I felt. Typically, knowing that is enough to make me happy enough too.

This is not a typical day.

Luckily, he seems preoccupied with his latest Lego creation. The kid is truly an artist, absurdist with his concepts, perhaps, but he definitely has a point of view.

I should tell him as much. I should extol his work and encourage his thirst for experimentation, but I'm feeling self-centered and self-loathing and all I can do is stare at the ceiling and think, *not enough not enough not enough.*

It's like a woodpecker tapping at my brain. Incessant and maddening. My groan of frustration comes involuntarily like a yawn, starting small and growing as it takes over.

"Mummy?" Fred's concern is etched in his brows as he peers over at me, his sticky fingers clutching a Lego in midair.

I might appreciate this aspect of motherhood the most. It's impossible to truly lose myself in self-pity with my child there to remind me the world does not revolve around my heartache. That for one soul, I am enough. Even when I feel the opposite.

"Sorry," I say, rolling to my side and propping my head up with my forearm. "I'm fine."

He's not convinced. "Did you hurt yourself?"

I shake my head, but I remember my commitment to parenting with transparency. There is something Fred might learn here, even if it's just that adults are not immune to complicated feelings.

I think about the simplest way to frame my current emotional state, a way he'll understand. "I'm obsessing," I tell him eventually. "I can't stop thinking about something I want very badly. It's making me feel a little insane."

His face relaxes. He can understand that. There is more than one tantrum that has occurred because of something he had to have Right This Minute. But there's still a question in his expression. "You're a grown-up. Can't you just get the thing you want?"

I open my mouth and shut it again, replaying his words in my head. *Yes, Camilla, can't you just get the thing you want? Who told you that you weren't allowed to be happy? The only one who ever did is gone now. Can't you get it for yourself now?*

Out of the mouths of babes.

* * * *

It's easier said than done, of course. But once the decision is made, it does seem less hard than I imagined to choose what to wear, to know where to go, to not worry about what I'll say. I simply remember the feeling and chase the effervescent trail it's left between me and the man who showed me how to find it.

It still takes a while to get ready. I primp in every manner of the word. It's been ages since I've taken this much care in my appearance, painting my toenails, plucking my brows, shaving every last blade of unwanted hair.

It isn't until I'm standing outside Nightsky that I have my first flutter of uncertainty, and it's not doubt about what I have planned, but that there's a possibility I won't get the opportunity to carry it out. It doesn't scare me as much as it should, because I'm finally starting to recognize that as much as I find my happiness in him, it's because that spark inside me has been lit. It's not a stranger to me anymore, this feeling. I might, someday, be able to chance this sprout growing into a vine of my own. But first, I want to see if this man who adored my child and looks at me like art would like to keep watering it with me.

I definitely won't have the chance standing out here, so with a prayer uttered under my breath, I push through the door and sweep my eyes across the room.

My gaze finds Hendrix almost instantly, even though his back is to me as he sits at the bar.

I allow the sigh of relief before heading toward him. He still hasn't looked behind him when I take the empty seat at his side. I feel how he notices me, how his back straightens and the air crackles like his body has just been turned on.

I also feel his hesitation, the worry that he might be overstepping by being here.

"Should I make it two?" he asks, picking up his near empty glass. He still hasn't turned toward me.

"No, thank you. I didn't come here tonight to drink."

Now he swivels in my direction so we're face-to-face. "Then why did you come here?"

"I wanted to see you. And so I came to where I thought it was most likely that would happen." I've quoted him, and it hits the mark.

He smiles, slowly but surely. He looks lonely, somehow, under that confidence.

My smile matches his without even trying. We're caught like that for several seconds, taking each other in, saying nothing.

Something hits me like a ton of bricks. The me he's seen that I wasn't sure was really me… Could it be that what he saw was us all along? Entwined, making each other better? Finding happy, discovering a new world?

Eventually, I realize I'm the one driving here, and so, gently, I put my foot on the gas. "Could we go somewhere?" I don't want him to assume I'm up to my old tricks, simply trying to get him in bed, so I add, "To talk?"

I'd offer my flat but I can't keep towing Freddie into my adult affairs, and besides, this discussion would be much more appropriate in a kid-free zone.

He considers for only a moment, though it's long enough to have my stomach in knots. "I'm subletting an apartment just a couple of blocks over. If you don't mind small…"

"Just so long as it's private."

"It's definitely that."

A few minutes later, we're outside and now my stomach's knots can be blamed on what I'm soon to share. I have my talking points memorized. They're only daunting because they're words I've never said outside a therapist's office. While they're always trapped inside me, they feel heavier as we venture from the commercial area of the neighborhood into the residential. I remind myself that bravery isn't a lack of fear. I remind myself that a loss leaves me the same, whereas the rewards leave me infinitely richer.

Then his hand finds mine swinging at my side, his fingers lace through mine and suddenly the burden lightens, like he's carrying it with me, and I'm no longer alone.

Romantic notion, I'm aware. It surprises me to find I'm capable of those.

By the time we're inside his flat and the door is shut behind us, it feels like we've had an entire conversation though we've spoken very few words at all. There's much that is said with hands clasped in silence. I gather a lot was said just by my showing up at all.

But now it's time to transition from that beat to the next, and I'm not as brazen as I was just a few minutes ago. I wipe my sweaty palms against the fabric of my skirt as I spin slowly, taking in his space. It's an open concept, which suits him, and though I'm sure the furniture came with the rental, there are pieces of him evident everywhere my eyes land. A jacket thrown over the back of the armchair. A tripod set up by the window. The photo printer sitting on the kitchen table.

It's been so long since I've been in a place where someone else lived, as temporary as that living arrangement might be. I've forgotten how to settle in.

"Can I get you something?" Hendrix asks, and I sense he's trying to help with my unease.

"Some water maybe?"

"Bottled or in a glass?"

"Either is fine."

He's back too soon, handing me a cold plastic bottle before gesturing at the couch. I take a swallow of the drink and sit down, but as soon as he sits down beside me, I pop back up.

"No, stay there, please," I say when he seems about to follow. I recap the water and set it on the side table, then reach for the tie on my wrap-dress. I have to do this now. Bravery always seems to cower in the face of comfort.

I can feel a protest pushing at his lips, but before he can voice it, I turn my back toward him and lower my dress so that my shoulder blades are exposed, pulling my hair to one side to be sure the scars aren't covered.

The sight renders him speechless. I get it. Sometimes when I catch a glimpse of myself in the three-sided mirror in my closet, I'm rendered speechless too.

I twist my head to glance at Hendrix. "Cigarette burns," I say, in case he can't identify the source of the constellation of angry red marks across my upper back. "My foster father's favorite form of punishment. Punishment being an excuse, really, since I rarely caused trouble back then. Making me wrack my brain trying to figure out what I'd done was part of his sadistic game, I think."

"Camilla..." he says, as he so often does, and I'm desperate to hear what he'll say next, but more eager to plow through the rest.

So I lower my dress farther, until the material is bowed down to my waist and the dark jagged stripe across my mid-back is exposed. "This one was Frank's doing. My husband. We'd been on a walk, and I smiled too wide at a man riding by on his bicycle so as soon as he was out of sight, I was pushed into the barbed wire fence at the side of the road. Later, he claimed it was an accident, but even if he hadn't held me down when he'd pushed...Well, let's just say there was a pattern of such accidents.

"There's matching streaks on the back of my thighs too, and here." I gather my hair high in a fist. "Very slightly you can see the one on the back of my neck."

Hendrix cranes forward so I perch myself on the ottoman in front of him so he can see better. His fingers whisper across the scars, skin that hasn't been touched in years. Certainly it's never been touched this gently.

"It seems stupid, probably, that a woman who was abused as a child would marry someone who treated her the same. Would stay with him." I swallow back against the shame. Even when I think I've overcome it, when I can stand to look at my reflection for days at a time, the feeling returns when I'm being observed. Shame is a weed. It always comes back. "Apparently it's not uncommon. So stupid, but not alone."

"I didn't say you were stupid." His tone is reverent. His tone is awed.

His tone is not full of pity, and that gives me strength to go on. "I have more, not all of them are as easy to see, and I don't remember where half of them came from, what injury left what mark." The breath I take in is shuddering. *Bravery is facing fear.*

On the exhale, I pull my arms out of the sleeves, letting my dress fall off completely as I pivot toward him. "It's these, though, that are the most humiliating."

He takes my outstretched forearm and gazes down at the short lines, stacked evenly on top of each other like rungs of a ladder or like the marks on the wall in Edward's nursery where Freddie stands once a month to measure his height.

Hendrix traces his finger across one. Now the next one. And the next. At the beginning of each stroke, I try to gather the courage to say the rest. At the end of each stroke, I fail.

"You did these," he says for me.

I nod, the ball too big in my throat for words. A deep breath, and it breaks up some. "I was at private school by then. Edward had sent me after he was granted guardianship. Someone had left a boxcutter in the common room."

I hadn't made them all at once. They'd come little by little over a term, each individual cut slashed into my skin when the complexity of emotion inside me became overbearing. It was that fizzy pop again, the way adrenaline poured out of me with the swipe of the knife. Like a release valve for my feelings. Unlike unwanted emotion, a wound had a start and an end, a finite amount of hurt. It was therapeutic. It was art.

But I've tried to explain the poetry of my actions before and been frowned at disapprovingly, so I don't try now. I know it was unhealthy. I know how it would break me to see Fred do it. I also know it was the only way I ever knew to process my pain, from the first burn on. A prescribed timeline. The promise of the end of the suffering. "Don't ask why," I say simply. "It's not something I can put into words."

"You don't have to," he assures me. "They tell a story all on their own."

I twist so I'm facing him directly, and though it's been a long time since I've sat in only my bra and pants in front of a man, the marks on my forearm are the only part of my skin that feel exposed. "What story do they tell?" I ask, because I'm honestly curious.

While I wait for his answer, I feel the same anxious anticipation that builds when waiting for a critic to explain what meaning they picked up from my latest photography exhibit. What is it he sees? A broken person? A crazy person? A stupid person?

I am all those things, but I'm also so much more.

It turns out, I'm also occasionally a happy person.

He sweeps his whole hand over the length of my arm and back, a soft caress that has my blood humming. He repeats the movement. "That you survived."

It's incredible how freeing it is to be authentically seen. I'd forgotten that graffiti is a form of art that often has a powerful message when it's truly understood.

Chapter Eleven

Composition: The arrangement of the individual elements within a work of art so as to form a unified whole. - *MoMA Glossary of Art Terms*

I shiver when Hendrix kisses the first of my scars.

He's not the first lover I've had who has seen them. Before Frank, I'd been guarded but less so around the men I was intimate with. I went through several boyfriends, most rebellious troublemaker sorts. Several had been quite extraordinary in bed.

But none of them—not my deceased husband, not the man who wanted to sweep me away to Brazil, not the one who broke into a pawn shop to buy me a diamond ring—not a single one of them ever pressed their lips to the raised welts scattered across my skin.

I'm stunned. And moved.

Goosebumps sprout along the path he makes. By the time he's kissed every mark on my forearm, tears are rolling down my cheeks.

He moves to my back where he lovingly kisses the cigarette burns and the barbed wire wounds and an unremembered mark he finds along my ribs.

This last one tickles, and I giggle.

Imagine me, giggling over *this*.

I'm still grinning when he gets up from the sofa and kneels in front of me. We lean into each other at the same time, our mouths meeting like old friends.

"You're beautiful," he says against my lips. "Every single inch of you."

I roll my eyes and kiss him again, a little less playfully. A little more greedily. If I am allowing myself to enjoy my body, I want to enjoy every sensation it's capable of immediately.

Hendrix doesn't seem quite as eager to speed things up as I am. "I want to kiss every place on your body you've been hurt. I want to kiss those places so many times that you remember them for that instead of anything before."

And I'm starting to remember another thing about bubbles.

He leaves my mouth to kiss up my arm again.

"When I was caught out about those—foolishly, I didn't think about the fact that the next term I'd have to wear a polo shirt for PE—I was assigned a counselor and told very strictly to stop with the self-harm." I have a reason to bring this up now. A fun reason. "Of course I pretended to comply. Really, I just started hiding where I cut."

Hendrix sits up, alert. He understands where I'm going with this. "Where are they?"

"My inner thighs." Heat rushes to my cheeks, knowing what will come next.

I'm already wet from the kissing. The rasp in his "Show me" nearly makes me come.

Making somewhat of a show of it, I lean back on my elbows and spread my legs wide. How long has it been since I've played like this with my sexual encounters? It's strange how easily it comes once I've given myself permission. I'm not even concerned about how well-lit the room is. It's a relief. It's freeing.

And that's the thing I'm remembering. That bubbles can come in streams. When you blow through the hoop. When you open a fizzy pop.

That maybe, unlike pain, these bubbles of happy weren't finite after all.

Like before, Hendrix runs his fingers tenderly across the rows of marks embedded in the soft skin at the tops of my inner thighs. There are more here. I'd discovered the delicate nature of this area made for a particularly painful cut. Since pain was what I was after, I'd done a lot of damage.

He studies each one carefully, as though trying to gather the story of each individual slice. "They're old," he remarks. "Do you still do this?"

It seems like I fight not to every day of my life. Like any addict, the more stressed I am, the harder the battle to not give in. But the help I got as a teenager taught me better ways to cope, and for the most part I've refrained since then.

I have to remain vigilant though. There's always the chance I'll fall off the wagon. Hendrix has to understand that if he really wants to be with me. Despite the happiness I find in myself under his gaze, there will always be sad days. Weeks, even. I am tentatively allowing a new future in, but it won't banish the past. "What would you do if I still did?"

"I'd kiss those marks too." As if to prove it, he bends down to place his lips on a jagged blemish at the roundest part of my thigh. "I'd love you."

I have to take a second to breathe before I speak. "The last time happened a while before Freddie was born. During a period when Frank was especially mean. It felt somehow empowering to hurt myself as well. It was pain I could control when so much of my pain came from chaos.

"After I got pregnant, though, after Frank died…" I pause to understand what I mean before I try to voice it. "I wasn't as interested in turning my body inside out anymore. I'm still tempted. But now I have more reason to not."

"I want to be one of those reasons." This time his tongue flicks across the scar. He must smell my arousal. The damp spot at the crotch of my pants is unmissable.

He kisses there next, soft and open-mouthed, his eyes on mine, seeking permission even as he invades my most private space.

I widen my legs farther in response.

I let him in.

He kisses me again, higher up. Through the silk material, he finds the swollen bud of nerves and sucks.

I let out a gasp. "Please!"

Quickly, he helps me out of my underwear and drags me to the edge of the ottoman, propping my feet up so he can take care of me properly.

And, oh, is he proper.

He's so proper, I'm already on the verge of orgasm, and it's only the third swipe of his tongue. I'd forgotten how fantastic being adored like this can be. I'd forgotten it was pleasurable at all. Frank's habit of using cunnilingus as an apology after a bad fight had, I thought, poisoned me against the act entirely.

I'm delighted to discover I was wrong.

It's only after I've come twice that Hendrix returns his mouth to mine. He's more frenzied now, tugging at the clasp of my bra as he kisses me. When my breasts are free, he plumps one with his palm while teasing and sucking the other nipple. He touched me like this in Paris, but not with his lips. The last mouth I had at my breast was my baby, and, oh God, have I been missing out.

Can't say I'm not living my life now.

It's the best life too, being cherished by a man so completely. Even when I realize I'm stark naked, and he's still wearing every stitch of his clothes, it doesn't feel uncomfortable. Of course I'm still eager for him to join me in the nudity. I pull at his Henley as he continues to feast on my breast.

Taking the cue, he abruptly stands and rips his shirt over his head. His pants tent out at his crotch, showing off a massive erection that I am eager to see in the flesh.

But when I reach for his zipper, he shoos me away. I'm bewildered until he gathers me in his arms and carries me to the nearby bedroom. He deposits me on the bed and leaves the light on as he works off his jeans.

"How long can you stay?" he asks, his eyes never leaving my body. It's amazing how they feel like they belong there, like they've always seen every part of me.

"I have the nanny until nine in the morning. I should probably be headed home by half past eight."

He glances at his watch. "Nine hours to do everything I want to do to you? I'll do the best that I can, but it's not even going to come close to being enough time."

My thighs clench with the promise. "Then, I suppose it will just have to be a beginning."

"The beginning. I like the sound of that."

Scary as it is to think, I like the sound of it too. So many of my recent stories have been rushed, begun and finished in the same night. There's a thrill in imagining how much more intricate this one can be with time, how deep and meaningful and divine.

I can see glimpses of it even now. As he rolls the condom on his cock, I foresee a night when we do away with it altogether, a promise to partner in whatever the gamble may bring. When he slides inside of me, I envision a time when it doesn't feel so new, when the excitement is overshadowed by the profundity of our love.

I see happiness that streams, even if no individual bubble lasts.

When we're sated and exhausted and he holds me against his chest, his fingers running up and down the length of my arm, I imagine this becoming routine. Imagine that it's our bed that we fall asleep in instead of his. Imagine that the sunshine that streams in the window in the morning belongs to both of us.

It's so real, I can see it. Which is exactly how art always begins.

"How much time do we have?" The sun is rising higher and the traffic on the street has picked up.

Hendrix has to shift his arm around me to check. "A little more than an hour."

I kiss along his sternum. My lips are swollen, but my mouth can't stop wanting him.

"Should we go again?"

He's noble for offering. We've already had three rounds. I've lost track of how many times I've come. My pussy is deliciously raw, and yet, I could go again. This wanting is a very deep well. It replenishes way before it's at risk of running dry.

But even though I'm as randy as a schoolboy, there is more between us than sex. And I'm very aware that my lover's attention is currently split.

"I think I'm too exhausted," I say, which is also true. I'm already working out how I'm going to trick Fred into letting us take an afternoon nap. "Besides, I feel your eyes wandering."

Hendrix plays dumb. "My eyes aren't wandering. What are you talking about?"

I twist my neck to motion to the camera sitting on the dresser. "You can't tell me you aren't thinking about it."

"Uh…" He lets out a nervous laugh before kissing me on the head. "I wouldn't dream of taking your picture without your permission."

I blush remembering my reaction in class. Was that really only yesterday? "That was...that was silly. It was about something else and—"

"I know what it was about," he says. "And I sense everything has changed, but I wasn't about to make any presumptions."

I love this show of caution, this hint that he isn't always as sure as I believe he is. It's comforting to not be alone in the awkwardness of a new relationship.

I wouldn't mind discussing that more, but this presses harder.

I prop my head up. "You see it don't you, though? What you want to capture?" I'm not sure if I'm teacher or lover in this moment. I just know what it feels like to itch with vision.

And, also, I don't want to be that woman I was yesterday. I don't want to be someone who shoves her photo albums on a shelf. I want to be the woman he sees.

He's hesitant. "Yeah, I do."

"Will they be erotic?" I tease.

"Some of them. Definitely. Are you saying yes?"

Whoa, this yes feels harder than the one when Frank proposed. When I'd thought that marriage would make him less brutal. When I'd hoped that I could settle him down.

But Hendrix isn't Frank. And I'm not who I was when I married him. Where's the proof? Everywhere.

"I am saying yes," I say, more boldly than I thought possible. Regret threatens instantly. "For your eyes only, right?"

"For *our* eyes only."

"Then...yes. Show me your best shot."

He jumps out of the bed as fast as Fred with the promise of crumpets. He throws on a pair of jeans sans underwear (hot) and strips the bed of everything but a single sheet that he allows me to use as a modest covering.

With determination in his eyes, he picks up his camera.

I'm a clumsy model, despite knowing what a photographer wants. I'm not used to being okay with the idea of being studied. But Hendrix is patient and knows how to settle the most frightened beasts. He takes his time, directing me this way and that, posing me in forms that feel strange. Pulling away the sheet entirely. Making me laugh. Over and over until my cheeks hurt from all the smiling.

When he's satisfied, he sits on the bed next to me, and without even scrolling through the pictures he's taken, he hands the camera to me.

"No self-editing first? That's brave." If he can be brave, I can be too. *Rewards.*

It's hard to look objectively at first, to not see everything I hate about myself in the foreground of every image. My pointy chin. My too-thin lips. My scars. So many times my scars.

But something happens—maybe it's Hendrix's mouth pressed to my collarbone as he peers over my shoulder or maybe it's the way he's framed the light or maybe it's the perfect composition of skin and sheet and smile. Whatever it is, I'm suddenly outside of myself looking in. I see what he meant to capture.

He's good. These pictures are so so good. An A plus if I gave grades. Exceptional and extraordinary.

And, like a good photographer, he makes me see the art instead of the artist.

So while the work itself deserves to be credited, it's not what strikes me most. What strikes me is the story he's trying to tell. What strikes me is what he sees in the woman who's me.

The woman who was always me. Always waiting for her chance in the aperture of just the right camera.

"Well?" he asks, revealing his nervousness. "Do you see it?"

I nod. I'm honest when I say the words I never thought I'd hear myself say. "I'm beautiful."

Epilogue

Perspective: Technique used to depict volumes and spatial relationships on a flat surface, as in a painted scene that appears to extend into the distance. - *MoMA Glossary of Art Terms*

As time goes by, my albums fill. Hundreds of photographs, both real and in memory form. I have favorites, of course. Images from the day Amelia, our first daughter, is born and all the milestones that follow. A series featuring Lily who pops into the world a year later with the loudest cry I've ever heard on a newborn despite being almost an entire month early. The day the adoption papers are signed and Freddie officially adds Reid to his name. The look on my husband's face when it happens, and I know no one has ever loved that boy like the two of us, together. The moment that Hendrix finally convinces me to put on his ring and make our family official.

But the albums aren't just filled with the big events. They are stuffed full of so many smaller moments. Moments that become routine. Waking up with Hendrix at my side. Clutching a baby to my breast while chasing after a toddler. Pages upon pages of child scrawled art. Picking wildflowers in the country. Watching the sunset—from the Eiffel Tower, from the Serengeti, from the beach in Myanmar, from the balcony of the flat we buy together.

I take a lot more pictures for moments and not for craft. I can't help it. I want anyone who walks into our home to see the happiness we share framed on every surface. It might inspire something in someone else who was missing it.

Becoming steady in my new self doesn't happen overnight. It

takes days added upon days. It takes tears and fights and lots of doubt, but it does happen. I can see the process as I flip through the snapshots in my head. Can see the blossoming of my character in stages. I learn eventually that the more collections of these photos I have, the less I revisit the darker images from my past. As though those albums are shoved to the back of the shelf, making way for newer, crisper memories. Making way for a life fully lived. A life that extends far ahead into a beautiful distance.

* * * *

Also from 1001 Dark Nights and Laurelin Paige, discover The Open Door, Dirty, Filthy Fix, Falling Under You, and Man for Me.

Author's Note

Dear Reader,

Camilla's story is one I've carried around with me for quite some time. I've known who she is and what her journey had to be, but when it came to actually writing it, I struggled with how much of what I knew about her was essential to this novella. After a lot of back and forth, I decided to trust in the character and followed where her voice led me. I was surprised by the way she wanted to tell her tale, by her noisy thoughts and the depth of her wounds. It isn't an easy story, that's for sure. It definitely was the story that I needed to write at this time. When the world feels fragile and broken and unsure, I needed to believe that fragile and broken and unsure is still beautiful. I found that reassurance in this writing, and I hope you found it in the reading.

Obviously there is more to Camilla's complex history which is only hinted at here. The circumstances that led to her being in foster care and the abuse she suffered at her husband's hands as well as the circumstances surrounding his death are important parts of her character but weren't important in the telling of this particular moment in her life. Those parts of her life are further explored from her brother Edward's point of view in the Slay series. If you haven't read those books, I invite you to discover more about the Fasbender family starting with book one, Rivalry.

As always, thank you for reading.

Laurelin Paige

Discover More Laurelin Paige

Man For Me

A Man In Charge Novella

Brett Sebastian is the very best kind of friend.

Who else would get me a job at one of the biggest corporations in America?

And hook me up with his uber-rich cousin to boot?

And let me cry on his shoulder every time said cousin blows me off?

Okay, it's pretty obvious that Brett cares about me in a different way than I do for him, but he seems fine with how things are, and our friendship works.

Until one fateful night when I'm mooning over his cousin, and Brett utters four words that should make me happy for him, should make me relieved, should balance out our uneven relationship:

"I met a girl."

Suddenly my world is crashing down around me, and I'm forced to ask myself—am I only interested in Brett now that he's taken?

Or have I been looking at the wrong man all along?

* * * *

The Open Door

A Found Duet Novella

I knew JC was trouble the minute I laid eyes on him.

Breaking every rule in my club. I never forget how he made me feel that night. With all the women in that room, all those bodies on display, but his eyes were only on me.

Of course I married him. Now years have passed. Kids have been born. We're still in love as always, and the sex is still fantastic...

And yet, it's also not. Like many who've been married for a while, I long for the high intensity of those days of the past.

I've heard rumors for years about the Open Door. An ultra-exclusive voyeur's paradise. A place to participate in—or watch—

any kind of display you can imagine.

My husband's eyes would still be on me. And maybe other eyes too. If that's what we want.

So when an invitation to come play arrives, how could we turn it down?

* * * *

Dirty Filthy Fix

A Fixed Trilogy Novella

I like sex. Kinky sex. The kinkier the better.

Every day, it's all I think about as I serve coffee and hand out business agendas to men who have no idea I'm not the prim, proper girl they think I am.

With a day job as the secretary to one of New York's most powerful men, Hudson Pierce, I have to keep my double life quiet. As long as I do, it's not a problem.

Enter: Nathan Sinclair. Tall, dark and handsome doesn't come close to describing how hot he is. And that's with his clothes on. But after a dirty, filthy rendezvous, I accept that if we ever see each other again, he'll walk right by my desk on his way to see my boss without recognizing me.

Only, that's not what happens. Not the first time I see him after the party. Or the next time. Or the time after that. And as much as I try to stop it, my two worlds are crashing into each other, putting my job and my reputation at risk.

And all I can think about is Nathan Sinclair.

All I can think about is getting just one more dirty, filthy fix.

* * * *

Falling Under You

A Fixed Trilogy Novella

Norma Anders has always prided herself on her intelligence and determination. She climbed out of poverty, put herself through school and is now a chief financial advisor at Pierce Industries. She's certainly a woman who won't be topped. Not in business anyway.

But she's pretty sure she'd like to be topped in the bedroom.

Unfortunately most men see independence and ambition in a woman and they run. Even her dominant boss, Hudson Pierce, has turned down her advances, leaving her to fear that she will never find the lover she's longing for.

Then the most unlikely candidate steps up. Boyd, her much-too-young and oh-so-hot assistant, surprises her one night with bold suggestions and an authoritative demeanor he's never shown her in the office.

It's a bad idea…such a *deliciously bad* idea…but when Boyd takes the reins and leads her to sensual bliss she's never known, the headstrong Norma can't help but fall under his command.

About Laurelin Paige

With millions of books sold, Laurelin Paige is the *NY Times*, *Wall Street Journal*, and *USA Today* Bestselling Author of the Fixed Trilogy. She's a sucker for a good romance and gets giddy anytime there's kissing, much to the embarrassment of her three daughters. Her husband doesn't seem to complain, however. When she isn't reading or writing sexy stories, she's probably singing, watching *Killing Eve* and *Letterkenny,* or dreaming of Michael Fassbender. She's also a proud member of Mensa International though she doesn't do anything with the organization except use it as material for her bio.

You can connect with Laurelin on Facebook at www.facebook.com/LaurelinPaige or on Instagram @thereallaurelinpaige. You can also visit her website, www.laurelinpaige.com, to sign up for e-mails about new releases.

Also From Laurelin Paige

Man in Charge Duet
Man in Charge
Man in Love

Slay Series
Slay One: Rivalry
Slay Two: Ruin
Slay Three: Revenge
Slay Four: Rising
Slash: A Slay Novella

The Fixed Series
Fixed on You
Found in You
Forever with You
Hudson
Falling Under You: A Fixed Trilogy Novella (1001 Dark Nights)
Chandler
Dirty, Filthy Fix: A Fixed Trilogy Novella (1001 Dark Nights)
Fixed Forever

Dirty Universe
Dirty Filthy Rich Boys
Dirty Filthy Rich Men
Dirty Filthy Rich Love
Dirty, Sexy Player
Dirty Sexy Games
Sweet Liar
Sweet Fate
Dirty Sweet Valentine
Wild Rebel

Found Duet
Free Me
Find Me

First and Last
First Touch
Last Kiss

Hollywood Heat
Sex Symbol
Star Struck
One More Time
Close

Co-Written Works:

Written with Sierra Simone:
Porn Star
Hot Cop

Written with Kayti McGee:
Miss Match
Love Struck
MisTaken: A Novella

The Dead Heat of Summer

A Krewe of Hunters Novella

By Heather Graham

Prologue

July

She was beautiful in death, as she had always been in life.

Lena Marceau lay with her blond hair fanned out like silk on the pillow. She wore a white nightgown.

Her hands were folded just below her breasts. She could have been an angel sleeping, filled with light and peace.

Ryder McKinley looked down at her, feeling numb.

"The medical examiner is ready to take the body," Braxton Wild told him.

Braxton was a detective with the New Orleans Police Department and had called Ryder. He was also one of the few people who knew there was an association between Ryder and Lena Marceau.

He had reached out to Ryder after Stephanie Harrow called him. She had been the one to find her sister. Had told Braxton that she'd gone to the house and assumed that since the baby was napping, her sister was, too. But after about thirty minutes, she realized that Lena wasn't just sleeping.

She was dead.

Stephanie was, of course, a mess. She was ready to take care of Lena's two-year-old daughter, Annette, but she had been crying so hard, she'd had to call in a friend—Vickie Carmichael—to take the child.

Before Ryder even reached the Marceau mansion, Stephanie had been sedated, and she and the baby had been whisked off to Vickie's house in the French Quarter.

There was no sign of any kind of trauma on the body; no sign of a break-in. Ryder knew Dr. Hugh Lamont, the medical examiner, and Braxton believed that Lena had committed suicide. Bottles of prescription medicine lay at her side. One was a strong sleeping pill she had started taking when her husband died a year ago.

Through her husband, Lena was the heir to a great estate. Not that there weren't other members of the Marceau family, but old Elijah Marceau had died just before his great-grandson, and he had loved Anthony and Lena.

They had loved him, too. Not only his money.

Lena had never been one to care about material things.

Ryder and Lena hadn't been able to catch up in a few years. When he'd been in NOLA recently, she had been in Europe. But they had communicated now and then on the phone, though mostly through email or social media.

"Ryder?"

"Yes, of course," he said, moving aside.

The memory of her, so angelic, would live in his mind forever.

He kept his face impassive as he asked, "The autopsy will be in the morning?"

"Yes."

"You won't mind if I attend?" Ryder asked Braxton.

"No, of course not," Braxton said and then hesitated. "We've worked with your Krewe people from the get-go down here, so my lieutenant had no problem with me inviting you along on a…routine investigation."

"Thanks."

"Ryder, it looks like suicide," Braxton said sadly. "Maybe she just couldn't endure the loss of her husband."

Ryder gave him a rueful smile. "No. Lena loved Anthony very much, and she mourned him deeply. But she was a mother, Braxton."

"Mothers aren't immune to the depression that kills," Braxton said gently.

"I don't believe it," Ryder asserted.

"Ryder, if all the M.E. finds is a mixture of her prescription drugs in her system, we're going to have no choice but to call it a suicide."

"Yes, I know."

"Oh. Okay," Braxton said.

Ryder gave him his best smile. "I'll be there tomorrow. I know what we're all expecting, but I'll be there."

"When do you go back to headquarters?"

"I have some time. We just chased down that drug runner who was targeting teens in the Southern cities. I have a bit of leave. I'll be around."

"I was afraid of that."

Ryder smiled.

"I won't step on local police. I'll be an angel," he said.

Then Ryder thought of her again. His beautiful, young cousin, lying there as if her dreams were sweet and wonderful.

Yes, an angel.

She had mourned her husband. Lena had loved Anthony. And he had loved her because what they shared hadn't been about the Marceau name or the money.

She had his daughter...

There was a commotion at the front door below. Ryder glanced at Braxton, turned, and hurried downstairs.

The police at the entry were speaking with two people. One a young man, perhaps thirty, dignified-looking in a business suit. He had dark hair that had been pushed back in his nervousness, soft brown eyes, and a medium build.

The woman was older, thin, and straight-backed, with gray hair queued at her nape. Ryder knew them. He'd met them at Lena's wedding. Justin Marceau, Anthony Marceau's second cousin, and Gail Reeves, the head housekeeper.

"Ryder!" Justin said. "Oh, my God, I saw the ambulance—"

"Where's the baby? What's happened?" Gail demanded. "I'm trying to tell these buffoons I work here. I manage the house. Lena! Where is Lena? Where is the baby?"

"Lena is dead. The baby is safe," Ryder said quietly. "Where have you been?" he asked Gail, looking at Justin to add, "And what are you doing here?"

Both burst into tears. Amidst it all, they learned it had been Gail's afternoon off. No, they hadn't been at the house earlier. Justin had come now because he'd heard that a few members of the board were coming by to explain a hike in the price of one of the drugs the company manufactured.

Ryder wondered if the display of tears was real. Justin was a Marceau...

But the estate and the company had been left to the baby, or rather her legal guardian, to watch over all until she was of age.

He didn't want to see Lena again, not even as she was, an angel. He had touched her...

And nothing.

Ryder left the Marceau mansion. He'd go see Lena's sister, Stephanie Harrow, as soon as he could. As well as his cousin's friend, Vicki, who had little Annette.

How that baby loved her mother. And how Lena had doted on her beloved child.

No.

No matter what anyone said, Lena wouldn't have left her baby.

He hesitated as he reached the SUV he borrowed from the local FBI agency when he was in the city.

Another car had just arrived. It was expensive, a Mercedes he noted. Three men emerged. The one who appeared to be the leader was in a gray suit that fit well with his white hair and well-groomed beard and mustache. The man behind him was tall and thin, probably in his early forties, wearing a blue suit.

The last man was young. He wore a sweatsuit, and his hair was damp. It looked as if he'd been pulled from the gym.

Ryder knew who they were. Barton Quincy, Larry Swenson, and Harry Miller. The three sat on the Marceau company's board of directors with Lena's late husband. Ryder had seen them briefly four years ago when his cousin, Lena, married Anthony Marceau.

One of you is a murderer! he thought. *One of you on the board of directors, or...*

Gail Reeves? The housekeeper?

Why?

Or Justin—also a board member—who was still weeping over Lena's death?

Ryder didn't know. All he knew was that his cousin had not committed suicide.

Braxton came to the front door to meet the first man, Barton Quincy, who seemed upset and then visibly angry. But Braxton was firm, not letting them enter the house.

The group departed in a huff. The older man in the gray suit paused as he reached the chauffeur-driven car, then turned to stare at the house.

Ryder could read the signs already. The medical examiner was going to declare Lena's death a suicide.

He would prove that it hadn't been.

Against the odds, he would prove it. Somehow.

And it wouldn't matter how long it took. Because her death would haunt him for as long as he lived.

Chapter 1

August

"Casey, I don't understand what you're looking for," Lauren Howard said. She stood and stared down a path of gothic tombs, all encased in the weeds and decay of the hundreds of years the cemetery had existed.

She was a pretty girl with dark hair, green eyes, and dusky skin. Clad in a colorful halter dress, she seemed at odds with the cemetery, even in the bright light of the rising sun.

"Looking for? Why, of course. It is Casey, medium extraordinaire. She seeks...yes! She seeks the walking dead," Jared Vincent told Lauren.

He grotesquely lifted his arms and stumbled forward, pretending to be a zombie. Jared was tall and lanky with soft brown hair that fell around his face. He made a strange-looking revenant.

Casey Nicholson sighed, then shook her head and smiled at her business partners.

This place was new to her friends. The graveyard was small compared to some of the other city cemeteries, which had become beautiful, haunted tourist attractions. There was only a small chapel in this one. It was built with funds raised by a priest through the Marceau family, who were grateful when a child made it through the yellow fever epidemic of 1853.

Casey had always loved the beauty of the city's cemeteries. And while St. Louis #1—and St. Louis #2 and #3—were the most often visited by tourists, along with Lafayette Cemetery in the Garden

District, St. Mary of Light Chapel and Cemetery was small, old, off the beaten path, and seldom visited.

It was still charming. Haunting, eerie, and sad in its decaying beauty.

"Who runs this place? The chapel was deconsecrated, right?" Lauren asked.

"Yes, I believe so," Casey said. "I think it's taken care of by the Marceau Foundation. Marceau money was used to create it. The family was Catholic and had been praying to the Virgin Mary. When the sick little girl in their family survived, they built the chapel and started the cemetery. They had the land for one, and..."

She stood and pointed across the cemetery. "The family mansion still stands just over there."

Casey wasn't sure who was running the company anymore. An elder family member had died, then the supposed heir apparent, and then his wife. But there were still members of the extended family all over the country. And the corporation had a board of directors. Someone would be claiming the corporation—and the money.

The money meant nothing in Casey's mind. Tragedy had struck the family. Including a young parent, so devastated by grief that she had taken her life.

Casey had met Lena Marceau a few times when she came into the shop. She had been sweet and unassuming. Casey hadn't even known it was her until she'd been given the woman's credit card for payment.

"And so, here we are. Hanging around the dead on a beautiful morning. You know, Casey, I love the shop. But, honestly, couldn't we have gotten something out of a really cool voodoo congregation or the like?"

"Jennie Sanders is coming today. She's my best client. And she feels that something from this cemetery is haunting her. I have to know what it's like in person," Casey said.

"Maybe it's because I grew up here, but when you've seen one cool and haunted *city of the dead*, you've seen them all," Jared said.

"Jaded," Lauren accused.

"The funerary art is similar but different," Casey nodded towards a statue.

"Right! Enjoy the art. It is beautiful," Lauren said.

"And rotting," Jared noted. He must have noticed how they

both stared at him and then added, "Hey, I'm here, right?"

New Orleans was famous for its atmospheric cemeteries, but Casey, Lauren, and Jared had been born and raised in New Orleans. The sometimes-eerie *cities of the dead* as the cemeteries were often called, were something they had grown up with. Casey's parents had lived across Rampart Street in the French Quarter, and she had been just a block or so from St. Louis #1 most of her life.

This wasn't one of the St. Louis cemeteries, though, and it was definitely off the beaten tourist track.

"Guys, I need to get a feel for this place. Like I said, Jennie Sanders is coming by the shop this morning for another reading, and I want to at least...well, to be able to say something," Casey explained.

"You aren't really a medium," Lauren reminded her. "And Jennie Sanders spends a lot of time on Bourbon Street and loves a few places on Frenchman Street. Not to mention, she loves to meet up with old friends at the bars on Decatur. She sees lots of *spirits*."

"That's right. You're not a medium," Jared noted.

"I never claimed to be."

"You're a psychologist," he added.

"Right. One who couldn't find work after college." Casey tried to hide her irritation with her friends. "And, again, I call myself a *reader*. I don't claim to be a medium. Come on! The place is called *A Beautiful Mind*," she added. "Art, music, and a sense of helping people solve their problems."

"You know, think about it. We could liven things up. You could call yourself a medium," Lauren said excitedly. "Oh, imagine. I could costume you in gypsy skirts and do a fantastic headpiece for you. We could stand on the street, and Jared could play his guitar, and we'd all sing *Lady Marmalade*. Imagine! We'd draw the tourists in."

Casey groaned—loudly. "Guys, give me a break. I just read the signs. And it works out fine. No singing on the street. Let's be happy, huh? Come on, you two. It's a miracle I found the shop and that we scraped up the money to buy it."

Jared elbowed Lauren, nodding in acknowledgement to Casey. "And, seriously, she's the best fake medium in the city because she *is* a psychologist. She tries to tell people to look at a situation and do the right thing."

"Nice, thank you." Casey grinned. "I'll take that."

She decided not to mention that none of them had received degrees that would help them much in the real world. Lauren had been an art major, and Jared had a degree in music— they both had fine arts degrees.

Lauren and Jared were both exceptionally talented, in Casey's mind, but they all survived because of the shop.

Jared often played his guitar outside. Sometimes, Lauren and Casey joined him, and they had fun—until someone went into the shop, and Jared had to finish up alone.

They sold Lauren's sketches and paintings and jewelry creations, along with tee shirts, and specially created NOLA souvenirs.

Casey glanced at her watch. New Orleans didn't tend to be an early city. They never opened the doors to the shop until ten, but it was almost ten now.

"Hey, look." Lauren pointed. "There. That tomb is freshly sealed."

Casey saw that the entrance to one of the more spectacular family mausoleums *had* been freshly sealed.

"Maybe they were actually getting ready to repair this place," Jared wondered. "My brother came through here once when one of the *oven* doors was cracked. Said there were bones sticking out. I did hear the upkeep of the St. Louis cemeteries and Lafayette has gotten a lot better in our lifetimes—though maybe Lafayette was kept up all the time. You said you think the Marceau Foundation runs this place?"

"I think so, with the church managing the daily operations. But Marceau Industries Incorporated helps too," Lauren said.

"Rich people there. But here...I mean, I don't know why the family doesn't donate the cemetery to a historical society or something of the like. It's all falling apart," Jared said.

They stopped and stared at the tomb. It was both Gothic and Victorian in style and resembled a small colonial mansion with arches and gargoyles with a winged angel cradling a cross atop the roof of the old structure.

Stone and metal plaques mentioned the names of those interred, from the first family member to the latest.

"Oh, my God," Lauren breathed.

"You're right. Look. This is the Marceau family mausoleum," Casey said.

"Someone was just interred here. Lena Marceau," Jared added. He whispered as if afraid he might wake the sleeping dead within the tomb. "Man, we should have thought of that.

"Lena Marceau. Of course," Casey murmured, thinking it odd that she had just been thinking about the woman. She had, of course, read about the young woman's death. Her sister had found her, looking as if she were merely asleep. The investigation was leaning toward suicide.

Lena's husband had died just the year before. It was presumed that she had never gotten over his death.

The facts were heartbreaking.

"This is so, so sad," Casey said softly, feeling the truth of her words.

"You knew her?" Jared asked.

"She came into the shop a few times. She was nice. She had a great smile, and was fun. She came in with her daughter. The baby is so beautiful. When we decided to come here, I had nearly forgotten all about...what happened. Though I figured the family had a really grand mausoleum in one of the major cemeteries by now."

"Sad, yes. And selfish." Lauren frowned and looked perplexed. "She had a two-year-old baby depending on her. If her sister hadn't arrived early, the baby might have...well, she might have gotten seriously hurt. You don't commit suicide when you have a two-year-old."

"Maybe she didn't commit suicide," Casey murmured.

"It was all over the news and in the papers," Lauren said. "She was alone. There was no evidence of a break-in. I heard there was supposed to be a board meeting at the mansion later that day, but she locked the baby in her supposedly childproof room for a nap and took enough pills to kill an elephant. What else could it have been but suicide? She overtook prescription drugs. There was no sign of violence. I guess I should have figured she'd be buried here. I remember once thinking the board for Marceau Industries Incorporated must be a bunch of really mean old men. They were probably so horrible to her, she couldn't stand it anymore. Maybe she even figured the baby would be better off if she was dead. She was alone with all those monsters. Her husband...yeah. Look. His name is here. He was interred here, too. I don't know why I didn't think anybody was buried here any longer."

"People who commit suicide usually suffer from terrible depression and believe others will be better off without them," Casey said. "And the family owns the place...I wasn't thinking either. I imagined she might be buried at Lafayette Cemetery. But, obviously, the family still has this beautiful mausoleum, so...it makes sense she'd be interred here."

"Weird. I think there are a few more of these smaller cemeteries that still aren't part of the major foundation that looks out for most of the historic cemeteries in the city," Jared said. "But nothing this size. Even if it seems tiny next to the St. Louis cemeteries or those in Metairie—some of which are huge. Anyway...it's good we came." He was trying to lighten the mood, Casey knew. "We all learned something we didn't know and came to a place we've never been—in the city we grew up in." He looked at Casey and likely saw the expression on her face. "Hey, it's okay."

She smiled. She didn't want to describe the sadness she felt for someone she had barely known.

"Now we know there was a recent interment. This is good," Jared said earnestly. "So, when our *spirited* lady comes in, you'll know how to direct her concerns."

"It just feels odd. I...I don't mean to be irreverent. We should have thought of it before. I mean, Lena Marceau died. As you said, it was all over the news," Casey murmured.

"Again, we didn't know she'd been interred here. Our client thinks she saw a ghost, and now Casey will know who the spirit was," Jared said and winked.

Casey glanced at her watch again, disturbed that they were making light of such a tragic death. People died every day, of course, but it was just that...Lena Marceau had left a baby behind. And her husband had died just the year before.

It didn't seem fair or right. And it didn't seem...plausible. Trying to think back, Casey thought Lena Marceau had been in the shop right before Mardi Gras.

"Why don't you two go ahead and get the shop opened? I just want to wander for a few more minutes," she said.

"You shouldn't do that. The family wasn't always known for being kind. Maybe the ghost is evil," Jared teased. "I think they practiced weird voodoo!"

Casey sighed patiently. "Jared."

"Oh, Casey, I'm sorry. I didn't realize...I'm sorry. It was tragic. No more cemeteries. We're next door to a voodoo shop, guys, with the nicest priestess in the world. Voodoo is not weird or creepy. Not real voodoo anyway. What Papa Doc did in Haiti was a perversion, just like Hollywood makes it all out to be. Our voodoo priestess is sweet and wonderful. Let's do stuff with her when you need to find some mojo to feed to a client," Jared said.

"Hey," Lauren added lightly, "you've left coins at Marie Laveau's tomb," she said as a reminder.

"Because it's the thing to do. Go. Please. You two are driving me crazy!"

"We're going, we're going. But don't blame us if the ghost of an evil voodoo priest gets his talons in you," Jared said.

"I promise you, I won't."

Casey watched them leave, laughing together as they headed down the main gravel path of the little cemetery.

She studied the tomb again. There might have been recent interments, but there were still vines growing all over the structure, and weeds had proliferated at the base.

Someone had left flowers at the iron gate of the tomb. Casey bent down for a closer look. The flowers had been there for maybe a day. There was a note with them. Simple.

It read: *Love you so much.*

Casey felt something on her shoulder and turned, startled and angry, thinking that Lauren or Jared had doubled back to tease her.

But it wasn't Lauren.

Or Jared.

A young woman stood there, blonde and beautiful with striking blue eyes.

Casey blinked. She had seen the woman before.

It was Lena Marceau.

Not dead at all? Or...

Then the woman spoke softly, and her words were almost like a rustle, her hand nothing more than air upon Casey's shoulder.

"You're not real!" Casey gasped.

She was suddenly angry.

They had done this to her—Jared and Lauren. They had made her feel as if the place were creepy and eerie, that spirits could roam the Earth.

It couldn't be happening. It wasn't even night. It was day, and a bright and beautiful one. The sun shone brightly...

Showing her a strange translucence in the woman before her.

"Well, yes. And no," the specter said.

"I'm not seeing you!" Casey protested.

"But you do see me," the apparition argued.

No, no, no, no, no!

Casey wasn't sure what happened next.

The world suddenly went dark.

She must have...passed out.

She'd never fainted in her life. But she was suddenly lying atop the step to the tomb, and she still wasn't alone.

The figure remained. The young blonde woman who was...who *had been*...Lena Marceau. The apparition. The figment of her imagination. The...

Here Casey was, with her psychology degree, going stark raving mad.

"Please!" the woman implored. "Please, please. I'm so sorry. But I need your help! Not for me, it's far too late for that, but please...my sister and my baby are out there."

Darkness seemed to surround Casey again, enveloping her in a stygian embrace.

How crazy...

Then, nothing.

* * * *

Ryder sat at his desk at Krewe headquarters in Virginia, concentrating on the last of his paperwork for the case he and Axel Tiger had just finished up in Colorado.

He hit the last letter key to finish his work and sat back.

He'd been glad to head to Colorado and work with Axel. His level of frustration had been high. The autopsy on his cousin had shown nothing the M.E. hadn't already suspected: an overdose of prescription drugs.

He'd spent a week with his cousin Stephanie, working with her and old Elijah's superb lawyer to make sure she had solid protection at the mansion and to ensure that the Marceau inheritance had been sewn up for little Annette.

He'd also researched the board, the family, and any others who might have had access to Lena and her home at the time of his cousin's death.

Someone had to have been involved.

He just didn't know who.

But he'd been spinning his wheels in New Orleans.

Bottom line, he knew that he had to find out who wanted control of the Marceau inheritance enough to kill.

Cunningly, and several times over.

And now...

Well, a baby was theoretically in charge.

Five people—all of whom he had seen on the day Lena died—might be involved. He had thought so then, and he still thought so.

People who were close to the day-to-day workings of the Marceau home and business—Gail Reeves, the housekeeper, who'd happened to have an afternoon off. Barton Quincy, director of operations at Marceau Industries Incorporated. Larry Swenson, Barton's second in command. Harry Miller, sales director. And Justin Marceau, another great-grandson, who had grown up in Baltimore, Maryland, but had taken his place on the board of directors.

Justin wasn't always in the city, but he had been in New Orleans on the day Lena died. And after the baby, Justin was next in line to inherit. Could Justin be involved? Or was he in danger just as the others had been because his last name was Marceau?

But even Ryder couldn't make sense of the fact that there had been no defensive wounds on Lena's body. There had been no alcohol by her side, either. Nothing to indicate that her mind hadn't been right, other than what everyone thought to be obvious depression enough to bring on suicide. There also hadn't been evidence that anyone had forced her to take the pills.

Ryder had seen video of the immediate property. He and Stephanie had gone over it together. On the feed, he saw Lena, holding little baby Annette and waving goodbye as Gail Reeves headed out. They never saw the housekeeper return.

At the estimated time of Lena's death, there was a mysterious blackout in the video.

Ryder had stayed in the city for two weeks, but a snag in a video reel—no matter how timely and mysterious—hadn't been enough for anyone but him to call Lena's death a murder. He knew Braxton had even pursued the matter with his superiors at the NOPD.

Braxton had let him watch as he interviewed Gail Reeves, Barton Quincy, Larry Swenson, Harry Miller, and even Justin Marceau. They'd all been brought in not as suspects, but in hopes they could give the police some indication of what might have happened with Lena. They all came in willingly, eager to help.

Or so they said.

And then...

Not even Jackson Crow, the field director for the Krewe, had managed to find a reason to home in on the investigation.

Eventually, Jackson had assured Ryder that they would pursue it further. But that meant a lot of research. Thankfully, Jackson had cooled Ryder down enough to work another case while the tech experts, Angela's incredibly talented group of *paper chasers,* had delved into the paper and digital trails.

But there had been a bright spot in it all. Adam Harrison, the assistant director over all of the Krewe and their magnanimous founder, had agreed with Ryder and Jackson that it was all far too suspicious.

A happily married man—Lena's husband, Anthony—had managed to fall off the roof of a building in the Central Business District after visiting a bank branch there when there was another branch just down the street from his home. And, equally suspicious, a young woman who adored her child and appeared to be in fine health committing suicide.

Not to mention the fact that a fortune was at stake.

The Krewe would not give up, but it was the kind of case where many people needed to be investigated, and a great deal of material needed to be reviewed.

Though none were better at that kind of investigation than Angela's paper chasers.

Jackson had suggested that Ryder take on the case in Colorado with Axel while he let Angela and the tech crew perform research on the people and events surrounding the murders.

Ryder couldn't forget seeing Lena lying there like an angel. Nor the hurt in Stephanie's eyes. Or the baby's confused tears and frustration. Annette was too young to understand what had happened.

It had been heartbreaking to hear the baby crying for her mother.

Thankfully, Annette loved her Aunt Stephanie.

Jackson had been right. Ryder was better when working a case. Right now, his head pounded. He pressed his temples between his palms.

And then...

Timing couldn't have been better. He gritted his teeth against the pain and hit *Send* on his latest report just when a tap sounded at his door.

Angela. She had been with Jackson when the Krewe first came together on a case in New Orleans. They were now married and the parents of an adopted ten-year-old boy and a baby girl. She was a beautiful blonde woman who somehow managed it all—parenting and working and answering the phone at odd hours.

"Hello," he said, looking at her hopefully. "Did you find anything?"

She smiled. "I do have something," she told him. "Not much, but something. Did you ever hear of or do you know anything about a man named William Marley?"

"William Marley...yes. Or no. I never knew him, but when I was studying some company papers with Stephanie, his name was mentioned. He was sixty-six, still working on the board, close to Elijah and Anthony Marceau, when he died of a heart attack."

Angela nodded. "I pulled his medical records. He didn't have a heart condition, but he did die in a hospital, and there was no autopsy."

"If he died in a hospital—"

"I don't believe the doctors were at fault. The ambulance got him to the doors of the hospital, but he died being transferred from the rescue vehicle to the emergency room. It was evident he had died of a heart attack. He was sent to the morgue but was quickly transferred to the Devereaux funeral home in New Orleans." She was quiet for a minute. "Lena Marceau arranged for his burial. She was close with William Marley, like she was with Elijah and Anthony."

"Can we dig him up?"

Angela sighed. "Ryder. You grew up in Kenner. William Marley was interred in the Marceau family mausoleum. And he died before

Anthony. If you understand New Orleans, which you must..."

"A year and a day," Ryder murmured. That was the time it took for the Louisiana sun to basically cremate a body. "Still, Angela. I was at a forensic workshop as a cop. Cremains can leave clues. The year and a day simply means the body has deteriorated enough to be pushed into a holding cell at the end of the vault to allow for another interment. There might be something in the bones or the ash. I'm not an M.E. or even a tech geek, but I believe certain things—"

"Can be derived from bone and ash. There might be. But we're going to need permission to open the vault."

"We can get that. That will be the easy part. And if we find something in the bones or the ash, they'll have to reopen the case."

Angela smiled at him. "It's better than that. William Marley was on a trip to play at the casino in Biloxi. He died right over the state line in Mississippi. If we find anything, we can claim the case ourselves."

Ryder hopped up and rushed over to her, crushing her to him and twirling her around. He did so just as Jackson Crow happened to come down the hallway.

"What?" Jackson asked, a curious look in his eyes and a smile on his face.

"Your wife is brilliant!" Ryder told him.

"I know that," Jackson said. "Ah. She told you what she found."

"She did." Ryder winced. He had the best job in the world, and he never wanted to lose it. It was the only kind of work that could keep a man like him sane—and, hopefully, create a better world by bringing justice to those robbed of life and bringing closure to the ones left behind.

But Lena's death would haunt him to his dying day.

He'd discovered that he could talk to the dead when he was young.

He'd been put in therapy, of course.

So he'd learned not to mention it to others.

Until he heard about the Krewe of Hunters.

He'd gone to Lena's autopsy. He'd attended the funeral. He'd prowled the Marceau mansion.

But he hadn't found any remnant of her spirit—and he'd

searched.

"Jackson, I'd like—"

"To go back to New Orleans. Go. You'll have to book a commercial flight; we have a team heading out to San Diego with the jet."

"Commercial is fine. I'm just a visitor. Stephanie can order the opening of the vault, and Braxton and his people are good; they just had nowhere else to go in their investigation. And I understand how others think Lena's death was a suicide. But if—"

"If we can prove William Marley was helped into his heart attack, we can take over the case," Angela finished for him.

"Book your flight," Jackson told him.

"I already booked him one," Angela said. She glanced at her watch. "Better move. Your plane leaves in three hours."

"I'll be on it," Ryder assured her.

"And keep in touch. We're always here—or somewhere—if you need us."

"Will do," Ryder promised.

He picked up his phone. He had to tell Stephanie that he was on his way and warn her what he needed to do.

Investigate a corpse.

She wasn't going to be happy.

But Stephanie wanted to live. And she wanted to protect the baby at all costs.

She would do what was necessary.

Even if they had a fight on their hands.

Chapter 2

It was a given.

Summer in New Orleans was hot. The dead heat of July and August hung on into the early weeks of September, and just stepping outside was like taking a bath in sweat. Thankfully, the air-conditioning in the shop worked well.

It wasn't that it was any different than usual. Not really. It was hot every year, and they complained every year. And then fall and winter finally arrived, and the temperatures were beautiful. But the fourplex where Casey lived had a lovely pool in back, and she was currently dreaming of jumping into it. It was even part of a screened-in patio so it kept the mosquitoes to a minimum.

But Jennie Sanders was in the shop again. And even if she weren't, it was Wednesday—one of Casey's nights to close.

Casey could dream about the cool splash of the pool all she wanted. Instead, she sat across from Jennie at a table in her room in the back of the shop, staring at tea leaves.

"What do you see?" Jennie asked anxiously.

What do I see, what do I see?

Tea leaves! Casey thought.

Jennie visited once a week and was a wonderful customer, buying items in the shop every time she came for a reading.

And Jared was right. The shop did well, but what Casey did most of the time was be the best listener she could—practicing psychology. While Casey knew that she was a total sham as a medium, she was equally convinced there was something unusual in Jennie Sanders. Jennie had a sixth sense, and her visits with Casey helped her recognize it in herself and deal with life's little difficulties more easily.

Jennie was in her late forties and had grown children. Her husband, a retired professor, was an indulgent man, and her children were off living and working in Atlanta. She made trips to see her grandchildren, but other than that, she had time on her hands. She was an attractive woman who kept fit and was as regular about attending her beauty salon and going to the gym as she was about visiting Casey.

"From what I'm seeing," Casey said, "if you drive and are careful, a trip to Atlanta to see the grandkids would be rewarding for you. They love you and miss you very much. Oh, and your daughter-in-law, Mike's wife, loves it when you come. It gives her more time to work on her macramé projects."

"Oh, thank you! That's what I felt, but...of course, I'll spend time with Mike and Sheila, and I'll spend time with Virginia and Al, too. And when I'm there, they get together more often."

"I don't think you need to worry. Your children will remain close to one another."

Casey had met them both. They'd come into the shop with Jennie a few times. Mike loved Lauren's artwork, and Virginia suggested bizarre songs for Jared to play on the street. Usually, Jared played a game of *Name that Tune*! or thought of ridiculous melodies and lyrics to go with whatever she challenged him with. It was hysterical.

Jennie had nice children who loved her. Casey didn't need tea leaves to know that.

"Great! Then I won't see you for a few weeks," Jennie said, getting up. "I'll miss you. I love coming in here—"

"I'm sure I'll be here when you get back," Casey said, rising and leading them both out to the main area of the shop.

"Unless," Jennie said dramatically, "a tall, dark, and dangerously handsome stranger appears and sweeps you off your feet and takes you far, far away. Honestly, I don't know how that hasn't happened yet. Sweetheart, you are lovely. So sweet and kind. I mean, I guess that doesn't equal sex appeal, but you're gorgeous, too. Hair like a blackbird, eyes like...something really blue."

"Luscious locks like a raven's wing, eyes like the sky at sweetest morning's dew!" Jared supplied, grinning at them both from behind the counter.

"Well, thank you both," Casey said. "Jennie, have a great trip.

We'll hear all about it when you come back."

"Oh! I need to buy a few things. I'm going to take some of the latest watercolors Lauren has on display," Jennie said. "And I will be gone for a bit, so I'd love for Jared to give me a sendoff. With you lovely ladies, if you don't mind."

"I have just the thing," Jared said, grabbing his guitar. "John Denver, *Leaving on a Jet Plane*," he said.

He played. Casey and Lauren had done the song with him dozens of times before. It was always fun, falling into the harmony part, and Casey realized she was smiling when they finished.

"How was that?" Jared asked Jennie.

"Superb! Except I'm driving," Jennie said.

Jared grinned and burst into a rendition of the Beatles' tune, *Baby, You Can Drive My Car.*

He finished the song, and the older woman clapped. Lauren got the canvases that their customer wanted down from their hooks and wrapped them, listening as Jennie chatted all the while.

When Jennie left, Casey wandered toward the door and the street, wishing *she* could leave. But the shop had been her idea and was her baby. And given where they were located in the French Quarter on St. Anne Street, staying open until at least ten was par for the course and necessary to stay in business.

Casey had suggested that they alternate working the late shifts. She just wished this was her night to go home early.

Lauren and Jared had gone to LSU with her. They were truly close friends, and if she had begged one of them to take her place, they would have done so. But she knew they planned on heading to Frenchman Street to see a band that one of Jared's old frat brothers had formed.

She'd just look out the window.

But Jennie came back, obviously determined to speak to her again.

"Have you been back to the cemetery where the Marceau mausoleum is?" Jennie asked in a soft voice.

"No, I haven't. I'm sorry, Jennie." She tried not to let the woman see how just the mention of the place gave her shivers.

"You need to go back. I told you, my dream was vivid. There was a woman there, sobbing. And I don't know if she was dead or alive, but she clearly needs help. I mean, if she *is* dead, then you're the person to go."

A sobbing woman.

Yes. If her crazy break with reality had any substance, the sobbing woman was Lena Marceau. And yet...

No. Never again. Casey still didn't know what she'd seen or imagined that day. She only knew that she had awakened in an ambulance with doctors desperately trying to figure what had caused a healthy twenty-four-year-old woman to pass out in a cemetery.

Heatstroke had been the verdict—and a common one. It had occurred in the middle of the dead of summer, after all.

"Jennie, the dead are beyond our earthly help. But I can find someone with the church or talk to someone at Marceau Industries Incorporated. Make sure they look through the cemetery and see that all is well there. I believe they're taking better care of it these days. I heard restoring her husband's family mausoleum had meant something to Lena Marceau. And her sister, Stephanie, is now guardian to Lena's little girl, Annette. She's been keeping up with her sister's intentions. So, all should be well."

"I still think you should go," Jennie said. "You have such a way. Well, you do what you can, and I'll call you with any more dreams."

Casey forced a smile. "You do that," she said.

At last, Jennie was gone again. Casey walked back into the center of the shop. Jared was back behind the counter, and Lauren was adjusting some framed work on the walls.

"Hey, you two better get going," Casey said, glancing at her watch. "Jennie stayed late. It's after six."

"The band doesn't start until eight," Jared told her. "We're good. But, Lauren, let's get out of here. I want to stop and get something to eat."

"Where?"

"I don't know. We'll head over there and wander. Okay?"

"Sounds good to me."

The two didn't actually leave for another few minutes. Lauren was intent on getting everything on the wall straight and precise, and Jared greeted two new customers who came in and set them up for a reading the next week.

When they left, Casey wished she'd set the shop's closing hours earlier than she had. Because of all the diners out in the area and the many other shops that stayed open late, they closed at ten.

Customers came and went. For the most part, they were nice. People tended to like tarot cards because so many of the decks were so artistic and beautiful, and it was fun to discover that a so-called bad card might not be bad at all, depending on where it fell.

Casey had a nice time with a group of college kids that came in, explaining a few of the cards.

Decks were also reasonably priced, and something people could afford.

A man in his early forties came in while the girls were still there. He spoke to Casey casually about her readings and said he was thinking about tea leaves because they fascinated him. He bought one of Lauren's prints and said he'd be back to schedule a reading.

Darkness fell.

An older man came in. He looked a bit like a well-groomed Santa. He didn't seem the type concerned with a reading, but he asked her about tea leaves and the tarot, then grinned and asked her about her crystal ball.

"The only one we have is in the statue over there," she told him. "Everything I do is learned from books, sir, and I haven't found one to explain what I'd be seeing in a crystal ball. Except, well, they are pretty."

"They are."

He was pleasant and curious and asked her if she'd been a music major. She told him it was psychology, and that seemed to amuse him. He said it clearly explained the shop.

After that, he bought a few of their tee shirts, thanked her, and left.

It was almost ten, and she sank into one of the comfortable chairs by the small coffee and tea station they had in the far corner. Most of Lauren's work could be seen from that vantage point. It was a nice little nook where they had the table with a pod machine and plush chairs covered in a very dark crimson material that added to the masks and art and other décor in the shop.

Casey closed her eyes. The bell would ring when someone came in.

The bell didn't ring. But when she opened her eyes, someone was facing her.

Lena Marceau.

She opened her mouth, but a scream didn't come.

"Please, please, don't pass out on me again!" Lena—or the ghost or specter of the woman—said. "I'm so sorry! But you're a medium. You should have known I might be here."

Casey didn't pass out. Maybe she was too frozen to do so. All she could do was reply with, "I'm not a medium."

"But—"

"I read tea leaves and tarot cards. I don't even have a crystal ball."

She was talking—and talking out loud. To a ghost. But no matter how she blinked, the apparition didn't go away.

Lena spoke again. "Look, I don't understand any of this, and I'm so sorry. I have no choice. You must help me! They're going to kill my sister and my baby."

Casey realized that she was breathing heavily. She pinched herself—it was what was done in situations like these, right?

The pinch hurt.

But Lena Marceau still sat before her.

"I've tried to reach my sister. I've tried so hard. But I...well, I don't know how any of this works. By the time I came to myself—as a spirit or whatever—the funeral was over, and people had gone. My sister comes to the cemetery, but she doesn't see me. I know she senses something is wrong, though. And, oh, Lord! Ryder was there. Ryder is with the FBI, but he was gone by the time I realized I had to try to reach someone. And this isn't easy. I go by some people, and they shiver. And I have tried voodoo shops and magic shops and churches. I really thought you would see me—and accept me. I have met a few others like me, and they told me I needed to find the right person. That some people can see us. Not many, but they do exist. Please, please, you have to help me!"

Was Lena—or Lena's spirit—really there? Or was Casey conversing with herself?

There was no reason for her to have a psychotic break. She'd had no trauma in her life. She had good friends, a great home, and super parents who now lived in Arizona but came to see her regularly and loved her very much. Both were well.

"Please!" the ghost said.

"Lena, I bought this shop because I was a psychology major. When I got out of college, the jobs I was offered would have barely paid back my student loans. I grew up here, and I have been in this type of shop before, and I know...well, I've studied people. I've studied books on the tarot. When I say I read cards, I just talk about what the books say, along with what I believe the client is looking for or needs. I don't have any special abilities—"

"But you're talking to me."

Casey let out a soft sigh.

"Yes. Apparently, I've gone crazy."

"No, no. You're not crazy. I'm here. Well, I'm not *physically* here, but... Please, help me!"

"How? You keep talking about *they*. Who are they? What—what happened?" She took a deep breath. "I'm guessing you didn't kill yourself. I never thought it made any sense, but there was something of an investigation. An autopsy. You didn't fight with anyone. You just took the pills. What happened, *who* is involved?"

"I don't know exactly. I just know someone in that wretched company Elijah left Anthony and me, killed us both."

"Lena. First, I'm still trying to decide if there's been a trauma in my life I didn't realize that caused a psychotic break, or if...if it's possible you're here. But after that, there's still a serious problem. I can't just go to the police and tell them your ghost told me you were murdered!"

Lena sat back, looking around the store. "I always loved this place."

"Thank you. Lena—"

"You need to go to my sister and warn her."

"And your sister is not going to hit me or laugh me off the doorstep?"

"Stephanie won't hit you. She's nice."

"But she will think I'm a crazy person and laugh me off the doorstep," Casey said.

"We have to do something," Lena whispered.

"Lena, how can it be you don't know what happened to you?"

The beautiful blonde ghost leaned back in Casey's chair and looked up at the ceiling, shaking her head. "I don't know."

"How can you not know?"

She shook her head again. "He—I'm sure it was a *he*—didn't want me to know who he was. Maybe he's a believer in the dead coming back to life, or he wasn't sure if there were cameras in the house. We never had cameras in the house. I was in my bedroom when a masked person broke in, holding the baby—Annette had been taking a nap in her room—and a knife. I—I bargained with him. Said I'd take the pills. I'd make it look like a suicide. But told him he had to let me lock the baby in her room first. Said he couldn't touch her." Her ghostly fists clenched. "I needed to say goodbye," she whispered.

The thought of making such a decision, of all that it cost Lena, broke Casey's heart.

"Only my sister and I know the code to that door, and I knew Stephanie was coming over within the hour. It wasn't ideal, but the room was babyproofed, secure, and it was the only thing I could think to do." She paused for a minute. "At least I saved Annette. He wanted to kill us both. I told him I'd fight tooth and nail, and everyone would know we'd been murdered. So, I bargained for her life."

"I'm so sorry," Casey whispered.

Lena shrugged. "Anthony inherited the house, you know. No one had lived in it for a while, and...the reason Elijah left him the company was because Anthony didn't really want it. He didn't care about the money—he was an artist. A good one. But he'd loved Elijah since he was a little boy, and Elijah loved him. When it all came up about five years ago, I said, 'Sure, we'll live in your old family house, and we'll try to do good things.' I damned us both with that."

"You're not damned."

"No, I don't think so. And I've heard people move on when...when they're ready. When the time comes. Into a beautiful light. But the thing is, Anthony and I...we're both dead," Lena said bitterly. "I wouldn't care so much, except..."

"You're worried about Annette."

"And my sister. Casey, don't you see? They'll kill her and Annette."

"Okay, so a man was there with a knife. You don't know who."

"He wore black—black pants, black hoodie, black ski mask...completely covered. And I never got close to him. I couldn't recognize a smell or anything like that. I'm not even sure about the color of his eyes because I think he was wearing weird costume contact lenses. I don't know who he was. I beg you, help me. At least get to Stephanie and warn her that she's in danger. And tell her that...he wanted to kill the baby when he killed me."

This can't be real.

But Casey could see Lena sitting there. Maybe it was her own strange sense of guilt. Or the way she had felt at St. Mary of Light Cemetery while seeing the Marceau tomb.

"I don't know how much help I can give you," Casey said. "But—"

"But?"

"Of course, I'll help in any way I can. Tomorrow...I'll find a way to see your sister. I'll warn her that she's in danger. She'll probably tell me I'm a quack who owns a mystic shop and thinks she's got a direct phone line to the Underworld."

"Stephanie isn't stupid. I believe she knows she could be in danger. I need her to know just how much," Lena said.

Casey nodded. "Okay, I...I'll do my best."

* * * *

"You're back," Braxton said, forcing a weak smile as he greeted Ryder.

Ryder had told Braxton not to worry about picking him up at the airport. Said he could grab transportation himself.

But Braxton had insisted on coming, and he was here now, waiting for Ryder in the baggage claim section of Louis Armstrong International Airport.

"Yes, I'm back," Ryder said, shaking Braxton's hand. His old friend looked at him with skeptical worry. "Ryder, you know that—"

"I'm not going to be a pain," Ryder promised.

"But you're here because of the Marceau incident," Braxton said. "Ryder, it's over. The M.E. found nothing but an overdose of prescribed sedatives in her system."

"Don't forget, Lena Marceau was my cousin."

"Second cousin. Your mothers were cousins."

"I don't care what kind of cousin."

"But no suicide note was ever discovered. You're my friend. I tried. But the medical examiner, as you know, found nothing else," Braxton said, his tone miserable.

"Right," Ryder said. "And still, the Marceau fortune is in the hands of a two-year-old child. But I know when Elijah died, they discovered his will was extensive and detailed. Control went to Anthony, and then to Lena, and then from her to the baby, Annette, controlled by her legal guardian until she comes of age. And Stephanie Harrow is the baby's legal guardian now. Everything is hers, held in trust. And after her husband died, Lena saw to it that her sister was added to the corporation's board of directors."

"That can't sit well with the rest of the family and board members."

"There are five other people on that board, Braxton, including Justin Marceau."

"Oh, come on. You think that—"

"I do," Ryder interrupted, speaking firmly. But then he hesitated. "Stephanie called me last night. She was out with the baby and realized she was being followed. She didn't head back to the house but went straight to Bourbon Street."

"With a two-year-old child?"

"She knew there would be people there, plenty of witnesses. She found one of your officers and said he was a good guy. She asked him to see that she and the baby got home safely, and he did. Braxton, I'm just going to hang around and see what I can find out. Anthony and Lena dead within months of one another—by accident or suicide—and that starting a year after old Elijah passed on? I'm not knocking the NOLA police, you know that I'm not, but I believe that something more is going on. Come on, Braxton."

"Yes, but..." Braxton paused, shaking his head. "We've gotten word the FBI is disinterring a fellow who worked for the corporation—who conveniently died in Mississippi."

"Yes."

"But, Ryder—"

"If his heart attack was induced, then even you will have to admit it's starting to look suspicious."

"Induced? But a heart attack—"

"William didn't have a heart condition."

"But a heart attack—"

"*Can* be induced."

Braxton sighed and shook his head.

"Braxton, Jackson Crow obviously knows I'm here. I'm not official, again, no one has asked us in. And I'm not going to get in your way. But I'm going to be around for Stephanie, all right?"

"I just want you to be careful. We have a great relationship with the Krewe down here. Your Krewe of Hunters started up in NOLA, you know."

"I do know that," Ryder said. And he did. He knew the history of the Krewe. He'd wanted to be FBI for as long as he could remember. His father was a retired agent. When he heard about the Krewe—through rumor, mostly—he'd known what he wanted. He'd been accepted into the academy when he made a point of finding Jackson Crow, knowing when the man would be at his son's baseball game.

But Jackson had already known about Ryder. He'd wondered about that until he passed the academy and became Krewe.

Then, he'd learned that Jackson had heard about the strange case in Alexandria that Ryder had solved as a young police detective.

He'd longed to be a part of a group that understood him.

As it happened, the group had been watching *him.*

"So, officially, you're what? On vacation?" Braxton asked skeptically.

"You could say that."

Braxton groaned but picked up Ryder's bag and headed to the elevators for the parking garage. "As far as the NOPD goes, the case is closed. Lena has been interred, and life goes on. Where am I taking you?"

"The Marceau house," Ryder said.

"You're staying at the Marceau mansion?"

"The baby invited me."

"Hey!" Braxton protested.

"The baby owns the house. Stephanie is her legal guardian. I'm here because Stephanie is afraid. She is convinced that her sister was murdered, Braxton. Doesn't it worry you? Anthony and Lena, both dead? Another man possibly murdered, and Stephanie all that stands between that baby and her life?"

"No one could want to kill a baby. Hey!" he exclaimed at Ryder's look. "When Lena died, the baby was fine."

"Fine. Because she'd been locked in a room, and only Stephanie had the code to get in. I think Lena was worried after Anthony died. I mean, think about it. Why would Anthony mysteriously jump or fall off a building in the Central Business District? He had a beautiful wife, a gorgeous child, and he'd just inherited an empire."

Braxton was quiet for a moment. "His death was ruled accidental. And we're all watching, just so you know. We're not stupid down here. If you can prove the Marceau exec was murdered, you're taking over the case."

"*Taking over* is strong. I expect we'll be a team, or possibly form a task force."

Braxton shook his head. "Okay, well...are you going to invite me to tea?"

"You want tea?"

Braxton grinned. "Isn't that what rich people do? Sip tea and eat crumpets?"

"As long as I've known Stephanie, she's been a coffee girl. But if you want tea, I'll get you some tea. And crumpets."

"What is a crumpet?"

"Something baked," Ryder said. "I don't know. Let's just get there. And then..."

"Then what?"

"I'm going to pay a visit to the Marceau mausoleum."

"Think Lena will tell you what happened?" Braxton asked dryly.

"You never know," Ryder told him. "You just never know."

Chapter 3

Casey stood at the gate before the Marceau house—or mansion rather.

Esplanade Avenue in New Orleans hosted some fine homes. This one was especially beautiful, combining Colonial and Victorian styles with a perfectly manicured lawn and charming fountains on either side of the grand walk to the porch steps.

There was a call button, and she hit it and waited. A minute later, she heard a feminine voice say, "Hello, may I help you?"

"Miss Harrow?" Casey said.

She was ready to run. The woman would simply refuse to see her.

"Yes, this is Stephanie Harrow. How may I help you?"

"It's a private and personal matter," Casey said and winced.

She wished Lena Marceau's ghost would appear now. She'd stayed late at the store, talking in general, enthusiastic terms about Lauren's art pieces and smiling about Jared's talent with music, saying that she'd seen him outside the shop a few times, though he hadn't been there when she visited. He could go from doing Beethoven to Broadway to heavy metal in a matter of minutes.

"He is extremely talented," Casey had said. "He was with a group, but they were doing heavy metal almost exclusively, and he felt he was burning out his voice. He likes being a solo act or telling Lauren and I what to do. He was the music major, so we never argue."

Lena had also talked about her daughter, laughing and saying how they hadn't lied when they'd come up with the term *terrible twos.*

It had been past ten when Casey yawned and closed her eyes, leaning back in her seat.

When she opened her eyes and started to apologize for nodding off, Lena was no longer there.

And Casey was left to wonder again if her own mind was haunting her.

She had decided that she wasn't going to approach Stephanie Harrow and the Marceau house unless she saw Lena again. But that night, as tired as she was, she had trouble sleeping. She tossed and turned and feared that everything the ghost—real or imagined—had said might be true. She couldn't imagine anyone wanting to hurt a child.

But it had to be true. Her husband's death. And her death. To Casey, it was just...

Too convenient.

"I'm sorry, but who are you?" Stephanie asked over the intercom.

"My name is Casey Nicholson. I own a shop in the French Quarter. I...your sister was a friend of mine."

She was greeted with dead silence for so long, she almost turned away.

Then she heard the grinding of gears as the gate opened.

She walked through and up the walkway to the front porch. As she climbed the steps, the front doors—beautiful wood and etched glass—opened.

A woman walked out.

Stephanie Harrow was a few years older than Lena had been. Her hair was a darker shade of blond, cut short in a bob to frame her chin. She was an attractive woman, but her face seemed somehow marred by the sorrow she had faced.

"Come in," she told Casey.

"Thank you."

"Coffee?" Stephanie asked.

"I never turn down morning coffee," Casey told her.

"Then please, come on through to the kitchen. The parlor here...it's too big for me."

The parlor was big. But it was the entry with its sweeping staircase to the second floor in the center of the room that seemed to dominate the space.

"I used to love this place," Stephanie murmured. "Lena came down those stairs in her wedding dress, and it was spectacular. Now... Were you at the wedding?" she asked, frowning.

"No." Casey glanced down. "We met when she came to my shop."

"I see." Stephanie walked into the kitchen, a place as elegant and large as the parlor, but there was a breakfast nook by the back door that seemed much smaller and cozier. A coffee pot was already on the table there, and Stephanie grabbed a mug from the counter and motioned for Casey to follow her.

A tall, thin woman, straight as a Martinet, walked into the kitchen, a frown on her face. Casey thought she had to be in her mid to late fifties, but she almost looked as if she had come from another era. Her hair was steel gray, and she kept it braided at her neck.

"Stephanie, do you need help with anything?" she asked.

Stephanie waved a hand in the air. "I'm fine. Thank you, Gail."

The woman remained.

"This is a private conversation," Stephanie added quietly.

"The baby is with the gentleman. If there's anything—"

"Gail. Enjoy yourself. Watch a program. Lie down, read a book," Stephanie said, smiling at the woman. "It's okay. You don't have to be busy every second. Trust me, you are appreciated."

The woman smiled, cast a suspicious glance at Casey, and then left at last.

When they were seated across from one another, Stephanie poured Casey some coffee and indicated that she should help herself to cream and sugar from the servers by the pot.

"So, did my sister owe you money?" Stephanie asked, sipping her coffee.

"No."

"Are you here to ask for some kind of money?"

"No," Casey said. She winced and stirred in the cream she'd just added to her cup.

"Did you even know my sister, or is this some kind of a prank...or worse?" Stephanie asked, staring at her hard.

"No, I swear it's not a prank." Casey winced inwardly again and then took a deep breath.

"Lena was worried," she said in a rush, trying to figure out how to tell Stephanie the truth. "She...she doesn't—didn't—believe Anthony just fell. And she was worried for herself. But more than that, she was afraid for the baby. And now, she's gone. But... I can't forget the things she said to me, and I felt I had to warn you. Tell you just how frightened she was and how worried she was. And that...well, it's inconceivable, but she believes even Annette could be in danger." She suddenly sat straighter. "The baby. Where is she?"

Stephanie smiled at that, yet it seemed she looked at Casey more warily. "Annette is fine. I'm always with her. I don't even leave her with the housekeeper. She's with a relative."

"Um..."

"A relative on *my* side of the family," Stephanie said. She was quiet for a few minutes.

Casey sipped her coffee, still feeling like a fool. She had said what needed to be said. Now, she had to get out—and hope she'd fulfilled the mission given to her by a ghost. She no longer wanted to be haunted.

Except...

It hadn't been that bad. She'd enjoyed talking to Lena.

Or to herself, if she'd made up the ghost in her head.

"You know, Lena wasn't born rich. We grew up in Gretna. My mother was a teacher, and my dad was an accountant. We didn't want for anything, but they were hardworking, and we grew up with that ethic. Oh! And Anthony—did you know him?"

"No, I'm sorry. I didn't."

"He was great." Stephanie paused to smile. "He was like a nerdy hippie, if that makes any sense. He would have done great things with the company. Part of the Marceau money is in prescription drugs. Anthony wanted to make sure prices went down. He wanted the company restaurants to donate food and supplies to food kitchens. He had plans...Lena meant to keep those plans, and I want to live up to their legacy, but I don't know how they battled that board of directors. They exhaust me. And I never wanted to be in business. I illustrate children's books. Or I *did*. I'm afraid money was never my high point—money or math."

"Miss Harrow, money means nothing next to life," Casey said. "I know that—"

"I'm the legal guardian. I was made Annette's legal guardian in the event that something happened to Anthony or Casey." Stephanie gripped her cup with both hands. "I can't leave this baby. I'm careful about what I do. I don't want the money. I don't know how well you knew my sister, and I don't know if you're a sham."

"A sham? I'm sorry—"

"Don't you run a voodoo or magic or ghost shop?" Stephanie asked. "I think I remember Lena saying something about your place. A Beautiful Mind. You're a medium, right? Well, I'm afraid I don't put much stock in crystal balls, Miss Nicholson."

"Stephanie, I'm not a medium. I don't even own a crystal ball. Oh, I have a cute little display with a beautiful gypsy holding one, but I don't—"

"Thank you for coming. I see you've finished your coffee. May I see you to the door?"

"Yes, yes. Thank you for seeing me. And please, I know your sister was afraid—"

"You think I don't know my sister didn't commit suicide?" Stephanie asked, angry. "But I can't go to the cops. Tell them that someone—without even touching her—forced her to take a bunch of pills. That, facing death, she defied a knife or a bullet, knowing it would at least prove she had been murdered. I can't even come up with an answer myself—"

"Annette. The baby..." Casey said.

"What?"

"She bargained. Lena convinced the killer it would be best to let her lock the baby in her childproof safe room and have her take the pills voluntarily—than have her fight and have defensive wounds, showing everyone that she had been murdered."

Stephanie gasped, and tears suddenly filled her eyes. But then she blinked them away and cleared her face of any emotion.

It was clear Stephanie didn't want to acknowledge that Casey might have had a little help coming up with the scenario. After all, she'd just said she didn't put much stock in things like that. The information possibly coming from her dead sister's ghost might be a bit much to take, especially right now. Casey didn't want to add to the woman's grief, so she didn't say any more.

"I'll...uh...see you out. Unless you think you can convince a homicide detective your words are true. Anyway...I...I need you to go now," Stephanie said.

"Of course. I'm so sorry," Casey whispered.

She stood. She didn't need to be shown to the door. She had done what she had been asked to do. There was nothing more.

She glanced at her watch. It was nearly ten. She drove to the shop, trying to shake the feeling that she wasn't done with it all yet as she drove. But when she got to A Beautiful Mind, Jared and Lauren were there. They had already opened and were speaking to a group of customers about one of their displays.

Casey found herself waving and retreating to her reading room. She kept her tarot cards there, and it was set up with a table and comfortable chairs.

And her computer. She began research on the Marceau company. She had been looking for just about an hour when Lauren came back, tapping on the door and opening it, looking concerned.

"Um, there's someone out here insisting they see you—" she began.

She didn't finish. A man came up behind her, shoving the door all the way open and turning to stare at Lauren.

"Thank you," he told her, not pushing her exactly, but urging her out.

Casey leapt to her feet, staring at him, frowning and angry. He was a very tall man, about six-foot-four, wearing a business suit—in New Orleans, in the French Quarter. He had dark hair cut short but a little longer across his forehead, and broad shoulders with a build to go with his height.

She didn't care. This was her shop.

"You don't have an appointment," she said icily. "And you have been rude to Lauren. I'll thank you to exit the store before I call the police," she informed him.

He wasn't daunted in the least. He leaned on her table and stared at her hard.

"What were you doing at the Marceau house? How are you involved? Who are you working for?"

"What?"

She sank back into her chair. To her horror, it was the wrong move. He walked around the table in two steps and stared at her computer.

"Right. You know nothing about what happened, and yet you're on the Marceau home page?"

"I—I—"

"I repeat, what were you doing at the Marceau house?" he demanded.

He was imposing. She was almost afraid. But to her surprise, her fighting spirit rose to the fore.

"Who the hell are you? And how dare you barge in here like this?" she managed.

She was a good eight inches shorter than him, but she squared her shoulders, set her hands on her hips, and stared him down.

"Did someone pay you?" he asked her.

"Pay me? For what?" she asked. He was accusing and questioning her. But about what? She was honest, they had good business practices. She couldn't begin to understand this man's problem.

She took a deep breath and said, "I don't know who you are. I don't know who you think I am. I suggest you tell me just what it is you want, and then perhaps kindly remove yourself from these premises."

"What do you have to do with Marceau Industries Incorporated? Why were you pretending to be friends with Lena Marceau?"

He had eyes that were such a curious hazel color, they seemed to burn as he stared at her. The sound of his voice was deep and harsh and determined. She could imagine him as a cop in an interrogation room, and she doubted many *didn't* shiver and garble out the truth when he looked at them like that and spoke as he did.

She sank into her chair.

"I don't have anything to do with the Marceau company," she said.

"What were you doing at the house? Did you even know Lena?"

She looked at him and said softly, "Yes. I knew Lena. She liked this shop."

He backed up a step, crossing his arms over his chest, still watching her like a hawk. "Are you friends with Justin Marceau? Related to or friends with or on the payroll of Barton Quincy, Larry Swenson, or Harry Miller?"

"Sadly, I'm not on anyone's payroll except my own," she snapped. "I don't know Barton Quincy, Larry Swenson, or Harry Miller."

"You were at the Marceau house."

"Yes."

"Why?"

"I should have gone before. I—I knew Lena, yes. And I know

she never believed her husband just accidentally fell off a building. Or jumped. And she was afraid. And she was worried for Stephanie and Annette. I went because...I think it's important for Stephanie to know that Lena was worried."

"What took you so long to go see Stephanie then?"

She shook her head. "I—I didn't know Stephanie. Just Lena. I was afraid Stephanie would think I was crazy or after something. Look," she said, "I—I woke up this morning and decided it was early enough, that I could try to speak with Stephanie. She just needed to know that Lena was worried—had been worried. Afraid. I know nothing about the company. We make a decent living here. We have a huge mortgage on this place, but between us—my two partners and I—we get by. I don't know why in God's name you think someone would pay me to go to the Marceau house. No one did. You can ask Stephanie."

"I did."

"Well, then, you know what was said."

"Right. A quack from a shop combining every mystical thing in history came and started warning her to be careful."

"I'm not a quack."

"But you're supposed to be some kind of medium?"

"Argh!" She let out a cry of frustration. "I am not a medium. I read tarot cards. I read people. I sing in the street or in here sometimes with Jared. That's it. That's...that's it," she repeated.

She wasn't about to tell this man that Lena's ghost had visited her.

"So, who the hell are you? And what right do you have barging in here to question me and make fun of my place of business?" she demanded.

He leaned on the table; his face so close to hers.

"I'm Lena's cousin," he said softly.

He straightened and took a business card out of his jacket pocket, letting it fall onto the table.

"I'm Lena's cousin," he repeated, "Special Agent Ryder McKinley. Contact me when you feel you have more messages from beyond," he snapped.

Then he turned and left.

She heard the bell ring above the door, and then Jared and Lauren were in the room, staring at her worriedly.

* * * *

Ryder left the shop, trying to get a grip on his temper. He'd had no right to burst into the store and advance on the woman as he had, but before taking the baby and trying to keep her quiet to home in on Stephanie's conversation, he'd gotten a good look at her.

He'd wondered if she would go back to her shop and put on a ridiculously colored turban and a gypsy skirt and call herself Madam Something or Other.

But she hadn't. He'd followed her, of course. He'd watched her go in, and he'd waited, observing the store and its surroundings.

Then he'd gone in.

And had gotten nothing.

She knows something—or worse.

She's working for someone.

One of New Orleans' best coffee shops was up the road, so he headed that way, glancing at his watch.

William Marley would be removed from his resting place in an hour and a half. Adam had a friend at the office of the district attorney over in Mississippi, and the body or cremains—whatever remained at this point—would be taken over the state line to be examined, and so those who had contact with him before, during, and after his death could be questioned.

Ryder knew it would serve no purpose for him to go to Mississippi. The tests would take time. It was unlikely there would be much soft tissue left, but whatever remained might well prove something.

And if not...

There was this woman. The interesting one. Intriguing.

She hadn't put on a turban. In fact, she had looked like a scholar studying her computer.

With the site for Marceau Industries Incorporated displayed.

He judged her age to be in the mid to late twenties—he didn't think she'd hit thirty yet. She was medium height with long, slim legs, brilliant blue eyes, and hair darker than his. A striking woman, and about Lena's age when she died. He had to admit, it was conceivable the two had been friends.

And still...

Why suddenly go to Stephanie with a warning?

He walked into the coffee shop, glad they brewed coffee so strong a spoon could almost stand up in the cup. But as he entered the queue for the outdoor seating, he noticed Justin Marceau sitting at a table with Barton Quincy.

The offices for Marceau Industries Incorporated were in the Central Business District.

It was curious that they were in the French Quarter.

They hadn't seen him yet, so he leaned against the counter, waiting for his order and trying to see if he could discern any of their conversation.

He only heard one line.

"Stephanie won't vote for it. She's following everything Lena wanted to a T."

It was Justin who spoke.

Barton replied in a hushed but passionate whisper that Ryder couldn't catch.

Ryder's coffee order came up.

He walked over to the table and greeted the men in a friendly fashion. "Hey, Justin. And it's Barton, right? Barton Quincy? We met at Lena and Anthony's wedding. Ryder McKinley," he reminded Barton.

"Oh. Oh," Barton Quincy said, frowning. "I thought you worked for the FBI or something. I saw you at the funeral, but I thought you were back in D.C. or wherever now. What brings you back to these parts?"

"Lena was my cousin, so Steph is my cousin, too. Obviously. I wanted to check up on her and make sure the baby is doing well," Ryder said easily. "I had a little time off. I just finished a case, and it seemed some R and R was in order."

He kept his tone light and friendly.

Justin seemed nervous. Barton tried to assure him that everything was going well.

"I hear you set up security in the house for Stephanie before you left," Barton said.

"He did," Justin said with enthusiasm. "Guards on the property twenty-four-seven. And cameras in every room."

"A little overkill, don't you think?" Barton looked up at Ryder, not a twitch in tone when he said the word *kill.*

Ryder grimaced. "Well, the girls and I—Lena and Steph—grew up close. We were friends, as well as family. It still bothers me I didn't realize Lena was that deeply depressed about Anthony's death. Of course, Stephanie is an aunt, not a mom, so she's a little paranoid about making sure nothing happens to Annette. The girl is a little whirlwind. This way, Steph can grab things from the kitchen and keep an eye on the baby up in the playroom." Ryder made a show of looking around. "You two are a little out of your neighborhood."

"I had some shopping to do on Royal Street," Barton said. "Thought we could meet here."

"You two don't go into the office every day?"

Barton laughed. "This fellow? Work?" he teased. "Justin's surname is Marceau, you know."

"Hey! I'm available whenever needed," Justin said. "I did a great job at the last marketing meeting."

Barton shrugged and glanced at his watch then rose. "Well, I've got to get back. It was nice seeing you again, um, Ryder. Are you going to be here long?"

"I'm not sure just how long yet," Ryder said pleasantly. "I never know when I'll get a call to be somewhere, so..."

He left off, grinning and shrugging.

"Anyway, I should be off, too," Ryder said. "Good to see you both. I'm glad to know that when I can't be here, Stephanie has great people to call on."

Justin lifted a hand in goodbye. Ryder went down the street and then slipped behind a colonnade in a building hallway.

He watched the two men as they rose and parted.

Justin started for Canal.

Barton Quincy paused, looking up and down the street. Ryder wasn't sure, but he thought the man was watching one shop. Just one shop.

"A Beautiful Mind."

Did he know Casey Nicholson? Was that why he was looking at the shop?

Or had he seen Casey head to the Marceau house? Was he—like Ryder—curious as to why the woman had gone to see Stephanie?

Curious, too, as to just what Casey Nicholson knew about the death of Lena Marceau.

* * * *

Casey left the shop that day as early as she could.

She had to forget Lena Marceau, Stephanie Harrow, and the angry FBI guy who had shown up in the store.

It was hot, and she was done early enough to head for the pool at her fourplex before the mosquitoes got too bad.

Her friends teased her that she lived at an old folks' home—retired people rented the other three apartments in the building.

She loved the three couples, though. They watched out for both her and the building.

Plus, they brought her baked goods all the time. Only Miss Lilly—who had been an Olympic swimmer in her day—spent much time in the pool, and that was early. Miss Lilly might be found in the water any time after 6:00 A.M. Her husband, Joe, would sit in one of the lawn chairs and watch her, waving a hand and smiling and pretending he didn't hear her any time she suggested he get in—he needed exercise.

But at this time of night, the place was hers.

And the water felt good. So good. The temperature had been in the eighties and nineties all day, and many people might have thought the water in the pool was a bit too hot—like a lukewarm bath.

It didn't bother Casey at all. She loved the heat. And there was something special about water. She swam a bit, then just floated on her back and watched as the sun disappeared, and night slowly came on.

She wondered if she should go back to the cemetery and see if Lena was there. Did ghosts hang out in graveyards when they weren't busy haunting people, asking them to take care of something for them? She had first seen Lena's ghost in the cemetery.

And she'd fainted. Like a true coward.

She was a chicken. She simply hadn't believed in ghosts.

But would she rather a ghost haunt her, or accept the possibility that she was totally losing her mind?

She wasn't sure which she'd prefer at that point. She just knew that the water felt good. She tried to turn her mind to life and her commitments. She had promised that she would give a NOLA history and cemetery speech in the shop in two days for Miss Lilly's granddaughter's small study group. She needed to brush up on a few facts.

She had managed to think about the city and its history and enjoy the feeling of just floating in the water, looking up at the darkening sky, when she heard a hushed whisper. She blinked.

Lena was back. And she seemed to be drifting in the sky.

"Get out. Get out of the pool as quickly as you can!"

"What?"

"There's someone here—someone's out there. And he's...he's dressed in black. He's stalking you. He's in the bushes in the back of the neighbor's yard, watching you. Get in and lock your door and don't come out!" Lena's ghost warned.

Whether she was crazy or not, Casey jumped out of the pool. She grabbed her towel off the lounger and raced for the back door to the fourplex, once a shotgun house with a hall that ran from the front to the back and offered doors to the four apartments.

She threw open the door and slammed into someone. She nearly screamed.

Someone tall and dark and ridiculously solid, yet still nothing but a hulking shape in the night.

But then the shape spoke.

"Miss Nicholson. I'm sorry if I startled you. A woman who said her name was Lilly let me in and said that I'd find you out back," he said.

Him!

The man from the shop.

"Oh, my God. What are *you* doing following me here? Coming to my home?" she demanded in a desperate whisper.

She only realized then that he was holding her, steadying her.

"Trying to make sure you don't get killed," he said, his tone dry...

And carrying a frightening ring of truth.

Chapter 4

Denial. Seriously. She couldn't really have spent the evening before chatting with a ghost. And if so, she had done what the ghost wanted.

She couldn't be in danger herself.

Casey shook her head, trying to make something that resembled sense and logic out of it all.

"Back up," she said. "I don't understand. There's no reason for anyone to want to kill me, to follow me," she said, speaking quickly, trying to regain her sense of balance.

She stepped back at last, realizing he'd still been holding her. She murmured, "I'm sorry. I'm sorry. I'm soaked, and I just got you all wet. But—wait! You're the one following me, you...how are you here? I don't...I don't owe you an apology. I..."

He couldn't have been whoever Lily had said was out back in the bushes. He was standing here.

He took her by the shoulders, calming her, and he met her eyes with his own as he spoke in a soft voice. "Why are you in such a panic? This isn't because I was at your back door just walking out. You were terrified of something else, Casey. What happened? What's going on?" He gently tightened his grip. "And why are you still shaking?"

"I'm not. I—"

She broke off. What did she say to an FBI agent who had already knocked her for being a so-called medium?

"There was a noise in the bushes. I guess it scared me. I—I thought someone was back there."

He froze and dropped his hands. A seriousness took over his

entire demeanor. "Get in your room and lock the door after you lock this one and the front entry. When I'm back, I'll ring."

She nodded.

"I mean it, Casey. Do it. You may be in danger."

"Yes."

He stepped out the back. She watched him as he raced around the pool and disappeared into the hedges.

Lock the front door.

She hurried to do it and then slipped through her own door and locked it as well. For a moment, she stood there panting. Then she wasn't sure what to do.

"Lena?" she called.

But the ghost didn't answer.

She leaned against the door, holding tightly to her towel. She listened, but all she heard were the sounds of night—a car passing, a motorcycle, her neighbor's too-loud TV. But that was okay, Joe was hard of hearing and noise had never bothered her.

Then the buzzer to her apartment rang. She hit the button. "Yes?"

"Come let me in, if you will. Please."

"Okay."

She hurried to the front and opened the door. The agent was brushing leaves off his jacket.

"May I come in?" He took a deep breath. "Look, I apologize. I was an ass today. I was telling you the truth, though. Yes, I'm an agent, and yes, Lena was my cousin. And—"

"Yes, you were an ass today."

"I just said that." His lips tipped up in a small grin. "But everything I'm saying is true, and you know it. Lena was my second cousin, and I cared about her, deeply. And I care about Stephanie and the baby. Even if they had been strangers, what's going on here is cruel and heinous and could keep happening to innocent people." His eyes became more earnest than she thought possible. "I'm sorry I behaved badly. But this is serious. May we please talk?"

"I—yes. I just..."

She looked down at herself. She was still wearing her skimpy bikini with nothing more than the towel draped around her shoulders.

He glanced down briefly and then his eyes came right back to hers and stayed there. "I can wait while you change."

She nodded and turned down the hall, opening the door to her apartment.

He followed her in.

"Um...there's just one bedroom, up the stairs," she told him. *Why?* "The kitchen, dining, and parlor are all right here, as you can see. Help yourself to anything. I'll be right down."

Upstairs, she shed her suit and rinsed off quickly then grabbed clothing—a pair of jeans and a tee shirt—and hurried back downstairs, towel-drying her hair as she did.

He was seated at the dining room table, looking at his phone.

He hadn't helped himself to anything.

"Um—coffee?" she asked, a bit flustered. "And did you find anything? I mean, you tried to find out if someone was outside, right?"

"They're gone."

She sat across from him, studying his features. She hadn't realized before that he was so attractive. He'd barged in like a large ape, and that hadn't called for much of a fair assessment. He had a great jawline. And he was, she had to admit...compelling. His look was rough and rugged, yet almost classical with the clean line of his nose, the set of his eyes, and his cheekbones.

And, of course, I'm sitting here like a drowned rat.

Did that matter? He thought she was in danger. Lena had been murdered. But as far as she knew, no one else knew that Lena had told her anything.

Why would she be in danger?

"I am sincerely sorry for being so angry today," he said again, his tone low and modulated, and she thought sincere.

"Okay," she said slowly.

"You really knew Lena?"

"Yes. I really knew her. Not well, but she did talk to me a few times before... She came into the shop quite a bit."

"Have you seen her recently?" he asked.

"She's dead," Casey said.

"I know." He paused and softened his voice. "So, have you seen her recently?"

"What?" she asked sharply. "Look, you have the wrong idea, but I'm sure that's my fault. I majored in psychology, but I didn't care for the work I was offered after I got out of college. My friends were having the same problem. But I never, ever say I'm a medium, if that's what you're getting at. I have a dozen books on reading tarot cards, and I like them because you can lead them to say what you want. I swear to you, I try to make people happier about themselves, and that is it. I don't—I don't summon ghosts. I don't run seances. But it's true, I also read tea leaves. I have a dozen books on that, too—"

"And dozens of psychology books, I see," he said.

Just outside what would be the partition between the dining room and parlor if one existed, were her bookshelves. They lined both walls.

"I love the human mind. Strangest thing is it's the hardest thing in the world to fathom when you're working on your own."

He nodded for a minute, studying her, his eyes enigmatic.

"Lena Marceau did not kill herself. You are right in that."

"Um...are *you* a medium?" she asked him. "Has she...come to you?"

"Are you mocking me?" he asked her.

"I wouldn't dream of mocking a federal agent," she said sweetly.

He was quiet, studying her for a minute, and then he said, "I don't know why she hasn't come to me."

"Pardon?"

He slid his elbows on the table and leaned closer to her. "I don't know why she hasn't come to me. And I have had your background checked. Graduated with honors, worked a few places, bought the shop on St. Anne. You don't even have a parking ticket. Now, that's not easy, living here. Your parents are Gerome and Marie, who moved to Arizona when your dad's doctor suggested he needed a drier climate. You were born here, and you've been here since, other than for a six-month European study session during your junior year. You seem to be aboveboard in every way. Then again, that's just the type of person certain criminal elements try to rope in. So..."

"Um—so?"

"Either you have been paid to cause trouble—I doubt that after tonight—you just want something from Stephanie Marceau, or my cousin came to you."

"Look, I knew Lena—"

"And she's still talking to you."

He said it flatly, staring at her hard. She felt a sizzle race through her, and she didn't know if it was a touch of ice or a bit of fire.

"Are you trying to have me committed?" she asked.

"No. Look, I am an FBI agent, but I'm part of a special division called the Krewe of Hunters. We investigate…unusual cases. I'm not a medium. Mediums claim to have the ability to summon and talk to certain spirits—and maybe they can in some instances. But in my experiences with the dead—and they have been extensive—not all stay around to be summoned. Many who remain do so because they worry about the future of their descendants. They feel they need to guard a certain place or even see to it that history is remembered. Or because life was stolen from them in one way or another, and they have to see justice is done and ensure other lives aren't taken."

She stared back at him.

Could this be legitimate? Or was he trying to see that she was committed to an institution? Could they do that to her just because she believed she had seen a ghost?

They'd have to lock up half of New Orleans.

"Please," he said quietly.

She winced. "You don't have any recording devices on you, do you?"

He shook his head. "No. I swear."

She took a deep breath and decided to trust him with the truth. "I saw her first in the cemetery. It freaked me out so badly, I passed out twice and landed in the hospital for the night. They thought I had heatstroke. I thought maybe I did, too, seeing a dead woman. Then she came to the shop when I was alone last night. We talked for a long time." She focused her eyes on his. "Yes, she was murdered."

"Why haven't I seen her yet?" It was an introspective question, and he seemed hurt. But he gave himself a shake—both mentally and physically, Casey thought. "So, how? That's the question I keep getting when I try to pursue this case. But it may get better."

Casey shook her head. "May get better?"

"We had cremains disinterred today. I don't think even Anthony was this killer's first victim. A man who was on the board may have been—an old and dear friend to Elijah. He had no heart condition and mysteriously died of a heart attack. Luckily, over the state line."

"Luckily?"

"For me, not for him. I'm sorry. For the Krewe. It's a good thing. We can step in if anything is proven."

"You dug someone up today?"

"This is New Orleans. We didn't dig."

She shook her head. "No, no. I mean—"

"Yes, we exhumed a body. Please, tell me what Lena has told you."

Casey let out a breath. "We talked a lot," she said softly. "I don't know if you noticed those chairs by the coffee and tea stand, but...she just showed up there and sat in a chair. And she begged me not to pass out again, and I didn't. I knew someone would think I was crazy if I went to Stephanie with Lena's warning, but she was so desperate for someone's help..."

"You're not crazy," he told her.

She stood suddenly. "Special Agent McKinley, she was here tonight. She warned me to get out of the pool, said that someone was watching me. That they were in black and...I wonder if she went off, trying to find the person, too." She hesitated, wincing again as she looked at him. "Do ghosts have...rules? Or I should say, they can't just get anywhere by twitching their noses or anything. Can they?"

He shook his head and studied her again. "My special unit of the FBI is comprised of people who are part of the less than one percent of the population who has the sixth sense, or whatever it is. And recognize what they have. There are degrees to everything. Some people get a chill. Some see or hear things in their dreams, which is really nice. For instance, a mom comes to her children in a dream and assures them she's fine, that she's back with their dad. That kind of thing. Others..." He paused and shrugged. "Ghosts have to learn how to get around. They're like children, discovering more every day. But from all my experiences and those that have been shared with me by my colleagues, they can't be in more than one place at a time. And have you heard that saying? 'Beware of hitch-hiking ghosts?' Well, yes, ghosts like to hitch-hike or slide onto airplanes. I have a friend whose brother died in an accident, and he loves nothing more than to find flights where first class hasn't been fully booked. He pretends he's kicking back and enjoying the champagne."

"He can't drink champagne," Casey murmured.

He smiled. "Lena was here. Tonight."

"As I said, she warned me to get out of the pool and lock myself in."

He shook his head. "She wasn't out there. I hopped a couple of fences and looked around the general area. Whoever it was is gone. And so is Lena," he said. "All right, did she explain to you what happened by any chance? I mean, she took pills. Why? Did someone force her? Who?"

"A man in black."

"A man in black?"

"She couldn't see his identity. He wore black. Pants, shirt, mask—one that covered his entire face except his eyes. But she was convinced her killer was male."

"How?" The word was almost a whisper.

"She bargained. She told the killer she'd fight him tooth and nail, and the world would know she'd been murdered if he didn't let her put the baby in the safe room and lock her in. I guess the killer figured he had time to see that the baby had an accident somewhere along the line. So, Lena took care of the baby, leaving her where only Stephanie could get to her, and she took the pills." She frowned then. "I wonder what stopped her from fighting back once the baby was safe."

"Torture, maybe."

"Pardon?"

"Maybe she was afraid if she reneged on the agreement, the killer would torture her until she couldn't bear it and gave up the baby again."

"But once she was dead—"

"The killer couldn't get to Annette. The lock on the door is computer-driven—you must have the code to get into the room. Only Lena and Stephanie have the code. And Lena could leave the baby in there because it's completely childproof. Annette's mattress is on the floor, the outlets have child plugs, there is no other furniture, just a plastic play desk and tons of toys. Annette could have cried herself to sleep alone in there until Stephanie arrived—

that's the worst that could have happened."

"Oh," Casey murmured. Then she shook her head. "That's what I know. And..."

"And?"

"I think she might have saved me tonight. But I still don't understand. Why would someone come after me? Unless the man skulking around my neighbor's yard is just your run-of-the-mill peeping Tom, creep, or burglar."

He hesitated again.

"Oh, please. Come on. I don't know you, and you just convinced me to tell you I had a long conversation with a ghost. You came here. You came to me. You accused me of all kinds of things, and everything you know about me is boringly true. Have the decency to tell me what is going on," Casey said. She hadn't realized she was so angry until she stood, slamming her palms down on the table and speaking to him with her face just inches from his.

"Sorry," she said, moving back.

But he was smiling. "Good. You need to be fierce. You know what's going on. My cousin was murdered. And you know more about it than I do."

"Yes, but—"

"I knew Lena wouldn't kill herself. But forensically and by law, there was absolutely no way to prove it. She took the pills, and there was no sign the house had been broken into, or she had been forced in any way. She succeeded in her objective—she saved her baby. But I do believe whoever is behind this intends to kill Stephanie and the baby *and* anyone who gets in their way. I'm not sure what they're afraid of. They must realize you'd be a laughingstock if you went to the papers or the police and told people that Lena came to you and told you what had happened. But now that we know, we look for a way to prove it. I was frustrated, but I work with great people. We found out about the death of William Marley. And the man who founded our unit happens to be in the right circles in politics no matter who is at the helm. He managed to get us an exhumation order. Besides that, I believed from the get-go that Lena's killer—and William's and Anthony's—had to be someone in the corporation. Someone not happy with the way it's being run, or who wants to take over completely. There's only one family member left on the board. Justin Marceau. But he has his title, and he takes part in their marketing and promotion. Right now, they're heavily invested in the pharmaceutical drug trade. Elijah, Anthony, and Lena weren't as concerned with profits as they were with the wonders the right drugs could do for people—curing illnesses and prolonging life. So, there's Justin for one. And then there's the rest of the board. Barton Quincy, Harry Miller, and Larry Swenson. Barton has seniority, and he's the director of operations. Larry Swenson is his assistant—basically up after Barton—and Harry Miller's title is sales director."

"How did they get into the house? I saw cameras—"

"Amazingly, there was a blackout in the footage around the time Lena was killed. And according to the board, they were all together at the offices in the CBD when Lena died. Except for Justin, who came over early to warn Lena about what the board planned to discuss at the meeting. And he and Gail Reeves, the housekeeper, ran into each other at the bookstore in the Garden District. Justin gave her a ride back to the house. It was her afternoon off."

"Is Gail still there now, with Stephanie and the baby?"

He nodded. "Don't worry. Her alibi was airtight. Her book club had a meeting. Three people let me know she was there the entire time. One problem, of course, is Justin. I don't know if he's outright guilty or guilty of collaboration. Or if he's in danger." He shrugged. "I have a full-time security guard at the house. I hired a few retired agents. I know three of them, and they're on duty twenty-four-seven."

"Good," Casey murmured. "But back to me—"

"I saw Barton Quincy staring at your shop today. He and Justin were together at the coffee shop by your place. It seemed a distance to go for coffee from the CBD. Barton said something about needing something in the French Quarter."

"Well, that is feasible."

"It is." He scrubbed a hand down his face. "I'm sorry. I do believe everything you've told me. I had to be...sure. You'd be surprised by the number of naïve people who need money and get suckered by criminals. And while you might have had a run-of-the-mill peeping Tom back there, burglar or whatever—you may be in danger."

They were both quiet for a minute.

"Aren't you going to tell me you can take care of yourself?" he asked her.

Casey laughed softly. "No. I'm good at a lot of things. My best defense against anything bad is screaming like a banshee. I've never taken Kung Fu, and I've never been to a shooting range. I don't even like carving up meat."

He smiled at that. "Okay. Good."

"That's good?"

"Yep. You won't give me a hard time when I want you protected."

"And what is your plan here?" she asked.

"I'm not sure yet," he told her.

"Okay."

They sat in silence for another few minutes. He was thinking—obviously. But she was beginning to feel a bit awkward.

"Uh, would you like some coffee?" she asked.

A slow smile crept onto his lips. When he wanted to be, he could be nice. And that slow smile of his was almost...charming.

Maybe *charming* wasn't the word.

Seductive.

"You would like coffee, right?"

"Dinner," he said.

"Oh, well, I'm not sure what I have—" She tucked a stray strand of hair behind her ear and licked her lips. His eyes followed the movement, and she could have sworn she saw his eyes darken.

"This is New Orleans. Restaurants abound. Let's go to dinner."

"Dinner. Oh. Okay. It's getting a bit late—"

"This is New Orleans," he repeated.

"Are you asking me out to dinner?" she asked.

"I am." He winked.

"I'm not dressed—"

"I do believe you're one of those people who could wear a potato sack and still look fine," he said lightly. "We won't go anywhere fancy. Just out. There's a place off Magazine Street—"

"Hmm, people sometimes dress up on Magazine Street."

"I said *off* Magazine," he told her. "Family place. The owners are friends. He's first-generation Italian, and her family is Creole. Great, casual food."

"You sold me," Casey said.

"Make sure to lock up."

She locked her door, and as they were leaving through the main entrance, Miss Lilly came out of her apartment, smiling as she saw them.

"I see you found Casey okay, Ryder," she said.

"I did. Thank you for sending me through, Miss Lilly. As much as I appreciate your help, please don't let anyone else in. There have been some break-ins in the neighborhood."

"Oh, my! Well, thank you for telling me. I'll make sure the place is locked. And I'll tell the others. My, my, what a pretty couple you two make! Good to see you going out, Casey." She looked at Ryder. "This girl just spends too much time working. Not that I don't love the shop. I do. Anyway, you two go on out on your date. I'll see we all know we need to keep the main doors locked up good and tight."

"Oh, Miss Lilly, we're not—" Casey began. But she *was* going out on a date...

"We're really just friends, Miss Lilly," she corrected.

They weren't even friends.

Miss Lilly waved a hand in the air. "Get on out so I can lock up and get back to my program."

"Will do. A pleasure," Ryder told her.

They walked down the path to the street. Casey automatically started toward her little hybrid car, but Ryder said, "Mind if I drive? I know where I'm going."

"Ah, fine."

He opened the passenger door for her, and she slid in. Her arm grazed his as she did, and she felt a current of sensation rush through her, nearly causing goose bumps. He walked around to the driver's seat and was quiet as he pulled out onto the street.

"So, hmm. How long have you been an FBI agent?" Casey asked him.

"Four years. Before that, I was a detective in Baltimore."

"Baltimore? I got the impression you were from Louisiana."

"I am. But I went to college up there and stayed and became a cop. And then a detective. And then I went to the academy and right into the Krewe." He was watching the road, but he shrugged and looked at her quickly. "I saw my first ghost when my grandfather died. We were close. My dad was a cop, and one day, my grandfather's ghost warned him that one of their supposed snitches was in on the hard stuff himself. Since my dad was suspicious, the snitch arranged for an accident. Because he knew, my dad avoided the shootout intended for him in an alley. The problem when I worked as a detective in Baltimore is a lot like the problem we have here. You can't go to court, claiming a ghost told you what happened."

"No, I read somewhere that they ruled out spectral evidence after the witch trials in the Massachusetts Bay Colony," Casey said.

"And it's a good thing. People can make up anything."

"But you don't think I'm making anything up."

He glanced her way again.

"I know you're not."

They'd reached the restaurant.

It was off the main street, rustic and charming with picnic tables outside and nicely manicured foliage. Casey couldn't believe there was a restaurant she hadn't been to in the city, but New Orleans was filled with quaint little neighborhoods within neighborhoods, and she believed the restaurant catered to locals rather than tourists.

A middle-aged woman met them at the hostess stand and greeted Ryder warmly, clearly delighted to see him. She seemed happy to meet Casey, as well.

"So, you finally bring a beautiful girl to my restaurant," the woman said. "I'm Felice Barone—Felice Beauchamp Barone since we are Creole and Italian. The best of both, I believe! My husband and I, we are the owners. Owners and operators, cooks, busboys, and bottle washers," she said cheerfully. "I am delighted to meet you," she told Casey. She grew serious, looking at Ryder. "I thought you went back north. Back to work after...I am still so sorry, *cher.*"

"I did, but I'm back to give Stephanie a hand," Ryder said. "And, of course, if I am trying to impress a friend, I bring her here."

They chatted for a few more minutes and were then seated at an inside table. Casey hadn't cared where they sat when offered inside or outside seating. Then again, Ryder hadn't asked her. He had pointed to the table he wanted, causing Felice Barone to laugh. "This one, he thinks he's Italian. The old mob men, they had to make sure they were facing the door. You never have your back to the door."

"She's right. I like my back to the wall," Ryder said.

"An FBI thing?" Casey asked him.

"No." He chuckled. "I think I saw *The Godfather* at an impressionable age. But yeah, just a smart thing when you never know who you may run into—or who may be looking for you."

Felice had given them a corner square table so both could have their backs to the wall and then left them, assuring them that their waitress was one of her best.

"You can't honestly believe anyone is after me in an off-the-beaten-path restaurant, do you?" Casey asked when Felice was gone.

"No. If you go through that kind of trouble to make a murder look like suicide, you probably wouldn't ruin it by publicly attacking someone."

"Good. It will be great to eat without...watching the door," Casey said.

Their waitress arrived. She was pleasant and knew Ryder and greeted him warmly. She gave them the list of specials, suggesting that one have a Creole dish, and the other an Italian specialty so they could split them.

Ryder looked politely at Casey.

"I don't care what I eat," she said. "I mean, I'm sure it's going to be wonderful, whatever it is."

"Crawfish etouffee—it's the best here. And..."

"Lasagna!" Casey said.

"You're fond of Italian food?" Ryder asked her.

"I watched a lot of *Garfield* cartoons."

"Pardon?"

"*Garfield*! The cat, from Jim Davis."

"Oh, right. The fat cat that loves lasagna."

"You watch *Garfield*?" She smiled.

"Two-year-old little cousin," he reminded her with a grin.

"Ah."

The food came quickly, and it was wonderful. They both tried to be polite and wound up trying to put helpings of each dish on each other's plates at the same time, touching, apologizing, and then spilling food. But they finally got it together.

Casey was especially enjoying the crawfish etouffee when she looked up.

Someone was coming in the front door—someone who slipped in as a man was exiting.

Someone who wasn't alive.

"Ryder, I see her. She's just coming in. Do you see her?" Casey whispered.

He did. He almost stood, but apparently controlled himself quickly enough. He watched as Lena came up, gave Casey a quick smile, and leaned across the table to envelop Ryder in her arms.

Then she sat across from him.

Chapter 5

Ryder felt a wave of emotion rush through him. He'd wanted to see Lena, even in death—her spirit rather than the angelic and still form of her body. He initially hadn't thought her spirit had remained.

And mature adult or not, he'd not been able to fight the feeling of hurt and anger that had swept through him when he realized that her spirit *had* remained, but she'd chosen to go to someone else.

She had known he saw the dead. She'd been the one to help him *not* feel crazy when they were kids. She hadn't seen what he had, but she'd sensed things. And she had believed in him.

Now, she looked at him across the table.

"First, Casey, thank you," Lena said. "Ryder, I'm sorry."

"Why didn't you come to me?" Ryder whispered. "I was there in the house...right after. I was at the autopsy. The funeral. I stayed..."

"Ryder, I'm sorry," Lena said again. "But...well, frankly, it's not easy becoming a ghost. Maybe we don't want to accept it. Perhaps we just don't want to believe we're dead. Or maybe it's like a new birth, and we need to figure out how to exist in the world. It took me a while to...to understand that I could move and try to speak with people. At first...it was like sleep—a deep, deep sleep. Then I was in the cemetery and so afraid and alone...and, well, I finally made a few friends. Um, dead ones. And they helped me. By then...you were gone. And then I saw Casey. I'd met her at her store, and I knew she was kind and honest and...I'm afraid I sent her to the hospital from fright. But then I tried again, and I heard you were back, Ryder."

"I'm here, and we're working hard on this," Ryder assured her. "Casey has filled me in. Lena, I won't let it go. I will not let anything happen to Stephanie or Annette, I promise. But can you tell me anything about your attacker at all? Casey said you're sure it was a man. Do you know how he got in?"

"I have no idea. I keep the door locked. Gail keeps the door locked. Ryder, I was so scared, but not for myself. If anything had happened to Annette..."

As she broke off, he noted Casey was furtively looking around, possibly wondering how Ryder was conversing so easily without worrying about looking at Lena.

Experience. He toyed with his food and glanced her way now and then.

He knew she likely realized it looked as if he were just talking to Casey.

"I will not let anything happen to Annette," Ryder said firmly. "I swear it—on my life."

Lena smiled at him. "I believe you. You're my Superman, cousin. 'Truth, justice, and the American way,'" she quoted. "And I know you, Ryder. You'd be in this if it had been me or someone else—it's what you do. And I'm grateful for you."

"Well, let's see where we get," he said. "I need help from you. I need to find whoever did this to you."

"And Anthony," Lena added bitterly. "I never believed he just stretched too far to look at something and fell off a twenty-story building. And he definitely wasn't the type to commit suicide. But then again, neither was I—though we know what happened there. Ryder, you're my only hope," she said softly. "I mean," she added quickly, looking at Casey, "Casey, you were wonderful. I know you went to Stephanie. You must have since Ryder is here with you. And I've tried. I love my sister so much. I think she might have sensed something when I tried to speak with her, but she just doesn't...she doesn't see...the dead."

Ryder almost forgot himself, reaching out across the table to touch Lena's hand. But he winced and then drummed his fingers and glanced Casey's way again. She gave him a forced smile as if she were learning the art of conversing with the dead in public.

"Stephanie has put her trust in me. She's still at such a loss. You were her only sister."

"Maybe you can convince her I'm...okay. I mean, I'm here, but I will be able to find peace. They've been telling me—my dead friends—there comes a time when we all go, and there is goodness and something after. A light. They claim they've seen loved ones come for other loved ones. I mean, I haven't, but...I'll be with

Anthony. I must be able to tell him Annette is going to be fine. Ryder... How could anyone want money so much they'd kill like this? Elijah would never have handed control of the company to Anthony if he'd known it was a curse. Elijah was a good man, such a dear man. He believed in business, but he was also fair. And he made things people desperately needed easily available to them. But...is that it, Ryder? This was all over money?"

"Money and power," Ryder said. "Or so I believe. But I need to know more. And I think we're dealing with someone who is a true psychopath. Someone organized, capable of appearing perfectly normal—even in relationships—but lacking any true feelings or emotion."

"Someone who could kill without blinking and make sure they did it right," Lena said dryly.

"And it had to be someone close to you, the house, the family, or the corporation. That's why I need your help. And any little detail will help."

Lena glanced at Casey before answering and said softly, "I'm sorry. I'm sorry I dragged you into this. I'm just so frightened now for my sister and my baby."

"I'm all right," Casey said. And, looking at her, Ryder thought she was. Yes, she had been panicked and in denial. That might indicate that she was a normal person. How else did one react to suddenly realizing there was, in an already strange world, another world around her?

And she might be in casual clothing, but he hadn't lied to her. She was a beautiful, young woman, her best feature being her eyes. Their color was so blue it hinged on violet, and the depths of them always seemed to speak volumes.

Admittedly, he'd first thought her a quack, using her looks to help lure those who might believe she had a *friend line* to the beyond.

And now...

"Seriously," Casey added softly. "I want to help."

Lena smiled and said, "Thank you," softly to Casey and then turned back to Ryder. "I think he was about six feet tall. And I believe he was wearing contact lenses, making sure I couldn't recognize him if things went south. I don't know. He was in black—sweats, I believe. All-encompassing black. His hood covered his hair. I think he even had a voice box. It was all raspy as if it were coming through something. And he had wires around his face and neck under the sweatsuit top. I could still see them. I don't know how he got in. Gail was out—it was her afternoon off. Stephanie was coming over, but not for an hour or so. All I could do was bargain."

"You saved Annette's life," Ryder assured her.

They all fell silent. Felice came back to their table, pointing at their dishes.

"What's the matter? Suddenly you don't like the food?" she asked.

"Oh, no, the food is delicious," Casey assured her.

"Delicious as always," Ryder said.

Felice was frowning. "I don't know why you like this table. It's cold here! There must be something wrong with the air-conditioner. We must get that fixed. Would you like to move?"

"No, this is my table, and I love it, Felice," Ryder said. "You know that."

Felice smiled suddenly. "Look at the two of you. So close and...*whispery*. I guess you don't feel the cold. Ah, young love. You two can cuddle for warmth."

She left, and Lena laughed.

"You two do make an adorable couple."

"We're not a couple," Ryder and Casey said in unison.

"Well, okay, but you're both beautiful people, so...you would make a beautiful couple. Hey, trust me. Don't mess around. Life is short. I learned that saying to be the absolute truth."

"Oh, Lena," Ryder murmured.

Lena frowned and spoke in a panic. "I'm going to fade!"

"What?" Casey asked. "Fade?"

Lena shook her head. "It takes...well, learning. I'm learning to be a good ghost with a lot of help. But still...thank you both. We'll talk tomorrow. Oh! Ryder, you have Annette and Stephanie. And now, you can't let anything happen to Casey."

The last was barely a whisper. Casey's name sounded almost like a soft hiss.

Suddenly, Lena was gone.

Casey stared at Ryder. "Ghosts fade?"

"I can explain what I think I know," he told her. "I know many spirits, but...I've never been a ghost, and it seems the experience can be different from...ghost to ghost. From what I understand, it's not easy for them at first to...materialize, I guess. She'll need to rest, to gain strength again. Old ghosts can stay for longer periods of time. Some can even push buttons and sometimes move things. It's like anything—we learn to crawl, walk, and then run."

"You're so easy with all of this," she whispered.

"You think it's hard as an adult? Try being a kid telling someone their grandfather had given him warnings when that grandfather had been dead and interred for two years." He shrugged and smiled at her. "It takes time," he said softly.

"You mean...I may see other ghosts now?"

"When they choose to be seen."

"Oh." She groaned.

"It gets better. For tonight, I guess we should finish dinner. Then I'll get you back home."

"Take your time. I have a feeling I'll be up all night."

She would be up all night—listening. Afraid.

Ryder noticed the tension creeping into her face and body. "Maybe you shouldn't stay at your place."

"I could go to Lauren's house," she mused. Then she shook her head vehemently. "No. She lives with her grandmother, and I wouldn't put either of them in danger. Even though I'm not sure I'm in danger, I'm not brave enough to find out. I will lock all the doors, I'll—"

"No. We'll go by your place, you can get a few things, and we'll go to the Marceau house."

"What?"

It seemed the logical answer, especially since Ryder had no other solution. And while he doubted that Lena's killer would break into a house and risk capture, he'd somehow gotten into the Marceau house before.

"Look," Ryder said earnestly, "I promised to look after Stephanie and Annette. But now I'm worried about you, too. And you have the common sense to accept the fact you *might* be in danger. So, if we are all in one place, it will be much easier on me."

She seemed to weigh her options. "I still need to go to work in the morning."

"I'll get you there. But you can't be alone. And tomorrow, I'll get some help."

"You have friends with the NOPD?"

"I do. But I'm not calling them."

"Then—?"

He grinned and shrugged. "I have people."

She frowned at that, curious—and seemingly unconvinced. "I can't just go and stay at the Marceau house. I mean, I'm not invited—"

"You're invited. I'm inviting you."

"I don't think Stephanie liked me."

"Stephanie is still hurt. She's grieving, and you freaked her out. She'll want you there. She can't know the truth the way we do, doesn't quite understand, but she always knew that..."

"That?"

"Sometimes, it runs in families. We had a mutual great-grandparent who... Well, if it is something in the DNA, she was the one who passed it down. Stephanie knows there are people who *sense* things. She knows that I do. I didn't know much about you when I left the Marceau house after you did—"

"You were the relative—her side of the family—watching the baby when I was there."

"I was."

"I can't—"

"You must."

She sat back, shaking her head and biting her lip. Then she bowed her head slightly.

"Please," he said.

Her head still lowered, she nodded. She looked up and noted, "You still have crawfish on your plate."

"I'll take care of that," he told her. "You're leaving lasagna," he added.

"I'll take care of that," she said.

He smiled, and they finished their food.

He paid the tab, and they both assured Felice that the food had been beyond wonderful. And that they'd be back. He was afraid during the drive, and even as he waited for Casey to pack up a few things, that she would protest again.

But she didn't. She was silent during the trip to the Marceau house, and he didn't try to make idle conversation. At the mansion, he used the remote to open the gates and parked in the drive at the side of the house.

Stephanie was on the steps, chatting with Arnold Benson, one of the old friends Ryder had hired to watch the house. Little two-year-old Annette was in her arms. Stephanie was frowning, but the baby called out, "Hi!" and stretched out her arms.

"I'll explain," Ryder said briefly as he took Casey's small case and walked to the door. He was ready to take Annette from Stephanie, certain that she was reaching for him.

She wasn't.

Her outstretched arms were for Casey.

"Um, sorry. Hi. May I?" Casey asked Stephanie.

Stephanie didn't answer. She let Annette go.

The child was truly adorable. Like her mother had been, she was blonde. Little ringlets of a sunshine color framed her face. Her eyes were powder blue. Annette was, however, a typical two-year-old, wanting what she wanted.

"She knows you. She likes you," Stephanie said.

"Lena had her in the shop a few times. I set her up with a little tea set, and we played This Little Piggy Went to Market and a few other games," Casey explained. She held the baby and smiled as Annette giggled, said something in her baby language, and then showed Casey her nose.

Arnold Benson cleared his throat. Ryder quickly apologized and introduced him.

"An old friend. Arnold Benson was with the field office here for years. Arnie, Casey, Casey, Arnie."

Arnie smiled at Casey. Casey smiled back. Ryder figured she approved of his choice for a guard.

Arnie had shaved his head and looked as if he were retired from the World Wrestling Federation rather than the FBI.

"Nice to meet you," Casey said.

"Pleasure. So, is this lovely lady what really brought you back to NOLA?" Arnie asked Ryder.

"Casey is a friend. And I've been honest with you, Arnie. You know what brought me back."

"Yeah," Arnie said softly, glancing at Stephanie. "I just came out to do a grounds check. I have a little nook in the library where I can see more than a satellite can. Ryder, you did one hell of a job getting cameras installed in this place. I almost feel like a cheat, taking your money. I spend most of the day just watching the screens, and this lovely lady over here"—he paused to indicate Stephanie—"keeps me fed way better than I tend to feed myself."

"I've been in the nook and checked all the screens myself," Ryder said. "It is a pretty good setup, if I do say so."

"It's fine for you to say so. And also fine that you keep paying me," Arnie said lightly.

"Not a problem," Ryder assured him. "Let's get on in, shall we?"

"I'm just doing my walk-around," Arnie said.

"Thanks," Ryder told him.

"After that, you can find me in my nook."

They went into the house.

Stephanie looked at Casey. "You have an overnight bag. Are you staying here?"

"With your permission, of course. Ryder suggested it made sense."

Stephanie glanced at Ryder but then smiled at Casey. "You really did know my sister."

"I did know her, yes. Not well. But she came to the shop several times. I wouldn't have lied to you."

"No one can lie to a two-year-old and get away with it," Stephanie said lightly. "And, speaking of the two-year-old, it's late. I'm going to get her to bed." Stephanie hesitated and glanced at Casey. "If he brought you here...well, I know my cousin. He's vetted you, and there's a good reason you're here, especially since I'm sure you have your own home."

Casey nodded.

"Okay then, go on up the grand staircase. It's a beautiful house, and I can't tell you how much I hate it. The strangest thing is...neither Anthony nor Lena was into money or material things. And here I am. But whoever did this isn't going to win." She dropped her chin, eyes downcast. "I'm a coward, so I'd consider taking Annette and running, but I'm afraid we'd be hunted down. Annette and I must be here. Especially until..." Her voice trailed, and she turned to Ryder.

"Put the baby to bed," he told her. "We'll talk after."

"I have her crib in my room," Stephanie said. "Right next to my bed."

"Then we'll talk in the morning," Ryder said.

Stephanie nodded and took Annette from Casey.

"Make yourself at home, Casey. Please. The kitchen is wide open. Gail Reeves lives on the property, but she has the old carriage house out back." Stephanie paused. "I don't even let Gail in anymore until she calls and tells me she's ready to come over. Anyway, sorry, I'm talking away. And this kid needs to go down for the night. I'll see you in the morning."

She turned and started for the stairs, but then turned back and looked at Casey.

"You've seen my sister, right? Her spirit or...ghost?"

"I—yes," Casey said.

"And now I've seen her, too, Stephanie," Ryder said. "We are going to solve Lena's murder."

Stephanie smiled. "I know you will. Just do so quickly, please. Okay? I'm going nuts here."

This time, she continued up the stairs.

Ryder looked at Casey.

"Come on up. I'll give you the Blue Room. Goes with your eyes." He winked.

"Great. I'm all into matching," Casey said dryly.

He carried her bag and led the way. The Blue Room was in the west wing, across from another guest room—the Gold Room in his case. All the rooms were named for colors except for the master suite—which had a plaque on it that said: *Master Suite.*

No one was in it now. Stephanie wouldn't sleep where her sister had died.

But Stephanie was in the baby's room, also in the west wing.

He liked being near those he was watching over.

Even with a trusted guard on duty.

Even with the elaborate system he'd installed.

"Blue Room," he said, opening the door and leading Casey in. The carpet and drapes were navy blue, the bed covering a softer pale blue.

"It is—blue," she said.

"I think it's probably comfortable—"

"Oh, no. It's lovely. I was just noting that it is well, blue."

He grinned at her. "Bathroom is right there to the side. The old man had all the old dressing rooms turned into bathrooms. Elijah." He hesitated and shrugged. "He was a good man. Anyway, you're welcome to prowl the kitchen below if you get hungry. I'm across the hall in the Gold Room if you should need anything. Or if you'd like something, I can get it for you now."

"No, I'm going to try to sleep, thanks."

"Okay, then."

He looked at her for a moment. He'd just met her. She'd angered him to no end when he thought her a fraud.

And now...

He liked her. *Really* liked her. And that was…unexpected.

He noticed how her hair fell around her face in soft waves. How her eyes studied everything intensely. She was thoughtful and quick-witted. Smart and intuitive.

And he'd seen her in a bikini. Ryder smiled at the memory.

But he'd put her into extreme danger. Unless she had already done that to herself.

It didn't matter. This was no time for his instinctive sex drive to kick in.

"Good night, then," he said quickly. "Um, just amble down to the kitchen in the morning whenever you like."

"Thank you," she told him.

He smiled and closed the door behind him, hurrying to his room.

He had worried so much when he first arrived. He hadn't wanted to leave Stephanie and the baby alone.

People would know about William Marley's exhumation.

His presence had been required at the cemetery. And before that...

He'd been so angry when Stephanie had thought a quack *medium* had come to her. He'd taken off, trusting in Greg Farley, the morning shift guard, to keep the home safe.

Hovering at the house wouldn't solve anything.

But...

He'd seen one of his prime suspects studying Casey's shop. And there had been someone in the bushes at her home when she was out alone in the pool. She'd known it—and Lena had known it.

And now, he knew what had happened from Lena herself.

He decided to put a call through. He could get help when he needed it.

And he needed it now.

* * * *

The bed was amazingly comfortable. She'd brought her own things, but she felt as if she were staying in a hotel room. Anything anyone might desire was available in the bathroom, from toothpaste to soap, to shampoo, conditioner, and a hairdryer.

She wondered if—in the past—company executives had stayed at the mansion. Or if they were due to come again.

Not anytime soon, she imagined.

Despite the luxury of her accommodations, she lay awake.

She wondered if Lena would show up, but she didn't. Maybe she was as polite in death as she was in life and not about to disturb anyone trying to sleep.

Casey still couldn't believe that she was here. Even after the shock of seeing and accepting Lena Marceau as a ghost, she had never expected a day like today. And the last thing she wanted to do was think about the strange ghost-seeing FBI agent, who had come into her life like an exploding volcano—and become her most curious ally.

As she had become his.

She stared at the dark ceiling, remembering his voice. The way he stood, the way he'd held her when she burst into her apartment building, dripping...

How he hadn't minded giving her a real apology, or the fact that he took her safety so seriously.

She was a link to Lena—and Lena's killer.

Still...

She liked him. Too much. She was thinking about him in many ways...

Too much.

Finally, she turned on the television and fell asleep at last to a rerun of *Cheers*.

She woke late, at least for her. It was almost eight o'clock. For a minute, she blinked and then remembered her surroundings and why she was there. She rose, showered, dug into her little bag, and dressed for the day.

It was still so damned hot. She had brought—ironically, she thought—a blue halter dress and a black sweater to wear when the air-conditioning kicked in.

Jared and Lauren really liked to blast it at the shop.

Ready for the day, she left her room and hurried downstairs to the kitchen, where she found Ryder and Stephanie and the baby.

Annette was in her highchair, playing with her cereal as much as eating it. The highchair was pulled up to a small kitchen table. Stephanie was on one side, Ryder on the other.

Apparently, Annette loved to say, "Hi!" because she greeted Casey with the word and a big smile and then said, "Hi!" again.

"Hi, you," Casey said, ruffling the little girl's hair.

Annette took her hand.

"Good morning. Did you sleep all right?" Stephanie asked her.

"Yes, thank you. The room is lovely."

Ryder was on the phone with someone, and he lifted a hand and gave her a smile, indicating he'd be off soon.

"Coffee?" Stephanie asked.

"I would love some. Can I do anything? You don't need to wait on me."

"No, no—the pot is right there. I'm not much of a cook. I'm afraid breakfast is cereal or toaster waffles."

"Cereal is great, thank you," Casey said.

Her cell phone rang as Stephanie poured her a cup of coffee. She excused herself and dug into her purse for her mobile.

It was Miss Lilly. She winced. She should have told her concerned neighbor that she'd be away.

"I'm so sorry, Miss Lilly. I'm fine. Just staying with a friend."

Ryder had finished his call and was looking at her.

"Oh, don't apologize, darling," Miss Lilly said. "Joe and I are delighted you apparently spent the night with that tall, dark, and devilishly handsome fellow. I've been telling you for ages you can't just work and read and swim. I mean, I love swimming, but—"

Casey wanted to sink under the table. Lilly was speaking loudly, and Casey was sure Ryder could hear every word.

"I mean, you're a young, lovely thing. Sweet as molasses, too. Oh, wait, not sticky sweet. I mean, you have a mind on you, and you're smart, too. But everyone needs a sex life," Lilly said with a giggle. "Even oldsters."

Casey knew she visibly winced.

"Joe and I...we just wanted to make sure you were okay."

"I'm fine, Miss Lilly. I may be away for a few days."

"Ah, you little scamp. You have fun! Life is short. You'll have to tell me all about it when I see you next."

"Um...sure, of course. Miss Lilly, I have to get back to—"

"Oh, get back to it. I didn't mean to interrupt."

Ryder was laughing. The baby was giggling, and even Stephanie must have heard Lilly because she was smiling, too.

"I'm so sorry," Casey said, explaining to Stephanie. "One of my neighbors. She's a sweetheart, worrying about me, really. And I...I'm sorry."

"Hey, what are you sorry for? It's nice that a neighbor cares," Stephanie said.

Ryder had a smirk on his face. He passed her the box of cereal as Stephanie set down a bowl and a cup of coffee.

"It is nice," he said. "She apparently likes us both. And me, from just meeting her at her main door."

Stephanie smiled and joined them again as she looked at Casey. "Have you seen Lena this morning? She must have liked you very much. I mean, Annette likes you."

"I haven't seen her this morning. But...I know how she loved you and appreciates you," Casey said earnestly.

"Well, I hope she comes to the house sometime," Stephanie said softly. "I want her to know how much I love her—will always love her. She was my only sibling. It feels like a part of me was cut away. I'm so grateful I have Annette. And so scared."

"Stephanie—" Ryder began.

They were cut short by the buzzer.

"That's Jackson," Ryder said, pushing his chair back. "Excuse me. I'll just let him in."

He left the kitchen to answer the intercom and open the gate.

"Jackson?" Casey said to Stephanie.

"Jackson Crow, Ryder's field director. He's going to hang with the baby and me today."

"Oh," Casey said and smiled. "Um, nice."

Stephanie laughed. "Jackson is great. He's six-foot-something of Native American and Irish and incredibly good-looking. And married. Very married, with two kids, and a spectacular wife who manages and juggles the Krewe of Hunters. You'd be amazed by some of the strange activities that go on around the country." She was quiet for a minute. "And the departed who stay because they need help or need to help someone else. Like Lena," she added softly. She squared her shoulders then and stood ready to meet the newcomer.

Annette started to cry, wanting out of her chair. Casey instinctively went to get her and remembered that Stephanie was her guardian. She asked, "May I?"

"Oh, please. I miss her little daycare most of all in this insanity of being so careful. She needs more fun than I can really supply."

Casey rescued the baby, who wanted to run out of the kitchen and to the door. She moved like lightning, but Casey kept up.

Ryder introduced her to Jackson Crow, who seemed to be everything Stephanie had said.

He was also good with children, saying, "Hi," to Annette in answer to her every "Hi!"

He studied Casey and was friendly and cordial, thanking her for being there.

"What a way to come into this," he said. "But then, it never is easy."

"We're going to head to the French Quarter," Ryder told him. "Casey opens the shop at ten, so I guess we need to get going. Bobby O'Hara is in the library now, keeping an eye on the video screens. Come in there for just a minute. I'll introduce you."

Annette raced after Ryder and Jackson, and Stephanie and Casey raced after Annette. Annette ran to the corner to play with some books. Jackson and Casey were both introduced to Bobby O'Hara, another of Ryder's old friends. Bobby, in contrast to Arnie Benson, had a full head of white hair and a cavalier mustache.

Casey greeted him pleasantly, but as she spoke, her eyes wandered around the handsome library before stopping to hear what was being said.

There was a row of pictures on the wall.

"Are you all right, Casey?" Ryder asked.

"Um, sorry. Who are those men?" she asked.

"They're all on the board of directors," Stephanie supplied.

"Why?" Ryder asked Casey.

"I—I've seen them. Two of them, anyway. They've been in my shop."

Chapter 6

Casey stared at the pictures.

Yes, she had seen two of the men. She walked toward the photos on the side wall. A desk sat against that wall, while the rest of the walls were filled with shelves and books—other than the security nook Ryder had created.

Above the desk hung a sign that read: *Past and present leaders of Marceau Industries Incorporated. We thank them.*

"They came to the shop when? Who came? Which men?"

Casey pointed to two of the pictures. One was of an older man, another of a man about forty. They hadn't come in together. They had come in at different times.

"That's Barton Quincy, the new CEO. And that's his assistant, Larry Swenson," Ryder said. He caught her gently by the shoulders and turned her around to face him.

"Casey, when did they come in? Did they see you...with Lena?"

She shook her head. "They were both in before I saw Lena in the shop. I mean, Lena's ghost. They were in that night, though. They both bought a few things and talked about a reading."

Ryder released her and then paused. His eyes were on the wall, focused on a section that included past leaders of the company.

"Ryder?" she said.

He pointed to another picture. "That's William Marley. The man we had exhumed, whose cremains are being studied in Mississippi."

"Oh," she murmured.

"We're still waiting on results, but tests take time, especially when you're dealing with a corpse that has been..."

"Baking in the Louisiana sun," Stephanie supplied.

"To put it gently, yes," Ryder said. "Jackson—"

"Angela has done extensive background checks on every man on the board," Jackson said. "Nothing in the paperwork helps. Justin Marceau was busted as a kid for pot. Larry Swenson had a lot of parking tickets. Expensive, but a far cry from premeditated murder. Harry Miller didn't even have a traffic infraction against him. After a month of searching, the only thing she could discover was the unusual way that William Marley died. Suffering from a sudden heart attack without having any problems with heart disease at all."

"Stephanie, I think you need to call a board meeting," Ryder said.

"But I—I don't know anything. I approve or deny decisions as the baby's trust officer, but I don't know much. I was never a businessperson. The only thing I ever knew was that both Anthony and Lena were passionate about keeping the price of life-saving drugs down as much as possible. And I believed it was all just a formality, naming me as Annette's legal guardian. Anthony and Lena were young. I never thought it could really happen. I heard Anthony arguing with one of the men once. I don't even know which one. He said that, yes, you had to pay staff and have laboratories, but they didn't need to make a lot of money off prescriptions that people need for heart conditions or diabetes or other such diseases. Anthony said he wasn't going to make money off the lives of others."

"It's okay. You'll just call the meeting to make sure the company can make money in other ways. Slight increases on their organic vitamins and other such items," Ryder said. "That will be it. The meeting will be to make everyone understand that you—as Annette's guardian—will veto any suggestion of a price increase in new or old drugs. Elijah was a smart old geezer. He created the board but kept ultimate control on all aspects. And that authority has now passed down to you and Annette. You can just say you're calling the meeting to make sure everyone knows the direction the company will be taking, and Marceau Industries Incorporated will honor the wishes of Elijah, Anthony, and Lena."

"Okay, but I don't think I can call a meeting for today. I believe Justin is in Biloxi, speaking with a chemist they want to hire," Stephanie said. "And I have no idea if the other guys are in the office or not."

"Tomorrow will be fine. For now, I'll head to the French Quarter with Casey, and Jackson will stay here and get some work done," Ryder said. He glanced at Jackson, and knew the man would have Angela dig deeper into every possible—and impossible—resource to find out more about Barton Quincy and Larry Swenson."

Casey looked at them all with a frown. "Wouldn't Justin be the one to benefit if...if he were the one who—?"

"Was around if something happened to me and Annette?" Stephanie said. "No, that's the odd thing. If something happens to both of us and there are only four board members left, it's an equal split. Elijah just wasn't close to Justin. When Justin asked for a job, he gave it to him. But he only got a position because he was a Marceau, and Elijah couldn't let a family member have nothing. So, he worked with Justin, and Justin *does* have a charming personality. It turned out he wasn't so bad when it came to marketing, advertising, and especially, personal appearances," she finished.

"I need to get to the shop," Casey murmured. "I open today."

"Okay, we're out," Ryder said.

"And we'll be on it from any angle we can find," Jackson assured him.

Ryder looked at Casey. "Time to get you to work."

"You're coming to work with me?"

He paused to let her see the seriousness of his words. "I'll be in or near the shop all day."

Her eyes rounded at his unspoken message. "You think someone might come after me. In a shop in the French Quarter?"

"I think someone will be watching you, and I want to see who. Also, with the meeting tomorrow, we may get something. And we should get some lab results back from the M.E. over in Mississippi. So for now...I'm your constant companion," Ryder said.

He was curious to see if she would object.

She didn't. She just glanced at her watch.

"Then we should get going."

* * * *

It was interesting, Casey thought, bringing Ryder into the shop with her, especially after what had happened the morning before. In the hours since, she had gotten to know him...

And it was strange that in the short time they'd spent together, she somehow felt ridiculously close to him.

Of course, he might end up saving her life. He was security.

But he was also more.

She really hadn't wanted to like him. But she did. And she sure as hell hadn't wanted to find him intriguing, compelling, and attractive.

Sexually attractive.

But she did.

She'd had a few weird dreams. They should have been about ghosts…being haunted.

They weren't. Her dreams hadn't been horror stories at all. Rather, they were fantasies. There had been something like an old disco ball sending rays of color everywhere, and she and Ryder had been dancing. He had been giving her that strange smile of his as if they shared something unique and special. It was an incredible secret and a bond that went deeper than any other could go. She felt the strength of him in every movement. In their dance, he pulled her close, his eyes both tender and aflame, and she thought they'd come closer and closer until... She had woken up.

Now, she was the first to arrive at the shop. Once she opened, Ryder took a seat in one of the comfortable chairs by the coffee and tea service until Jared and Lauren arrived.

He stood to greet them. "Uh—hi."

"Hi," the two said in unison, staring from him to Casey.

"It's all right," Casey said quickly. "We had a chance to speak yesterday. Ryder is with the FBI." She hesitated. "He and Lena Marceau were cousins."

Jared still looked protective and fierce, as much as someone who was almost a throwback to a love-all hippie could.

Lauren seemed curious and wary.

"And how does that affect you or the shop in any way?" Lauren asked. She looked at Ryder. "I have a cell phone on me, and I can hit *emergency call* with the twitch of my hand."

Casey laughed and went over to hug her and then Jared.

"What's going on? Really?" Jared asked.

"Lena Marceau was in the store several times," Casey explained. "We...we wound up having some serious conversations. I'm good with kids, so...we talked. She talked about her husband and about it being crazy having so much money. She didn't believe her husband fell off a building, and she was frightened for herself and Annette. I told her to talk to the police. She told *me* she had planned to. I was sad when I heard she'd killed herself. You know Jennie was convinced she saw ghosts at the cemetery. Then...I went to see Stephanie Harrow, the baby's guardian. And Ryder thought that..."

"I thought she was a sham, just tormenting Stephanie. Or worse," Ryder said. "I thought she might be part of something horribly devious like getting rid of Stephanie and the baby, too."

"But..." Lauren spoke and then looked confused. "Hey, I'm not FBI or anything—art major here—but even I know you look at the person who would benefit."

"There are four people who would benefit," Ryder explained. "But there's also murder for hire. Whoever is doing all this is in for the long-haul. But we discovered that another person in the higher-up section of the company might not have died of a simple heart attack. And I think someone started watching Casey. So...I'm here for a bit."

Lauren and Jared looked at each other.

"Well, we'll be nice and safe," Lauren said.

"Not that we've had trouble," Jared put in.

"But you never know. New Orleans is not without crime," Lauren said, but then she frowned. "You can't just arrest the four people?"

Ryder smiled at her. "Well, there's the Constitution. Innocent until proven guilty. And proving anyone guilty in this...it hasn't been easy. Anyway, I'll be in here for part of the day, and scouring the area the other parts. If I can help anyone in any way, just let me know."

"Nice. Thank you," Lauren said.

"I'm going to hang a few large canvases if you want to pitch in," Jared said.

"Sure."

A woman came in to browse the tee shirts, souvenirs, and jewelry. Casey spoke to her, showing her which goods were local, and explaining what some of the symbolic jewelry meant. Lauren spoke to another woman about a sketch of Jackson Square.

Ryder worked on the canvases with Jared. The two talked easily.

She heard Ryder tell Jared at one point, "Yeah, I have a degree. Criminology. I'm afraid I haven't an artistic bone in my body, but that doesn't mean I don't love art and music."

"Everyone has music," Jared assured him. "It's in the body, the blood, the mind, and the soul."

Ryder's phone rang, and he excused himself, walking outside and down the block. Casey watched him go.

Lauren was next to her where she stood behind the counter.

"Okay...nice!"

"Yes. I mean, it turns out he was just really upset. I guess I don't blame him. I suppose it was just something eating at me. We do have a shop where I do readings, and people often think that means you assume you're something you can't be. Anyway, Ryder was protecting his cousin, Stephanie Harrow, Lena Marceau's sister. And—"

"I'm glad he turned out to be nice. Because he is...well, he's employed, for one."

Lauren had been engaged for a while to a man who turned out to be using her for room and board.

"He's employed, yes," Casey said and laughed.

Lauren grinned. "And he has a damned good body."

"He seems to be in shape."

"Great face. Those eyes of his..."

Casey knew where this was going but smiled at her friend. "He is nice-looking."

"And he likes you."

"He's protecting me," she made clear.

"No, he *likes* you. You can see it in his eyes."

Casey thought about the short time they'd spent together. Their chemistry and conversation. The way he was not only with her but with his cousin and little Annette. He was kind, with a protective streak a mile wide. She knew it was fast, but she trusted what her feelings were telling her. "And I like him."

"Hmmm…" Lauren mused. "He's probably honorable and ethical and all that."

"I imagine he has some good qualities." Casey chuckled.

"Men like that don't come around every day, Casey," Lauren said, a seriousness replacing the levity of their conversation. "And you never just go out, which means the last time you were with someone was when you were seeing Sam Tourneau. He was nice enough, employed, good-looking..."

"And he only loved football." Casey remembered the sting of that breakup. "I like football. But I also enjoy music and my friends and...books and art and things besides sports. But we're still friends."

"Right. And he was a decent guy. But you don't go out a lot. I think this guy is cool, and you should get something going."

"He lives in Virginia or somewhere in that area," Casey reminded Lauren.

"Okay. So maybe he goes away in a bit. Seize the moment, my friend. I know what you should do if you worry about where things might go." Lauren's eyes widened. "Go mad for a few days. Don't let it get awkward. He's an agent. A guy on the move. So, premeditated sex."

"What?" Casey almost choked on her laughter.

"Just agree to sex, sex, and nothing but sex." Lauren giggled.

"I think you're mixing up your courtyard dramas." Casey rolled her eyes.

"I'm just talking about being upfront and honest. You like him. He likes you. Birds do it, bees do it... Have a thing while he's here."

"Oh, Lauren."

Casey hadn't realized Jared was standing nearby until she heard him laugh. "I like it! That may be my line. If Lauren would just be a good wing woman, I may try it on the hot girl playing the washboard at Pete's one of these days. Premeditated sex."

Casey groaned and was grateful when the shop door opened. A few members from a local retirees' club came in. They chatted, and then one turned to Jared and asked, "Where's our song?"

"Your song? Oh, you want your song," Jared said. He looked at Casey and Lauren. "Ready, ladies? This is one of our finest harmonies."

Casey winced inwardly. Their favorite song was from Blue Oyster Cult. *Don't Fear the Reaper.*

They did do excellent harmony with it.

But Casey didn't get a chance to answer. Jared had already gotten his guitar and started strumming. She and Lauren were behind the counter. Lauren flung an arm around Casey's shoulders and smiled, and they began the song.

Casey hoped Lena Marceau would not pick this time to come

by.

Luckily, she didn't see the ghost. Ryder, however, returned at the end of the tune, and while he had a strange expression on his face, he clapped along with the retirees. The group chatted and talked, and a couple of their members bought a few pieces.

The store emptied, and Ryder looked at them, moving his gaze from one to the other.

"Hm, do you people have a lunch or dinner break? Or whatever meal it is one has in the afternoon?"

"Oh, yeah, we cover for one another," Lauren said. "Why don't you and Casey go on out and get something? I had a big breakfast."

"I didn't," Jared said and then gulped as Lauren nudged him in the ribcage.

"But I'm not hungry yet," he added quickly. "You two go. And get back. Then, we'll go."

"Okay with you?" Ryder asked Casey.

"Sure."

"She has something to ask you. Or suggest," Lauren said.

Casey cast Lauren a scathing glare. Lauren smiled.

They started out of the store, and Ryder asked, "What would you like? We're in the French Quarter. Most places are wonderful."

"I'm not... I don't care. I'm not that hungry. I'm actually a little on edge." She looked at him searchingly. "Have you seen Lena?"

He shook his head. "Not today. I believe she'll find us by tonight. We know she's been to the house. She sees Annette that way."

"Of course," Casey murmured.

"So, what did you want to ask or suggest?" He looked at her with concern.

She shook her head. "That was just Lauren being silly."

"She's talented. There are wonderful artists working all over this city. It's a magnet for creative types, I think. But Lauren's work has something special in it. Heart. She has a true feel for everything unique and wonderful about this city."

"Did you spend a lot of time here?"

"I did. Growing up. I was born in Gretna. Anyway, food. I *am* hungry."

"Okay. Wherever. What about your call? The one you left the store to take."

"Ah, that." He smiled tightly. "That was my ticket into serious delving. The medical examiner from Mississippi called." He winced. "I was there for the exhumation, and I have to say, I think I'm going to be cremated from the get-go. William Marley was embalmed, and the work was good. So, he decayed in the heat, but...there were remains. Enough for the M.E. to discover there had been a massive dose of cocaine in his system. He was well-known and had never been a drug user in life. At this point, the M.E. couldn't find the delivery system, but he's convinced the heart attack was brought on by the cocaine."

"So, he *was* murdered."

"Yes, and Jackson is going through the proper channels to see that the investigation into Lena's death is reopened with the FBI. With me heading up the investigation."

"I'm happy for you. But where do you go from here?"

"I have a friend locally who was one of the detectives on the original case. I'm going to bring him back in. And after Stephanie's meeting tomorrow, I'm going to go after the board of directors one by one. Nobody else benefits from these deaths. I wish it was as easy as Lauren's suggestion that we just arrest them all, or that Lena could just appear in front of a judge and demand they all stand trial. But we need evidence."

"How did he get into the house—whoever the man in all the black clothing was?" Casey asked.

"Whoever got in knew the security code for the gate and the front door. Either that, or Gail Reeves let him in. But she was at her book club meeting. Several people vouched for that. Muriel's."

"Pardon?"

"For lunch. Muriel's, Jackson Square. I've always loved it."

"Fine with me."

They were about a block or so away after having ambled somewhat aimlessly.

Casey had always loved Muriel's, too. The place was rumored to have several resident ghosts, mostly past owners of the property. There had been a building at the location soon after the city was founded, *La Nouvelle Orleans*. The great mansion that had stood on the spot had been horribly damaged in the great fire that swept the city in 1788, though it had been rebuilt. The property was still prime real estate—caddy-corner from Jackson Square.

"You know they have séance rooms," Ryder said dryly.

"And they really have seances." She smiled.

They were only interested in eating today, and a friendly hostess quickly gave them a table.

They were served iced tea while their entrees were prepared. As they waited, Ryder leaned close and said, "I really am sorry."

"You don't have to keep apologizing. I understand."

"Okay."

"Good."

"I was wrong about you."

"I guess I was wrong about you also. Too bad you don't live here. At some point, I could have taken you to see some amazing bands. Jared is friends with just about every musician in the city."

"Maybe I'll stick around long enough for you to take me out."

She grinned. "Are you picking up our late lunch or early dinner?" she asked.

"I am."

"Okay, then. I'll take you out."

"Sounds good. We'll be almost like a couple."

He was still close, and she could see a light in his eyes, both teasing and serious. "I was really wrong. I like you and admire you," he said softly.

"Um—thank you."

He leaned back, smiling. "You could tell me how much you like and admire me, too."

She laughed softly. "I do like and admire you, even knowing what an ass you can be. But that's okay. I understand." She took a sip of her tea.

"So," Casey murmured awkwardly, "what's your life like when you're not chasing down devious killers?"

"The Krewe is an amazing unit. According to the papers that define us, we go in when there are unusual aspects to a case. Adam and Jackson have drawn together an incredible group that has gotten larger over the years. We have our own separate headquarters, an array of forensic investigators, and some of the best computer forensic people to be found."

"Your life is work?"

He shrugged. "A lot of us are friends. We know and understand each other. We go to ballgames. Adam owns a non-profit theater.

Several spouses and significant others actually work there. We see lots of wonderful shows. We go to concerts, movies...and we have a Friday night poker game for whoever shows up."

"Nice. I thought you were going to say you worked all the time."

"I do work a lot. But you work all the time, too."

"Work is fun. Lauren is an amazing artist, and I help with her projects. And we have a great time with Jared. He has some original work, and Lauren and I are going to help out when he records."

"Are those two together?"

"No. They're just best friends. We all are. We decided in college that we'd never screw it all up by dating each other."

"So none of you is married or about to be married?" He leaned in closer.

"Are you?" she volleyed back.

"No."

"Why not?"

"What?"

It was his turn to back off. Then he shrugged. "I came close. But...yeah. Work. I should say it was never going to work. She's a good woman. We're still casual friends. But she was..."

"Clingy?" Casey suggested as he looked for a word.

"Yeah. I'm a decent guy. If I were going to do something, I'd just say it. But she was suspicious every time I got a call in the night, and I don't believe in a life without trust."

"I'm with you there. I never came close to marriage. I guess I tend to back off quickly, and Lauren complains I don't give things a chance. But there needs to be some common ground when you're looking at long-term." She winced slightly. "Well, anyway...the food is great, as always. I should get back."

"I'm going to go in with you and then head back out to the street."

"Okay. You really think someone is watching the shop?"

"I really do. You already told me you had seen both Barton Quincy and Larry Swenson in A Beautiful Mind."

"But that was before Lena came to me that night."

"I'm guessing they knew Lena had been there before."

"But just because she was there—"

"You don't claim to be a medium. But you *do* read tea leaves and the tarot. If they knew she had been to your shop, they might have been trying to find out if she'd come to you with her accusation that someone helped Anthony off that building. And if so, even though it's a bit of a stretch...maybe they were trying to make sure she didn't give you information from the beyond."

"Wait. You think our killer believes in the occult? Even I didn't believe that a ghost delivering a message was possible until Lena appeared."

"Either the killer believes or doesn't want to take any chances with loose ends." He smiled at her. "But don't worry, I promise you…until I know you're safe, I'll be close to you at all times."

Casey smiled weakly. She wasn't sure how close she wanted him to be. The more they were together, the more she felt the strength of simple attraction.

No...

Not simple. He had proven to be decent, ethical, and even courteous. There was no denying his appearance, the shoulders, the slim hips. His long legs, great face...

She couldn't shake Lauren's words.

Premeditated sex!

But she couldn't see herself just suggesting that to him since neither of them had anything else going on. *How about some recreational sex?*

"Ah, yeah." She cleared her throat. "We'd better get going."

He paid the tab, and they left, walking side by side the few blocks back to the shop.

Their arms occasionally brushed as they walked. He caught her hand to steer her to his side when a kid on a bicycle almost ran them off the sidewalk. It was good to feel his hand surrounding hers.

And to wonder just how good it would feel elsewhere...

Chapter 7

Ryder left Casey to wander, moving across the street and then up the other way.

The concept that someone was watching her at the shop might be crazy, but if Barton Quincy and Larry Swenson had been in her shop, it gave credence to the idea that someone was suspicious of her.

Finding out who among his list of suspects might believe in the occult would be an interesting aspect to the case.

He had wandered down two blocks, pretending to look in shop windows, when he saw a woman entering Casey's store—Gail Reeves, the Marceau's housekeeper.

He didn't think Casey had met the woman when she was at the house. She'd seen Stephanie that day, and only Stephanie. Gail had been out, or so he thought, and he had been with Annette.

He strode back, wondering if he should go in. He might as well. Gail knew Casey had come to the house. Stephanie had gone on about being accosted by the city's *mystics*, so Gail knew about Casey.

Which meant, she must know he was watching over Casey and the shop.

He strode toward it, pausing when his phone rang.

It was Braxton.

"Hello, Detective Wild."

"Hello, Special Agent McKinley. I guess I'm working for you."

"Working *with* me," Ryder said.

"Apparently, they're quietly reopening cases—William Marley, Anthony Marceau, and Lena Marceau."

"Someone helped William Marley have that heart attack," Ryder said.

"Evidently. Can you tell me what's new?"

"I'm on the street. Jackson Crow is in the city, but we'll be calling on your people for help. Of course, we have our field office here, but we want the NOPD to be equal partners with us in finding out what the hell is going on."

"Right. I don't know—"

"I'm on St. Anne. There's a coffee shop—"

"Thirty minutes?"

"Sounds about right."

Ryder ended the conversation in time to see Gail Reeves leaving Casey's store. He walked in a few minutes later.

"Gail was just here," Casey said.

"I saw."

"She said she'd heard about me and mentioned she loves shops like this and knew I had to be good if Lena came here. She wanted to set up a tarot reading. I told her Lena had not come in for a reading. And she said Lena had mentioned the shop and how much she loved it and how she felt an affinity toward me."

"Ah."

"So?"

"I'm not sure. But that's interesting. I'm going to walk over to the coffee shop and meet up with Braxton Wild, the detective called in when Lena died. He'll be working with us on this. I need to bring him up to speed. I can see the shop from there."

"Thanks," she told him, smiling as a woman walked into the store.

"Jennie! Hey, I thought you were on vacation," Casey said. The woman was a customer Casey obviously knew well.

She was older, slim, and attractive, and made no pretense of doing anything but staring at Ryder.

"Hi!" she said, ignoring Casey's question.

"Hi." Ryder smiled at her. "Ryder McKinley," he told her.

"I like it," she said, looking at Casey. Then she added, "Oh, sorry. Jennie Sanders. I love this place—and Casey. She's the best. Did you come for a reading?" she asked him.

"I just love the shop, too," he said lightly. "And Casey, of course. She *is* the best. I'll see you in a bit, Casey. I'm off for coffee."

"You aren't from around here, are you?"

"Actually? Originally from Gretna. Nice to meet you, Jennie. Later, Casey."

He still heard the woman as he walked out of the store.

"Good thing I came in. I did say you might not be here if someone tall, dark, and dangerously handsome walked in. And did you hear? It almost sounded like he said he loves you. What? Don't give me that look. Oh, Casey, I hope you jumped all over him."

The door closed behind him, and he laughed, surprised that he could. It seemed his every waking minute had been bound by tension for too long...

And then Casey had come into his life. She wasn't really *in* his life. More, she was letting him into hers. For now. But...

Braxton must have been in the French Quarter or at least near it. He was already waving to Ryder from a table at the coffee shop. It seemed he'd ordered. Ryder could see he had gotten two large cups of coffee, and Ryder knew one was for him.

He joined the detective, sliding into a chair that allowed him to easily see Casey's shop.

"I'm glad you're in charge of this thing," Braxton told him. "Because I don't know where to go. We questioned the men on the company's board of directors—especially Justin, since he is a Marceau, but he doesn't benefit any more than any of the others. He was not a beloved grandson like Anthony. I checked that out. He didn't seem bitter about it and said he hadn't cared about it or even Elijah much when he was younger. He was just glad his name had given him a position since he hadn't been stellar in any career he undertook himself. We questioned Gail Reeves, too. And, yes, the woman was with her book club. How are you going to get anywhere from here? You said Jackson is here, but can you really babysit Stephanie and Annette for the rest of your life? And even if you could...there could be that one slip, one moment..."

"I could use some help keeping an eye on the shop right there," Ryder said, pointing across the street.

"A Beautiful Mind," Braxton said. "Someone with a beautiful mind did all this?" he asked dryly.

Ryder grimaced.

"Okay, my humor isn't great."

"Before she died, Lena visited the shop several times. She said something to the owner, Casey Nicholson. Casey finally went to

Stephanie's house, feeling like a fool but determined to let Stephanie know Lena had been afraid her husband's death had been no accident. Anyway, I found out Barton Quincy and Larry Swenson were in the shop, too. Separately, just looking. I don't think they were shopping. I think they were trying to find out if Casey knew anything."

"So, both men are guilty."

"Maybe."

"Conspiracy theory?"

"Braxton, we know William Marley was helped into a heart attack. We know something happened. Maybe Larry was just doing something for Quincy. Perhaps they're both involved. Didn't the board members give the board alibis when the investigation began?"

Braxton nodded. "But how...?"

"I don't know. We need to find out. Anyway, I need to be at the board meeting Stephanie is calling for tomorrow. So, I need you on the shop."

"All right. On it. What about the baby?"

Ryder grinned. "Jackson is great with kids. He has some of his own."

"All right," Braxton repeated.

"The shop opens at ten. Casey works with two friends from her college days. It's pretty cool. The female is an artist—a damned good one. The male with them is a musician, and they all perform in the shop when customers ask them to. You'll be fine."

"I'll be fine. But you don't have anything else?"

"Actually, I do. I think someone was trying to get to Casey Nicholson the other night. I couldn't catch him. He was wearing black and crawling around in the building's shrubbery."

"You couldn't catch him? You're slipping, my friend."

Ryder gave him a dry smile. "Oh, I will catch him. Trust me. I will catch him."

* * * *

The day passed quickly. Not a bad one. Customers came in and out. Casey and Lauren sang with Jared a few times, and she convinced Jennie that Ryder was a visiting friend, and that she wasn't being whisked away. Said he'd be going back to work in Virginia.

He hadn't stated his title when he introduced himself. She didn't want to go into it all with Jennie anyway, so she was as casual as she could be.

"Don't let that one get away!" Jennie told her.

Casey smiled and patiently explained, "I don't have him, so he can't get away."

"If you don't have him, do something. You should have him," Jennie told her. "Anyway, I just stopped by because my car needed a little work. I'm leaving in the morning."

"That's good. Family is good, Jennie. Give us a call and let us know you got there okay."

"Ah, you're sweet. I will do so," she promised.

Then she was gone.

Lauren and Jared returned, and friends from one of Lauren's art classes came in while Jared was talking to a friend he knew from a band.

Restless, Casey glanced at Jared and said, "Running out for just a minute."

She wasn't sure Ryder would appreciate it if she honed-in on his meeting at the coffee shop, but she just needed out of the shop for a minute.

Being anxious was something that seemed to grow within her.

She had barely started down the street when someone slipped out of a narrow alleyway between the storefronts, taking her hand and drawing her back, whispering quickly at the same time. "It's me. It's okay. But come back here."

Ryder. He had her hard against him. She turned in his hold, confused. He was looking down the street. She saw one of the men she had seen before in her shop. She remembered the pictures in the Marceau house library.

Larry Swenson. She twisted in Ryder's arms, so close that she was looking up into his face. He looked down at her. It was almost as if they were in a lover's embrace. He grimaced, then glanced back down the street before looking into her eyes again. He touched her face gently. "I'm sorry. I want to see what he's up to."

She nodded, staring back at him.

Larry Swenson paused in front of A Beautiful Mind.

He looked in the shop, frowned, and moved on.

"Go back in. Do you mind? Braxton is watching the place. I

want to follow Swenson."

She nodded.

"Quickly, okay?"

She nodded again. Then, he was gone, long strides taking him behind the man who had looked into the shop.

She hurried back as she had promised.

The afternoon sun was starting to set when Ryder arrived back at six.

"Hey, girls, get out of here," Jared commanded. "My night. And, Casey, you lucky devil, you're back on the late shift tomorrow."

"All right, then," she said, glancing at Ryder. He hadn't said anything about his excursion following after Larry Swenson.

"Yep, I'm getting my things," Lauren said. Then she added, "Hey, Casey. Don't forget, Miss Lilly's granddaughter's group is coming in tomorrow," Lauren reminded her.

"I won't forget."

Casey noted that Ryder had been talking to Jared, and both were laughing.

"What's up?" she asked, but Jared waved a hand in the air and bid them goodnight. They waved goodbye to Lauren at the door and then started to Ryder's car.

"What happened with Swenson?" she asked.

"He stopped on the next block and made a phone call. I couldn't get close enough to hear without being seen, but he looked at the shop the whole time he talked. He had to have reported he didn't see you in there."

"I could have been in the back in my reading room."

"True. The thing is, it hasn't been happenstance or simple shopping trips. Larry Swenson has an interest in the shop. And you. And he called someone else to report."

"Do you think he knows you're watching over it—and me?"

"Maybe. But Braxton and his people will be watching tomorrow; I'll be at the board meeting with Stephanie."

"So, now—"

"Now, we wait until tomorrow."

They reached his car. As they got in and he pulled out into traffic, Casey remembered she had a long and busy day coming up.

"So, since we're on hold, may we drop by my apartment? I'd like to pick up one of my books."

He arched a brow at her. "You've seen the library at the Marceau house."

"A particular book," she told him. "I'm giving a speech tomorrow to a group of school kids."

He smiled. "Sure."

He was silent then, but it looked as if he were inwardly laughing about something.

"What? What were you and Jared laughing about?" Casey asked.

He shrugged. But he was...smirking.

"What?" she prodded.

He glanced her way and then shook his head before laughing out loud.

"Premeditated sex," he told her.

"Oh, God!" She groaned.

"It's okay. I told him not to worry. I haven't known you long, but it's been long enough to know you'd feel horribly uncomfortable in Stephanie's house, so...no premeditation."

On the one hand, she was mortified. On the other...

She remembered the way his eyes had roamed over her. And the feel of his hand as he touched her cheek. The thrill she felt at even the simple brush of his arm. The strong feel of his body against hers.

"You're right."

He nodded.

She took a deep breath for courage and spoke while looking straight ahead. "But we are going by my apartment."

He glanced her way, arching a brow.

"Premeditated sex?" he asked her.

She looked at him and saw the intensity in his eyes. "What do you think about the idea?" she asked softly.

"Wow."

"Is that a...?"

"I'm all into that kind of premeditation, Casey." His voice had deepened, and his fingers tightened on the steering wheel. But then he seemed to force himself to relax. "I mean, Jared made me laugh, telling me about Lauren's terminology, and I never would have presumed anything. You must have some idea how attractive you are, which has nothing to do with the fact I really do like and admire you." He licked his lips and turned to pin her with his gaze. "But the idea is beyond appealing.”

She thought over all she’d been through the last few days. The death of a friend, the possibility of murder, the fear of being targeted. “We don’t know where we’ll be tomorrow, Ryder. Which is fine with me. I mean, we’ll both be in New Orleans, but—”

“We have no guarantees,” he said.

Casey looked at him then said softly, “If I’ve learned anything from all this, none of us even has a guarantee there will be a tomorrow.” She winced. “I didn’t say that to be hurtful in any way—”

They had reached her neighborhood, if not her building. He pulled the car off the road, reached over, touched her face, and kissed her.

“No guarantees,” he whispered. “And life is beautiful. I would like to experience it with you tonight, Casey. Intimately.”

She smiled, touching his face, letting her fingers trace the fine contours of his cheekbones, and then running a fingertip lightly over his lips.

“We should really get a room.” He smiled.

“I have a room,” she breathed.

“We should really get in your room.”

“Drive.”

He chuckled and drove the rest of the way to her place. He parked, and they got out quickly, Casey reaching for her keys as they did so. She opened the main door.

Miss Lilly was there, and they both came to a dead halt.

“Hello. Lovely to see you both. Casey, I wasn’t sure—”

“I’m just stopping by for some things...”

“And I have some calls to make. Important business calls. I can’t be disturbed, I’m afraid. We may be a while. Right, Casey?”

“Yes, we may be here a while. But I will be spending the night out again.”

“Wonderful!” Lilly said, clapping her hands together. “I’m so delighted to see such lovely young people together. But I wanted to remind you about the children tomorrow.”

“I’m all set, Miss Lilly. They’ll get their speech.”

“Great. Well then, you two go on,” Miss Lilly said, turning to head back to her apartment. But she called out to Casey, beckoning to her.

"Honey, don't you read too much or let him work too long. Hang on to that one. I mean, you need to make the most of your time, if you understand me."

Casey smiled. "Thank you."

"And don't worry, you won't be disturbed."

Casey gave the woman a weak smile. As she returned to Ryder and opened the door to her place, she murmured, "Well, that was a surprise to put a stop to—"

She'd opened the door and started through. He moved her forward more quickly, closed the door, and then spun them and pressed her against it.

"No," he murmured. "There are no stops to premeditated sex."

His body leaned hard against hers. The kiss then was nothing like the tender and soft exploration in the car earlier. Ridiculously hot and wet, tongues battling, their hands fumbling with each other at first.

"The bedroom's upstairs," she said when their lips parted.

"I remember." He moved back, his smile now beautiful and seductive.

But he paused to make sure the door was bolted. As he did so, Casey turned and raced up the stairs. He was right behind her. He caught her inside the bedroom, flinging them to the bed together, where they laughed for a moment. Then their laughter faded as they looked at one another.

When they kissed again, the passion of the kiss seemed to radiate and take hold. Shifting, they began to disrobe, and then they were laughing again as they tried to help one another, pausing for Ryder to put his holster and gun aside, then falling upon each other once more. Rolling, lips touching body parts as they were bared, until they were naked at last. He was above her, looking down into Casey's eyes. They kissed, and then his lips traveled the length of her as her fingertips played over his shoulders and back, soft brushes that teased and evoked. Until she rose against him, caressing, kissing, and discovering his body as he had hers. Eventually, they turned again, kissed some more, teased and caressed and seduced and enchanted one another with every brush of their fingers and lips until they came together at last.

Life was beautiful. Being together like this was part of what could be amazing between human beings. Casey briefly thought the future didn't matter. They had bonded in their brief time together, and this...between them...was somehow right. She would never regret this time.

They moved, tossed, arched, writhed, and a rhythm rose and fell between them, becoming sweetly frantic and urgent. Then the world seemed to explode, and it *was* beautiful. As if honeyed crystals filled the night air around Casey. They stilled and lay together, entwined, touching, breathing, just holding tight.

"Casey," Ryder murmured softly.

Suddenly, she was afraid. This had been her choice. She didn't want the night marred by any regrets or worries on his part.

She leaned against his chest and teased lightly, "Premeditated sex. Wow. I really liked it."

He smiled. "Liked? I loved it. I loved it so much, I'm willing to take a chance and go for it again."

She laughed and snuggled against him, caressing his cheek.

But he was serious. They made love again, and finally, regretfully, he said, "We need to get to the Marceau house."

She nodded. "And I need to get my book."

With a deep sigh, she rose and hurriedly gathered up her clothing and dressed as he did the same. She raced down the stairs before him, finding the book she wanted. She waited for him at the front door and then locked it behind them as they moved on to the main entrance.

Miss Lilly's door opened, and the woman peered out. "Take care, my young lovelies!" She looked at Ryder with a straight face. "I do hope your calls went well."

"My calls were great. Well, at least on my end, they went great."

He looked at Casey. She kicked him, hoping Miss Lilly couldn't see the motion.

As the door to Miss Lilly's apartment closed, Casey heard her laughing softly.

She sighed.

"Don't forget, we have her approval," Ryder reminded her.

They went out to the car.

"You know,"—he paused before opening her door—"premeditated is great, but it doesn't always have to be that way."

She didn't quite know how to respond as he ushered her into the car and closed the door. It took a few minutes of driving for her to form the question. "What does that mean?"

He looked at her and grinned. "You know where the door to my room is."

"Ryder, it's Stephanie's house—"

"I think she'd approve. But your call," he told her.

They'd reached the mansion.

"And now, Jackson Crow is here—"

"Jackson is always telling me to get a life." Ryder put the car into park and turned to her. "And what you said tonight is all too true. Life doesn't come with guarantees. For anyone."

"We should live," she said softly. "But I do need to read and shower. And you need to see Stephanie and Jackson—"

"And, therefore, we seize the moments," he said, grinning.

She might very well do that.

But then...

They approached the house. The historic home where Lena had lived.

And died.

Casey looked up at the house and made a silent vow.

She would be like Ryder. She'd never let it go. She'd do anything she could to help find whoever had stolen the beauty and life and goodness of Anthony and Lena Marceau—and William Marley.

Lena had come to her.

And she would not fail the gentle ghost.

Chapter 8

Ryder had poured his second cup of coffee in the morning when he turned to see that Lena's ghost was in the kitchen.

"Hello," he said softly.

"I'm learning, but I'm afraid I'm just slow as a ghost."

Stephanie walked in then with the baby. Annette immediately smiled and laughed and said, "Mama!"

Stephanie looked at Ryder with hope in her eyes. "She's here? Lena's here?" she asked.

"Tell her how much I love her, and thank you," Lena said, striding across the kitchen to take her sister in her arms.

"That's her, that's her! Right, this feeling?" Stephanie asked.

"It is," Ryder said softly.

Lena Marceau then wrapped her arms around her daughter. Annette giggled.

"Casey is here, right?" Lena asked Ryder anxiously.

He nodded. "She'll be down soon." He looked at Stephanie and said, "She asked about Casey."

Ryder had left her sleeping. They'd had a long night. He hadn't gotten much sleep himself, but he felt better this morning than he had in...a long time. Everything about this situation screamed that life—and love, human kindness, caring—were not to be taken for granted.

"Thank goodness," Lena said. "I never meant to make her life a nightmare. First, I popped in on her. And then, I popped out. Oh, Ryder. I am so sorry. It's just the strangest thing. I mean, I can feel it when I'm appearing and when I'm not, and it's almost like being alive. You have to rest sometimes to get your mojo going so the living can see you and...anyway."

"What's she saying?" Stephanie asked Ryder anxiously.

"She disappeared on us the other day, and she's explaining that it's difficult to appear when you're a new ghost," Ryder said. "I'm going to fill her in on what we're planning for the day." He turned back to where Lena stood. "I'm going with Stephanie to the board meeting today. She's going to insist they find another way to improve profits. There will be no charges above cost for necessary drugs. I'm going to watch for reactions from the foursome around her."

"But the baby—?" Lena said worriedly.

"That will be me," Jackson Crow said, entering the kitchen. "Lena, I'm Jackson Crow, field director for—"

"Oh, I know who you are," Lena said and smiled. "And you see me so clearly and hear me, and...well, of course, you do. Ryder told me all about you when he started with the Krewe. He was so excited. I didn't understand. In life, I had what Steph has, a sense, but nothing more. But I believed Ryder and I was so happy when he found work with people like him. But—wait! You're going to watch the baby?"

"I have two children of my own, thank you very much. I can play an excellent game of This Little Piggy Went to Market with a variety of ages. Annette and I will be fine," Jackson assured her.

"Plus, he has a Glock and is an excellent marksman. Not to mention, we'll still have one of the friends I hired to watch the cameras, and our suspects will be in the CBD," Ryder reminded Stephanie. "I'll be with you—every second," he told her.

Lena shook her head.

"What about Casey? I never meant to—I was just getting so desperate. But she's in danger now, too."

"We're going to see her to the shop. She'll be there with her friends and co-workers and Detective Braxton Wild."

"The detective believes in all this now?" Stephanie asked.

"He's known about ghosts for a while now. Comes with the territory of knowing about the Krewe. And he always did believe that what went on with Anthony and Lena was suspicious. He just didn't have anywhere else to go," Ryder said. "And the case is now in the hands of the FBI. So, you'll have us, and Braxton and the NOPD on this until it's solved."

Stephanie sank into a chair and looked around the table. "Thank you," she said. Then tears formed in her eyes, and she said softly, "Hug me again, Lena. Hug me, please. I miss you so much. So very, very much."

"Oh, Steph. I miss you too," Lena said and hugged her sister.

Jackson cleared his throat. "I'm here with Annette. The rest of you need to get going. Casey should be delivered safely to the French Quarter, and then Ryder and Stephanie need to get to the Marceau offices."

"I'll go up and make sure that Casey is ready," Lena said.

He hadn't wanted to move.

"I'm taking the baby to the safe room. If anything should happen, she'll be protected," Jackson murmured. He looked at Ryder, shaking his head. "This operation never took brawn. They play on people. Anthony was either pushed off the building after being lured to the roof or was told it was his life or Lena's or the baby's. I don't believe anyone will be getting through me."

"I don't believe so either," Ryder assured.

"But my baby is the key," Lena whispered. "She was always going to grow up privileged. Anthony and I wanted so badly to continue with Elijah's legacy, using all he had for good. I knew I could trust Stephanie to raise her. Anthony and I chose Stephanie and asked her the day the baby was born... We never thought we were putting her in the path of homicidal maniacs."

The killer—or killers—aren't maniacs, Ryder thought. They had a clear agenda. A takeover of Marceau Industries. They were organized, devious, and cunning.

"Lena, stay with us and have faith in us," Ryder said.

She smiled. "I do have faith in you," she said. "So..."

"We begin the day," Ryder said.

* * * *

Lena was back.

Casey saw the woman's ghost floating up the stairs just as she came down the hallway.

"Casey!" Lena said.

"Hey. You're good, huh?"

"Well, I'm dead, but I'm a stronger ghost now."

"I'm so sorry—"

"I'm joking. I mean, it's not a joke, just...well, a sense of humor helps us get through almost anything, huh?"

"True," Casey said softly. A sense of humor was...human.

Love, enjoyment, friends—all of those were human gifts. Longing to be held...

And to take it other places. That was human, too. *And okay*, she told herself.

The situation remained tense and dire. But it was okay to have had a beautiful night. She'd awoken feeling as if the sun were radiating through her and from her.

Lena's ghost hugged her, and she felt the strange yet comforting almost-there sensation. "I can't apologize to you enough—"

"Lena, it's all right. I've met wonderful, interesting people. And Detective Wild will be looking after me all day. Everything is good."

"'Sundrops, lollipops, and rainbows,'" Lena said dryly. Then she grinned. "Lemon drops! I always loved them. I still feel like I smell them now and then. Anyway, I'm holding us up. Time to go."

The baby was safely with Jackson.

Stephanie and Casey got into the car with Ryder, and Casey offered Stephanie the front passenger's seat.

"Lena is still here, isn't she?" Stephanie asked. When Ryder nodded, she added, "I'll sit with my sister." She crawled into the back and asked, "Lena can hear me, right?"

"She can," Ryder assured her.

"Lena, give me another hug. I love hugs," she said. Then, as Ryder pulled the car out into traffic, she said, "I can feel hugs. I can't do what you two can, but I can feel hugs."

Casey was happy as they drove to the French Quarter, where, while it was almost ten, there was still parking available.

Ryder wanted to make sure that Detective Wild was at the store.

He was. The detective greeted Ryder and Stephanie and had a special smile for Casey, telling her it was going to be a great day. He planned to sit in one of the chairs and look at the art and smile at all the people who came in. "I've been by here before. We'll get your friend to play and enjoy some good music," he said. But then he looked at Stephanie, his expression full of remorse. "I swear, we tried everything in our power."

Stephanie smiled at him. "I know. It's okay. I had nothing, either. Only the fact I knew my sister."

Lena's ghost gave Detective Wild a hug. He shivered.

"This is a really good guy," Lena said. "I know he tried to do the right thing."

"All right. If all is well, we're going to head over to the Central Business District and the Marceau building," Ryder said, but he was looking at Casey.

Had she really only known him for two days? Had they really just spent an incredible night together?

A *premeditated* night?

She wanted to touch his face. She wanted to respond to the light—and the worry—in his eyes. She refrained.

He didn't. He pulled her into his arms and held her for a minute, then lifted her chin and tenderly kissed her lips.

"They'll know," Casey whispered.

"Yeah, they will," he answered.

They were both startled when Stephanie and Detective Wild—and Lena's ghost—applauded.

"I could have told you that you two would hit it off. In fact, I was going to bring you here, Ryder, the next time you came to see me. At least...well, I put Casey in danger, but at least I put the two of you together," Lena said happily.

"And now, we will get going," Ryder said.

"You need to open the door to the shop," Detective Wild said. "They frown on police opening doors without probable cause."

"Yes, yes, of course," Casey said. She turned the bolts as Ryder and Stephanie turned to go back to the car.

Ryder turned again and waved. Casey waved back. She wondered if she'd have a chance—with Detective Wild in the shop—to tell Lauren she'd taken her up on the concept of premeditated sex, and it had proven to be an excellent idea.

She walked in and told Detective Wild to make himself at home. He did. He looked around and enjoyed the art and the little souvenirs before sitting down in one of the chairs by the coffee service. Casey pulled up the computer and unlocked the cash register and card reader.

She noted it was after ten, and neither Lauren nor Jared had arrived.

They were seldom late, but maybe they'd met up at ten to head to a music venue. They did that now and then.

She was rearranging a jewelry display when her phone rang.

She didn't usually answer numbers she didn't know, but with Lauren and Jared both running late, she was worried.

"Hello?" she said.

"Miss Nicholson, don't hang up, and don't let that cop in there know anything is wrong at all. Just listen..."

The voice, coming through a distortion machine, broke off.

Then, she heard a scream. A terrible shriek of pain. And then Lauren's voice, "Casey, don't do whatever it is...they can't get away with it. They can't—"

"No."

The word came out as a whisper.

"Shut the hell up and quick! It would be so easy for me to kill her in the blink of an eye. You'd better not even make the kind of face that cop can read. I *will* kill her. I have a knife at her throat. If you tell the police? You may be fine. But I promise you, this little artist lady will be dead. Escape the cop somehow in the next few minutes. Get to the cemetery. And if you alert anyone—cops or FBI—we'll know. Do you want to hear the guy scream, too? I can make that happen. Get out of the shop and get to the cemetery unseen if you want these two to live."

Whoever it was hung up.

Casey stood there, frozen. She sank onto the stool behind the counter and tried to remain impassive.

This was how they got away with murder. They used a person's loved ones against them.

Casey had known that. And she knew that obeying the voice would be doing exactly what they wanted.

Be at the cemetery. New Orleans had dozens of them.

But she knew which one.

Call Ryder! her subconscious screamed.

She wanted to call him. Desperately. But someone was watching. And she knew she couldn't risk Lauren's life. Or Jared's.

She couldn't save her own...to risk theirs.

* * * *

"None of this has made any sense to me," Stephanie said. She was still riding in back. Ryder had assured her that he didn't mind looking like her chauffeur. "I mean, why would they want to get rid of all of us? Oh, I know those guys want to increase the prices on a lot of necessary drugs. But still, if something happens to Annette, it's not like the money goes to one person."

"Stephanie, do you remember if Anthony—or you, Lena—ever offended any of them personally?" Ryder asked as he drove. They'd been over the question before with Stephanie, but it didn't hurt to revisit the situation. Stephanie had been so lost and in such deep mourning when Lena died, she hadn't been thinking straight.

Lena might remember more now.

"Anthony was the nicest man in the world," Lena said. "He was so careful never to offend anyone."

"I can't think of anything," Stephanie said and then sighed. "I do know Barton Quincy thought Anthony was a flake. I heard him telling Anthony one time that he couldn't run a major corporation and act like St. Theresa at the same time."

"But Barton wouldn't just get everything," Lena protested. "Not even Justin would get everything, and he's a Marceau. And besides, Justin isn't like those guys. He's a free spirit."

Stephanie couldn't hear Lena, but her mind must have worked along the same lines. "Not Justin. I can't see it, I just can't."

"Money can do very strange things to people. And I don't think one person could have managed all this alone," Ryder said.

"Conspiracy theory?" Stephanie asked. "Seriously, Ryder. You think that many people can be that horrible?"

"If frightened for their own well-being, possibly," Ryder said.

"But all four of them?" Stephanie asked.

"Maybe not. I don't know. But I believe with my whole heart that at least one of them is guilty. None of this makes any sense at all otherwise," Ryder said. "Maybe one is seriously psychotic—death means nothing to them."

"Trust me, it means something," Lena said bitterly.

"When you have a person like that, and others who have an agenda and are willing to go along with something heinous if they don't have to perform any bloody acts themselves, you can easily have a conspiracy."

"Only one man threatened me and forced me to take the pills," Lena murmured.

"And we're back to the fact that the property video went blank at just the right time. And one of these guys must have figured out a way into the house. Maybe they managed to copy Anthony's keys and get code information off his phone... I don't know." Ryder grimaced.

At the Marceau offices in the CBD, they headed straight for the meeting room.

As they paused to check in with the receptionist, Lena murmured, "I'm going on ahead, to see what they're up to."

Stephanie chatted a minute with the receptionist while she checked to make sure the other board members had arrived and were going to the conference room. She was still talking when Lena's ghost came back to Ryder.

"This is going to be interesting. I heard Barton Quincy talking to Larry Swenson. He was saying that someone had 'gone off the rails.' That the 'idiot believes in ghosts!' Then they said they had suspected all along that 'she' needed to be taken care of, that 'she' shouldn't have been on it or that they should have dealt with 'her' earlier. Ryder, it doesn't sound like they're talking about Casey. So, who could they be talking about?"

He glanced at Lena and pulled his phone from his jacket pocket, pretending he'd gotten a phone call.

"There's only one other person I can think of...someone who could have helped them in what they needed to do for the right sum. Don't mock my conspiracy theories, cousin."

"Ryder, we can go on in now," Stephanie said.

They walked down a hallway toward the conference room.

Ryder was just about to enter when the phone he was still holding rang.

It was Braxton.

"Ryder, I swear I don't know how Casey did it, but..."

"Did what?"

"She's gone. Casey is gone. Her friends and co-workers never showed up for work. No one took her, Ryder. I know that much. She was here with me, and she stepped out to clean something off a window, and then...she was gone. No one took her. She ran. Away from me. On purpose."

Ryder felt his heart flip, and a burning sensation cascaded through him.

Fear.

He looked through the glass wall enclosure of the conference room, thinking that one of the four members besides Stephanie had to be absent.

But they were all there. Barton Quincy was at one end of the table. Justin was next to him, talking to him earnestly. Larry Swenson was sitting back, playing with his pen and looking bored. Harry Miller was writing notes on a pad.

If they were all there...

It still had to be someone connected.

She. The someone who was going off the rails.

He grabbed Stephanie by the shoulders. "Get in there. Be tough. Carry out the agenda just as we planned. I'm sending cops, and unless they get you out of the offices, you're going to be fine. Don't let them tell you the baby is in danger, or that I'm in danger or anything. Don't believe any threat if it comes to it, and don't leave the offices. You understand? Hang tough."

Workers were busy at desks in the main room, and the conference room was visible to all of them through the glass.

"Lena is with me?" Stephanie asked.

Ryder nodded.

"I won't leave her," Lena promised.

Ryder nodded again. He could hear Braxton, still on the line, calling his name. He put his phone back to his ear as he left the offices. "I need police at the Marceau offices, Braxton. Now. Those bastards can't try anything against Stephanie. I'm going after Casey."

"But where? I ran down the streets, Ryder, I swear. I didn't want to fail you. I called it in. She must have moved like lightning, and she knows how to zig and zag these streets and is aware of every little nook and cranny to hide in if a cop comes. I've got the city searching. I don't see how you're going to find her—"

"I will," Ryder said. "I will. Because I think I know where she's headed."

"I'll get the force out—"

"No. We can't. Not if everyone is going to come out of this alive. Just get here. Stephanie is in danger. I'll find Casey," he said.

He was already running out to his car.

He used his emergency vehicle lighting to make it through the French Quarter to Rampart.

Then he turned the lights off.

And prayed he was right.

Chapter 9

Casey ran, dodging tourists, glad they were closer to Esplanade than Canal. There seemed to be more tourists towards Canal and Jackson Square, but she was running away from there and the river toward Tremé. As she ran, she heard a jazz band playing, caught the sound of laughter and applause, and thought about the city—the unique architecture, the beauty of the cathedral, the colors, the laughter, and the unique décor that made up New Orleans. She felt the *life* of the city and kept running, arguing with herself all the while.

Whoever this is will just kill them all.

She was a psychology major. She would use psychology. If she didn't save her own life, it would be okay if they at least let Jared and Lauren go.

She ran almost all the way to Rampart and paused to catch her breath. The first order of business had been to escape Detective Braxton Wild. She was sorry for what she had done to him. He'd been there to protect her. He was nice, determined. He'd just never expected the woman he was supposed to be guarding to turn on him and run.

She took several deep breaths and started off again, this time at a quick walk. Could this person really have eyes everywhere? Would they have known if she had spoken to Detective Wild? But what if he'd tried to stop her? What if his interference had caused Lauren's death?

Again, and most logical, what if she got there and the murderer just killed all three of them?

That was definitely possible. But...

She had no choice. And she knew just how Lena had felt the

day she had taken pills rather than watch her baby die.

There was still a ways to go. She crossed Rampart and quickly ran down a side street. She suddenly saw several police cars and wondered if they might be looking for her. Detective Wild would have likely called in her disappearance immediately.

But she bypassed them and reached the cemetery, running through the entrance as fast as she could. Like most cemeteries in the city, it had been laid out in lanes with small mausoleums lining each side, and occasional patches with in-ground burials, wall vaults or *ovens*, and single, aboveground tombs.

She knew the way to where she needed to be.

The gates were open. The Marley family mausoleum had not been properly resealed since William had been exhumed.

But she didn't head straight there *or* to the Marceau tomb. She was probably a fool. She remained torn, wondering how many killers were involved, if they really would have known if she had spoken to Detective Wild, and where they were now...

Did they know she was coming? That she was here?

She edged around the vault in front of her, trying to determine if she had been right about her destination. Did the killer want her here? And did the killer really hold Lauren and Jared?

Tangled vines surrounded the tomb, but she carefully crept around it. As she was doing so, she realized that she was being followed. Someone was behind her.

She reached into her bag, wishing she had a gun—and that she knew how to use one—and sought her phone.

She stopped and swung around, holding her cell high.

Someone stood in front of her, entirely clad in black like a child who had found a black bedsheet with which to play ghost.

Man? Woman? A smaller person, she thought. *Medium in stature but small for a man.*

"You're holding a cell phone on me?" the person demanded. The voice was amused and still coming to her distorted.

"I have the FBI on speed dial. You make a move toward me, my finger twitches, and they're all over you in two seconds."

How had this tiny person held Lauren and Jared and caused Lauren to scream?

Easy. He or she held a small gun in one hand.

And a large, glinting knife in the other.

"You let them go this instant. And you're an idiot. If you kill me, it won't get you any closer to Stephanie and the baby. It will only get you caught."

"You didn't talk to the cop. I know you didn't."

"They're closing in on you anyway."

"Oh, they'll never get to the bottom of it."

"I want to see Lauren and Jared."

"You'll see them. You just need to get into the tomb."

"No. I need to see them out here. I will hit speed dial. If we're all going to die, so are you."

If she kept this person talking, was she buying time? Detective Wild would have called Ryder by now. The police would be scouring the city.

But would anyone know to look in a small, almost-forgotten cemetery in Tremé?

"Why are you after me anyway?" she demanded. "I'm not a Marceau!"

"You know," the black-draped creature told her. "You know... Lena talked about you. She said you were amazing. I've—I've felt things. The bitch came back. Lena came back. And she came back to you. Eventually, you'll know, and you're going to tell them what happened and—"

"You think Lena came back? If I knew, I would have told them by now. Listen, no one knows who you are. Let my friends go. Let me go. I mean, I don't know how you pulled the rest of it off—"

"Me? Oh, not alone, my dear. We all played our parts. All for one and one for all. That's the only way you can ever trust anyone. Absolute loyalty comes when anyone is in danger of the death penalty. When the guilt is shared evenly. Ah, the challenges were great. The danger was great. But the rewards...endless. We all had alibis, absolutely ironclad. And there you have it."

Suddenly, it all made sense.

Keep her talking, keep her talking! she told herself.

"I see. Well, I'd watch it if I were you," Casey said.

"What are you talking about? You need to get in that tomb. That's where you'll find your friends."

"So you can shoot us all? That's not such a great idea either. A small cemetery...you figured no one comes here. No one will hear the shots. But that's a small enclosure. You're a small woman. If you want to kill me, you didn't come up with the best idea. I'm surprised the foursome let you in on this. I mean, whoever managed to get William Marley chock-full of cocaine to induce a heart attack...that was brilliant. Even if there had been an autopsy, how do you prove that someone forced him to overdose? And killing Anthony? Lure him to the roof, and he falls over. No cameras, no one there, and it was probably staged to look like an accident or a suicide. If there had been a stray weather chopper or someone up on a taller building, it could have even appeared that Anthony was going to jump, and they were trying to talk him down."

"Foursome?"

"Well, they paid you, that foursome. Obviously. I guess your part in it all—for a handsome reward—was to see that one of them was able to get in, cut the video system, and go after Lena. That didn't take a rocket scientist. Threaten a baby, and a mother will do almost anything."

"You think you're so smart. It wasn't a foursome."

"Barton Quincy approached you, right?" Casey asked pleasantly.

"No, Miss Smarty Pants. Larry approached me. He said Anthony and Lena were ruining the company, and we'd all wind up on the streets if things were done their way. I worked my rear off for years for those people. Member of the family, they called me. Lena never even trusted me with Annette. She was always with that kid. Anthony barely knew I existed. Such good people! I was nothing to them. I was like the air. So, when Larry came to me and said he needed to get into the house and told me what he was going to pay me to help, I made sure he got in."

"Interesting that you felt that way. I saw how kind Stephanie was to you. But let's see. Barton Quincy warned you to make sure you were at your book club. Did you know then that he was going to kill Lena? Did you know about William Marley or Anthony?"

She shrugged. "I suspected, but... Stop it. And that family—not nice! They were patronizing. You need to get into the tomb."

"*You* need to figure out another plan. While you're shooting one of us, the other two will jump you. The tomb is too tight. So, two of us are dead, but so are you," Casey said.

"You think you're so smart!" Gail Reeves screamed and ripped off her mask and voice modulator. "You thought that up all by yourself. Sorry, it won't happen that way. Barton told me you're just a nut job despite how Lena said she loved your store and you. She said there was something so special about you. That you saw things."

"And you're trying to kill me—without permission from the guys—because you think Lena's ghost will tell me everything? Oh, Gail. Lena didn't even know you were the one who let her killer in. Who was it by the way? Justin?"

Gail waved her gun in the air. "Justin? Don't be an idiot. I don't think he could successfully set out to kill a cockroach. Justin wasn't in on this."

"Who killed Lena?"

"Who cares if you know? You know I will kill you. Larry took care of William. Harry Miller was responsible for seeing that Anthony went off the roof. And Barton Quincy took care of Lena—and he was anxious to do it."

"But they don't know what you're doing now, do they? Because if you weren't freaked out by the fact that I saw Lena's ghost—I do see her, by the way—you'd never have made this mistake. And it is a mistake. It will bring the cops down on all of you like locusts."

Gail Reeves smiled. She was nothing like a kindly grandmother.

There was malice—and lunacy—in her eyes.

"I have my money. I'll be long gone. Go, get into the tomb. If you die like a nice girl, I might let your friends live."

She will never let anyone live, Casey thought.

But she was trying to buy time. Heading for the tomb could buy her more.

"Lena, hey! There you are," she said.

Lena wasn't there, but Casey wanted to see the effect her words had on Gail Reeves.

Gail glared at her.

But as Casey reached the gate, it began swinging as if there were a breeze. She frowned.

Lena had gone to the board meeting. Could she be here? If she was, did that mean Ryder was here, too?

But it wasn't Lena. Casey saw the ghost of a World War II soldier by the gate. Given his uniform, he had been United States Air Force.

She blinked. A second ghost. One helping her.

This time, she wouldn't pass out. She was fighting for her life.

"Dante Marceau, Miss Nicholson. Friend of Lena. I'm sorry to say I didn't make it back from Normandy, but I'm delighted to be here today to help you in any way I can. Lena has told me all about you."

Yes, of course, Lena had friends now who were ghosts.

"Thank you!" Casey said aloud.

It was almost pitch-black inside the tomb. Only a small stained-glass window at the rear allowed in shards of colored light.

It was enough.

Gail Reeves had managed to get Jared and Lauren inside. They were tied back to back and seated just below the stained-glass window.

Gail had used her blade on Lauren, leaving a bloody slash across her cheek.

Her friends both looked at Casey as if they were heartsick. Terrified, but sick that she had come.

That she would ultimately join their fate. Casey closed her eyes briefly. Her life didn't flash before her. She smelled the moldy scent of the tomb, saw the niche where William Marley's body had recently lain. The floor was dusty, spiderwebs teased the walls and crypts. It was truly the home of the dead.

"Go, go, get in!" Gail said harshly.

"Wait!" Casey said. "She's here. Lena is here. Be careful—"

The gate didn't just jiggle or sway. It slammed hard, separating Casey from Gail. Unnerved, Gail fired a shot. It slammed into stone.

She took better aim to fire again.

But the gun was suddenly ripped cleanly from her hand as Ryder leapt out from behind a neighboring tomb, his movements smooth and easy.

Gail screamed as her fingers twisted, and she fell to the ground in front of the mausoleum. But she bolted up, the knife in her hand, raving mad as she lunged at Ryder. He caught her wrist and grabbed the knife. When she tried to strike him, he ducked and struck back.

"Ryder, thank God!" Casey breathed, starting to come out of the tomb.

"No, no, get back in there for a minute. Let me get Gail in there and then close the gate," Ryder said.

"What—?"

"They know I left. And they know Gail is a whack job."

Casey edged back into the tomb, hunkering down as Ryder

lifted Gail's unconscious body, slid her in, and closed the gate. Then, he disappeared.

Casey moved closer to Lauren and Jared, bringing a finger to her lips in the strange and eerily colored darkness that was the realm of the dead.

"She's got to be here. I told you we needed to do something about her!"

Larry Swenson was doing the speaking.

"We needed her. We had to get to Stephanie and the baby, and she was our shot. If we can't kill them, this has all been for nothing."

Harry Miller was with Larry Swenson. They were walking through the graveyard, hurriedly coming toward the tomb.

"What if the cops get here?" Larry asked.

"We lay it on Gail. Say we were getting suspicious. Barton should have been here, too, but he's always keeping himself out of the way. Bastard! Thinks if we get ourselves killed, he'll take the whole prize. Then, he'd have to kill Justin Marceau, too. And he hates getting his hands dirty," Harry said disgustedly.

"He got his hands dirty. He killed Lena," Larry mumbled.

"He thought he could control her. When he couldn't...he really hated her."

The two were almost at the mausoleum.

Ryder suddenly stepped out in front of them.

"Gentlemen," he said. "I'm afraid you're going to have to stop there. You're under arrest for murder."

Casey inched forward, moving over the prone shape of Gail Reeves.

She saw both men draw guns.

But Ryder, who had sounded so easygoing, who hadn't even been holding his Glock, got both men before they could fire their weapons. Larry Swenson spun around and fell as a bullet ripped through his shoulder, and Harry Miller screamed like a crazed banshee as his hand was shattered.

By then, cops and FBI agents were running through the cemetery. Ryder opened the door to the tomb, and Casey leapt up, anxious to free her tied and gagged friends. Casey hugged Lauren and Jared as the pair cried with relief. They garbled out words to explain how Gail had been hiding in the back of Lauren's car and had forced them here at gunpoint, and then bound and forced them to gag each other.

Gail had secured them together in the tomb and then cut Lauren so she would scream, and Casey would come.

It was bedlam.

Lauren and Jared were taken away in an ambulance to be checked out, and so Lauren could receive stitches.

Larry Swenson, Harry Miller, and Gail Reeves were taken away.

Ghosts milled about and watched the activity. Lena Marceau stood with Dante Marceau, the apparitions arm-in-arm.

"I don't think this place has ever seen so much life," she said, grinning.

Braxton Wild walked over to Casey and hugged her tightly. "You're all right. You're all right!" Then he frowned. "Young lady, don't you ever do such a thing again."

"I'm sorry, Detective Wild," she said.

He grinned. "Call me Braxton. I hear we're going to Frenchman Street together later tonight to listen to some kickass bands."

Casey smiled at him. "Okay by me."

Braxton looked at Ryder and said, "The police picked up Barton Quincy. He's busy blaming it all on the housekeeper, claiming innocence. And we also have Justin, who is also claiming innocence."

"From everything I heard, Justin *is* innocent," Casey told him.

"Well, we'll see about talking to him and letting him go this afternoon. The others...they'll face state and federal charges." He looked at Ryder. "You could have killed them. You let them off easy."

Ryder shook his head. "They'll be in a maximum-security prison. They'll never get out. They need to suffer a long, long time for what they did."

Ryder put an arm around Casey. "Should we be going out tonight? Are you all right? What about Lauren and Jared?"

"Yes, we should go out tonight." She grimaced. "Life is short. Let's live it," she said softly.

Epilogue

They didn't go out that night. There was far too much paperwork. And too many people who had to understand a great deal. Jackson worried at first that they might have trouble in court, but they quickly learned that every one of the conspirators was ready to turn on the other.

They all wanted deals.

The best the conspirators would get was the death sentence taken off the table.

No, they didn't go out that night. Or the next. But now, a few weeks later, it was finally time to put everything behind them and celebrate.

Even Stephanie came. It was going to be a long time before she trusted leaving Annette with anyone, but there *was* one babysitter she had come to trust and love.

Jackson Crow.

And Jackson had insisted that Stephanie get out.

Justin Marceau was with them. He and Stephanie were going to have a hell of a time trying to remake the company and find good people to help them. But they both believed that good people were out there. And Justin was both terrified and grateful.

He knew he would have eventually been on the hit list.

"Really, the only way it broke was Gail Reeves going crazy believing in ghosts," Justin said. He shook his head, and Casey smiled. "Some people."

Jared and Lauren came. And Braxton had ridden with Ryder and Casey. Jared even sat in with a few of the bands they stopped to see, and it was great to see him happy and in his element.

Toward the end of the evening, and after much thought and discussion with Ryder, Casey asked Lauren and Jared what they thought about taking over the shop. It was their shop, really. They were the art and the music.

"But," Lauren told her, "you were always the beautiful mind."

"I knew it from the moment I walked into the shop," Lena's ghost said, and Casey smiled, though the others couldn't hear Lena. "You were, but these two are its heart. Just like Ryder is yours, and you are his." Casey smiled wider.

"So you're moving in with Ryder?" Jared asked.

She nodded. "But we both love NOLA. We'll be back."

The night with friends was wonderful. The next day was better.

They went back to the cemetery—Jackson, Stephanie, Annette, Ryder, and Casey.

They stood by the tomb as other ghosts made appearances.

Lena had shared with Casey that she'd sensed Anthony's presence when the arrests were made in the cemetery, but nothing since. Still, she had a feeling she might go with him when the time was right.

It was daytime, but it seemed a streak of light stronger than the sun shone down by the tomb. And a misty, almost golden image of a man appeared in that ray of light.

He reached out a hand to Lena.

Lena paused, and a collective gasp of fear went through the group as the ghostly mother managed to take hold of her child and then race to the light with the baby.

"Annette," Stephanie whispered.

But the group seemed to be just a burst of light for a minute as Lena and Anthony held their beloved daughter.

Then, Lena ran back with the baby, hugging Stephanie and returning the child to her guardian's arms.

"I love you. Please understand. Please love her as I would. As I will always love you both. And everyone, thank you. Thank you!" she said.

The light was gone, and Lena with it. Stephanie sobbed softly, and Ryder set his arm around her. He assured her that he and Casey would stick around for a while. There would be more paperwork and additional things about the case to untangle. And Casey knew he would do whatever was necessary to make sure everything was locked up tight, that the board members and Gail got what was coming to them, and that his family was never harmed again.

Later that night, lying together, Ryder seemed thoughtful.

"Are you sure you don't mind picking up and leaving, giving up everything to come with me?" he asked her, not for the first time.

She smiled and stroked his face.

"Jared and Lauren will be fine with the store. Jennie Sanders will know she has special powers now." She laughed. "Someone tall, dark, and dangerously handsome *did* enter my life to sweep me off my feet. We have learned so much about death...and life. Let's seize it and live it," she said.

He smiled, straddling her.

"You do have a beautiful mind. And...hmm. A beautiful rest of you, too."

She laughed softly. "Thank you. And as for life..."

"Let's get to it!"

He kissed her.

Life.

She had come close to losing it. She had discovered that she could help someone who had lost it. And now...

It was a gift. And she would cherish every minute of it.

Especially with Ryder.

* * * *

Also from 1001 Dark Nights and Heather Graham, discover Blood Night, Haunted Be the Holidays, Hallow Be The Haunt, Crimson Twilight, When Irish Eyes Are Haunting, All Hallows Eve, Blood on the Bayou, Haunted House, and Descend to Darkness.

Discover More Heather Graham

Descend to Darkness
A Krewe of Hunters Novella
Coming October 11, 2022

Angela Hawkins Crow awakens to find herself in total darkness. Despite her years as a Krewe agent, she is first seized with panic, but her life and her training kick in. She knows that she must stay calm and go back in her mind to find out how she got where she is…and where she might be.

Meanwhile, an eerie phone call comes in at Krewe headquarters, warning them all that Angela has been kidnapped, describing her ordeal, and lamenting the fact that she can't be saved.

But there is no such thing with the Krewe. In the dark and in the light, the fight is on.

Angela determines that she might know what has happened to her, and she is prepared when her kidnapper can't resist the temptation to check in on her.

By following his wife's expertise with research, Jackson discovers what just might be happening—and in the darkness of night and the silence of the graveyard, he'll risk everything to find the woman he loves.

* * * *

Haunted House
A Krewe of Hunters Novella

Halloween! Strange things are going to happen and every year, while loving the holiday, members of the Krewe of Hunters also dread it.

Something somewhere is bound to happen.

And it does.

Krewe member Jon Dickson's fiancée Kylie Connelly is contacted by an old friend who has just moved to Salem, Massachusetts, when the unimaginable happens as the holiday approaches.

Jenny Auger has just managed to buy the historic home of her dreams. But it comes with far more history than she ever imagined—the skeletal remains of seven victims interred in the old walls of the house years and years before—along with a threatening curse.

And strange things are happening in the city. Bizarre attacks…murders that mimic days of old.

With Halloween on the way.

Kylie has a history with the city of Salem, and her strange talent for being within the minds of those under attack—first realized in the city—remains sharp.

But the situation is far more dire than what they have discovered, with strange events and attacks occurring.

And with all their talent for crime solving—with help from the living and the dead—it still remains to be seen if they can solve the murders of the past before Halloween, and the bloodbath that just might occur if the sins of a time gone by cannot be brought to light.

* * * *

Blood Night

A Krewe of Hunters Novella

Any member of the Krewe of Hunters is accustomed to the strange. And to conversing now and then with the dead.

For Andre Rousseau and Cheyenne Donegal, an encounter with the deceased in a cemetery is certainly nothing new.

But this year, Halloween is taking them across the pond—unofficially.

Their experiences in life haven't prepared them for what's to come.

Cheyenne's distant cousin and dear friend Emily Donegal has called from London. Murder has come to her neighborhood, with bodies just outside Highgate Cemetery, drained of blood.

The last victim was found at Emily's doorstep, and evidence seems to be arising not just against her fiancé, Eric, but against Emily, too. But Emily isn't just afraid of the law—many in the great city are beginning to believe that the historic Vampire of Highgate is making himself known, aided and abetted by adherents. Some are even angry and frightened enough to believe they should take matters into their own hands.

Andre and Cheyenne know they're in for serious trouble when they arrive, and they soon come to realize that the trouble might be deadly not just for Emily and Eric, but for themselves as well.

There's help to be found in the beautiful and historic old cemetery.

And as All Hallows Eve looms, they'll be in a race against time, seeking the truth before the infamous vampire has a chance to strike again.

* * * *

Haunted Be the Holidays

A Krewe of Hunters Novella

When you're looking for the victim of a mysterious murder in a theater, there is nothing like calling on a dead diva for help! Krewe members must find the victim if they're to discover the identity of a murderer at large, one more than willing to kill the performers when he doesn't like the show.

It's Halloween at the Global Tower Theatre, a fantastic and historic theater owned by Adam Harrison and run by spouses of Krewe members. During a special performance, a strange actor makes an appearance in the middle of the show, warning of dire events if his murder is not solved before another holiday rolls around.

Dakota McCoy and Brodie McFadden dive into the mystery. Both have a. special talent for dealing with ghosts, but this one is proving elusive. With the help of Brodie's diva mother and his ever-patient father—who were killed together when a stage chandelier fell upon them—Dakota and Brodie set out to solve the case.

If they can't solve the murder quickly, there will be no Thanksgiving for the Krewe...

* * * *

Hallow Be the Haunt

A Krewe of Hunters Novella

Years ago, Jake Mallory fell in love all over again with Ashley Donegal—while he and the Krewe were investigating a murder that replicated a horrible Civil War death at her family's Donegal Plantation.

Now, Ashley and Jake are back—planning for their wedding, which will take place the following month at Donegal Plantation, her beautiful old antebellum home.

But Halloween is approaching and Ashley is haunted by a ghost warning her of deaths about to come in the city of New Orleans, deaths caused by the same murderer who stole the life of the beautiful ghost haunting her dreams night after night.

At first, Jake is afraid that returning home has simply awakened some of the fear of the past…

But as Ashley's nightmares continue, a body count begins to accrue in the city…

And it's suddenly a race to stop a killer before Hallow's Eve comes to a crashing end, with dozens more lives at stake, not to mention heart, soul, and life for Jake and Ashley themselves.

* * * *

Crimson Twilight

A Krewe of Hunters Novella

It's a happy time for Sloan Trent and Jane Everett. What could be happier than the event of their wedding? Their Krewe friends will all be there and the event will take place in a medieval castle transported brick by brick to the New England coast. Everyone is festive and thrilled... until the priest turns up dead just hours before the nuptials. Jane and Sloan must find the truth behind the man and the murder--the secrets of the living and the dead--before they find themselves bound for eternity--not in wedded bliss but in the darkness of an historical wrong and their own brutal deaths.

* * * *

When Irish Eyes Are Haunting
A Krewe of Hunters Novella

Devin Lyle and Craig Rockwell are back, this time to a haunted castle in Ireland where a banshee may have gone wild—or maybe there's a much more rational explanation—one that involves a disgruntled heir, murder, and mayhem, all with that sexy light touch Heather Graham has turned into her trademark style.

* * * *

All Hallows Eve
A Krewe of Hunters Novella

Salem was a place near and dear to Jenny Duffy and Samuel Hall -- it was where they'd met on a strange and sinister case. They never dreamed that they'd be called back. That history could repeat itself in a most macabre and terrifying fashion. But, then again, it was Salem at Halloween. Seasoned Krewe members, they still find themselves facing the unspeakable horrors in a desperate race to save each other-and perhaps even their very souls.

* * * *

Blood on the Bayou
A Cafferty & Quinn Novella

It's winter and a chill has settled over the area near New Orleans, finding a stream of blood, a tourist follows it to a dead man, face down in the bayou.

The man has been done in by a vicious beating, so violent that his skull has been crushed in.

It's barely a day before a second victim is found... once again so badly thrashed that the water runs red. The city becomes riddled with fear.

An old family friend comes to Danni Cafferty, telling her that he's terrified, he's certain that he's received a message from the Blood Bayou killer--It's your turn to pay, blood on the bayou.

Cafferty and Quinn quickly become involved, and--as they all begin to realize that a gruesome local history is being repeated--they find themselves in a fight to save not just a friend, but, perhaps, their very own lives.

About Heather Graham

New York Times and *USA Today* bestselling author, Heather Graham, majored in theater arts at the University of South Florida. After a stint of several years in dinner theater, back-up vocals, and bartending, she stayed home after the birth of her third child and began to write. Her first book was with Dell, and since then, she has written over two hundred novels and novellas including category, suspense, historical romance, vampire fiction, time travel, occult and Christmas family fare.

She is pleased to have been published in approximately twenty-five languages. She has written over 200 novels and has 60 million books in print. She has been honored with awards from booksellers and writers' organizations for excellence in her work, and she is also proud to be a recipient of the Silver Bullet Award from the International Thriller Writers and was also awarded the prestigious Thriller Master in 2016. She is also a recipient of the Lifetime Achievement Award from RWA. Heather has had books selected for the Doubleday Book Club and the Literary Guild, and has been quoted, interviewed, or featured in such publications as The Nation, Redbook, Mystery Book Club, People and USA Today and appeared on many newscasts including Today, Entertainment Tonight and local television.

Heather loves travel and anything that has to do with the water and is a certified scuba diver. She also loves ballroom dancing. Each year she hosts a ball or dinner theater raising money for the Pediatric Aids Society and in 2006 she hosted the first Writers for New Orleans Workshop to benefit the stricken Gulf Region. She is also the founder of "The Slush Pile Players," presenting something that's "almost like entertainment" for various conferences and benefits. Married since high school graduation and the mother of five, her greatest love in life remains her family, but she also believes her career has been an incredible gift, and she is grateful every day to be doing something that she loves so very much for a living.

Also from Heather Graham

Krewe of Hunters series

Phantom Evil
Heart of Evil
Sacred Evil
The Evil Inside
The Unseen
The Unholy
The Unspoken
The Uninvited
The Night is Watching
The Night is Alive
The Night is Forever
The Cursed
The Hexed
The Betrayed
The Silenced
The Forgotten
The Hidden
Haunted Destiny
Deadly Fate
Darkest Journey
Dying Breath
Dark Rites
Wicked Deeds
Fade to Black
Pale As Death
Echoes of Evil
Christmas, the Krewe and a Large White Rabbit
The Summoning
The Seekers
The Stalking
Seeing the Darkness
Deadly Touch
Dreaming Death
Horror-Ween

The Best Christmas Ever

Other Books by Heather Graham

A Dangerous Game
A Perfect Obsession
Flawless
Waking the Dead
Let the Dead Sleep
Night of the Vampires
The Keepers
Ghost Moon
Ghost Night
Ghost Shadow
The Killing Edge
Night of the Wolves
Home in Time for Christmas
Unhallowed Ground
Dust to Dust
Nightwalker
Deadly Gift
Deadly Harvest
Deadly Night
The Death Dealer
The Last Noel
The Séance
Blood Red
The Dead Room
Kiss of Darkness
The Vision
The Island
Ghost Walk
Killing Kelly
The Presence
Dead on the Dance Floor
Picture Me Dead
Haunted
Hurricane Bay
A Season of Miracles
Night of the Blackbirds

Never Sleep with Strangers
Eyes of Fire
Slow Burn
Night Heat

From 1001 Dark Nights

Blood Night
Hallow Be The Haunt
Crimson Twilight
When Irish Eyes Are Haunting
All Hallow's Eve
Blood on the Bayou
Haunted Be the Holidays

Wild Fire
A Chaos Novella
By Kristen Ashley

Acknowledgments from the Author

As ever, my love and gratitude to Liz Berry, MJ Rose and Jillian Stein for their unwavering support, generosity of experience and stalwart dedication to me and the romance community.

Chapter One

Movie Star Gorgeous

Dutch

Dutch's phone rang while he was in the T-U-V section at Fortnum's Used Books.

He pulled the cell out of the back pocket of his jeans and checked the screen.

Jagger Calling.

He loved his brother, but it was hit or miss if he'd pick up a call from the guy.

This was only because Jag was all about good times. Getting drunk. Getting laid. Getting out of town for a change of scenery, doing it on a long ride, and doing it in order to get drunk or laid in a fresh locale.

Jag was twenty-six, it was his time to carouse.

At least that's what their ma and Hound said.

Dutch was twenty-eight, and apparently it was his time to carouse too.

At least that was what their mother and Hound urged him to do.

Dutch just wasn't feeling it.

Not anymore.

Not that he ever did. That was not the kind of guy he was.

He could see getting a buzz on, and he did.

But being around dudes who were so drunk, they were either sloppy or turned into assholes, not so much.

Jag never took it that far. His brother just got happy(er) and (more) sociable when he got a buzz on.

Jag's puking-and-being-an-asshole days ended that night their motorcycle club, Chaos, voted Jagger in as prospect. Then they made him drink to the verge of alcohol poisoning. After that, with the mother of all hangovers, they made him clean up after himself and everyone else who'd over-imbibed.

Come to think of it, that was when Dutch's getting-drunk, puking-and-being-an-asshole days ended too. Before Jag's. When the brothers had taken Dutch on as a recruit and made him do the same thing.

These were the ways of Chaos, Dutch had learned.

Even shit that didn't seem to have a purpose, had a purpose.

Tack, their retired president, was that kind of guy, that was where he led the Club, and he'd cemented them there, all so he could hand that kind of Club down to his son.

Something he did.

In other words, no man wanted to be around another man who could not handle his booze. Who didn't know when to stop. Who got to the point he was puking and being an asshole.

So you learned right away in Chaos that wasn't the brother to be.

And they found a way to teach that lesson and made you that kind of brother.

He ignored the call, shoved the phone back into his pocket and slid the volume from the shelf.

Vonnegut. *Bluebeard.* Hardback.

Dutch opened the book and saw, in subtle pencil written at the top right of the opening page, *$5.00.*

Vonnegut hardback, five dollars.

A freaking steal.

He set it on top of *Rabbit, Run* and retraced his steps to the M-N-O section.

He checked and it was a negatory.

They almost never had a copy of *Confederacy of Dunces*, which sucked.

So he retraced to E-F-G and hit gold.

Ellison. *Invisible Man.*

He snatched that up and headed to the Young Adult section, even though he knew it was a fool's errand. He'd checked every time he'd come to Fortnum's for the last year.

He was right.

It wasn't there.

He hit up the T-U-V section again, just in case it wasn't in Young Adult.

Nope.

Not there either.

Dutch then walked back up to the front and saw Duke, as usual, was behind the book counter.

The man's eyes came direct to him the instant he'd cleared the stacks.

Duke was a mainstay at Fortnum's. An ex-English professor who, decades ago, left the university politics, track to tenure and rat race behind, dropped out and made his life about his wife, his bike and his job at a used bookstore.

Dutch liked Duke, respected the man, but he didn't like the look in Duke's eyes these days when Dutch would come to the store. He further wasn't big on the looks Duke and Tex would exchange when Dutch was around.

Tex was a Vietnam vet, an ex-recluse, and an inveterate cat lover. So much of the last, there were dozens of pictures of cats, all Tex's, tacked haphazard on the wall behind the coffee counter under the shelves of cups and mugs.

The man was also a lunatic. And it was against all odds that huge, loud, bad-mannered, cat-loving dude was the best barista in the state and at least everyone in Denver knew it, so even now, when it was one in the afternoon, there was a line ten strong in front of the coffee counter.

But even with all that, Tex was a good guy. Solid.

Like Duke.

Family, the folk at Fortnum's. Duke, Tex, Indy (the owner of the store), Jet, one of Indy's best friends who also worked there, their large posse.

Dutch had a family like that. A big one of MC brothers and their women and their children.

Good, solid folk, down to their bones.

And yet…

"*Invisible Man*, this for you, or someone else?" Duke asked, taking Dutch's attention, and Dutch realized he was so lost to his thoughts, he was working on autopilot and hadn't noticed he'd approached the register and laid down his books.

"Someone else," Dutch answered.

"You read it?" Duke asked.

"Yeah," Dutch told him.

"Whole world should read it," Duke muttered, jabbing a thick finger against the screen of the tablet that stood in for a till.

"Yeah," Dutch agreed. "Listen, you wouldn't have any copies of *The Hate U Give* by Angie Thomas that haven't been shelved yet, would you?"

Duke shook his head. "Not many givin' up that book. We get one, you want me to call you?"

He could go to Barnes and Noble, easy.

With Tex as her barista, not to mention Indy and her crew all being the subject of those books that had been published, so folks came in all the time, Indy wasn't hurting for customers, or cash.

Still, Dutch bought his books exclusively from Fortnum's.

And he had a lot of books.

He had no idea why Fortnum's was his go-to. It wasn't about buying local or any of that other millennial shit.

Thinking on it, it was the fact he liked the vibe.

It was the fact that walking in there was like walking into someone's house.

Like coming home.

To family.

Shaking off his thoughts, he agreed, "That'd be cool."

"You wanna stay for a cup o' joe and a talk?" Duke asked, and Dutch hid his surprise.

The man hadn't approached. Not in word or deed.

There were the looks he gave Dutch, the ones he exchanged with Tex.

But he never said dick.

"No, got shit to do this afternoon," he lied.

He had no shit to do that afternoon.

Or at all.

Ever.

"Boy—" Duke started.

"I'm not a boy," Dutch bit.

His temper wasn't usually short, but these days, it could be.

This was why Duke blinked.

He then said, "Son—"

"I'm not your son either," Dutch returned.

"Right then." Duke's voice was no longer a friendly rumble. It was tight. "First, my age can't have escaped you, considerin' all this gray hair and wrinkles, so you are a boy to me, and you will be until you're sixty and I'm dead. And second, any man's a man at all, a man that's younger than him and obviously struggling is his son. A son he looks after."

Christ, was he not hiding it?

"I'm not struggling," he lied again.

"Dutch—"

"Brother, just ring me up so I can get on with my day," Dutch demanded.

Duke was silent a beat.

He then finished ringing him up, and Dutch paid.

"No bag," he grunted.

Duke slid the books over the counter toward Dutch.

Dutch had turned, avoiding Tex's eyes as he did, and started heading toward the door when Duke called, "You know that door is always open, but the one to my cabin in Evergreen is too, man."

Duke was good people and Dutch had acted like an asshole.

So he lifted a hand and flicked out a finger to indicate he'd heard Duke's words before he walked out the door.

It was early November, and cold, and he'd had a trip planned to Fortnum's on his agenda that day, so he was not on his bike.

He was in his truck.

And right then, he walked the five blocks to his vehicle huddling into his leather cut. A spot that even five blocks away was considered a score in an area that had grown popular over the years, to the point all the good shit was smushed in with all the trendy shit.

Trendy, like there was a fucking tiki bar, for fuck's sake.

As the years had gone by and the new edged out some of the old, Fortnum's had become the bastion of old-school cool on South Broadway in Denver.

And Dutch hoped like hell the millennials—of which he was

one, but he wasn't a fan of his membership—got bored with Broadway and returned it to the freaks and geeks and antiquers and gays and hip cats and hipper pussycats who knew true cool came from a vintage clothing shop, not a Free People catalog.

He climbed into his truck as his phone rang again.

He checked it.

It was Jagger.

He ignored the call, started up his truck, and embarked on the only other item on his agenda that day.

He headed to King's Shelter, a safe place for runaway kids.

King's provided food. A bed. TV. Some counseling if you took it. Some tutoring, if you took that too.

Mostly, it was a no-pressure place for kids who couldn't hack home so they wouldn't be on the streets. They could get a decent meal, sleep in a clean bed, take a shower and catch up on their reality programs.

Right, that wasn't entirely accurate.

There was food, clean beds, and a huge TV.

But also, there was pressure.

That said, Juliet Crowe, the woman who ran the place, made an art of making pressure seem like no pressure.

If there was a way to reconcile shit at home, she'd find it, and reconcile that shit.

If there was no way, she'd figure out an alternate avenue for a kid that didn't include hanging downtown, falling into dealing, using, or whoring.

It was just she was a dab hand at finessing that shit.

He parked at the shelter, got out, grabbed one of the books, and headed in.

Chances were probably seventy-thirty the kid wouldn't be there.

Dutch's day looked up when he saw him there.

He didn't hesitate moving right to the guy who was not at one of the couches around the big sixty-incher, watching some show where three bitches were wearing skintight mini-dresses and four-inch heels, shouting at each other and pulling each other's hair.

He was sitting at a table on the outskirts.

That was Carlyle.

The outsider.

Even at a shelter for runaway kids.

"The wig's gonna go, wait and see," he declared as Dutch made the table.

Dutch turned his head and looked at the TV.

Carlyle was right. One of the women was shrieking because another one had pulled off her wig.

Dutch sighed and looked back to a boy who was really no longer a boy.

The kid was six nine if he was an inch. Three hundred pounds if he was an ounce. Dark skin. Brown eyes hard as marbles.

He was also seventeen, and if something wasn't done, soon, he'd be free to do whatever he wanted.

And Dutch did not see this going in the right direction.

He knew why Carlyle was there.

And Dutch could be the only guy in Denver who could get him out of there.

And he needed to get this kid out of there.

Outside the obvious, Dutch had no idea what was at stake for the future.

The cure for cancer.

A Nobel Prize.

Or just this kid becoming a billionaire.

All he knew was that whatever was at stake was big.

He tossed the book on the table.

Carlyle didn't look at it, kept his eyes glued to the TV.

"Your mind's gonna turn to mush, you stare at that shit too long," Dutch warned.

That brought Carlyle's eyes.

"Yeah?" he asked, the word short and belligerent.

"Yeah," Dutch confirmed.

Carlyle said nothing.

"I'm adding to the shelter's library," Dutch told him, dipping his head toward the book.

"And why would I give a shit?" Carlyle queried.

"Because you'd do better reading a decent book than watching zombie television."

Carlyle's heavy brows went up. "Zombie television?"

"There's nothing worthwhile to TV like that. It rots your mind. Turns you into a zombie."

Carlyle straightened in his chair, and to a man who had not

spent his formative years under the wing of the entirety of the Chaos MC, particularly a brother called Hound, Carlyle straightening might make his sphincter tighten.

But Dutch knew how to handle himself with fists, with a blade, with a piece, in most any situation. Chaos had seen to that.

More precisely, Hound had seen to that.

So when Carlyle's attention focused more fully on him, Dutch didn't twitch.

"Man, who gives a fuck?" he asked.

"I think me standing here is pretty good indication that I do," Dutch replied.

Carlyle looked back to the TV, muttering, "Fuck off."

"Carlyle—"

That was when he got the treatment he'd given Duke at Fortnum's.

But Carlyle style.

"Do you think I'm invisible? Do you fuckin' think I'm invisible?" Carlyle spat.

Somehow, even without looking at it, the kid had seen the cover of the book.

"What I think—" Dutch started.

"I've already read this book, motherfucker, and even if I hadn't, hear me, I don't need some white guy to show me the way of my people."

With that, he shoved the book off the table. It fell to the floor, and Dutch and Carlyle had the attention of the room even before Carlyle pushed his chair back so hard, it fell over as he stood and stalked to and out the front door.

Dutch drew a sharp breath into his nose, put his hands to his hips, and stared at the closing door thinking, *That didn't go very well.*

Then again, every approach he'd made for the last three months hadn't gone well.

"Dutch."

He heard her call his name, but he knew she was there before he heard it.

He turned, saw her standing about ten feet away, and serious as shit, Juliet Crowe was the most beautiful woman he'd seen in his whole goddamned life.

Movie star gorgeous.

Fuck.

He went to the book, bent, picked it up and set it on the table, headed to the chair and righted it, all before he moved her way.

He'd barely stopped in front of her when she asked, "You all right?"

"Tryin' to find a way to get in there, like we talked about."

"What was the book?" she asked.

"*Invisible Man*."

She nodded, and even though he didn't sense any disapproval, Dutch kept talking.

"It's not lost on me he's a Black guy, but it's just a really good book."

"He read *Skinny Legs and All* last week," she shared.

Dutch felt something in his chest loosen.

As far as he knew, nothing he'd tried these last months had gotten in there, and it wasn't just books. He'd offered Carlyle his time. He'd offered to share his story. He'd asked the kid if he wanted to work out with him at his boxing gym.

Nothing got in there.

But he'd brought *Skinny Legs and All* the week before.

"Shoulda brought in *Bluebeard*," he muttered.

"Cops came yesterday, looking for him," she went on.

Shit, shit, *shit*.

"Any news?" Dutch asked.

She shook her head, letting the concern leak into her eyes. "I talked to Eddie, the case is cold. They're closing loops, moving on."

Shit, shit, shit.

Dutch just stared at her, but he did it meaningfully.

She got closer so he knew she read his meaning.

"Dutch, every time a kid with promise, which is every kid that walks through those doors, comes here, and there's a situation, I have to weigh whether or not I ask my husband and his band of badass brothers to wade in and sort out that situation. Carlyle is no different. And Vance and the guys cannot spend all their time sorting out the problems of the kids at King's. They all have mortgages to pay, for one. For another, that's *my* job."

"Carlyle is a kid with a one hundred and forty-nine IQ who has full rides to MIT, Stanford and Columbia whose dad was shot dead while saving the life of a neighbor who had an intruder who was set on doin' more than stealin' from the woman. Carlyle is this fuckin' close," he held a thumb and forefinger in front of her eyes to demonstrate a point she knew better than him, "to flushing his entire life down the toilet. So I think Vance, Lee, Luke and company should tap in on this one and find the person who killed Carlyle's dad because the cops obviously cannot."

Vance—her husband—Lee, Luke and company being part of the band of badass brothers that made up Nightingale Investigations.

And while the cops had limited resources and rules they had to abide by, the boys at Nightingale did not.

"You know that I know about your dad, Dutch," she said softly.

He dropped his hand and stepped away.

"I know he was targeted because he was fighting the good fight," she kept at him.

"We're not talking about my father," he bit out.

"Aren't we?" she asked carefully.

"I had a mountain of support and I'm not a certified genius," he shot back.

"Carlyle has the same support, it just takes some kids time to work the hurt out, and the best we can do is make sure they don't stray too far while they're doing it," she returned.

"And what if he strays too far?"

Her eyes narrowed.

Her husband might be in a badass brotherhood, but Juliet Crowe used to be known as The Law. Years ago, she'd gone rogue when one of her kids overdosed, and she'd set about vigilante-ing the shit out of the drug dealers of Denver.

She'd been good at it.

She'd refocused her attention to King's, but the Lore of The Law had not died, which was most of the reason why she had so many kids there, they'd had to build onto the shelter.

And her years with the kids, her husband, her own brood of boys she and Vance had made, and her time on the streets meant she didn't miss much.

And she wasn't missing much now.

"What do you know?" she asked.

"He's not keeping good company, Jules."

"And you know this…how?" she pushed.

"I know it because when he clocked me, I saw him slip out the back of Shady's when he's too damn young to be in Shady's in the first place. Shady's is Resurrection's hang. I asked one of the Resurrection brothers who Carlyle was talkin' to and he shared it was a dude I did not want to know, and he wouldn't be comin' back to Shady's because Resurrection wasn't down with his presence there. And he hasn't been back. And neither has Carlyle."

She pressed her lips tightly together before she unpressed them to ask, "What? Drugs?"

"Black market."

"Black market what?"

"Black market everything. Designer gear. Pharmaceuticals. Maple syrup. Freakin' sperm. Anything and *everything*."

She looked surprised. "Maple syrup?"

"Yeah. That was my reaction. I looked it up. It's a thing in Canada. Farmers sell it under the table."

"Whoa," she muttered.

"This guy is part of a bigger operation," Dutch told her. "An operation that gets their hands on a kid like that, with a brain like his, he's hacking for the Russians at a million dollars an hour or worse."

He now saw humor in her expression as she said, "You have a very inventive mind."

He saw no humor in this situation at all and therefore laid it out.

"No, my dad's throat was slit in the parking lot of a pizza joint when he was gettin' into his truck to bring dinner home to his family. This put my mother in a tailspin it took nearly two decades for her to haul herself out of, which meant the man who loved her who was breathin', a man she also loved, didn't have her until it was almost too late for them to make their own family. And I know, along that road, no matter how much support I had, I asked myself the question of what the fuck's the point? A good man tries to do good, and gets his throat slit. A good man tries to do good, and gets a bullet to the neck and bleeds out on his neighbor's bedroom floor. So my mind isn't inventive, Jules. I know that dark place it goes when you think this world is so fucked, the only course you got is to get what you can for yourself and fuck everyone else."

"Point taken," she murmured.

"Talk to Vance," he ordered.

She shook her head. "I had Roam come in, chat with Carlyle, the wall he has up…" She paused, got closer, lowered her voice, and kept going. "I'm not saying I'm giving up on him. I don't give up on them even if they walk out that door and give up on us. I'm just warning you, Dutch, that sometimes, there's no help they'll accept. Sometimes, they're so set to stay in that dark place, you could run yourself ragged, and there's no pulling them out."

Roam used to be a kid in that shelter.

Roam was now known off the street as Roman, and he was a member of the badass brotherhood at Nightingale Investigations.

"It isn't a Black thing," he told her, because Roam was also Black.

"Roam was in this shelter. Roam gets it."

"It's a murdered father thing, Jules."

She nodded.

"I fucked up, making it a Black thing," he said.

"Yes," she agreed quietly.

"Fuck," he muttered.

She read his face again and went back on what she'd said earlier. "You could still get in there, Dutch. I mean, he was reading Tom Robbins last week."

"Yeah, but now I'm that well-intentioned, clueless, white dude biker so I'm out before I was ever really in," he returned.

"I don't think so. Roam told him about your dad."

Dutch clenched his teeth.

Jules kept talking.

"Roam told him about your dad, and he picked up that book, Dutch. There are different kinds of brotherhoods, and sadly, you two belong to an unusual one. And Carlyle is not one of those smart kids who's so topped out in brains, he's got no room for logic. He'll put it together that a biker wearing a cut isn't coming to a shelter and focusing on him because he wants to brag over cocktails that he's giving back to society. Just give him time."

Dutch looked over her head, something he could do, because the woman was not short, but he was six two.

"Vance dropped that bug in your ear about Carlyle for a reason, Dutch," she said.

He looked right at her.

It was not lost on him they'd played him. It was not lost on him that Vance, who was sober, was hanging at the Chaos Compound while the guys were throwing some back, when he rarely hung at the Compound, and he was talking about one of Jules's kids for the exact reason he was hanging at the Compound, talking about one of Jules's kids.

He was maneuvering Dutch's ass to be right there in an effort to get shit sorted with one of Jules's kids.

Nope, Juliet Crowe never gave up on any of her kids.

"I'll figure something out," he said.

She smiled at him.

And taking that smile in, knowing the woman she was, the heart she had, the grit, he had no idea how old she was, he just knew she was older than him by more than a decade.

But if she was not married to a man who she made clear was her heartbeat, and the mother to their three kids, Dutch would want in there.

Permanently.

He nodded, muttered some words of farewell, and moved out.

His phone rang as he made his way to his truck.

He pulled it out again, saw it was Jagger, and felt a frisson of disquiet slide up the back of his neck.

Three calls in less than an hour, that wasn't about going out and tying one on.

It could be their mother. Hound. Their little brother, Wilder. Any brother, really, in Chaos, their woman or one of their kids.

This on his mind, he took the call as he angled his ass into his truck.

"What's up?" he asked.

"Hey, you busy?" Jagger asked in return.

That wasn't the lead-in to trouble.

And regrettably, he was not busy.

Though Jag could need or want anything, most of that something Dutch wanted no part of, so he didn't share that news.

"What's up?" he repeated.

"Listen, I'm elbow deep in a build with Joker and unless we bust ass, we're not gonna make the deadline on this ride. And Carolyn has taken an extra shift because her landlord's an asshole and raised the rent. Again. So we need someone to go to the airport and pick up her sister. Carolyn thought I could do it. *I* thought I could do it. But we can't get this bitch to turn over and we don't know why, so I can't do it. Which means I need to ask you to do it. Her flight lands in an hour."

Dutch did not like this.

Carolyn was Jag's on-again, off-again girlfriend. There was no future to it, and both of them were down with that. They gravitated to each other when one of them was lonely or one of them wanted a good time or something familiar.

Carolyn lived in an apartment that was outside her reach because Carolyn had champagne tastes and a Diet Coke budget. Though one thing you could say about Carolyn, she worked for what she wanted. Which meant extra shifts as a CNA in a nursing home, a lot of house sitting, dog walking, babysitting and anything else she could do to earn a buck to pay for her trendy pad and her designer shoes.

Eventually, though, Carolyn would marry white picket fence. That wasn't Dutch's judgment. The woman was honest to the point of bluntness. She made no bones she was enjoying some rough trade before she pursued, then settled in with the real catch.

For some reason, Jag took no offense to this.

Dutch did.

He'd been around Carolyn a lot.

He'd never met the sister, but he'd heard about her, seeing as the sister was not a big fan of Carolyn's lifestyle and all that entailed and that bugged the shit out of Carolyn, who was a fan of sharing just about anything, including how much of a pain in the ass her big sister was.

Carolyn could loosen up enough to find her good times.

But from all reports, the sister had a stick up her ass lodged so high and tight, it'd take surgery and a miracle to extract it.

In other words, he had zero desire to drive to DIA to pick that woman up.

"Can't she Lyft?" Dutch asked.

"She's got some issue with Lyft, and Uber, I forget what it is. Reports of driver attacks on women or they're not paid enough or whatever it is with her, which is always something," Jag answered.

Yeah, from what he'd heard, it was always something.

"Right, so she can take a taxi," Dutch pointed out.

"It'd cost a mint."

"Light rail goes out there, Jag," Dutch kept at it. "It also comes back."

"Dude, if you've got nothin' on, can't you do your brother a solid?" Jagger demanded.

This was a good question.

Shit.

"Yeah, I can do you a solid."

"Thanks," Jagger replied. "I'll text her flight details and I'll get Carolyn to send a picture of her so you know who you're looking for."

"Great."

"Seriously, appreciate it, Dutch."

"Yeah."

"Later, brother."

"Later."

He disconnected, fired up his truck, and was at a stoplight before he checked his phone after he heard several texts come in.

The flight details, her name and…

Fuck.

A picture, and she couldn't be any different than her blonde-haired, blue-eyed sister.

It was a candid, no doubt taken in portrait mode on an iPhone.

It looked like it was a posed shot done by a top-notch fashion photographer.

Goofing off, head slightly turned, brown eyes twinkling, wind in her dark, curly hair, sunshine lighting her flawless skin, making a kissy face with full lips.

Georgiana Traylor was movie star gorgeous.

"Fantastic," he muttered, shoved his phone back into his pocket, and headed to DIA.

Chapter Two

Carry-Ons

Dutch

With what seemed like a thousand other people, Georgiana Traylor was spewed out of the wide opening that was at the top of the escalators from the underground train at DIA.

Flight details indicated she'd come direct from DC.

A long flight.

And she looked bright, rested, and way more gorgeous IRL than in her picture.

Dutch approached.

She took him in as he did, walking in a way she did not intend to stop, the expression on her face all he needed to know.

Beautiful.

And a bitch.

One look at his MC cut, she thought she had his number, and she didn't like it.

Even though she could read the patch stitched into the leather on the front of his cut that said Chaos, and she had to know his brother was in the same Club. And he knew she knew Jag.

He also knew, as he watched her opening her mouth to say something, he'd better get there first or the woman was going to have to get over her issues with Lyft.

"Yo, I'm Dutch. Jagger's brother. Carolyn and him got tied up, so they asked me to come and get you."

She made a show of stopping, blasting him with an unhappy look, then drooping a shoulder to allow a beat-up leather backpack to fall off. She caught the strap in her hand, dug into the pack, pulled out her phone, then made a further show of taking it out of airplane mode and waiting until it binged with her texts.

"Should turn off airplane mode the instant the wheels touch down like every other loser who can't breathe without an electronic connection," she mumbled irritably to her phone then looked at him. "Carolyn shared. Thanks for coming all the way out here to get me."

She said that last like she wasn't thankful even a little bit.

"Not a problem," he lied right back.

Her eyes narrowed like *him* not meaning what he said was rude, but her doing it when he'd just met her and was doing her a big, freaking favor was a-okay.

Jesus.

This was Carolyn's sister, all right, totally the pain in the ass Carolyn had described her to be.

"You gotta pick up a bag from baggage claim?" he asked in order to get this show on the road.

"Yeah," she answered, her gaze scanning for the screens that shared baggage claim info.

"You're on seven."

"Right," she muttered and started motoring.

He watched her go.

More accurately, he watched her ass as she went.

Okay, he'd give friendly a try.

"Not a carry-on person?" he asked, falling into step beside her.

She was tall-ish. Maybe five six. Five seven.

And something the photo didn't share, she was curvy as fuck.

Carolyn was tall too, but reed thin, no tits, but even he had to admit she had a great ass.

Georgiana had it all. Tits. Ass. Thighs. A belly.

She was Ashley Graham and then some.

And just as fuckable.

Fuck him.

"I like to shampoo my hair, and sadly, I can't shake my dedication to mascara and foundation. Too many liquids to get through security," she said to the space in front of her, like she was talking to air, and he didn't exist. "And I *detest* all those jerks who cram all their crap in the overheads, making boarding last a million years instead of twenty minutes. They act like getting one over on the airlines and not paying to check a bag is akin to their own personal V-E Day."

Right, well, it wasn't like he didn't know she was opinionated.

He definitely knew that.

And now it was confirmed.

"And when they shove their stuff in the bins over first class, and they don't sit in first class, it makes me want to scream," she ranted on. "I mean, the folks in first class either pay through the nose for those seats or travel so much, they have the miles to upgrade and earn a guaranteed section of overhead bin. It isn't like the flight attendants won't find a place for your bag because every other blockhead has taken up all the remaining space. And they'll use first class if they have it. And a bag checked at the gate does not spontaneously combust when it's put in the cargo hold. But you didn't pay for that privilege, and you take it anyway, because you somehow think it's your due, so how the world revolves around you, I do *not* know."

Okay then.

He'd given it a shot by asking what he thought was an innocuous question.

He decided it was quiet from here on out.

"Needless to say," she carried on even though he'd given her no indication he wanted to hear more, "I'd upgraded once, long flight, like this one. To New York. I was running late, got to the plane, so I didn't get to board at the beginning. I had my laptop bag, which isn't very big, mind you, and my backpack, and I had to put one in the overhead bin, no way I was going to check either. The plane wasn't fully boarded, but some buffoon in the back had shoved his bag in my bin and the rest of first-class stowage was totally full. The guy sitting next to me was already there, saw it and told me. So I had to shove my laptop bag in a bin halfway up the plane. It sucked. I had to work on that flight, and it was a nuisance walking back there to get my laptop. *Jerk.*"

They'd made it to carousel seven, and as they stopped to wait, Dutch kept his trap shut in hopes she'd catch his drift and stop bitching about shit that did not matter.

He was feeling optimistic about this when she was silent for long beats.

Unfortunately, this didn't last.

"Do you not travel?"

He looked down at her. "What?"

She was staring up at him. "Are you not a traveler?"

"I got somewhere to go, I get there on my bike."

She visibly fought a lip curl before mumbling, "Of course."

"Though, I've been on a plane more than once and I don't care what other people do with their bags. I check. It's less hassle. The rest is not my business."

What made him share that, he had no idea.

It was a mistake.

"It's literally impossible, not only scientifically, for the world to revolve around seven point seven *billion* people," she declared.

"What?"

"The world's population," she informed him.

"You do know, you bitchin' about this shit means you think the world revolves around your opinion about it," he returned.

Her eyes got huge.

It was cute.

Goddamn it.

"You got the power to just let it go," he told her.

Now she looked like she was going to be sick.

Somehow, that was cute too.

Shit.

"I'm not one to *let things go*," she said, and he honest to God thought the last three words were going to make her gag.

And he had never before felt the sensation, but all at once he wanted to laugh, kiss her, tell her to chill the fuck out and share he was going to go get his truck and bring it around to pick her up, and then walk away from her.

In that order.

"Like you cursing," she went on. "You don't even know me and you're using foul language. I could let that go, but that's not in me."

Hang on a second.

He turned fully to her. "Seriously? You're gonna give me shit about my language when you don't know me either, and *your* language since we met, both the shit that's been comin' out of your mouth, and your body language, has been nothin' good from the start?"

She didn't deny either.

She stated, "I haven't cursed at you. And you're *still* doing it with me."

"But you *do* throw attitude and negativity around with no shame. In my estimation, it's not the words you say, it's the way you say them and the meaning behind them that holds the power, good, or in your case, bad."

She simply *couldn't* deny that.

But even if she kept her mouth shut, for some reason, he didn't let it go.

He asked, "You don't use cuss words?"

"Not with someone I don't know."

"You're not the kind of woman to let things go, I'm not the kind of man to let anyone tell him how he can be."

Her eyes dipped down to his cut then back up. "Right."

"Like that, Georgiana," he told her. "Carolyn's like you and she says it like it is, so it isn't like I don't know about you, because she's shared. But I love my brother and he needed a favor so I'm here when I could be doin' a lot of other shit. Now you got a tick in your skin about MCs or bikers or whatever, and you can't let shit go, even when some guy you don't know is doin' you a solid when he could be doin' a lot of other shit that's far more preferable than listening to you bitch about shit that makes no difference. And just acting like a bitch because you got some shade to throw about how I live my life when you have no clue the man I am or how I live that life."

"I have a clue," she told him.

"Oh yeah?" he retorted. "You get that clue watchin' *Sons of Anarchy*?"

"No, I got that clue when Carolyn told me who she was dating, and I watched *Blood, Guts and Brotherhood*."

Well, hell.

Blood, Guts and Brotherhood was the documentary—more accurately, the *award-winning* documentary their now-president Rush's wife Rebel made about the Club.

"If you did, then you know what we're about, so what's with the attitude?" he asked.

"The director of that movie, Rebel Allen," she told him Rebel's name like he hadn't sat down to dinner at the woman's table two nights ago, which he had, "wore a leather jacket that said 'Property of Rush' on the back of it to the premiere of that film. And women are *not* property."

"Well, Rush wore his Chaos cut to that, but he has about a half dozen tees he wears all the time that say 'Property of Rebel' on the back. You got a problem with that?" he shot back.

She snapped her mouth shut so hard he heard her teeth clatter.

"Unh-hunh," he muttered, turning toward the carousel that had begun to churn. "You don't know dick."

"Knowledge of MC culture is not hard to come by, Mr. Black."

Yeah, she knew Jag enough to know his last name.

And his brother might be a guy who enjoyed a good time, but who fucking didn't?

Like Dutch, Jag had earned his patch, served the brothers, ate shit, did the grunt work, pulled his weight, and then some. Jag worked on the builds at the garage with Joker and he worked hard (Dutch didn't work in the garage, somehow—mostly because he was good with numbers, and people (just not Georgiana Traylor, or Carlyle Stephens)—Dutch had become the *de facto* manager of the auto supply store attached to Chaos's custom-build garage, both called Ride).

Jag was a good son. A good brother, of the blood and the patch. A good guy.

He wasn't a loser or a user or a cheater or a dick.

And so…

Okay.

She knew his brother, she knew him.

He was done with this woman.

When he looked at her again, he only twisted his neck before he bent it to give her his eyes when he said, "How 'bout we get your bag and get you home, Miss Traylor."

"*Ms.*," she returned.

Of course she'd have something like that to say.

Fortunately, she then nodded.

Their agreement to ride a stalemate until he could get shot of her lasted about seven minutes.

That being, until she moved forward, and he wanted to be able to ignore it, but he couldn't.

Because when his father died, Hound stepped in and became his dad. And when Hound wasn't around, Tack was. Or Hop was. Or Dog. Brick. The list went on.

In other words, he'd been trained well.

So when he saw the bag she'd clocked, he moved. And when she reached for it, he shouldered her out of the way and nabbed it.

"You did not just—" she began to hiss.

He strolled away, pulling her bag behind him, and saying, "Protest to the other libbers who give a shit. Let's just get out of here."

He felt her following him mostly because he couldn't miss she did it seething.

Dutch further did not miss the irony—and if he wasn't so pissed, he'd laugh at it—that her bag was a goddamn carry-on.

When they made it to his truck (fortunately, the way there was silent), he stowed it in the cab behind her seat.

He then nearly broke her hand when she made a show of reaching for her door to close it after she'd gotten in, but he was making a show of standing there, holding it, waiting for her to get her round ass in, then he made a further show of throwing it to.

Luckily, she had quick reflexes and got her hand out of the way.

They were headed to the parking booths when she declared, "I'm paying for parking."

And he would admit, though never to her, that it was plain stubbornness when he replied, "Absolutely not."

"Caveman," she snapped.

"Battle-axe," he returned.

She gasped.

He hit the button to roll down his window to pay for parking.

Of course, her being her, she did not let it go and they were barely riding free on Peña Boulevard when she stated, "You could have just swung through arrivals and avoided parking fees altogether."

"I was picking up someone for my brother, woman or not, and my momma and daddy, both Chaos through and through, raised me better."

He heard her huff.

But she said not a word.

Yeah.

That shut her damned mouth.

In fact, it shut her mouth so good, she was silent for so long, he got tweaked enough to look her way.

She had her head turned and was staring out her side window.

And she was a serious pain in the ass, but the look on her face that he caught even in profile, which wasn't annoyed, frustrated, obstinate or haughty, but something softer, and definitely something concerning, made him wonder what she'd been doing in DC.

And if maybe something that happened there, or was the reason why she went there, was not only putting that look on her face, but also putting her in a shit mood.

These thoughts being why he asked, "You okay?"

He'd turned back to the road, but he glanced and saw she'd done the same and was looking out the windshield when she answered, "I will be when you drop me off."

Right.

No.

"We don't get along," he pointed out the obvious. "And we don't have to. This is a one-shot deal, this time we're spending together. It's soon gonna be over, so set that aside because I'm asking genuinely. You okay?"

She didn't answer.

"Right. Whatever," he muttered.

She said nothing for so long, they were nearing the highway when she finally spoke.

"My trip was unfun. And I'm supposed to compartmentalize, and usually, I can do that. But this time, I'm not finding it easy."

"I know you're Carolyn's sister. I know you don't let shit go. I know you got serious issues with the way people deal with their carry-ons. But other than that, I don't know dick about you, Georgiana, so gotta say, I don't know what any of that means."

"The story I'm on," she explained. "The story I have to write tonight and turn in so they can post it in the morning. It's not a fun story. And I should lock it tight where it's supposed to be, until I let it out to write it, and then lock it back up and move on. I can do that, normally. I've actually been on worse stories, and I could do it. This time, for some reason, it's messing with me."

"Story you're on?"

"I'm a journalist."

That explained the not-letting-go part of her personality.

"*The Post? The News?*" he asked. "*Westword?*"

"No. Online. National. Or international. *The Worldist.* We're redefining news. Or bringing it back to its roots. Like *Vice* on HBO. Where it's about news, information. Not graphics and makeup and hairstyles and graying men with bushy mustaches standing up in front of screens with attractive women thirty years younger than them who'll be cast out the second they reach a certain age, but the guy will be up there until he keels over. News that is not news because it's shaping a narrative, even if that narrative is hooey crafted carefully to gain ratings. But a narrative isn't news. Isn't information. It's a point of view. And news does not have a point of view."

Well, shit.

He'd heard of *The Worldist,* and after getting over its relatively stupid name, he'd checked it out. When he did, not only for their video reports, but their written ones, for the last year or so, if he wanted the real story, he went there. To the point he had a subscription.

"That's the problem," she carried on. "My job is not to have a point of view. My job is to gather facts and write them in a manner they're relayed in a way that people can understand them. The end. But this story, I have a point of view. It happens. I'm human. But this one…"

She had more to say, she just didn't say it.

"What's this one?" he asked quietly.

"The student loan crisis."

"And?"

"Well, there's aid. Not a lot of it, but there's aid. The thing is, you can't tap into it if your parents have money."

"Yeah, and that makes sense."

"Yeah, it does. The thing is, some parents aren't parents. But the aid agencies regard them as parents. So, say your mom looks after you in all ways, including financially, and you're barely scraping by. But you want to go to college. She can't pay for it. You can't pay for it. You apply for aid you can't get because your dad's a high-powered attorney in DC, who makes seven figures, but he's not given you or your mother a single dollar or even seen your face or asked to do so since he took off when you were two years old. But his salary is calculated, and you have no shot at aid. So you have two choices. Don't go to college, or eventually start your life weighed down by crippling loans. And it's alarming how many kids pick door number one."

"College isn't the only choice and it isn't the only road to a good life," he told her.

"You're correct," she replied. "But schooling to learn to be a plumber, an electrician, a hair stylist, an HVAC tech, a vet tech, a massage therapist, and the list goes on, isn't free either."

She was right.

"So, you're back from DC after meeting with a filthy-rich, deadbeat dad whose kid is deciding not to go to college because he's a deadbeat," Dutch surmised.

"Yeah. And he wasn't big on the way our chat went, and I assume with his demonstrated prowess in the courtroom he has a great command of the English language, but in communicating that to me, he chose to use words far worse than the ones you use."

"You blindside him?" he asked.

When she answered, the snap in her tone was back.

"Of course not. I told him the article I was working on and why I wished to speak to him. Prior to me flying out, he had a great many things to say about 'making your own way in the world,' when he's a trust fund baby, his college and law school were paid for by his folks, and his parents also have chosen not to claim the results of his first marriage, a marriage they did not approve of. He thinks she…his daughter, that is…will improve her character by having to work for her future. Not that he has any clue what her character is, considering when he left her, she couldn't form sentences."

Dutch was of a mind, if you had it, and it didn't make them spoiled brats, you gave it to your kids. Otherwise, what was the point of having kids in the first place, if you didn't give them the things they needed to have a decent life? If you didn't give them whatever you had to in order to give them a good life from the start until you dropped dead.

What his mother had given him and Jag.

What Hound had given them.

What Chaos had given them.

But bottom line, no kid of his would be a kid he'd ever walk away from.

"He was unprepared for the fact that I *was* prepared," she went on. "Benefit of the doubt, it was my age. But the truth of it, it was probably my gender and he underestimated me. So he didn't think I'd dig and find out that, being a five-hundred-dollar-an-hour attorney and all, he'd managed to come out on top every time the mom took him to court to get some support. He stuck to the line he had no responsibility for a girl he did not know, he did not want, even before his wife got pregnant, something he alleges he told his wife before she conceived against his will, and was happy to allow to be adopted, if his ex would simply move on and stop harassing him. How this made it through in this day and age, I have utterly no clue. Except he makes a lot of money, he comes from even more, and knows the legal system and those who work in it like the back of his hand. Credit to the woman, she didn't give up, until the trying nearly bankrupted her and she had no choice but to go it alone."

"What a dick," Dutch muttered.

"Correct again," Georgiana agreed. "Needless to say, he wasn't a big fan of me mentioning all of that in correlation with the life his daughter is leading, which hasn't been bad, because she has an awesome mom. But it certainly isn't what it would be if he just paid child support. And matters deteriorated when I questioned him about how he felt about his part in the decisions she's now facing."

"Sucks for the kid," Dutch noted, not having anything else to say.

Georgiana had more to say, though.

One thing was certain, she had a weight to get off her chest.

In other words, her trip to DC was seriously unfun.

"The daughter wanted to be a midwife. Certified midwives can earn anywhere from forty-five to one hundred and twenty K a year, depending on their experience and where they live. She's now downgraded her goal to patient care technician, and even if that's the most in-demand job in the US, and a necessary one, they make about twenty-five grand. That's double the single-person-family poverty level, as defined by Federal Poverty Guidelines, but almost half of the lowest salary she'd make if she did what she's been dreaming of doing. I don't make much more than that. So I know the tough financial decisions you have to make, earning that much. Decisions you wouldn't have to make if you brought in twice as much as you do."

Dutch still didn't have anything to say, except what he'd already said.

This was the way it was.

And it sucked.

"So how do I write this article without making the father out to be what he is, a total jackhole?"

Dutch didn't quite clamp down on his bark of laughter before he asked, "A jackhole?"

"What would you call him?" She asked the question, but didn't let him answer. Instead, she kept talking and doing it fast. "Don't tell me. I can guess."

"I bet you can," he mumbled, smiling at the busy highway he was navigating. "It's the truth he's a jackhole. So tell the truth."

"My editor requires objectivity."

"Okay. So then objectively, he's still a jackhole."

There was a moment of silence and then she busted out laughing.

And that just cut it.

Because the woman had a generous mouth, a generous head of wild, dark, curly hair, a generous body…

And a generous laugh.

She also had a generous amount of attitude, he reminded himself. And not a lot of it was good.

He could see she'd had a shit trip.

He could not see her taking it out on a stranger who was doing something nice for her.

"My dad was…not around, maybe that's it," she muttered like she was talking to herself.

Christ, he shouldn't have asked if she was okay. He didn't need her to give him reasons to understand why she was behaving like a bitch.

"But I think it's that somehow, I got on the kids beat," she kept at it. "And it's wearing me down."

Even if he knew it was no good for him, Dutch again couldn't stop himself from asking, "The kids beat?"

"If it has to do with kids, they assign it to me," she told him. "The state of CPS. Foster care. Social media shaming. Vaping in schools. Now this. Meeting this young girl with good grades that don't set the world on fire, but she also has a part-time job to help mom out at home, not hours to kill to do extra credit or go the extra mile. Her mom works a data desk at an insurance company, and she doesn't do badly, she just doesn't have tens of thousands of dollars to toss around. She doesn't even have what it takes to make sure her daughter has the most recent iPhone and the bevy of other status symbols kids find important these days, to the point the girl's prom dress was rented. And good or bad, that kind of thing matters to a kid."

"All of that's a lot to compartmentalize, Georgiana," he pointed out.

"Yeah, well, it's my job. I know journalists who've been at it far longer than me and they don't act like harridans, raving about freaking carry-ons because they met a douchebag who was all down to make a kid, and even more down to walk away from her."

Yup.

He shouldn't have asked if she was okay, because he sure as shit did not need to like this woman.

His brother was dating her sister, for one.

And even if there was a reason behind it, she absolutely did not make a good first impression. No man (or woman, undoubtedly) wanted to be someone's punching bag on a consistent basis when that someone was in a bad mood.

Then, of course, there was her bullshit about bikers.

He knew she was looking at him when she asked, "Did I blow your afternoon?"

"My plans got sidetracked so I was free," he told her.

"What were your plans?"

"Seems we share a theme," he muttered.

"What?" she asked.

"I've been recruited to try to help reach a kid at King's Shelter who's fucking up his life."

"King's Shelter? You?"

And there it was.

A reason why he wasn't going to be able to like this woman.

"Yeah, bikers do more than get drunk, bang biker bunnies, start bar fights and get arrested," he said sarcastically.

"It's not that—"

He cut her off.

"You ever heard of BACA?"

"Sorry?"

"BACA. Bikers Against Child Abuse."

"Yes, I have. They do good work."

"Well, essentially, they're an MC. An MC that does good work. Not all bikers are Hells Angels and the Bandido Nation. That's the fuckin' point of the term 'one-percenter.' Ninety-nine percent of bikers are just bikers. One percent are outlaws. Chaos is not a one-percenter."

"You were, though," she said softly, not an accusation, a fact.

And she was right.

That was a fact.

The operative word being *was*.

"We're not anymore."

The cab fell silent.

She broke it.

"Who's this kid you got recruited to help?"

"Listen, I'm sorry you had a shit trip, but maybe we should—"

"Dutch, you haven't asked me where I live."

He felt his brows go up because he hadn't.

"Did Carolyn tell you?" she asked.

"No," he grunted.

"So, where are you taking me?"

And now her words were threaded with humor, which was almost prettier than hearing her say his name for the first time.

"On autopilot," he muttered.

"Because I came off the plane and acted like a bitch? Or because your work with this kid somehow got sidetracked?"

He wasn't going to answer that.

"You're headed in the right direction anyway. I live in Governor's Park," she told him.

"Great," he mumbled.

"It's the kid," she decreed.

She wanted it?

He'd give it to her.

"Yeah. Seventeen. One-hundred-and-forty-nine IQ, and he's been tested, so that's not a guess. Scholarships lined up to top schools. And I mean *top*. Top in terms of MIT. His dad gets murdered, the cops can't find who did it, he's so pissed at the world, he wants off the grid. And he's headed that way."

"Your dad," she whispered, correctly ascertaining why he'd been recruited.

It could be Jag shared with Carolyn and Carolyn shared with Georgiana.

But it definitely was *Blood, Guts and Brotherhood.*

Graham Black, his father's story was out there.

Everyone knew.

Or at least everyone who'd seen that film.

What everyone didn't know was right then, in the cab of his truck, sitting next to a gorgeous but paradoxical woman, he was wearing the leather cut his father was wearing when he'd had his throat slit.

"Yup," he grunted.

"How did this kid's dad get murdered?" she asked.

"They live in a duplex. Him, that being Carlyle, his little sister, mom, dad, and it's the middle of the night, and the dad hears a racket coming from the other side. The mom calls the cops, but the noises aren't good, so the dad grabs a baseball bat and heads over. Busts in. Tears up to the bedroom. He's shot dead interrupting an attempted rape."

"Oh my God," she breathed in horror.

"That about sums it up," he agreed.

"A boyfriend? An ex? A hookup?"

"What?" he asked.

"Did the woman who was being raped also get—"

"No, she survived."

"So, it's a stranger? A break-in? Did the dad hear the breaking-in part?"

"That's the rub," Dutch told her. "They heard the fight, not the break-in, and there was no evidence of a break-in, outside what Carlyle's dad did to get in. But the woman contends it was a stranger. She'd never seen him, had no idea where he came from. She was sleeping and then he was there. There was hope in the beginning, they thought. The woman, their neighbor, she was cagey. They think she knows more than she's letting on. And Carlyle, his mom, and his younger sister said there were folks who visited her that they weren't real hip on, and the dad flat-out did not like having around. They just don't know who they were."

"And she's not talking."

"No."

"Or she's lying."

"Yeah."

"And this kid ran away from home because his dad died next door and he probably heard the gunshot that killed him."

Dutch swallowed, feeling that for Carlyle in a big way, before he said, "Yeah."

"What's she saying about these folks who came calling?"

"That they're just friends. Acquaintances, whatever. They have nothing to do with the incident."

"Do the cops believe that?"

"I don't know what they believe. I just know months have passed with no leads, no DNA that wasn't supposed to be there, nothing this guy left behind, no other witnesses, but the dad, who can't share what he saw, and the case will stay open, but they're moving on because it's gone cold and they got other shit they gotta do."

"And you're not getting through to the kid," she surmised.

"Nope," he confirmed.

"Maybe he just needs some time," she suggested.

"Yeah. Time to get himself hooked up in shit he shouldn't be hooked up in."

"Is that happening?"

"Yup."

"Well, damn," she whispered.

"And she finds a reason to curse," he muttered.

When he did, he felt a faint slap, but heard a definite one against the leather at his arm when she whacked him gently, like a man's woman would whack him gently as a joke, all as she said an amused, "Shut up."

Mm-hmm.

They needed to get to Governor's Park.

Yesterday.

"How do you know he's turning to the dark side?" she asked.

"Saw him with some dude who deals black market crap."

"Sorry?"

"Saw him, at the back of a bar, with some dude who deals black market crap."

"What do people involved with black market crap want with a seventeen-year-old kid?"

Dutch felt his innards seize.

Because that was a good fucking question.

"Dutch?" she called when he didn't say anything.

"Deal it for them," he pushed out.

"Is he doing that?" she pressed. "Dealing for them? Do you know that?"

"No," he forced through his lips.

"Okay, I'm no authority on this, but I've done a few articles on gangs. And gangs deal, and they'll use a seventeen-year-old to deal. Non-gang suppliers supply kids who deal in schools. These are easily picked-off, expendable soldiers in that war. One goes down, three pop up. But black market…"

She trailed off.

"No?" he asked.

"What's their market?"

"Pharmaceuticals. Sperm. Maple syrup. Designer shit."

"Okay, designer stuff, I can see. Kids want that. But Dutch, who is a seventeen-year-old runaway going to deal sperm and maple syrup to? He hardly has those connections and there is no way anyone who wants that kind of thing wants to see a seventeen-year-old front man. And maybe they need all hands on deck, they have so much product to move, but that's thin. Especially considering they've got their fingers in so many pots, there's way too much at stake to take on a recruit who's so young, and green, what he can move would not outweigh the dangers of him being a weak link that could lead to it all falling apart."

He could see she was a good journalist.

He could also see a hella smart kid who was witness to whoever walked into his neighbor's house before his dad died, now out of that house, out of school, lots of time on his hands, spending that time picking at threads until he found one that led him somewhere.

Dutch's dad died when he was five.

But straight up, if he'd been twenty-five, or seventeen, and the cops, or the Chaos brothers, did not take care of business…

He'd do it.

"Dutch?" she called.

"What?" he answered.

"You're thinking about something."

"It's nothing," he lied.

She didn't say anything for a few beats before she asked, "Now…uh, are *you* okay?"

He was not.

But this might lead him to being okay.

At least about Carlyle being something closer to it.

"All good," he said.

"Since we're on Speer, maybe I should give you my address," she noted.

"That'd be smart," he joked.

She gave it to him, and he drove her there, both of them quiet.

Dutch was reflecting.

Georgiana was not.

He could actually feel her watching him and trying to dig into his head.

When he got to the address, he saw she lived in a high-rise condo complex. An ugly one that was probably put up in the '70s or '80s, and it would take at least another thirty, maybe forty years to make it retro cool.

Still, it was a hip location, even if the units probably sucked.

He pulled into the loading area in front of the building and stopped.

He also got out, even though she was out, standing on the sidewalk, with her backpack over her shoulder and her bag on its wheels at her side.

She smiled at him and he wished she didn't.

"For once, I was faster than you," she teased.

And he wished she didn't tease either.

"You're home safe, good luck with the article," he said as his goodbye, and began to turn to walk away.

"Dutch," she called, and he really hated how her kinda husky, but still lilting voice carried his name.

It was like she was touching it…

Him.

Like a tap on his shoulder, a brush of his jaw, her lips skimming his ear.

He turned back to her.

"I was a total bitch, and it's totally worth using a curse word.

I'm sorry. I'm thinking I need a change in direction, that meaning career, because I obviously can't hack this, and if I can't hack this, no way I'm going to get where I want to go in journalism. And it's been bothering me, because I'm not rolling in the dough in a way I can take a year's sabbatical full of martini lunches with my girlfriends while I write the next Great American Novel before I try to find another position again. And it's freaking me out."

"Just ask for a different beat," he recommended.

Her brows inched together. "Sorry?"

"Tell your editor you need a break from the kids and ask for a different beat. You need something fresh. I can tell you're good at what you do, you care about it, you clearly got a passion for it. It'd suck, you gave it up because you had a tough story that tweaked you, for whatever reason it tweaked you. Move away from that beat. You got something fresh to sink your teeth into, you'll be fine. Even Dan Rather sat at a desk after being a correspondent for years. Everyone needs change, and now's that time for you."

Her expression was open, and no other way to describe it, *glowing* by the time he got done talking.

"So you're a young budding biker guru," she said on another smile and more teasing.

"No, I'm just not neck deep in it so I see it clearer," he replied, not smiling and wanting to get the fuck out of there, because her smiling, teasing, *glowing* meant he *needed* to get the fuck out of there.

She must have sensed his desire because her smile faded, he wasn't thrilled to watch it go, but he didn't say dick.

"Your wisdom I feel made my apology get lost, so I'll repeat it. I was a bitch, Dutch, and seriously, I'm sorry. There's no excuse for it. I guess I was just at my end, and you caught that."

"I'm a biker, something you got issues with 'cause you got a stick up your ass about shit you don't know, issues for you, and undoubtedly with your sister having fun with one. A biker who walked up to you, so you felt open to smack me with your shit because I don't matter. I'm just a biker. *That* is what happened and *that's* what you're apologizing for."

At his words, she was the one who looked like she'd been smacked. Her head jerked with it, the whole thing.

Jesus, shit.

"Right, well, okay, guess I deserved that," she whispered. "But thanks, truly. And good luck with Carlyle. I hope you break through."

She yanked up the handle on her bag and had started rolling it away when he called her name.

"Georgiana."

She turned back and gave him no shot to apologize.

She said, "You know, you were right. This was a one-time thing, thankfully short, and now over. But really, good luck with Carlyle and…whatever else you do with your life."

He didn't call out again as she jabbed a code into a box, shoved through the front doors and went right to the elevators.

When she disappeared in one without even glancing his way was when he rounded his truck and got back in.

She'd been a bitch, and she'd apologized.

He'd been a dick, and it was left at that.

And as much as that burned in his chest, and fuck, but it burned and he had no idea why it burned so hot and so deep, leaving it like that…

He was going to leave it like that.

Whatever else you do with your life.

Yeah, there it was.

Whatever else he did with his life.

Which was nothing.

He was doing nothing with his life.

He had no drive.

He had no goals.

He had no mission.

He had no passion.

He had dick.

On that thought, he started up his truck and headed for the Chaos Compound.

There was beer there. Tequila. Brothers.

He wasn't big on getting drunk.

But for once he was feeling like tying one on.

* * * *

Dutch did as he planned.

He didn't get puke-and-act-like-an-asshole drunk, but he'd

gotten to the point he'd had to crash in his room at the Compound instead of getting in his truck and going home.

But after he woke up the next day, brushed his teeth, splashed water on his face and got dressed, he went home.

To his laptop.

Which he opened while the coffee was brewing.

And he pulled up *The Worldist* website.

Then he read an article about student loans that had Georgiana Traylor's byline.

He found he was right.

She was good at her job.

Because the article was succinct, but thorough, he was keen to read the next installment that was coming the next day, and the father didn't come off as a total jackhole.

He came off, subtly, as a complete bastard.

Dutch read the article again.

Then he made himself a cup of coffee and took it to the bathroom, since he was going to shower.

And after that, go to the offices of Nightingale Investigations.

Chapter Three

Meanwhile

Meanwhile…

As Dutch Black was getting drunk with some of his brothers at the Chaos Compound…

Georgiana Suzanne Traylor had written the first five hundred words of what would be a fifteen-hundred-word series that would run on *The Worldist* over the next three days.

She'd turned it in.

Half an hour later, she'd had a twenty-minute phone conversation with Cristina, her editor.

Five minutes of that was about changes Cristina wanted in the article.

Five minutes were Georgiana telling Cristina what she could expect in the next two installments.

Three minutes were Cristina approving and giving Georgiana food for thought.

Seven minutes were Georgiana explaining, and Cristina agreeing to give her different stories and take her off the "kids beat."

Georgiana had hung up and then given herself some time to feel relief that a huge concern that had been bugging her since she met seventeen-year-old, midwife-hopes-dashed Madison McGill in her bid to find an angle on her student loan piece.

However, she did not allow herself time to give silent,

ineffectual (considering he was gone, gone, *gone*) thanks to Dutch Black for (apparently, time would tell) solving a problem that had been plaguing her now for weeks.

She'd done her tweaks to the article.

And she beat the deadline of the final submission by forty-seven minutes.

Which heralded her opening a bottle of wine.

She knew what she was going to do before she pulled up Grubhub and ordered from Little India.

And while she waited for Little India, she unpacked, started a load of laundry, changed her sheets, and took a shower to wash off the feel of the plane.

Through this, she sipped wine and accepted the icy chill from her roommate's Scottish fold cat.

A cat which had—considering her roommate had unexpectedly taken a second stint with *Médicins Sans Frontières*, which meant she was supposed to be gone for a year, but now it would be two—officially become Georgiana's.

Or so said Georgiana.

Because when (if?) the woman ever got back, Georgie was claiming the damned cat.

"It was only a day," she told Murtagh, who her roommate Cela had named Angus, but Georgie had renamed Murtagh after her favorite character from the *Outlander* TV show.

Murtagh turned his bushy gray body and showed her his butthole.

And thus, Murtagh shared neatly that he was not a fan of being left alone overnight.

This was not news.

Though, apparently, like she'd been that day when she got off the plane and saw her sister had blown her off…*again*, Murtagh was at an end with his substitute momma taking off.

Georgiana made note of that, and since she traveled a lot, and when she didn't, she was out of the house a lot, she finished waiting for Little India by putting the clothes in the dryer and then sipping wine while mentally compiling a list of friends she could ask to hang out with Murtagh while she was gone so Murtagh would have someone to love.

Because Scottish folds were very affectionate.

And anyway, Murtagh had already experienced the trauma of losing his first momma and now he was saddled with Georgie.

Reason one (but the list was much longer), why Cela wasn't reclaiming her cat.

When the food came, she ate on the sofa with the bottle of wine close, Murtagh not close, and John Oliver cracking her up, pissing her off, and giving her the needed reminder of why she decided to do what she did even though what she did didn't make people laugh.

But hopefully it made them think.

Then Murtagh forgave her and cuddled up as Georgiana settled in with her real plans for the night.

It was stupid and she knew it.

She just couldn't stop herself.

So she rented it to stream.

She remembered him from when she'd seen it before. She remembered him being like his brother, good-looking (in a biker guy way).

But she hadn't met him the first time she saw *Blood, Guts and Brotherhood.*

And now she'd met him.

She also didn't remember him being in it that much. The film was mostly about the history of the Club, juxtaposed with footage of them now. At their business. Working on their builds in their garage. In their hangout lair. Their homes. With their wives. Kids. Bikes.

Each other.

The brothers Chaos.

But the majority of it was Ken Burns *Civil War* style.

Narrative, and some spoken-word interviews, over pictures of days of yore.

Though there was a small amount of old VHS and phone video footage.

And the first time she watched it, her heart stopped, knowing Carolyn's boyfriend had lost his father in the way explained by the film.

This time, she made everything stop the first time a picture of Graham Black came on her TV screen.

He was crouched down, elbows to knees, and you could see the muscles through his jeans tightened over them in his position. Head turned to almost, but not quite full profile. Dark hair longish, a mop of messy curls and waves. Skin tanned. Lines fanning out from his deep-set, hooded eyes. Huge, white smile.

And there was no mistaking it physically.

Dutch Black had his father stamped all over him.

Graham Black had been an exceptionally handsome man.

His son was no different.

She was about to hit play, but then she didn't.

And Murtagh gave a concerned "Mwrr?" when the noise came from her throat.

But she'd taken out her contacts and now had her glasses on because her eyes were dry and scratchy from wearing the contacts on the plane.

It might be a trick of vision.

But she had to check.

So she took Murtagh up super-close to the screen, shoved her glasses up on her head, all so she could see.

"Yes," she whispered staring at a specific spot on the screen. "Oh my God," she kept whispering. "Yes."

She cuddled Murtagh closer and walked back to the couch.

As they settled in, Murtagh started purring and kneading.

Georgiana didn't hit play.

She stared at the patch on the leather jacket Graham Black was wearing in that picture.

Through the threads on the border around the patch that said Chaos that was positioned over the heart, there was some unraveling, and on the leather, there was a scratch on either side of the minimal damage to the stitching on the patch.

The same as on the jacket Dutch wore that day.

It was his dad's jacket.

It was his dad's patch.

"Muwrrrr," Murtagh said.

"Yeah," she whispered, "I really, really, *reallyreallyreally* messed up today, baby."

"*Murrr*," Murtagh told her.

"No, it isn't okay," she replied.

"Mwrr?"

"I don't think so. I think it's who he is, to his bones, his blood, his DNA, so he'll never forgive me."

"Muwrrr," Murtagh decreed.

"I love you too, honey."

Murtagh's job was done (or so Murtagh thought), so Murtagh shut up.

Georgiana hit play.

As she watched, she paused a number of other times.

All when *he* was on screen.

Even when it was pictures of him as a little kid, or a baby.

Held in his father's arms.

She noted there was something stamped all over Graham Black too.

Unmistakable.

He loved his wife.

And his sons.

Georgiana couldn't hold it in and got another "Mwrr?" from Murtagh when she made a sad noise at a photo of Graham Black wearing a proud papa smile as he was caught on film in the middle of pulling his oldest son off his back.

The dark-haired toddler was arms and legs akimbo, like he thought he was flying through the air, even though his dad's arms were raised high, his son held tight on either side in both hands.

The toddler's eyes were aimed down at his father, face filled with glee.

It took some deep breaths to get through that one.

Thankfully, only once did she rewind a creeper, stalkery ten times. And this was when the camera had caught Dutch Black in the present (or a few years ago).

Laughing.

When the film was over, she didn't think about what she intended to do.

She just started on the road to doing it.

Thus, she took Murtagh direct to her backpack, dug through it, got her notebook and pen, brought it back to the sofa, had a think, and while she did, she made her usual list.

And after finishing off the wine, the list and a couple of Zzzquil gummies, she and Murtagh went to bed.

First thing in the morning, after she made coffee, she grabbed her notebook and reviewed the list.

It read:

1) Jackson. DPD.

- Carlyle Case. Status. Future. Details.

+++NEIGHBOR!!!!

Who else saw who came and went from her house?

Names?

No DNA in bed, on skin or under nails with a rape?

- Market (sperm, syrup, pharma)

Players????

2) Banga -n- Kraken. Street.

- Market (players, locations, warehouses?)

- Where to buy?

- Who?

- If not them...who to ask?

3) King's Shelter?

- ED? Juliette — (last name?)

- Rock Chick books — read.

4) Charge taser/check expiration on Mace.

Cover:

Sperm the ruse.

Single.

Independent.

Too much $$ for insemination (How much does that cost? Find out.)???

Lame...build on this. ↑↑↑↑

Once she reviewed it, Georgiana grabbed her phone and started at the top.

She called Jackson, one of her sources in the Denver Police Department.

When he said he was all in for a mid-morning coffee break (and she knew what he meant was he was all in to stare at her breasts while they sipped coffee, he asked her for a date, she politely declined while telling him how much she valued their friendship, all this happening through her delicately pumping him for information or maneuvering him to get it for her), she slapped on some makeup, did something with her hair, tugged on some clothes that showed absolutely no cleavage, promised Murtagh she'd be back…

And she headed out.

Chapter Four

Cute

Dutch

"Get twenty feet from this truck, you're on camera. Most of the entire perimeter," Vance said.

It was late at night.

They were in his truck, outside a warehouse, at the back, both their eyes to that warehouse that wasn't big, but it wasn't small, it wasn't well-lit, but it also wasn't dark.

And even from their distance, which was the same as the rest—not far, but not close—you could see the cameras.

"Except there," Vance continued. "The back north corner. There are no doors or windows there to breach or see in, so they left it unprotected. But you only got about ten feet of leeway, then you're fucked because you're on camera."

Dutch turned his head to look at Vance Crowe, Juliet's husband, and one of the Nightingale men.

Vance was also looking at him.

"They send a man out. Random. To do a check. They'll clock you in a vehicle. We're takin' a chance right now, bein' here, and them seein' us. That happens, they probably won't approach. Guys like this, they don't want mess, distractions or problems. But the minute you go, they'll pack up everything in that warehouse, it'll be gone within an hour and we'll be back to square one."

Dutch nodded. "So park elsewhere, get to that back corner, hunker down around the side, and watch from there?"

Vance nodded. "You wanna see if the guy the kid was meeting at Shady's goes in or out of that building, then follow him, that's your only shot. Good news, they don't use the front door so if he comes around, that's where you'll see him. Bad news, it'll be seriously uncomfortable staking out like that, it could take days for the guy to show, if he ever does, and you run the risk every time of being seen if the guy they send out decides to do a full perimeter check."

Dutch didn't ask if Vance knew if the guy often did a full perimeter check. This situation was in its infancy. Recon had been swift, and it was patchy. He was lucky Vance had this much information to relay. He was lucky Vance and the men at Nightingale Investigations had waded in at all.

But this was about one of Jules's kids, so maybe it wasn't that lucky.

"You're gonna have to melt, brother," Vance advised. "That guy comes out, you have an exit strategy planned. Which means no watching in the daylight. You can become a shadow, but even I can't do that shit when the sun is shining. If they catch you, they won't make an approach if you're sitting a vehicle. You're close to their operation, they'll deal with you fast and no one will ever see you again."

That caught Dutch's attention.

"You know who these guys are?"

Vance shook his head. "I know *how* these guys are. But you do what you do, and we've got Brody looking into who owns that warehouse, running the plates of vehicles I took down, and the guys will be gathering word we pick up on the street. When we get something, I'll relay that to you."

Dutch nodded.

"We don't got a lot of man hours to help you out with this," Vance warned. "Your brothers gonna pitch in?"

Dutch had already decided.

He was not taking this to Chaos.

First, it'd have to be discussed at the table and voted on. And honest to God, after the nightmare his Club had been picking its way through for decades got sorted, and they finally were free and clear of all the shit that included drugs and guns and porn and whores, kidnappings and death, he did not know how that vote would go.

And he didn't know how he'd feel if the vote didn't go his way.

Second, he also didn't know what he would be asking them to do and how deep it would get.

They weren't a highly trained, skilled, experienced investigation team, like Nightingale. They were bikers. And they could take care of business, they'd proved that often. But this was not riding close to the bone where your motivation was keeping yourself breathing, your brothers the same and your families safe.

But last, and most importantly, this was his.

It was his and Carlyle's.

And for some reason he was not currently evaluating, he wanted it to stay that way.

At least for now.

"Don't know what I'm asking them to do and it'll need to go for a vote," Dutch told Vance. "So, until I know, not right now."

Vance, who had pulled himself into Dutch's passenger seat when Dutch met him there, gave him a chin lift before he looked beyond him, back toward the warehouse.

And then everything about the man changed.

This made Dutch return his attention to the warehouse.

And at what he saw, he was pretty fucking sure he experienced his head exploding even if it didn't actually explode.

Because first, she was there at all.

And second, she could get caught on camera, and then just get *caught.*

"The *fuck*?" he bit out.

"Seems we're not the only ones interested in this building," Vance said.

Yup.

It seemed that way.

It also seemed he told a goddamned bitch of a journalist about a tragic situation with a kid and she was tired of her beat, so she took the information he gave her and was looking into the black market in Denver.

He heard the fury in his tone, even as he watched her and felt his heart start to race, as he said to Vance, "You go, I'll take care of her."

"Take care of her?" Vance asked.

"I know her. She's a journalist. Not thinking she'd nose around this, I told her about it."

"Shit," Vance muttered.

"Right," Dutch agreed.

"You need my help with her?" Vance asked.

"I got it."

"Take care they don't see you first," Vance advised. "They see her before you get her, she can deal. I'll keep an eye. You get her out of here, then I'm gone. You catch trouble, I'm in."

She couldn't deal, he could tell by the way she was moving she had no idea what she was into.

"You got it," Dutch said, thinking fast and moving faster.

He opened his door just as he heard Vance open his.

Then he moved swiftly.

Trying to stay out of camera range, which Georgiana was wandering close to, he took as direct a route to her as he could.

She was wearing all dark clothing, a knit cap over her hair, fluffing out the dark curls at the bottom, and she was slinking through the night, staring up at one of the cameras.

He approached from behind, and she was so bad at this, she didn't hear him until it was too late.

He had her, one arm around her stomach, the other hand over her mouth.

She screamed behind it, arched hard and started to struggle, so he hissed in her ear, "Quiet! It's Dutch."

She stilled, twisted, he semi-let her go, keeping an arm around her, and his hand lifted so he could clamp down again on her mouth if he needed to.

And for some fucked-in-the-head reason, she caught his eyes in the dim light, hers got bright and happy, as did her entire gorgeous face.

She smiled huge and began, *loudly*, "We had the same—!"

"Shut it," he bit. "They're gonna see. Or hear. Let's go."

Only then did he take his arm from her, but he did it to grab her hand and drag her ass to his truck.

He practically picked her up and dumped her in before he jogged around the front bumper, got in himself and started up.

"Dutch, we—"

He turned to her, leaned her way, she reared back at his actions—the way he made them and probably the look on his face—and he ground out, "Serious to God, Georgiana, shut the fuck up."

"You're angry," she whispered, looking surprised at this fact.

But she was wrong.

He was not angry.

He was enraged.

He could not believe anyone would hear Carlyle's story and use any part of it to further their own career.

She'd figured it out, like he had.

And if she investigated it, blew it open for her news website, she'd get off the kids beat for certain.

"Yeah, I'm fuckin' angry," he replied. "And you best pray I get a lock on it on the way to my place."

"Your place?"

"Christ woman, *shut up*," he hissed.

With big eyes, she closed her mouth.

He turned back to the wheel, checked his mirrors, slid out of the spot, and drove the ten minutes to his crib.

He parked at the side, got out, walked to the hood of his truck, and saw she was out, moving hesitantly toward him.

He gave a fake-gallant sweep of his arm toward the side door.

She looked at it like a doomed woman looked at the gallows on her way to the noose.

Then she took in a big breath and marched her sweet ass toward his door.

She stepped aside so he could unlock it.

After he did, he stepped aside so she could precede him.

She'd stopped in his mudroom and he moved past her, going into the living room, doing it walking around, turning on lights.

He did this deliberately, taking his time, because he sure as shit didn't get a lock on his temper on the drive there.

When he finally turned his attention to her, she was looking around the room, her mouth hanging open.

"Yeah, bikers read," he said snidely.

Her eyes snapped to him.

"Dutch—"

"Shut your mouth, I'm talking."

She shut her mouth, but she did it with her expression changing.

She didn't look confused or concerned.

She looked like she was getting angry.

What this fucking woman had to be angry about, he had no clue.

But he was about to ream her with what was pissing *him* off.

"I cannot believe you sat in my goddamned *truck*—" he was losing it, he clamped down, and started again, "—with me doing you a goddamned favor, driving all the way out to fucking DIA to pick your ass up, and I told you about Carlyle, and you were struggling with your job, your own shit, when this kid is struggling with his dad getting shot fucking *dead*, and you used me sharing that with you to do something for yourself."

"What?" she asked, back to looking confused.

"Investigating the black market info I gave you to write something for your website," he rapped out. "Bet the crime beat is more interesting than the kids beat. Bet it also has a fuckuva better career trajectory too. Staff writer writing stories about vaping in school make squat. Investigative reporters probably make a bucketload more."

She took a step back, honest to fuck, like she'd been sucker punched.

"You didn't think I figured it out the minute I saw you there?" he asked cuttingly. "Bikers don't read. Bikers don't volunteer at runaway shelters. Bikers don't got brains in their heads?"

"Stop it with the biker stuff," she whispered.

"Fuck you, Georgiana," he bit.

Her head jerked.

And then…

"No, Dutch, fuck…" She took in a huge breath and screeched, "*YOU!*"

After that, she started marching toward his back door.

Oh no.

She was not going to go and fuck his mission to get Carlyle some justice.

He began walking toward her, stating, "We are not done."

She whirled on him and declared, "We *so* are."

He stopped two paces away and he didn't even attempt to

disguise the disgust in his tone when he asked, "You think you got moral ground to stand on here?"

"Yeah, Dutch," she said sharply, taking a long stride to him, and he braced because she was noticeably so pissed, it was sparking the air, zapping his skin, and he thought she was going to shove him.

She didn't.

She halted so fast, she swayed and kept talking.

"Because I cannot fucking *believe* that you thought…because I was temporarily a bitch. Because I thought I was in a career crisis. And granted, me taking that out on you was totally *not okay*. Even if you have no *freaking clue* any of the other shit that's going on in my life, not just with my job, but with my *sister*, and…and…*whatever*. I cannot *believe* that *you* would believe that I would do something so low and scummy as what you're accusing me of doing."

"So what were you doing there?" he asked.

"Carlyle is investigating his father's murder."

"No shit?"

"And my guess is, I was there for the same reason you were there. I was trying to find the guy Carlyle was talking to so I could figure out what connection he had to what happened that night so I could tell the cops and then they'll have a lead. And that might mean finding Carlyle's father's murderer."

He didn't believe her, which was why he drawled, "Right."

But then…

Shit.

She stared at him a beat, still pissed as shit, before that slid out of her face, and fuck…

The hurt shone clear. Hurt she could not be faking because it shimmered in the wet gathering in her eyes.

"You know, Carolyn is using Jagger," she whispered.

He wasn't expecting that, and both her words and tone made his chest get tight.

"What?" he whispered back.

"He gives her money. She's got, I don't know, four, five guys on the hook that come and go depending on who's up next to give her a loan and who needs a break from her asking. She says she'll pay it back. Ask your brother. But I'll bet she hasn't paid back a dime."

Dutch could not believe his ears.

But champagne tastes, he knew Carolyn had those, she didn't hide it, tricked out the way she always was.

What he couldn't believe was that Jag was falling for that shit.

"And I'm worried," she went on, "because the other guys are just guys. But he's a biker. And pardon me for thinking it, but I'll bet, woman or not, good guy biker or not, you don't fuck over a biker. And for years, she's been fucking over your brother. I don't think he's too dumb to get it. I think he likes her and thinks he's helping her out. But it's gonna get old and then he's gonna wonder where his money is going. Which is to designer shoes, handbags, Dior makeup palettes and a nasty little relationship she's got going with cocaine. And depending on how much he's given her, who knows what his reaction will be."

Cocaine?

He didn't get into that.

He got into something else.

"Jagger would never hurt a woman," Dutch said through his teeth.

"There are different ways to hurt people and the vast majority of them do not involve physical pain," she fired back. "Of all the guys she's taking for a ride, I think the only one she genuinely likes is your brother. So yes, when Carolyn hooked up with Jagger, I did a deep dive into MC culture and Chaos. She's my sister, and she's messed up, but I love her, so excuse me, because you might be you, and Chaos might be Chaos, but even you can't stand there and deny hardcore MCs are what I think they are. Yours might be a different kind of hardcore, but Chaos is hardcore, and you know it. But I didn't, until I met you. So I got worried. And maybe I developed an attitude about bikers. She's my sister and she's screwing up her life in a number of ways. Sue me."

"Georgi—"

"*And*," she cut him off, "you're right. I'm off the kids beat. I talked to my editor and she agreed it was time I explored new horizons. She said I have talent, and she wants to see me stretch myself. So thank you for that, because that was a load off. We're going to try a few things, see where I land in the New Evolution of Georgiana Traylor, Ace Reporter. And the crime beat was discussed and it's an option. But I am *not* using a seventeen-year-old's heartbreak to further my career. And just you thinking that, Dutch, says it all about what you think of me."

On that, she whirled again and headed to the back door.

He was faster, and taller, so even though she got it partly open, he reached over her shoulder, palm flat to the door, and he slammed it shut.

"I'm leaving, Dutch," she told the door.

He felt pressure on it against his palm and knew she was trying to open it, so he leaned into it.

And her.

She smelled like cherries and almonds.

Christ.

"I fucked up," he said softly to the back of her head.

"Agreed."

"Babe, let go of the door. We'll go back inside and talk this out."

"No, thank you."

"Okay, let go of the door, let's go back inside so I can apologize for being such a colossal dick."

"You know, I thought you were mad at me because you were being protective."

Again, not what he expected to hear.

"What?" he asked.

"When you dragged me here. I thought you were mad because you thought I was putting myself in danger and you're an alpha biker guy who'd get ticked because some woman was somewhere she shouldn't be, even though he was at the same place for the same reason. And I thought…insanely…that wasn't annoying. It was cute and kind of sweet."

At the end of that, she let out a little *huh* puff of air that stated plain she felt all kinds of fool he turned out not to be cute or sweet.

Fucking fuck.

"Georg—"

"Let me go."

"We need to talk."

"I did it for you."

She turned her head, tipped it back, giving him big, brown, wounded eyes, and goddamn it.

He barely knew this woman.

And she was unraveling him.

"I was such a bitch to you it made you be mean to me and I'm not sure that's you so I wanted to do something that would make you think I wasn't a bitch and—"

"Baby, come inside with me so we can talk."

"—you thought I was there to get a story and—"

"Please, Georgie."

"—I've got some stuff. I talked to my source at the DPD and he's getting me more and I'll deal with that and—"

"Christ, Georgie, *please*."

"—I'll give it to Carolyn when I get it and she can give it to you and then I'm out and you never have to see me again."

He told her what she needed to know. "I'm not holding this door shut, darlin', because I don't ever wanna see you again."

She just stared up at him.

"Come on, take off that hat, your jacket, I'll get us a beer and we'll work this out."

"Insult to injury, I've been reduced to saying words like '*made you be mean to me*,' like I'm seven years old."

Dutch engaged his other hand to put gentle pressure on her hip to try to turn her from the door, urging again, "Come on."

"And just so we're clear, I wasn't only doing it so you wouldn't think I was a bitch, because that makes it about me. I was also doing it because I want Carlyle to go to MIT."

Words weren't working. His hands on the door and her hip weren't working.

It was time to take a different tack.

And the one he chose was bending his head and kissing her.

She jerked away, shifting fast, and slammed a shoulder into the door.

"Sorry, baby, but you wouldn't shut up and you wouldn't come into my hou—"

He didn't finish that.

Because she was on him.

Clutching the sides of his head in both hands, she pulled his mouth to hers, curved her back so her soft body was pressed to his, and that was all Dutch needed.

He moved into her. One hand up under her hair then buried in that soft mane, his other arm curled tight around her waist pulling her closer, he pinned her against the door just as she parted her lips to invite him inside.

He accepted the invitation.

She wrapped her arms around his neck and shoved her body further into his.

She smelled of cherries and almonds, her mouth was hot and sweet and greedy, and when she quit trying to duel with his tongue to take over the kiss, her capitulation was sucking it deeper into her mouth.

The result, his cock, already stiffening, got rock-hard.

Fact: Georgiana Traylor could kiss.

And she had the sweetest draw he'd ever felt.

He wanted that on his tongue, and elsewhere.

Which meant this had to stop, immediately, or he'd fuck her on his mudroom floor.

He pulled slightly away to get them both under control.

But when her mouth went after his again, her hand curling tight around the back of his neck, he adjusted so his left eyebrow was to hers, his mouth was out of shot, and he sucked in a ragged breath.

"Why'd you stop?" she said, her breathy voice doing a number on him.

As an answer, he tightened his arm around her waist, and since there already was zero room between them, she couldn't miss what she was doing to him since the indisputable evidence of it was pressing into her belly.

She didn't miss it.

"The question bears repeating, Dutch, why did you stop?" she asked.

That made him smile.

And also answer.

"Georgie, you're the kind of girl I need to take on a date. Buy you dinner. Tell you how pretty your hair is. Your mouth. Your voice. How much I like your ass. All that before I fuck you."

She made a noise that was half soft gasp, half gentle whimper, and his dick actually started to hurt, straining against his jeans.

"Not to mention, we might need to sort through a few issues before we rip each other's clothes off and get busy," he finished.

"Am I in danger of you ripping off my clothes?"

"Absolutely."

Her eyes got bigger, then they got sultry in that hot way a

woman who knows she's got control of your cock gets, before she suggested, "Okay, just a suggestion, but maybe if you want to cool things down, you should let me go."

He got on that, but he did it shifting them so his back was to the door and his body was barring it.

Only then did he let her go.

She stepped away, now appearing amused.

"After that kiss, I'm hardly going to run into the night," she told him.

"I'm not taking any chances."

"Whatever," she mumbled, turned, started to sashay back into his house, and did it saying, "You promised me a beer?"

He watched her move, which did nothing to help him contain his raging hard-on.

But when she was out of sight in his living room, he sucked in another breath, got some damned control, turned, locked the door, shrugged off his cut and hung it on a hook by the door, and then followed her.

Dutch went to the kitchen that was open plan.

By the time he pulled two brews from the fridge, she'd followed him and was standing opposite the bar, living room side, hat gone, jacket thrown over the arm of his couch.

He knew she was wearing black jeans, now he saw she had on a tight black turtleneck.

And even covered from chin down, she looked great in it, and her tits looked fucking amazing.

"How many books do you have?" she asked.

He looked beyond her into the living room that was decorated in nothing but books.

He, Jag, Hound, Snap and Boz had built them after he bought the place.

Now, every single wall, except, obviously, where the kitchen was, was floor-to-ceiling bookcases that were, for the most part, filled with books.

There were some framed pictures his mom had given him. One of him, Jag, his mom and Hound on Hound and Ma's wedding day. One of him and Jagger with their arms slung around each other, both of them wearing their cuts, the night Jag was patched in. Another one of him in his mother's hospital room holding his newborn brother the day Wilder came into the world.

And one of his dad, the dad that was no longer breathing, leaning forearm to the bar in the Chaos Compound, smiling big at a camera that was in front of the face of the woman of his dreams, the mother of his children, his wife, Dutch's mom, Keely Black Ironside.

The shelves were also punctuated by things like lamps and a candle one of his ex-girlfriends gave him and he liked the scent of it, so after they were over, he'd bought another one.

But mostly, yeah, it was books or space where more books would go when he bought them.

Though, there were three shelves that were all albums because he liked the sound of music from vinyl, which was, as far as he knew, the only millennial thing he could get on board with.

He grabbed his bottle opener, popped the caps on both of the Fat Tires, came to stand across from Georgiana, slid hers to her and waited until she took a sip, something he did not do, before he spoke.

"First, before we get into inane things like my book collection, I was a dick. It was out of line. You did not deserve it. And I'm sorry that shit came out of my mouth."

"Okay," she said quietly.

"I was a dick two days ago when I dropped you off too. You didn't deserve it then either."

"Okay, Dutch. Though, I'm not sure that's correct."

"It's correct," he said firmly.

She pressed her lips together then let them go and whispered, "Right. Okay."

"Second, that kiss was hot. So I'm takin' you out to dinner tomorrow night, somewhere nice, good food, maybe even fancy, then plan to spend the night here."

Her brows went way up, she sucked her lips in so far between her teeth they disappeared, it was cute as *all fuck*, something he felt in his dick, throat, and the fact his mouth got dry with the need to take hers again, before she rearranged her face and asked, "Is that a biker's way of asking a girl on a date?"

"No fuckin' clue. It's just what's happening tomorrow night."

"Righty ho." She was whispering again and now looking like she was about to crack up laughing.

"So, we on the same page with all of that?"

"Well, um…yes, of a sort."

"What's the 'of a sort' part?"

"I can't tomorrow night."

"Why?"

"Well, you see, my source in the DPD chose this unfortunate time to realize I was using his fascination with my breasts to semi-kinda-but-mostly-definitely score information from him and he pressed the issue. So, in order to learn what the cops know about Carlyle's dad's case, I have to go out to dinner with him tomorrow."

Dutch took a beat.

Then he took two.

Then he said gently, "Right, baby, you know that biker research you did?"

She nodded.

"And that hardcore stuff you learned?" he continued.

She nodded again.

"Well, there is a definite Chaos version of that," he told her.

"Do I want to know?" she asked.

"Maybe not, but after that kiss, and what's gonna come next, you need to anyway."

She took her own beat before she invited, "Right then, sock it to me."

"You are not going out on a date with a guy who has a fascination with your breasts when you're in my bed."

"I'm not in your bed yet, Dutch, and pointing out, it was you who put a stop to that."

"I'll amend. You are not going out on a date with a guy who has a fascination with your breasts when it's a certainty you're *gonna* be in my bed."

"Dutch—"

He asked a question he did not want to ask.

"You into this guy?"

She scrunched her nose.

She was not into this guy.

He straightened, and he'd never heard it come from his own throat, but he could not deny it was an actual growl when he started, "Georgie—"

"He's not a cop, but he has electronic access, and he can give me good stuff, Dutch."

"Yeah, and I know actual cops, a number of them, who also have access, who not only won't mind sharing, I've already got a sitdown planned with two of them tomorrow."

"Oh," she mumbled.

"Cancel your plans."

She tipped her head to the side. "I kinda can't."

"You absolutely can."

"Well, see, now, if I screw this up, he's gonna be mad, and I'll lose my source in the DPD. I know someone else who's got loose lips, but they don't have his kind of access. And, as previously mentioned, I'm soon to be assigned articles on the crime beat, so I need a good source. So I *have* to go, regardless."

Dutch looked to the ceiling.

"I was right," Georgiana said.

He looked back to her and saw her grinning.

"It's totally cute, the protective, and in this case, possessive thing," she explained.

"I'm not feelin' cute," he informed her.

"Well, you are," she muttered to the neck of her beer bottle before she took another sip.

"You go, you're done, you come here to me," he demanded.

"There's a problem with that too," she admitted.

Jesus.

"What?" he asked.

"I have a cat, that's not really my cat, but I'm claiming him. He was not a big fan of substitute momma leaving him overnight to go meet a douchebag, deadbeat attorney in DC. So, in order to assist him in getting over his trauma of spending the night alone, I really shouldn't make him spend the night alone again so soon."

For the second time with shit she was saying, this time especially after that kiss, he couldn't believe his ears.

"You're not gonna come to me because of your cat?"

"Again, not my cat, though he is because I'm claiming him. He's my roommate's cat. She's a doctor without borders. And I suspect, since she's on stretch number two, she's never returning home. So I'm taking this as an abandonment issue even though all of her belongings are still in my apartment, including her cat. But if by chance she does return, and she tries to reclaim my-cat-not-my-cat, I might have to catnap him and go on the lam."

After she delivered that, so they didn't have sex for the first time on his kitchen floor either, in that moment he considered it a very good thing the bar was between them.

"Are you always this cute?" he asked.

"I hope so. Are *you* always this cute?" she asked back.

"I'm not cute, babe."

"You so totally are," she mumbled, again to the neck of her beer bottle.

She took a sip and then grinned at him.

Okay, what the fuck?

Why was his dick getting hard just watching her grin?

"So, how many books do you have?" she returned to her earlier question.

"Bring your cat here, before your date-not-date."

She huffed out a disbelieving laugh and asked, "You're going to hold my-cat-not-my-cat hostage so I'll come to you after my date-not-date?"

"Yup," he confirmed before he took his first sip of his own beer.

"And you want *me* to serve my-cat-not-my-cat up as hostage by bringing him to you before my date-not-date?" she asked, now smiling huge.

He leaned into both forearms on the bar, his hands cradling his beer between them.

She hesitated only a second before she did the same thing so they were close enough to start kissing again.

He didn't kiss her.

"So we got our plan," he decreed, because, as funny as she was, he was done talking about her cat. "You come to me before you go to him and bring your cat. Then you come to me after. We talk. We drink beer. We watch TV. Whatever. We sleep together but do not fuck. And I'll take you out to dinner the night after, and that's when we'll sleep together, after fucking."

"I guess we do have our plan since the brand-new biker guy in my life has just declared that's the plan."

"Affirmative."

She started laughing soft and quiet and hella pretty.

And he knew they had their plan.

Only then did he relax.

"And I have no idea how many books I have," he told her.

"Have you read them all?"

"Not yet."

"Is that a goal?"

"Yeah."

"Impressive," she whispered, not looking amused.

Looking into him and wanting to be kissed.

He pushed forward and touched his lips to hers.

She followed him a little when he pulled away, then quirked her lips in surrender when she realized that was all she was going to get.

For now.

"So what do you know that brought you to that warehouse?" he asked.

It was then she realized they were out of the flirty banter and into the heavy, so she sighed, but didn't hesitate sharing, "I have other sources. Kids, or not-so-much kids anymore, that I met from past stories. When Jackson, the DPD guy, held out on me, I moved down the list to them and told them what I wanted. They were good kids who got disenfranchised, they liked me, thought I was cool, and fortunately as time passed, they didn't quit doing that. So they poked around a bit and gave me some leads. The other stuff I checked out and it led to dead ends. I'm assuming, since you were there, that what I was about to look into tonight wasn't a dead end."

"Full disclosure, I was into you when your sister texted me your picture, and stayed into you even when you got off the plane in a bad mood—"

"You're being generous now, honey," she whispered. "It wasn't just a bad mood. I was awful to you."

He kept going like she didn't talk and like hearing her call him "honey" in that sweet voice of hers didn't hit him warm in the gut.

"So tonight was part about me making a fucked-up assumption and part that Vance had just warned me that if I got caught close to that warehouse, I'd disappear. So it was also part me pissed as shit you were bumbling around in a dangerous sitch that might get you hurt, or worse."

She pushed up and asked, "Bumbling?"

He pushed up too and asked in return, "Did you know you were onto something that might get you disappeared?"

She didn't answer, though she did, since she took an annoyed sip of her beer.

"Right," he muttered.

She rolled her eyes.

That meant it was his turn to grin.

"I want in on your talk with the cops tomorrow," she declared.

He was about to slug back more beer, but that stopped him.

"Georgie, you're out. I got this."

There was a serious chill on her, "I'm sorry?"

Fuck.

"This shit is dangerous and there's a dead man to prove it," he pointed out.

"Well, I'm not asking to be a part of the takedown team when the cops go in and bust this black-market ring. I'm just saying I want to be there when you talk to the cops. And I want to keep on what I'm doing. Because I have things to contribute and most of it might come to nothing. But some of it might help Carlyle find some closure, if not peace."

Goddamn it, he couldn't argue that.

"Fine," he said.

"Fine," she snapped.

"I'm in on your shit too."

Her expression softened in order to soften her words. "Dutch, you can't come on my date-not-date with me. That'd definitely make Jackson clam up."

"I get that, baby, but the other shit. The street kids. Whatever."

She seemed to be contemplating this. "Work as a team?"

"Why not?"

She smiled at him. "Cool."

Yeah, it was.

"It might be fun," she said.

Yeah, it would.

He grinned at her and took another sip.

Then, regrettably, he had to get into more heavy.

So he leaned back into his elbows, and he saw her mentally brace, which meant she read him, as he meant her to, before she leaned into hers.

He tried to cushion his words as best as he could when he gave it to her.

"You know I'm gonna have to tell my brother about Carolyn."

She dropped her head and stared down at her beer.

He lifted a hand and curved it around her jaw, so she looked at him again.

"I can give you two days to prepare her. In that time, she can come clean. She can do whatever. But after those two days are up, Georgie, I gotta give Jag what he needs to have, and I'm gonna warn you, he's gonna lose it and scrape her off."

"Yeah," she said sadly.

"He won't hurt her, at least not—"

"I know."

"He's also not gonna get shitty about getting his money back. But she'll be dead to him."

"I know," she repeated.

"It's not all about the money. Drugs are a no-go with us, baby."

"Me too," she whispered. "I don't know what to do about her. She's a hot mess, and not only in this way, which is saying something."

And more of her bad mood at the airport was explained, and this shit was even bigger.

With regret, he took his hand from her and said, "We can talk about that tomorrow night after you get here from your date-not-date. Now, 'cause I wanna kiss you again to take your mind off shit things, and if I do, that'll take us where we shouldn't go until we get to know each other a little better, I gotta get you home."

"Back to my car, you mean."

"Then I'll follow you home."

"I can drive myself home, Dutch."

"I know that, Georgiana. But you'll be driving away from a warehouse full of black market shit, and the bad guys who deal it, where I do not know if we wandered into their camera range and they saw me drag you out of there. So they might be even more vigilant. So I want to make sure you're not followed. With me?"

She nodded.

"Quick kiss, then finish your beer, then we're out of here."

She gave him that got-your-cock look again which caught the attention of his cock, as it was meant to do, and said, "You *so* want in my pants."

He arched a brow. "And you don't want in mine?"

She inched forward a little. "I *oh-so* want in your pants."

He chuckled.

She leaned into him and gave him a quick, hard kiss, before she pushed back to straight and he watched, unmoving from his lean into the counter, as she tipped her head back and downed more than half a beer in one go.

"Talk about impressive," he teased on a smile when she finished.

"I'm this close to jumping your bones because you're being so cute, so you best get me home, bad boy."

"I'm not cute."

"Whatever."

Someone was going to get their bones jumped, and in order not to jump that gun, because they started out way wrong, and he was going to lead them forward all right, he pushed up, socked back another slug, but didn't down the whole thing. He set his beer aside, rounded the bar, caught her hand, and led her to her jacket on his couch.

As she pulled it on, she said, "It's super cool you're letting me give Carolyn a heads-up that you're gonna tell Jagger."

"If you don't want to be thrown under that bus that Jag knows because I know because you told me, then we can do it whatever way is your way, but it's gotta get done, and sooner not later."

She nodded. "Can I tell you at our cop talk tomorrow?"

He returned her nod.

He also took her hand again to lead her out to his truck.

But she tugged on his and he stopped moving.

"When is that?" she asked.

"Lunch. Noon. Eddie Chavez and Hank Nightingale."

She nodded.

"I'll pick you up at eleven-thirty," he told her.

She nodded again and said, "I'll need your cell number."

"You can program it in, in the truck."

Another nod then, "Dutch."

"Right here," he stated when she didn't say anything else.

She looked weird for a beat before she blurted, "I like you."

He felt his lips twitch as he shifted, getting closer, and his voice was low when he said, "I hope so."

"I just…well, it…" She cleared her throat. "Carolyn played

Jagger and—"

He interrupted her.

"We're here, finally."

"Uh…sorry?"

"We're at the good part to being in the biker world."

"What's that?" she whispered, staring up at him.

He got even closer, dipped his head to hers, and with their mouths close, and eyes locked, he answered, "Live and let live, Georgie."

"So you're saying, if we…you know, if something comes of us—"

"You're you, she's Carolyn, and Jag will know the difference. And no offense to your sister, but he's not that into her, so it might sting, that'll mostly be to his pride, but he'll get over it, though he'll get over her faster."

"Okay," she said breathily.

He liked the way she said that.

He liked the way she was staring up at him, like she could stand there for a year and do it and be totally down with that.

So he changed his mind.

"I think we need to kiss again," he told her.

"And I think you're absolutely right," she replied.

She pushed up on her toes.

He bent down.

They both wound their arms around each other.

And they went at it.

He managed (mostly) not letting his dick get (too) hard.

But it wasn't easy.

Then he ended it, walked her to his truck, took her to her car, followed her home and waited outside until he saw the light go on in the unit she told him was hers and she texted, **All good.**

He waited some more and got, **Murtagh is looking forward to his adventure.**

He waited even longer and got, **Murtagh is my cat-not-my-cat. FYI.**

Only then did he reply, **Go to bed, baby.**

And on his way home, he got, **Cute.**

Chapter Five

The Right Stuff

Dutch

Dutch was in a moderately bad mood at eleven twenty-seven the next day when he knocked on Georgiana's door.

It didn't take long before she opened it, and she did that with her face happy and eyes alight, a big smile on her mouth.

"Hey!" she greeted.

"Babe, you gave me the code to your building," he stated irritably.

Something she did, via text, that morning, half an hour ago, not at his request.

The smile wobbled. "What?"

"We barely know each other."

"Dutch, you've had your tongue in my mouth."

"I know."

"And maybe doing that again would be a better way to greet your New-Style American Girl You're Gonna Start Seeing."

At the vague but hilarious reference to *Sixteen Candles*, and Georgie just being Georgie, he moved fast, hooked her around the waist and hauled her so hard to his body, she let out a high, adorable squeal.

He then laid a wet one on her, shuffling her back into her pad as he did it, hearing the door swing shut behind him.

When he ended it, she was visibly dazed and blinking.

He made note of that since, with the way she ran her mouth, it might come in handy.

"You buzz strangers up," he ordered.

She recovered and retorted, "You're not a stranger."

"We could go bad and I've got your code."

Georgie tipped her head to the side. "Are we gonna go bad?"

"No."

She got that look he liked way too much, pressed close and moved her hands so they were curled around either side of his neck. "Dutch. We have a new building manager and he's King of Security. He changes the code randomly and often."

That made him feel better, and he gave her a squeeze to communicate that.

"He's also installed more cameras, which means our HOA payment has gone up, and I'm down with more security. The rise in HOA fees, though, bites," she went on to share.

This surprised him.

"Your landlord makes you pay the HOA?" he asked.

"Since I'm my landlord, yes," she answered.

This surprised him more. "You own this place?"

It wasn't tactful, but she didn't take offense and showed him that by busting out laughing.

Through it, she said, "I don't know where that comes from, either you don't think my pad is all that hot and don't understand why I bought it, or you don't think I have it together enough to be a homeowner."

"Babe," he muttered, lacing that word with apology.

She ran a finger along the stubble at his jaw and said softly, "This pad isn't all that hot, but it was what I could afford when I got a bee in my bonnet about getting on the property ladder. It took a lot of scraping money together, a couple years of seriously frugal living, and a loan from my dad, but I managed it. Though, I continue to manage it by having a roommate who was in med school when I found her, then took off to save the world, somewhat literally, but still pays half the mortgage."

"I haven't seen it, still know it's a good investment."

That made her look surprised. "Sorry?"

"You'll move on, but you can rent this until you die. It'll be a tidy source of income. I got the same. Two rental properties. My brother Snap makes a mint off stuff he owns, I followed that road."

More surprise from Georgie. "So you own a house and two rental properties?" She didn't let him answer, but quickly said, "And that isn't about you being a biker. It's about…" She didn't finish that either, in a way. She also did by asking, "How old are you?"

"Twenty-eight."

Now she looked stunned. "And you own three properties?"

"I'm patched in, so I take full cut of monthly earnings from Ride. But Ma got Dad's cut the whole time after he died, until she got hitched to Hound, who's also a Chaos brother. She set some aside for Jag and me. And when they sold the house we grew up in, they split that in half, and gave it to Jag and me. Though, not right away. She held on to it until we were old enough not to blow through it doin' stupid shit. But when she did hand it over, it was substantial, and to make it work for me, I invested it."

"So you're Wise Biker *and* Real Estate Mogul Biker?"

He grinned down at her. "Snap's the mogul. I'm not there yet."

"You've got more than me," she mumbled.

"Georgie," he called.

She refocused on him.

And blurted, "I'm thirty-one."

She said that like it was a dirty little secret.

When she didn't say more, he prompted, "So?"

"You act older than twenty-eight."

More prompting from him. "And?"

She was watching him closely when she asked, "Does it bother you that I'm older than you?"

"Did it bother you when you thought I was older than you?"

Her bright smile came back. "So my New-Style American Biker I'm Starting to See is Wise Biker, Budding Mogul Biker *and* Enlightened Biker."

He grinned again and gave her another squeeze. "Yeah."

"Awesome," she whispered, pressing close.

He was about to kiss her again when they both heard, "*Mwrrr!*"

She jerked in his hold, looked down and cried dramatically, "Baby!"

She then pulled free of Dutch's arms and Dutch watched her bend down and pick up a cat that was sitting at the sides of their feet.

She turned it in her arms, cradled it like it was her child and started speaking to the animal, sharing big, but doing it in a cooing voice that was straight-up hilarious.

"You can see, he's gorgeous, and he's a good kisser, so there's reason I forgot all about you. But I'm so sorry I forgot about you. I'll introduce you to him right away." Her eyes came to Dutch. "Dutch, this is Murtagh." She looked to the cat. "Murtagh, this is my New-Style American Biker I'm Starting to See, Dutch Black."

"Mwrr," Murtagh replied.

It took some effort, with Georgiana showing him more of the good that was Georgiana, to tear his eyes from her to look at the cat.

But when he did, he experienced a sensation he'd never felt in his life.

Love at first sight.

Big round eyes. Poofy round face. Tons of thick, gray hair. Folded-over ears.

It was the cutest damned feline he'd ever clapped eyes on.

Not even knowing what he was doing, he took the cat from her arms and held it the same way Georgie had been doing.

"Yo, Murtagh," he greeted.

"Murr," Murtagh replied.

"You're gonna hang with me tonight."

"Mwrr?"

"Yeah. Make sure Mom brings some toys. We'll live it up."

"*Mwwwwrrrr.*"

He turned his attention to Georgie and declared, "We're all good."

He then clamped his mouth shut.

Because she was staring at him in a way no other woman had looked at him.

But he'd seen that look.

His ma looked at Hound like that.

Tack's wife, Cherry, looked at Tack like that.

Shy's woman, Tabby, looked at Shy like that.

Hop's wife Lanie.

Joker's wife, Carissa.

Snap's wife, Rosalie.

High's wife, Millie.

This list could go on.

Georgiana was similarly frozen, and like two lovestruck idiots, they stood close, a cat held between them, staring silently into each other's eyes.

But so many words were flying, all of them full of meaning, it was not funny.

Dutch broke the spell.

"You got a bag and coat, baby?" he asked quietly. "We gotta go."

"Yes," she whispered.

She then moved awkwardly, like she didn't know how to use her limbs, and gave Murtagh a head rub before she moved away.

Dutch started stroking Murtagh's belly, and Murtagh shared he dug that by starting to purr.

At the same time, Dutch used that opportunity to take his first look around.

He didn't know what he expected to see, but what he saw was not what he would have thought would be Georgie's living space from what he knew of her.

Or what he'd assumed.

Erroneously.

And last night, damagingly.

He had thought, career woman, and ambitious, probably often on the road or at least out of the house, her space would not matter and that would show.

He was again wrong.

It was cluttered, but tidy, with a freestanding, open-backed bookshelf that made one room, two: a living area and a dining area.

The space was roomier than he would have guessed. The couch had a gallery wall above it that looked interesting enough he knew he'd take a closer look at what she had up there later. The coffee table had a big wicker basket under it, probably to tuck away throws. There was a chair that was definitely there for looks, not comfort, made of clear plastic. And the look worked, it was sheer cool. Toss pillows that ranged from animal prints to florals that somehow worked.

The coffee table was completely covered. Stacked with books, some in a tray. A small decorative bowl, a squat vase with a pink puff of fake flowers, a single taper candle adding dimension.

The bookshelves were totally books, though artfully arranged, and not clogged, you could see through to the dining area which was a small round table with steel-legged, plastic-seated bucket chairs. With those chairs it was truth, it was kind of a marvel, how she'd made something cheap look chic.

He'd furnished his own crib, so he knew the cost of shit, and the scale of quality that money bought you, and none of this was top-of-the-line or even middle-of-the-road stuff.

But she'd made it work, it had personality, and it stated plain there was more to Georgiana.

She dove deep into her job, it meant something to her, and she was good at it.

Her roommate had abandoned her cat, and Georgie had adopted it.

She'd blown it with Dutch, liked him, and went *way* the extra mile to make up for it.

She was loyal to a sister that didn't deserve it.

She had guts.

She had spunk.

She was hilarious.

She knew how to use her mouth, and almost better, when to stop using it and let Dutch take what he wanted, and in doing it, give her more.

And she cared about the space around her, made it hers, stamped it with her style, and it was interesting.

He turned his attention to her and finally took in what she was wearing.

Another black sweater, this one a crewneck. A tan skirt. Pencil, fitting close to her hips, ass and thighs. Black boots, high heels, not ridiculous drag-queen high, but still hot. She had a little scarf tied around her neck that had a pattern on it that was black and cream with some pink thrown in. Her hair was up in a messy bunch at the back top of her head, with tendrils floating down. And she had studs in her ears that were little clusters of tiny pearls, and other than a watch glinting from under her long sleeve, that was the only jewelry she wore.

Class. Professionalism. Personality.

Jesus.

Thank fuck Jag and Carolyn blew off picking her up from the

airport.

She'd pulled on a lightweight feminized peacoat and was grabbing her beat-up, cognac-colored leather backpack.

"Ready," she said.

He jerked up his chin and looked down at the cat. "We're outta here. Catch you later."

He got a buzzing "mwrr" before he put the cat down.

"Be good, Murtagh," Georgiana ordered.

Sharing the affront he took at this, Murtagh turned his back on her and jumped on the couch, not bothering to reply.

Outside the apartment, after she made sure the self-closing door latched, Dutch took her hand and held it all the way down the hall, while tagging the button to the elevator, waiting for the elevator, and then in the elevator.

It wasn't until then that Georgie spoke.

"You're a hand-holder."

He looked down at her, starting to let go, asking, "You're not?"

She held tight to his hand before she lost it. "I wasn't. Until now."

He smiled at her.

She smiled back.

They held hands the rest of the way to his truck.

"What's for lunch?" she asked when he'd pulled out of his parking space.

"Las Delicas."

"Excellent," she muttered.

And she had good taste in food.

"So, I've been thinking about Carolyn," he began.

"Ugh," she grunted.

"Baby," he murmured.

"It's okay. I've been thinking about it too. It's time. High time."

"In the past, before this, have you talked to her about it?" he asked.

"When we met, you said something about how Carolyn had spoken about me, so you knew about me, and my guess from how you said that, what she told you about me wasn't stellar. What do you think?"

"So you're a pain in her ass because you ride her ass."

"Dutch, she…*God*."

She was struggling, she didn't hide it, but instead of pushing it, he gave her time.

It was the right call, because she didn't take much of it before she said, her voice pained, "Essentially, she's whoring herself for material items and dope."

Essentially, she was correct.

Dutch kept his mouth shut.

"Mother thinks it's a phase."

Dutch said nothing.

"Mother is wrong."

Dutch had a question about that. "You call your mom 'Mother?'"

"My mom *is* a 'mother.' Dad's a *dad*. Mom's worked hard at being *Mother*."

"You said your dad wasn't around—"

"He wasn't. They split. He traveled for work so there were reasons he was absent in the beginning. He also found another woman, married her, they had a kid. Through all of this, Mom put a lot of effort into making his life hell. So he made the decision that life was too short to deal with her, and he put great effort into omitting her from it. The side effect of this was, to do that, he had to omit us. Carolyn and me."

"The fuck?"

And back was the growl.

"There's that cute again," she whispered.

"There is no excuse to pick yourself over your kids. Christ, *your daughters*."

"A son would be different?" she asked curiously.

"Okay, get this, it's important. I don't have any kids. I still know I'm gonna be protective as fuck if I get girls. Not that I won't love and protect a boy. But it's gonna be stratospheric with a girl. So my advice, file that away, and if you got a problem with it, get over it."

"So…crazy…*cute*." Again with the whisper.

"Georgie," he warned.

"Dutch," she replied, sounding amused.

"Haven't met the man and already not a big fan of your dad."

"He paid support. He sent us money, a good deal of it, on birthdays, Christmas, even Easter and Valentine's Day, and sometimes we'd get a card with cash in it just because."

"Money isn't love. In this case, and brace, because this is harsh, it might be about guilt."

"You're right, honey, but he wasn't totally absent. And when we got older, had some independence and could get away from her, we reached out and he latched on. He helped me with college, for one. And I told you he floated me a loan to buy my condo. What I didn't tell you was, that loan is being deferred, month to month every time I contact Dad and tell him I've got his check, and he says, 'What're you gonna do without this month if you give me that, sweetheart?' Then even if I say, 'Nothing,' he still refuses it."

"Was he there to take pictures of you when you went to your prom?"

"I skipped my junior prom and went to my senior prom with my posse of chicks and we wore Doc Martens and combat fatigues in protest to the patriarchy."

Dutch busted out laughing.

He kept doing it when she added, "That was my militant feminist phase. Somewhat *literally*. At least in terms of garments." And he didn't stop when she went on, "I'm over that now."

"Those heels are hot, darlin', that skirt is hotter," he told her.

She whacked his arm like she did the first time they were in his truck, he liked it just as much as he had back then, except this time he could admit that to himself, and she said, "Shut up, Dutch."

He grinned at the road, but did it knowing he had to get them back on track.

Something he did.

"Georgie, Carolyn."

"Right," she mumbled.

"What I was thinkin' is that Jag doesn't have to throw you under the bus. Carolyn doesn't have to know you told me and I told him."

He saw her hand coming his way, but even if he did, it surprised him when she ran it down his jaw before she stretched across the cab and he felt her kiss his cheek.

She stayed stretched when she said, "You're unbelievably sweet."

"Just lookin' out for him and tryin' to do the same for you," he pointed out.

"Yes, and I appreciate it, but file this away, honey," she used his words and kept on, "I don't do that. It's a white lie for kind reasons but it's still a lie. And I don't lie."

That said good things about her and what might become of them.

But in this instance, it was inconvenient.

"Babe."

She sat back in her seat and carried on, "What *I* was thinking is that whatever we've got going is happening with us and eventually Carolyn is going to know about it. It's not cool what she's been doing and it's not cool I've kept my mouth shut she's doing it. I'm not going to make the rounds of her guys and tell on her. I'm also not going to maybe start a relationship with someone that interests me a whole lot and have her mess sit there between us. She knows I'm that kind of person so she's going to be angry, but she's not going to be surprised. And the bottom line, maybe she needs some drama to shake her out of the disaster she's making of her life. And losing your brother is going to shake her."

"Interests you a whole lot?" he teased, did it careful, because he could tell not only by her words, but by her tone that this shit was heavy, and he wanted to lighten it for her.

She reached out a hand and squeezed his thigh, but she didn't say anything.

Dutch didn't say anything either, because even though she removed her hand, he still felt it.

And the touch on his jaw.

The kiss on his cheek.

Her hands curled around his neck earlier in her pad.

Her fingers tightening around his in the elevator.

Hell, just the way she looked at him when she opened her door.

Years ago, Hound had told Dutch and Jagger to watch their mother to know what kind of woman to look for to make their own.

And after watching Keely Black grieve for nearly two decades, at the same time watching his mom and Hound dance around each other, both feeling deep for the other, neither going there, and now them having what they had, it wasn't nauseating, the love they had they did not bother hiding.

His mother was not cuddly and gross.

But she was affectionate and loving and open about it to all her boys. The ones she made and the one she made hers.

He and Georgiana hadn't even been out on a date, and she already communicated with more than words.

Communicated the important stuff.

The deep stuff.

The right stuff.

Georgie couldn't be any different than his ma.

Keely Black Ironside was biker babe through and through.

But yeah.

Evidence was coming clear Georgiana Traylor had the right stuff.

Through and through.

"So I'm gonna talk to her tomorrow," she said, cutting into his thoughts.

It occurred to him she was in his truck, working Carlyle's situation with him, and now was dealing with her sister, and she had a job.

"Is your latest story suffering because of all this?" he asked.

"Well, uh…" She did not answer.

"Babe," he grunted.

"Okay, so I am who I am, and once I got my teeth into Carlyle's case, and because I, uh…well, watched *Blood, Guts and Brotherhood* again and I'd been so awful to you, I kinda got obsessed and called my editor and asked for some time off."

Dutch again held his silence.

"I haven't had a vacation in over a year, and our PTO accumulates, all the way up to eight weeks, so I have a ton of it. I think she was actually relieved to give me a couple of weeks off. And she said that I needed to do this more regularly, or burnout wasn't a possible, it'd be an inevitable."

"You watched that film again?" he asked.

"Yeah," she answered.

He smiled big at the windshield. "You are *so* into me."

She whacked his arm again with her, "Shut up."

But he caught her hand this time before she took it away and held it against his thigh the rest of the way to the restaurant.

Eddie and Hank weren't there yet, so they got a table, regrettably. He'd prefer a booth and to have her cornered in it, his thigh pressed to hers and her close enough to touch. But they needed a table for the discussion. Better and freer eyelines.

They got chips and salsa, their drinks.

But neither of them even opened a menu.

If you knew LD, you knew what you were going to order at LD.

The end.

Hank and Eddie showed, introductions were made, and it wasn't only Dutch who noticed the intensity of interest they had in Georgie.

And it wasn't about her being with Dutch.

Eddie, the more direct of the two, cut right to it.

"You're a reporter."

"I'm on vacation."

"And you're here because…?" Hank asked.

"Because she's with me and she's helpin' me out by using her sources," Dutch answered.

His tone was undeniable, and these men were cops, neither of them even owned a bike, and the cloth they were cut from might be a different color, but it was the same cloth.

So they read the tone, understood it, and that was the end of that.

Hank nor Eddie looked at the menu either before they all ordered and then they didn't waste any time with it.

"We both read through it before we came here and the Khalon Stephens case stinks, man," Eddie started it.

Dutch straightened in his chair. "Stinks how?"

"Fishy," Hank said shortly. "From start to not-quite-end."

"What do you mean?" Georgie asked.

"I wouldn't know where to begin," Eddie answered.

"How about the beginning," Dutch suggested.

"Well, first, cops at the scene report, and pictures prove it, the resident of the duplex opposite the Stephens family had visibly been beaten. Bloody nose. Swelling. Contusions on face and arms. Like she'd been held by them and hard. There was also sign of a struggle in the room," Eddie said.

"Or a fight," Hank added.

Dutch knew that distinction meant something, but Hank left it at that, and Eddie carried on.

"Bed had been slept in, but it does not appear there was a struggle there. The covers were thrown back like she got out. Not like she was awakened in surprise by an intruder and was pulled out."

Dutch glanced at Georgie.

Georgie gave him big eyes.

The Stephenses had not heard a break-in and there was no evidence of one.

How the intruder got in was a mystery.

Unless he was let in.

"She wiped herself down before going for the rape kit," Hank shared. "So there was no point in doing a rape kit, and as such, none was done."

Dutch's eyes leapt to Hank.

"Say what?" he asked.

"She contends she was not thinking clearly," Hank told him. "Even though the rape was interrupted, material can still be gathered. A rape kit is performed in a hospital and not only did she wipe herself down, wash her hands and brush her hair before she showed, she changed clothes and the nightgown she was wearing mysteriously disappeared. To this day, it has not turned up."

"That's pretty freakin' thorough grooming before heading out to have your rape kit done," Dutch noted sarcastically.

"It's not unheard of that happens," Eddie noted. "Victims of violent crimes are rarely in an emotional state to think straight."

"But wasn't she warned not to do that?" Dutch asked.

"She was," Eddie answered.

Before Dutch could respond, Georgie spoke.

"By process of elimination, since three people were there, one's missing, one's dead, and she's the last, she's the only one reporting there was an attempted rape."

"Yeah," Hank affirmed.

"And there were officers at the scene, was she not offered an escort to the hospital?" Georgie went on.

"She wasn't only offered that, it was pressed, but she was adamant that she would make her way there herself," Hank told her.

"And they let her, in her home, which was the scene of a crime that resulted in a death, wash up and then go to the hospital?" Georgie sounded shocked.

"She did not wash up or change clothes at home. She found somewhere along the way from home to the hospital to do it," Hank shared.

"So the woman went out of her way to clean up," Dutch asked, also shocked, and pissed.

"Yeah," Hank said.

"It unheard of *that* happens?" Dutch put to Eddie.

Eddie grunted unhappily.

Fishy was damned right.

"You have *got* to be kidding," Georgie snapped, beyond disbelieving, or irate.

She was furious.

There was a lot of emotion behind that, some deserved, but this was past that, and Dutch wanted to know about it.

"Where's that come from, darlin'?" he asked.

"She said she was being raped," she replied.

He drew out his, "Yeah."

"And from what we've heard, there is a distinct possibility that's not the case."

"Yeah," he repeated.

"I'm sure this is arguable, but in my estimation, the worst kind of woman is the woman who makes a false allegation of rape, or attempted rape. Every one who does makes the ones who actually endure that nightmare have to travel a road that already is going to be arduous, one that's so horrendous, the majority of victims refuse to even take that path."

Dutch felt the truth of that in the back of his throat and swung his eyes to Eddie and Hank.

"She's right," Hank said low.

"So that's why no DNA was found," Georgie rapped out.

"Yup," Eddie said.

"She's lying. Covering for the murderer," Georgie spat. "She knows him."

"Yup," Hank said.

"The fuck?" Dutch murmured angrily.

"Where is this woman?" Georgie demanded.

All of the men looked to her, but it was only Dutch who reached out and wrapped his fingers around her wrist.

Sparks had flown from her last night because she was pissed as shit at him.

It was not lost on a single man at that table she was about to explode, and she wanted to aim the grenade that was her at Carlyle's neighbor.

"Take a breath," he urged.

"Carlyle's dad went over in the midst of a lovers' spat or a conspirators' fight or a bad guy argument because he thought a woman was being harmed and he was the kind of man who would do something to put a stop to that and he got dead because of it and this *bitch is not talking*?"

He leaned her way. "Baby, take a breath."

"How can the worst situation in the world get even *worse*?" she demanded to know.

"We don't know her story, Georgie."

"I'm thinking I do, Dutch. She's covering her and/or this guy's ass and Carlyle's dad is dead. Benefit of the doubt, she was in a bad situation. Carlyle's father still charged in, in order to save her from it and the thanks he gets is her letting his murderer go free."

"Get a lock on it, darlin'," he ordered gently.

"No," she snapped.

"Georgiana, you losing your mind on this woman is not gonna help Carlyle."

She caught his eyes and stared into them, deep and for a long time.

Then she took in a shuddering breath, tore her hand free and raised it toward a passing waitress.

"Margarita, double shot of tequila," she ordered.

The waitress nodded.

Georgie then dipped a chip, ate it angrily, and talked while munching, muttering, "Fucking bitch. Fucking fuck her."

"I see you're over your no-cursing-around-people-you-don't-know gig," he noted.

This time, she punched him in the arm.

He caught her around the back of her neck, pulled her to him, and kissed her hard. No tongue, unfortunately. She still tasted good.

When he let her go, she declared, "You're a good kisser, Dutch, seriously, but your kisses don't wring miracles."

"I'll have to work on that," he replied.

"Whatever," she mumbled.

"Luke has got to meet this one," Eddie said.

"Tex," Hank said. "Tex is gonna adopt her."

Christ, that couldn't happen.

Tex would take one look at Murtagh and there'd definitely be a catnapping and Murtagh would be lost to them forever.

"Who are Luke and Tex?" Georgie asked.

Both Hank and Eddie stared at her.

Then Hank asked, "Have you not read the *Rock Chick* books?"

"No. They're on my list," Georgie answered.

"Please, God, don't," Hank begged. "I think you're the only woman in Denver who hasn't, and I cannot tell you how refreshing it is to sit at a table with someone who does not already know the names of my kids."

"And other shit about you," Eddie murmured.

"And you," Hank returned.

Their food came, along with Georgie's margarita.

They tucked in but Dutch did it pushing, "So the cops know this woman is shady and that's it?"

"We also talked to the detectives in charge of the investigation, and to describe them as being frustrated, with the case and especially her, is an understatement," Eddie told them. "They're pissed. But they can't waterboard her in order to get her to talk."

"Though they discussed it," Hank muttered.

"I'll fill the buckets," Georgie also muttered.

Hank shot her a grin and Eddie gave her a big, white smile.

"What about who the Stephens family saw go in and out?" Georgie asked. "Canvassing other neighbors? Is anyone recognizable as persons of interest to the police?"

"You'd be surprised how little detail people have about things they've seen, even things that don't sit right with them, when it comes down to that detail being important," Hank shared.

"So no luck with that," she surmised.

"Sadly, no," Hank confirmed.

"So everything leads to a dead end."

"Everything leads to the neighbor," Eddie corrected.

"She's just not talking," Georgie said flatly.

No one answered that because they'd already been over it.

"What does she do?" Georgie asked.

"She manages a restaurant," Hank answered.

"Who owns the restaurant?" Georgie asked.

Hank smiled a respectful smile and told her carefully, "Those leads have been followed and there's nothing there. If there was something hot, it wasn't uncovered when it should have been, and it's gone cold. The detectives on this case are solid and they did the work. I hate to admit it, any cop does, but even if this was my case, I'd keep the file on my desk, but I'd have no choice but to move on."

"Same," Eddie grunted. "And not just because we're partners."

"What's her risk here?" Georgie kept pushing.

"Her risk?" Hank asked.

"Giving a false report to the police," she stated. "And since it's likely she knows this man, let him in, and is covering for him, abetting a crime. Because it's a crime, yes? Even if Carlyle's dad forced entry, he didn't do it for nefarious reasons, so a crime was committed. One that's punishable."

"There would be discussion about that if it was a lovers' spat that he interrupted and they mistakenly shot him, thinking he was an intruder," Eddie said. "But how this is looking like it actually went down, it'd be hard to stick murder one on them. Though, if the prosecutor got creative, and there was something dark they're hiding, darker even than her covering for a lover, or other, that something being the reason she's not talking, they could get murder two and she could get hit with false reporting and accessory."

"So if this guy is found, and if she's found out, they'll go down," Georgie concluded.

"If the evidence is there, the prosecutor doesn't screw it up, no deal is struck, yeah," Hank confirmed.

Georgie then looked to Dutch and there was a light burning so bright in her eyes, he felt it scorching his skin.

But it didn't hurt.

It was beautiful.

"How's the kid?" Eddie asked.

Dutch tore his attention from Georgiana and looked to Eddie. "Not good."

"I can imagine, seein' his dad like that," Eddie murmured.

Dutch's blood ran cold.

It was Georgiana this time who wrapped her hand around his wrist, but it was like a phantom touch, his focus was hyper-alert on Eddie.

"Seein' his dad like that?" Dutch asked, his voice sounding funny to his own ears.

Choked.

He felt both Eddie and Hank's attention sharpen on him but that was phantom too.

He was staring at Eddie like taking his eyes off the man would mean he'd forget how to breathe.

"Yeah," Eddie said slowly.

"Carlyle saw his father dead?" Dutch pressed.

"Dutch, honey," Georgie whispered, squeezing hard at his wrist.

He ignored her.

"Followed his dad," Eddie said carefully. "Didn't you know?"

Oh Christ.

Followed him?

"Followed him…how?" Dutch forced out.

"His mother tried to stop him, but he followed his dad to his neighbor's. He spoke to the police at the scene, said his dad was down by the time he got up there. He wasn't dead. When the police got there, the kid was still pressing on the wound, but it was too late. The carotid was hit. The man was gone," Eddie shared.

Dutch dropped his head and stared at his lap.

"You didn't know that?" Georgie asked gently.

"No," he said to his lap.

Carlyle watched his father die.

And his father watched his son watch him die.

"Dutch," Georgie hissed urgently.

They'd shared that moment when they both knew life was over.

Carlyle's life as he knew it, with a good man who was a good dad in his home, raising him up, molding the man he'd become.

And his dad knowing he'd never see that man because his life was just over.

His body jostled and he came to seeing Georgie semi-crouched beside him. She had a hold on his leg and his neck, and she was shaking both.

"Look at me, baby," she whispered.

"I'm all right."

"Okay, then humor me by looking at me for a sec, okay?"

He slid a hand along her neck and repeated, "I'm all right, Georgie."

She gave him a good once over, took her time, and only when

she was satisfied did she let him go and resume her seat.

Dutch cleared his throat and gave the men his attention. "Sorry."

"Understandable," Hank replied.

He felt Georgie now in hyper-focus, but on him, and he made a show of forking into his burrito.

But when he got it to his mouth, he didn't taste it.

Because new thoughts were forming in his head.

Including the fact that the cops had come to the shelter, looking for Carlyle.

Did they do that just to share the case had gone cold, apologize they had to get on with other shit, pat him on the back and tell him to keep his chin up and maybe get his ass home?

No.

They wanted to go over what he saw.

And now Dutch wanted to know what he saw.

But the bottom line was, they all *needed* to know what he saw.

Because he fucking saw something.

But he was keeping it to himself, and Dutch got that.

Fuck him, he got it.

But as smart as Carlyle was, this was not his job. He was too young, and he didn't have the skills to see it through.

Making matters worse, if this was tied up with other shit, and that woman knew that Carlyle saw what he saw, the kid was flat-out in danger.

Which could be another reason why he refused to go home.

He was keeping his mother and sister safe.

Fuck.

"You got something for us?" Eddie asked.

Dutch had food in his mouth.

He chewed, swallowed, felt Georgie's continued hyper-vigilance on him, but he locked eyes with Eddie.

"Yeah, I do. But I got work to do on it so can you give me a few days? Then I'm handing it over."

"Chaos got your back?" Eddie asked.

"Nightingale does," Dutch answered.

Eddie nodded. That worked for him.

Dutch looked to Hank.

Hank was eating like nothing was weird. It worked for him too.

Dutch understood this.

Lee Nightingale, who owned Nightingale Investigations, was Eddie's best friend, Hank's brother, and they both knew Lee, nor his team would leave Dutch blowing in the breeze.

They finished their meals shooting the shit.

At the end, there was a brief but annoying discussion about who was going to pay that Georgie did not participate in, but she won it by walking up to the register and paying herself. Something which Dutch knew was going to lead to another discussion about how she was never going to do that again.

Hank urged Dutch to take Georgie to meet Tex.

Georgie looked intrigued.

They said goodbye on the sidewalk.

And Georgie called it when they were in his truck on the way back to her place.

"Carlyle saw something."

"Yup."

"We have to find Carlyle."

"Yup."

"Shit," she whispered.

Dutch drew a sharp breath into his nose.

Then he repeated, "Yup."

They settled into unhappy silence.

Dutch broke it.

"You ever pay the bill like that again, I'm spanking your ass."

She said nothing.

Until she did.

And it was…

"Cute."

Chapter Six

Butch and Sundance

Dutch

Dutch lay on his back on his couch with a book in his hand and a cat on his chest.

The only reason he was there and not out on the streets looking for Carlyle was because they'd spent the afternoon searching for Carlyle.

They'd checked everywhere they'd known to check, and being on the kids beat, Georgie knew even more spots than Dutch did.

They'd also put bugs in as many ears as they could talk into, including Vance Crowe.

And Georgie had phoned her two street kids-not-kids to ask them to keep on the lookout and do that with a purpose.

These dudes called themselves "Banga" and "Kraken," and just that made Dutch's stomach tighten at the thought she was associating with whatever lunatics these guys were.

Because seriously…

Kraken?

He listened over her speakerphone as they assured her they were on it.

And then it started to get late, and Georgie had pitched a fit about Dutch continuing to look while she was on her date-not-date because, "Who's going to keep Murtagh company?"

He was in love with her cat, but he wanted to find Carlyle more.

Georgie impressed upon him he couldn't run himself ragged or they'd never find Carlyle.

She then told him they had to let the folks they'd roped in to help have time to do something about it, adding something about a watched kettle never boiling.

She ended all this on what really did it.

That if Murtagh did not have time to get used to his house before she got there, no way she could spend the night with him, because if she brought Murtagh over, he would be disoriented in a new space and she wouldn't be able to concentrate on Dutch.

Obviously, on that, he gave in.

It was when Dutch was hanging at her pad while she got ready for her date-not-date, already having taken all of Murtagh's shit and Georgie's overnight bag down to his truck, that things got iffy.

Because she came out looking shit-hot in a little black dress that was way off the shoulder, had long bell sleeves, the hem hit her just above the knees, it was skintight, and the capper was the pair of sexy black stiletto sandals on her feet.

He had, he thought, justifiably lost his mind and told her to go change.

She had, he thought, totally insanely lost hers and told him he couldn't tell her to change her clothes or tell her to do, say, *anything.*

"You're wearin' that to get info from this guy? And you walk out *to me* wearin' that dress and I know you're wearin' it and up to that? Are you serious with this shit?" he demanded to know.

"No, dummy," she retorted. "I'm wearing it *for you.* I mean, who am I going home to at the end of the night?"

Well then.

"He's still gonna see you in it," he pointed out a lot less heatedly.

"Who cares? He's the means to an end and that's all. And seriously, Dutch, you gotta trust me, *that's all.*"

"I know that's all, but the way you describe this guy, I don't got a good feeling about him."

"He's a lech, but he's also a good source, and I can handle myself, and you have to trust that too."

Shit.

He did.

And right then, that blew.

"Don't call me a dummy," he said.

"I will when you're being ridiculously bossy and a dummy. I mean, *gross*. I'd never wear something sexy for *Jackson*. Or anyone for purposes such as that. I want justice for Carlyle, but there are certain lines a girl doesn't cross. At least this girl doesn't."

"Good to know," he muttered.

"And anyway, this is just a cute dress. It's not sexy. You just like me."

"Babe, when you grow a dick, you can say shit like that. Trust me, it's sexy."

"Really?" she asked, looking down at herself.

Fucking hell.

What was he going to do with this woman?

He knew.

"Get over here. I wanna kiss you stupid so you don't forget who you're comin' home to at the end of the night."

She shook her head and added rolling her eyes. "Like I'd forget, Dutch. You're the hottest guy I've ever dated, and I'm saying that peremptorily, because we haven't actually been on a date. And I'm not counting lunch with two cops as a date, no matter how good my burrito was."

"Okay, now you gotta get over here so I can kiss you stupid because what you said was so sweet and you're bein' your usual hilarious."

"You just want to kiss me because I'm in this dress."

"I wanna kiss you all the time, but I need to kiss you now because you're in that dress."

"There you go, Dutch, the reason I'm *in this dress*."

He was seeing he needed to have his head examined because he *was* a total dummy getting hooked up with a woman who was absolutely *not*.

In the end, he went to her to kiss her stupid.

He then crated her cat, grabbed her laptop case, she went off on her date-not-date and he came home with Murtagh.

The cat had something to say about his new environs, and he said that something continuously.

Until his food was down.

Then Murtagh couldn't give that first shit where he was.

And now, the only thing that had happened that night was he'd avoided two calls from Jag, one from his mom, and got a text that read, **Call your mother** from Hound.

To which he'd replied **Is everything okay?**

And got the response, **Don't know, you tell us.**

He wasn't going to go there, and he wasn't feeling great that they were wondering, but he'd thought he'd ended it (for now) with**, Later. We'll do a family dinner or something.**

When Hound didn't text back, he was left with counting down the hours until Georgie came to him, of which he was giving her two, and he was barely at the end of the first one.

"It's gonna be a long night," he told Murtagh.

Murtagh's responding "murr" was interrupted by a banging on his front door.

The cat sunk his claws in, and Dutch had to hand it to the little bugger, he was Sundancing this shit, not leaving Dutch and looking at the door with an angry "*Mwryow!*"

"Open up!" Hound shouted.

Murtagh stood up, somehow gaining twenty pounds—in each foot—and shouted, "*Mwrrryow!*" back.

"Right, Sundance, Butch is gonna go open the door," Dutch said, picking up the cat, getting an angry noise, putting the cat down on the couch after he angled off it, and hearing the thud of him jumping to the floor and following Dutch to the front door.

He opened it.

And he had no choice but to step aside when his entire family stormed in.

"*Mwryow, mrr mrr, myow, myow, mrr,*" Murtagh demanded to know why they'd interrupted his quiet night.

"What the fuck?" Jagger asked, staring down at the cat.

"Oh my God, that cat is the cutest thing I ever saw," his mom declared.

"*MWYOW!*" Murtagh shrieked.

"What's the matter with it?" Hound asked.

Dutch bent down, picked up the cat, and because big brother shit never died, he fell in love with it even more when he stretched out a paw, claws extended, scratching toward Jagger like he wanted to eviscerate him.

Dutch started laughing at the same time encouraging, "Atta

boy."

"What'd I do?" Jagger asked.

"Give him to me," his ma said, and didn't let Dutch move. She came to him, entirely unafraid of Murtagh's murderous intent toward her middle son, and she took the cat. "Look at you," she cooed, cuddling Murtagh close. "My first grandbaby."

Murtagh immediately started purring and butting his mother's jaw with his head.

"Jesus Christ," Hound grunted then scowled at Dutch. "You know now I'm gonna have to get her a fuckin' cat."

"What are you all doing here?" Dutch asked.

"When did you get a cat?" Jagger asked in return.

"What are you doing here?" Dutch repeated. Then he looked to his mother. "And where's Wilder?"

"We *do* know how to get a babysitter for your little brother, Dutch," she replied. "Bev and Tad are with him. It's getting late. Close to his bedtime. And anyway, his presence during this visit is unnecessary."

His five-year-old brother's presence wasn't necessary during this visit?

"Okay, then someone answer my first question," Dutch demanded.

They all looked at each other.

"Do I need to read minds? Go out and get some tarot cards? What the fuck?" Dutch prompted.

"Cool it, son," Hound said.

"Not feelin' cool with you all here, acting weird," Dutch returned.

"We're not acting weird," his mom said.

"No one's answering my question, that's weird," Dutch replied.

"Gotta admit, it *is* weird," his mother said under her breath to Hound.

"Oh, for fuck's sake," Dutch said to the ceiling.

"You haven't been to the shop in five days," Hound declared.

Dutch looked to him.

"And you came to the Compound, got toasted, when you never get toasted, and crashed there, when you rarely crash there," Jag put in.

"On top of not being in the shop for five days," Hound said.

"In fact, you haven't been back on Chaos at all since you tied one on."

"A brother does what he does. The shop not been covered?" Dutch asked.

"You know it has, but that's not the issue," Hound answered.

"What's the issue that means you all show up unannounced at my house and act weird?" Dutch pushed. "I haven't disappeared. It's not like I'm not answering texts. I've just been busy."

"With what?" Jag asked.

"That's my business," Dutch answered.

"Dude, we're just worried about you," Jag replied.

"There's nothing to worry about," Dutch stated.

"Now, Dutch," his mother said.

And that was all she said.

Shit, shit, *shit.*

"I'm good, Ma," he lied.

She gave him a look that said she knew he was lying.

Fuck.

"Listen, I just got something I'm workin' out. I'm on it. It's cool. And when I feel like sharing, I'll—"

Dutch didn't finish that.

His back straightened.

Jag and Hound both looked toward the side door.

Murtagh called, "Mwrr."

And Georgie could be heard shouting, "Oh my *God*! Remind me *never* to agree to do anything like that *again.* I do not care how righteous the cause. You were *so right.* That Jackson guy is *pond scum.* He—"

She stopped speaking and stopped moving when she was one step into the living room, her face going pale as she stared at his family.

But Dutch's vision was blurry, his head was fuzzed, and his palms were itching when he turned her way and barked, "*What?*"

She jolted and looked to him, whispering, "What, what, baby?"

He prowled to her, asking, "What'd that Jackson guy do?"

"Uh," she mumbled, eyes huge in her face and aimed up at him as he stopped in front of her. "Your family is here."

"What'd he do that you're here barely an hour after I left you?" he demanded.

"Can we just say he wasn't a gentleman?" she tried.

"No," he bit.

She put her hand to his sternum, leaned in and said, "Your family is here, honey, like, *right here*."

"Um, hello there. I'm Dutch's mother, Keely. And who might you be?" his ma said close to his left side.

"Jesus, Georgiana, what're you doin' here?" Jagger asked from close to his right.

"Everyone out," Hound ordered at his back.

That was Hound, always at his back.

Definitely literally, and now figuratively.

"Not on your goddamned life, cowboy," his mother decreed.

Shit.

"I'm thinking there are other good reasons I wore this dress tonight," Georgie muttered.

He wanted to think she was funny.

He was not finding anything funny.

"You okay?" he asked her.

"He just made a pass. I deflected. Took off. But, uh..." Her eyes went side to side, before she finished, "my mission was not accomplished."

"Hound, my love, my husband, father of one of my sons, dad to all, do you know how interesting I find all this?" his mother called, even though Hound was probably three inches away from her.

"Baby," Hound grunted like he was trying not to laugh.

"*Very* interesting," his mother answered herself.

"Hi." Georgiana jumped forward, extending her hand toward Keely. "I'm Georgiana Traylor. And Dutch and I are, um...we're, uh..."

Dutch shifted, slung an arm around her shoulders, and said, "It's Georgie's cat, Ma."

"I see," Keely said, lifting a hand and taking Georgie's. "Nice to meet you, Georgiana."

"She's Carolyn's sister," Jagger shared when Keely let her go.

"Is she now?" Keely asked, her eyes narrowing.

And it was the first time Dutch had any indication his mother had Carolyn's number.

Jagger was grinning massively, shoving his way in front of

Hound, arms crossed on his chest. "Did you two hook up after Carolyn and I couldn't give Georgie a ride from the airport?"

"Jag—" Dutch started.

"Jives," Jagger noted. "Seein' as it's been about five days."

"Jagger—" Dutch tried again.

"Fuckin' hell, man, you and me with sisters," Jag stated and burst out laughing.

"Oh my God," Georgie mumbled super low, pressing her hip hard into his to indicate that this was not a good sitch and it was getting worse.

"Murr," Murtagh butted into the conversation.

"Hullo, my baby, hullo, my precious," Georgie cooed to him as he threaded himself around her stilettos and the hems of Dutch's jeans.

"This is like a Hallmark movie," Jag said.

"Hallmark in hell," Georgie said, again under her breath.

Now that was funny.

Dutch choked down laughter.

"Okay, I'm done. What the fuck is going on?" his mother demanded in Mom Voice.

"Shit," he muttered.

"Oh boy," Georgie mumbled.

"Baby," Hound tutted.

"It's just that Dutch hooked up. I told you two he was cool," Jag declared.

"Is that it, Dutch?" Keely asked. "You just found a girl? Who's your brother's girlfriend's sister? Who tonight apparently was out with another man, wearing that dress, a man who made a pass at her? News that's surprising in itself, considering she left him and came right to you. News that further made me wonder if we'd have to tie you down so you wouldn't go out and commit murder? Is that *just* what's going on?"

Dutch looked to Georgie and asked, "Babe?"

She got him.

"I don't know, honey," she said. "Your call."

"Not all of it," he reminded her.

"It's gonna have to be done eventually."

"*Jesus Christ!*" Keely screeched, Georgie jumped, and Dutch looked to his ma to see her eyes on Hound. "They're talking *in code.*

This is so deep between them they can talk *in code*. And his mother is just now meeting this girl?"

"Woman, lock it down," Hound growled.

She leaned toward Hound. "*In code*, Shepherd."

"He's a grown man, Keekee," Hound replied.

"So you're okay with this?" she demanded.

"Well, yeah," Hound answered. "Because *he's a grown man*, Keely."

"Oh for fuck's sake, we're investigating the murder of the dad of one of the kids at King's Shelter. Georgie is a reporter and she's using some of her sources to find out whatever she can," Dutch told them. He looked down at Georgie. "And obviously, that did not go well tonight."

"It's over. I'm fine," she assured.

"Right," he grunted.

"You're investigating a murder?" Keely asked.

Goddamn it.

"Ma—" he started.

"When did you take the detective's exam?" she queried.

"Listen—" he tried again.

"Strike that, when did you become a cop at all?" she kept at him.

He went silent but did it looking to Hound and Jagger for support.

And found none.

He would discover why immediately.

"Got a brother at your back?" Hound asked.

Fuck, fuck, fuck.

"Hound—"

"Do you?" Hound bit.

"No," Dutch bit back.

"Are you fucking shitting us?" Jagger demanded.

"Okay, now, let's just—" Georgie tried.

"Quiet, girl, you're not in this," Keely ordered.

Now, wait a fucking minute.

"Do not," Dutch clipped.

His mother blinked.

Hound got closer to his wife.

Georgie pressed closer to his side.

"This is my home, and this is my woman, Ma. Do not speak to her like that in my home. Or ever."

"Your woman?" Georgie and Keely both asked at the same time.

"We're new," he said to Georgie and looked to his mother. "She's new. But the point still stands."

Keely couldn't argue that and didn't.

She asked, "How new?"

"We haven't even been out on a date," he told her.

"And she's coming in your side door?" his mother inquired.

"Keekee," Hound warned.

Keely shut her mouth.

"Respect, I love you, but how many dates did you go on with Hound before he was at our breakfast table?" Dutch asked.

There was utter silence, until Hound chuckled.

"Gotcha there, Ma," Jagger said.

"When you all have children, I will be laughing," Keely stated.

"Maybe I should—" Georgie started.

"They're leaving, you're not," he told her.

She sucked in her lips and lifted her brows.

"Right, about this murder," Hound said.

Dutch looked to him. "It's mine."

"Dutch—" Hound began.

"It's mine. I'm doing what I have to do. It's mine."

Hound stared into his eyes and Dutch knew this bit. It stung. It pained him.

This man took them out to get candy on Halloween.

This man sat them down and gave them their sex talks.

This man put their names forward to be brothers at Chaos.

This man gave them a baby brother and made their mother happy again.

But what Dutch was doing for Carlyle was about Carlyle.

It was about Khalon Stephens.

And it was about Graham Black.

Dutch knew it would not erase his father's death or Carlyle losing his own dad.

He also knew, for whatever reason, he had to do this.

If he didn't, he'd never be right again.

He sensed Georgie knew it.

And looking in Hound's eyes, it didn't surprise Dutch in the slightest that Hound knew it too.

Hound Ironside knew his boys down to the soul.

So he knew this.

Keely sidled closer, whispering, "Dutch."

"It's mine, Ma," he said firmly, now staring her straight in the eye.

She halted, nodded, her expression troubled.

"Maybe it should be mine too," Jagger put in.

He looked to his brother.

Jagger got it too.

And he would go there because Jag deserved the shot to have whatever Dutch was going to get out of this.

Except…

He looked to Georgie.

She shrugged and bit her lip.

She then nodded and said, "It's not fair. They're on again and it's not right, Dutch."

He nodded back and asked, "You or me?"

"What the fuck?" Jagger cut in.

Georgie looked to his brother. "Okay, I'm sorry. So sorry. But, well…"

She faltered.

Dutch stepped in.

"She's usin' you, man. Carolyn. She's got a bunch a' guys she mooches from and it's not life-is-tough shit. She's got a cocaine habit."

Jagger's upper body swayed back.

Shit, Christ.

"Brother, I'm sorry," he said quietly. "But it's true."

"I'm not a pain-in-the-ass sister, Jagger," Georgie added. "I've been on her for a while to get herself cleaned up and to stop…uh, what she's doing with, um…using you and the, uh…other guys."

Fuck.

"I told you, boy," Hound said.

"I did too, honey," Keely put in softly.

Whoa.

He had no idea his parents had figured shit out about Carolyn.

Dutch looked to Jag.

Jag was staring at Georgiana.

"The other guys?" he asked.

She jolted again and then asked back carefully, "You didn't know?"

"I knew, but she takes money from them?"

"Yes."

"All of them?"

"All of you."

Jagger's tone was not right when he asked, "Cocaine?'

Shit, this sucked worse than he already knew it would.

"It was recreational at first, and I was still concerned," Georgie said. "But I don't think it is anymore. She used to not hide it. She hides it now. And she sometimes sells handbags, or shoes, when she's in between guys, I suspect so she can keep supplied."

"So the money I've been givin' her is goin' up her nose?" Jagger asked. "Not to pay her rent?"

Dutch let Georgie go because he could tell by the line of Jag's body and the deterioration of his tone that shit was going south.

Hound also adjusted his position.

Keely went to Georgie.

"Son," Hound said low.

"Don't, Hound," Jagger warned.

"Let's take this outside, brother," Dutch suggested.

Too late.

Jag's body tightened tight.

"Goddamned *fuckin' cunt*!" Jag shouted.

Then he twisted, reached an arm long, and pointed his finger at Georgiana, and Dutch braced to intervene.

He did it with difficulty, because he would lose it if his brother was a dick to Georgie, and he did not want that between him and Jag, nor have that dragging on what he wanted to build with Georgiana.

But this was Jag.

He should have known better.

"Sorry," Jagger forced out. "Sorry you heard that. But she's a goddamned *cunt*."

Dutch relaxed.

Hound relaxed.

Keely stayed close to Georgie.

"I should have said something earlier," Georgie noted, and she sounded miserable.

"Can't rat out your own sister," Jagger replied.

"I tried to stop her," Georgie told him.

"Babe, this isn't on you. This is on your user, loser, junkie bitch of a sister," Jagger stated.

"I should have—"

"Stop it," Jag hissed. "This is the goddamned damage of assholes like Carolyn. She makes me feel like a chump, I gave her money. She makes you feel like shit, you didn't shield people from her bullshit. And it's all *on her*. So fuckin' shut up about it."

"Jagger," Hound said in a warning tone.

"Fuckin' shut up about it, *please*," Jagger amended.

Georgie let out a startled laugh and said, "You got it."

Okay then.

Done.

"You need a shot?" Dutch asked. "I got all sorts of shit. You call it."

"I need to find Carolyn and tell her she's dumped and if I see her face again, we got issues," Jag replied.

Dutch looked to Georgie.

But she shook her head. "It's his now. And he's right. It's not his job, or my job, or yours, or anyone's to cushion her from whatever's coming. It happened how it happened and now it's Jagger's," she said. "So I'm not going to ask any of you to let me cushion her from this."

"She's gonna be pissed at you, babe," Dutch warned.

"Well, I've been pissed at her for a few years now, it's my turn, I guess," she returned, and then she looked to Jag. "But if you want me to talk to her—"

"No, I got this," Jag bit out.

Georgie nodded.

"I know I need a goddamned shot," Hound declared, walking to the kitchen.

Keely gave Georgie a look, Dutch, Jagger, then she followed her husband.

"Mwrr?" Murtagh asked, batting at the leg of Jagger's jeans with his paw.

"So now you like me, after you know the piece of ass I was

tagging was taking me for a ride?" Jagger asked.

"*Mwrrrrrrr*," Murtagh answered, butted Jag's leg with his head before he ran his whole body down it.

Which meant Jag bent and picked him up, muttering, "You're nuts."

"Murr," Murtagh retorted.

"Don't deny it. You totally are," Jagger said, and Murtagh gave up on the conversation and started purring when Jag started scratching behind his ears on his way to carrying Murtagh to the kitchen.

"Does your whole family speak cat?" Georgie asked Dutch.

"Until now, I'd have said no. Now, I gotta say yes."

She smiled at him.

And it was huge.

Chapter Seven

It's Family

Dutch

Dutch woke as usual, on his stomach.

Not as usual, he felt something weighing on his lat and across the small of his back.

It took a second before he smiled.

Georgie.

She was pressed up to him, cheek to his lateral, he could feel her soft hair there, her arm was around his back.

He liked her just like that, but he had a feeling he'd like something else better.

So he shifted, which made her shift, and he instantly found there was more to be into with Georgiana, because she made cute sleepy noises as they both moved.

This being Dutch turning to his side to face her, Georgiana giving him room to do that, then burrowing in, tangling her legs with his, wrapping her arm tight around his waist, shoving her face deep into his chest then sliding it up, so it was in his throat.

This left him with his chin on top of her hair which was contained in the poofy ponytail she'd put in it before they'd crashed the night before.

He slid both his arms around her, gave her a squeeze, and murmured, "You awake?"

"Mm," she hummed.

He grinned.

"Baby, good morning kiss," he prompted.

"No," she denied. "Morning breath," she explained.

He let his hands start roaming. She arched into him.

"I'll brave it," he said.

She moved her head up, her lips on him now, along his throat, to the side of his neck.

"Dutch," she whispered under his ear.

Christ, he liked how she said his name.

His hands began to roam with a purpose.

Her lips moved down his jaw.

"Rough," she mumbled.

"You like smooth?"

Her eyes found his. "I like *you*."

Well, fuck.

Enough play.

He kissed her.

He did not go in easy and he didn't do that because he had a morning hard-on.

He did it because he'd woken up for the first time with Georgie in his bed.

He took her to her back, Dutch on top, and they both got busy with hands and mouth and tongues.

And she didn't have anything to worry about. She tasted of a hint of last night's toothpaste and Georgie.

All good.

Real good.

He found more to like about her when she demonstrated she was a woman who wasn't afraid to use her nails.

She eventually went for his ass.

He went for her tit.

It was generous, way more than a handful, the bud of her nipple hard against his palm.

Dutch liked the feel of that so much, he tore his mouth from hers, angled, and gave it another occupation.

He drew her nipple in over her nightie and the noise that bought him meant he disengaged, dragged her nightgown down, exposing her to him, and he went back in.

She glided her fingers into his hair, moaning, "*Dutch.*"

Christ, they'd barely started, and he needed her pussy.

He returned to kissing her mouth, deep and wet, and when she gave over to his tongue, he guided a hand up her nightgown, over her hip, her belly, and down.

She gasped around his tongue.

He ended the kiss but didn't move his lips from hers.

"Yeah?"

"*Yes.*" It was a plea.

This woman.

His woman.

Always more and more to her.

All of it good.

He obliged, sliding his hand in the top of her panties and *in.*

She opened her legs a little to give him more of that wet heat.

"Fuck," he muttered, toying at the heart of the lusciousness of her.

"Dutch."

He rolled her clit.

"*Dutch.*"

He slid a finger inside.

Wet, hot and *tight.*

Christ.

It was going to be heaven, sinking in there.

"Ohmigod, *Dutch.*"

He stroked her, her hips moving with his rhythm, then he pulled out and rolled her clit again.

"Ready for you," she breathed.

"Unh-unh," he denied.

Her eyes were hooded, hazy, but they semi-focused on him when she asked, "What?"

"First time I make you come, gonna watch."

"Watch while you're inside."

"No."

"Dutch."

He put more pressure on her clit, her gaze hooded again, her back arched, and he ordered, "Baby, just roll with it."

She either didn't have a choice because of what he was doing, or she gave in, because that was what she did. Making hot, sweet little noises he instantly became addicted to, clutching him, she rode his hand.

Yeah, it was going to be heaven, riding that.

And he watched the show as the heat swept over her, her face so goddamned gorgeous, his cock beaded and he couldn't stop himself from putting his mouth to hers to swallow her sharp cry while he buried two fingers up her cunt to feel it spasm with her orgasm.

When her body yielded, carefully, he slid out, skated a hand over her hip and turned them to their sides.

He hooked her leg around his thigh and wrapped her up in his arms, holding her close.

She cuddled closer.

Neither of them spoke for long beats.

Until she did.

"Are we done?"

"Yeah."

"Yeah?"

"Yup."

"What about you?"

"Tonight."

"You're waiting?"

"Worth the wait."

She stiffened in his arms, relaxed, and mumbled, "Never had that."

Say what?

A man had never taken her there?

"A guy has never given you an orgasm?" he asked.

She tipped her head back and he looked down at her.

"Not without taking his own."

"I'll get mine tonight."

Something washed over her, she didn't hide it, she gave it to him, all of it.

And then she gave him more, lifting her hand and running her finger along his jaw in that sweet way she had, looking deep in his eyes, hers filled with, well…

Fuck.

They were filled with everything.

"What's happening here?" she whispered.

"A lot," he stated the obvious.

She melted further into him. "Yeah."

He grinned at her. "Good we got that understanding."

"I like your family," she said.

"They like you," he replied.

And they did.

After the drama, the night did not go as he'd planned.

That being Dutch having Georgie to himself without Carlyle or Carolyn or anything taking their attention, and they'd take that time to get to know each other better.

It had gone to a different plan, with his ma finding out neither of them had dinner.

She'd then commandeered the kitchen, and her husband to help, and made him and Georgie food while Jag, Georgie and Dutch alternately drank beer and took shots of tequila (of which Jag had more, but that was understandable). While they did this, Georgie and Dutch talked Jag down from feeling like a sucker for not reading the signs Carolyn was sending.

The night ended with the men doing the dishes and Georgie, Murtagh and Keely on the couch, the two non-felines in that scenario cackling and talking in low voices. The feline just laid in Georgie's lap, purring like he was in hog heaven.

In other words, watching her with his brother, and his mother, Dutch got to know her better, and as with everything he was learning about Georgie, it was beyond good.

It'd been late when they'd left and they did it because Dutch, not to mention Hound, had noticed that Georgie looked tired and was trying to hide yawns.

So Hound rounded everyone up and took them home, leaving Jag's truck because he wasn't smashed, but he wasn't good to drive himself.

And Dutch had wasted no time and gotten his girl to bed.

And now was now.

She shoved her face back into his throat and said, "I don't want to leave this bed." But before he could concur, she yanked her head back and spoke fast. "But I know we gotta get back on the case. It's just, you've got a great bed."

He did have a great bed.

But it wasn't his bed she didn't want to leave.

He beat back his smile and spanned her cheek with his hand. "Baby, I know you're not a selfish bitch. You've proved that repeatedly. You don't have to keep reminding me of it."

Dutch felt the heat against his palm even if he saw the rose bloom in the apple of her other cheek and she muttered, "Good."

"And I don't wanna leave this bed either. But mostly you in it with me. So how 'bout we make a deal?"

"A deal?"

"Today is Friday. We give Carlyle today. We got a reservation tonight, that's ours." He grinned at her. "We're gonna get busy after that, and I'm gonna get mine."

"Yeah, you are," she promised on a whisper, shoving closer.

He kept grinning as well as talking. "We give tomorrow to Carlyle, but even if shit is not sorted, we get Sunday morning just for us. In this bed. You and me. Work for you?"

"Totes," she replied.

He felt his body move with laughter even if it wasn't audible, except for the shake in the one word he said.

"Totes?"

She smiled at him.

He couldn't get lost in her cute.

They had to get a move on.

"Another deal," he continued. "You get the bathroom first and I'll make coffee."

Her smile died and she said, "Okay, but before we hit it, we talk."

They'd been talking.

"We are talking."

"A different kind of talk," she said.

"About what?" he asked.

She wet her lips, pressed them together and rubbed.

This did not give him good thoughts.

"About what, Georgie?" he pushed.

"About you," she said softly.

He tensed.

It came soft again when she said, "Please."

"What about me?"

"You know, Dutch."

And he did know.

He also knew she gave him Carolyn.

She gave him history about her mom, her dad, her roommate, her cat, her condo purchase, her job.

Open. Honest. Out there.

This was happening with them.

And she was asking for this.

What was happening between them was a lot.

He had to give her this.

Fuck.

"You get the bathroom, I'll get coffee," he muttered.

"Then you get the bathroom, and I'll pour us coffee. How do you take yours?"

"Two sugars."

"*Mwrrr!*" came angrily from the side of the bed.

They grinned at each other.

"Quarter can wet food, honey," she ordered. "Be sure to break it up."

"Gotcha," he replied.

He touched his mouth to hers, then he got that cute, little squeal when he dragged them both out of bed.

They each did their thing, and apparently, she did really like his bed because they were going to talk there.

He knew this because, when he was done in the bathroom, he came out to see her cross-legged in it, Murtagh curled in her lap, her fingers hooked through a coffee mug, his steaming on the nightstand.

He moved that way.

She checked out his body when he did, and pure Georgie, did not hide she liked what she saw.

He was wearing a pair of dark-red sleep shorts with a black drawstring and that was it.

Last night, and right now, he'd not missed she was making another play with her wardrobe decisions considering he doubted she usually wore what she had on now to bed.

Halter top, all lace up there, cut low, lots of cleavage, semi-sheer skirt, not lace, but super short.

His girl.

He smiled at her, got into bed, put his back to the headboard, legs stretched out, and Murtagh made what Dutch thought was a lunatic decision.

This being, he defected from Georgie's lap to take residence on Dutch's abs.

"You're stealing my-cat-not-my-cat," Georgie accused.

"Cut the crap, babe, he's your cat," Dutch replied, simultaneously reaching for his coffee and stroking the cat.

"Whatever," she mumbled and shifted so she was angled his way, one knee resting on his hip.

Okay.

Here we go.

Shit.

"Dutch—"

"No offense, darlin', but you won't get it," he said gently.

"I know that, but I think you need to explain it to me anyway," she returned, just as gently.

He drew in breath and let out a big sigh.

Then, instead of explaining, mostly because he had no clue what to say, he took a sip of coffee.

"I'm gonna say something and you tell me if I'm off base," she declared.

"Shoot," he invited.

"I watched that movie, now twice," she began. "And your father…"

He felt his body grow taut.

Murtagh mrr'ed.

Georgie persevered.

"He was…I suspect this is not lost on you…he was revered by your Club, Dutch."

"It's not lost on me," he grunted.

"That's a lot to live up to."

He stilled.

"And then there's Hound," she said.

He stared at her.

"Your Club has four pillars that hold it up," she stated. "Kane 'Tack' Allen, the president, the visionary. The man who would stop at nothing to guide them to being the Club it was intended to be. Cole 'Rush' Allen, his son. The man who would take the reins and lead the Club into the future when they were as they were meant to be. Graham Black, the example. The man who exemplified everything they wanted to become. And Shepherd 'Hound' Ironside, the dependable. The backbone. The man who would sacrifice whatever he had to in order to get them there."

Now Dutch was finding it hard to breathe.

"Two of those men are your fathers."

"I know," he pushed out.

"I don't know, but I assume it's hard being the son of either of those men. Never mind both."

Good fucking Christ.

"Dutch, do you have any clue how unbelievably amazing you are?" she asked.

Good fucking Christ.

"Georgiana—"

"They made you that, blood and guts, they made you that, Dutch. And *you let them.* You became you, not someone else, because of them and because *of you.*"

"Stop talking," he growled.

"No," she denied.

Shifting out of cross-legs, she leaned over him to put her coffee on the nightstand, took his and did the same, and she stayed close.

"They had a war to fight and you grew up under their example and you're searching for your war when they gave everything so you wouldn't have to do that."

"I'm not a man who can't *not* have something to strive toward."

It came right out of his mouth, what was bugging him, and he didn't even know it was that until that moment.

"Okay, you know that isn't a bad thing."

"I manage our shop. The auto supply side. The inventory. I do the books and give them to Rush. I make sure the shelves are stocked. I do the ordering."

"Dutch—"

"It's suffocating me."

And those words sounded like he was suffocating.

Georgie didn't miss it.

"Stop doing it," she whispered.

"I gotta. It's my part of being a brother."

"They would not want you to suffocate."

"They got mortgages to pay and families to feed."

"It's driving you away from them."

Fuck, she was right.

Fuck, she was so right.

He averted his gaze.

She grabbed both sides of his face and made him look at her.

"You can't be you without them."

"I joined them because I wanted to be a part of something."

"You are."

"I wanted to be a part of who they were…are."

He meant his dad.

And his other dad.

She pressed in on his face. "*You are*, Dutch."

"It isn't there anymore."

"Because you're not letting it be."

"What?"

"You and I are going to find Carlyle. We're gonna figure this out for him. Do you know how much faster that would go if a motorcycle club whose members know the streets better than the cops helped us out?"

He sat up straighter, losing her hands, and Murtagh jumped off with an annoyed *"Muwrrrr."*

"Babe."

"Quiet, please, and listen—"

"They've been through too much. We vote on shit like this and they'll vote it down."

She sat back and asked a shocked, "Have you lost your mind?"

"Watchin' a documentary, even twice, does not mean you know my Club, Georgiana."

"No, but I stood in your own damned living room, with your brother and your dad, both in pain because you hadn't shared, you hadn't asked them to be at your side through this, and I figure it isn't a stretch that every brother who wears your patch would feel the same way."

He shut up.

"They are not going to vote this down, Dutch. They're going to feel angry and betrayed you went this alone. And they're going to feel pain too, because you're drifting away when you are the bones of them."

Her words made something in his chest squeeze.

Hard.

"What?"

"You're him."

And at that, his stomach started to churn so much, he thought he'd be sick. "I'm not."

"Dutch, both of you are."

"Georgiana, don't talk shit you don't know."

"My God, Dutch!" she exclaimed, throwing up her hands in exasperation. "Carolyn has been *stealing* from your brother *for years* to feed a *drug habit* and Jagger was *justifiably angry* when he found out. He called her an ugly name and within seconds *apologized to me* because he said that about my sister when I was around. That is your father. That is Jagger. That is *you*."

Dutch stared at her.

"You're right, I never had and never will have the absolute *honor* of meeting your father. And you're right times two, all I know about him is that film, and getting to know *you*. You look like him. And you look at me like he looks at the camera in pictures I've seen of him—"

"Stop talking."

"And you held Murtagh like he held you—"

"*Stop talking*."

"And Murtagh is just *a cat*. God works in mysterious and sometimes hideous ways that are still wondrous. He took away Graham Black. But when He did, He left the world with two of him. Jagger *and you*."

He surged up, taking hold of her, and landed on her with her on her back.

She let out a puff of air.

"Stop fucking *talking*," he bit out.

She stopped talking.

He scowled at her until, like he couldn't hold it up anymore, his head dropped, his forehead slamming into hers.

She didn't make a peep.

He shut his eyes, tight.

And then she spoke.

"You miss him," she whispered.

His throat closed, he moved to shove his face in her neck, and it came out strangled when he said, "Yes."

He'd been five.

But he never forgot his dad.

You don't.

You don't forget that kind of love.

It's planted in you in a way that never dies.

She slid her hands down his back, murmuring, "Baby."

He pushed his face in deeper, tightening his arms around her.

When he felt she was having trouble breathing because she was bearing all his weight, he shifted so he had it in his forearms, but he didn't take his arms from around her.

"Talk to your brothers," she urged gently.

"I'll talk to them," he agreed.

"About helping us with Carlyle…and other."

"Yeah," he grunted.

She glided one hand up to his neck and gave it a squeeze.

He read her request, lifted his head and gave her his eyes.

"You'll find your passion, Dutch."

He wasn't sure about that.

But he nodded anyway.

She took her hand from his neck, curled her fingers in and used the backs of them to stroke his jaw.

He took her warning and was glad he read it before she asked, "Do you feel guilt you miss him so much when Hound gave you so much in his stead?"

Christ, how was she driving to the meat of everything?

"Yes," he answered.

"Hound was his brother. Do you think he wouldn't have given you the same thing, perhaps not in those proportions, but in the way he could even if your dad had not died?"

Jesus, he hadn't thought of it like that.

"No, he would have given it," he told her. "They all did and do. They did it with Rush. Tabby. With Cutter and Rider, Tack and Cherry's kids. Nash, Lanie and Hop's boy. All of them."

"It's family," she whispered.

Fuck, it was in front of his face.

It was what they fought for, what his dad died for.

And it took Georgie to point it out.

"Yeah."

"You can't drift away from family, honey," she said, smiled and finished, "ever."

"No."

"No matter what path you take, they'll have your back."

His forehead dropped to hers a different way before he said, "Yeah."

"Okay, good we have this sorted out," she muttered.

He lifted his head. "You paid some serious extra attention to that movie the second time around, didn't you?"

"Well," she shrugged on his bed, "I was into you."

Thank fuck, that made him smile.

"I was gonna make you a quick breakfast before we hit it," he told her. "But it's gonna have to be fast food on the way to the Compound. I gotta call a meeting of the brothers."

She eased under him. "Good."

Yeah, what was happening here between them…

It was *a lot*.

Dutch bent his head and kissed her.

And after all of that, what she gave him, where she took him, the release he felt inside, down deep, still not knowing what it meant to his future, but at least understanding what was there, his kiss was not quick.

Since she was Georgie, she responded wholeheartedly.

They got lost in it, some serious groping was happening, when a questioning, "Mwr?" semi-penetrated right before there was a hammering on his front door.

He lifted his head, aiming his eyes to the door of his bedroom.

"What—?" she started.

He looked down at her.

"Do you think Hound or Jagger told the Club about what we're doing, and someone is here, angry about it?" she asked.

"No fucking way," he answered.

The hammering kept coming.

He saw Murtagh bounce out, clearly kitty-ticked at the disturbance.

Dutch felt him. He was biker-ticked.

"I'll get it. You stay here," he ordered.

"Dutch—"

He kissed her, this time quick. "I'll handle it and be back."

Then he rolled off her and out of bed.

When he got to the door, and opened it, it wasn't a huge

surprise, what was on the other side.

It also was.

Last, it was aggravating.

But apparently, Jagger didn't waste any time.

"Where is she?" Carolyn demanded, landing a hand in his chest and shoving him aside as she stomped in.

He took a breath to control his temper, a mistake, because it took too long before he began, "Caro—"

"Bitch, I know you're here!" she shouted down the hall. "Get your traitor ass out here!"

Dutch closed the door and moved between her and the entryway to the hall at the back of his house.

"Calm down," he ordered.

"Fuck you and fuck her!" she spat, then leaned to the side to scream around him, "*Georgiana, get your fat ass out here!*"

Uh…

No.

Fuck…

No.

"Get out," he demanded.

"Fuck you," she repeated.

"Out of my house, Carolyn."

"*Fuck you, Dutch!*" she shrieked.

"For heaven's sake, keep it down. Dutch has neighbors," Georgiana said from behind him.

He twisted at the waist, saw she'd put on a mauve satin robe that had a subtle print of purple and white flowers with black stems. It had billowy sleeves, was super short so it showed her long legs, and was gaping open at the top, so it also showed her generous cleavage.

Even without makeup and her ponytail messed up from them making out, or maybe because of it, she looked like she was ready to step in front of a camera for a catalog shoot.

"Ohmigod, I cannot believe you're doing Dutch Black. Fuck me over and take the brother!" Carolyn accused.

"Go back to the bedroom," he demanded Georgie's way.

"Dutch, honey, this is mine to deal with," she replied, arriving at his side.

"Dutch…*honey*?" Carolyn asked snidely.

They both turned to her.

She homed in on Dutch. "FYI, she thinks bikers are trash. So she might like what you do with your dick, but you're just rough trade to her."

This did not affect Dutch in the slightest because he knew the kernel of truth behind it was gone and the rest of it was just Carolyn pissed that her own shit was blowing up in her face and she was lashing out because of it.

However, in the mix of the second drama they'd had that morning, he'd momentarily forgotten that his Georgie had a temper.

And she liked him.

So what Carolyn said was not a match strike to create a flame.

It was a lighter to a powder keg.

"You…goddamned…*bitch*!"

Her last word was pitched so high, it was a wonder his windows didn't shatter.

But Dutch didn't have time to shake off his ears ringing.

Georgie launched herself at her sister.

He just managed to catch her at the waist and then he pulled her back three feet.

She strained against his hold and yelled, "Let me go!"

"You couldn't take me," Carolyn taunted.

"Skin and bones and drug addled? You don't think?" Georgie returned.

Oh shit.

"Baby," he whispered, wrapping his other arm around her and pulling her tighter to him as she kept fighting his hold.

"I'm not drug-addled!" Carolyn shouted.

Georgie gave up the fight but kept up the lean.

"You're a goddamned cokehead," she retorted.

"Georgie," Dutch warned.

"*Am not!*" Carolyn shrieked.

The front door opened.

"And a *whore*!" Georgie yelled.

Oh fuck.

Jagger walked in, along with their Chaos brother and bud Roscoe, who was undoubtedly bringing Jag to get his truck.

They both read the situation immediately, thus both wasted no time positioning. Roscoe at Carolyn's back for possible containment purposes. Jagger at her side, for the same and for a better view of the action.

"I'm not a whore!" Carolyn yelled, but looking the woman's way, Dutch saw that got in there.

"What do you call taking money for services rendered, Carolyn?" Georgie asked.

Christ.

"Ohmigod, you did not just say that to me," Carolyn stated, looking struck. "In front of Jagger, no less." She jabbed a finger at Jag.

"You didn't think to keep Georgie out of it?" Dutch asked his brother.

"I didn't say her name, or yours. She figured it out," Jagger replied.

Shit.

"Yeah, I figured it out, because she's up in my shit so much, like *now*, saying whacked crap to me, it doesn't take a brain surgeon to jump from that, know we asked Dutch to pick her up, and she was all over running her mouth to him like she does to me," Carolyn supplied.

"It had to end, Carolyn," Georgie pointed out.

"You can't see me happy. You could never see me happy," Carolyn accused.

"What are you talking about?" Georgie's tone was confused.

Carolyn pointed at Jag again. "He makes me happy and you took him from me. You don't get it, but Chanel slides make me happy, and you don't want me to have them."

"It's not about the Chanel, Carolyn, and you know it," Georgie retorted.

"Bullshit, I'm just not into the same things you're into and you don't get it," Carolyn returned.

"Girl, if I could afford Chanel, I'd be all over it. I just can't…so *I don't*," Georgie shot back, and Dutch took note of what she said.

He'd heard of Chanel, had no clue otherwise, but his woman, like everyone else, had birthdays, and Christmas was not far away, so he'd talk to Lanie, or Elvira, and figure it out.

Carolyn changed tactics and said pathetically, "You took him away from me."

"You do coke?" Jagger asked unemotionally.

Carolyn took a step his way. "Jag, sweetie."

He took a step back and she halted.

"Do you snort coke, Carolyn?" he pressed.

"Just a bump every now and then. I work a lot, Jagger. You know that. A girl's gotta do what she's gotta do to keep going."

"When we were beginning, you pulled out a vial, and we had this conversation," Jagger reminded her.

Carolyn's jaw moved as she clenched her teeth.

They'd had that conversation.

"I told you dope was a dealbreaker," he went on.

"You smoke pot," she accused.

"Pot is not coke," he stated.

"It's a drug," she said.

"It's rare I do it, like, how many times have you seen me high?"

She didn't answer.

"Yeah," Jag said. "Maybe what? Three? Four? And I've known you that many years?"

"Jagger—"

"And to get my buzz, I don't suck anyone's cock," Jag went on.

"Oh boy," Georgie whispered the same time Dutch muttered, "Jesus," and this was the first time Roscoe verbally entered the scenario and he did that with a grunt.

"That's a whore, Carolyn." Jag was relentless. "Like it or not, you made me a goddamn john to get your fuckin' fix and you into dope was already a dealbreaker, and you knew it. You puttin' me in that position, we are dead. Like we didn't exist. And you know that too. So don't pile shit on Georgiana she doesn't deserve. And *really* do not take your fucked-up mess into my brother's home and spread it around. This is not gonna win me back. Nothin's gonna win me back. What it's gonna do, instead of bein' dead to me, you're not dead. But I'm gonna hate you, which I do at this moment. Can't stand the fuckin' sight of you. And that's on you too."

"Jagger," Carolyn breathed, horrified, hurt, even destroyed.

But Jagger just sounded over it when he sighed, "Get out, Carolyn."

Carolyn didn't move for what seemed like years before she slowly turned to Georgie and declared, "You're dead to me too."

Georgie's body jolted and Dutch tightened his arms around her to hold her close.

Jagger got her attention back when he shared, "And my hatred just grew. 'Cause you're blaming your sister, who loves you, worries about you, has tried to do right by you, and you're all right to stand there and gut her. Fuck off, Carolyn. Honest to Christ, it might take Dutch and me a little while, but I bet it won't take us long to talk Georgie around to understanding she's better off without you."

All right.

Time to end this.

"Brother," Dutch called.

Jag looked at him. "Am I wrong?" He then looked to Georgie. "Am I wrong, sweetheart? You got family now, the good kind that doesn't spit on you. You get that? Yeah?"

"Can this just be done?" Georgie asked in a small voice.

Yup.

This needed to be done.

Dutch gave Jag a look he could not misinterpret.

In turn, Jagger looked to Carolyn and raised his brows.

"I think I loved you," she said.

"I know I don't care," he replied.

Fucking hell.

"Jag," Dutch bit out.

Jagger nodded, went to the door, opened it and held it that way.

Carolyn looked to him, to Georgie, her face started collapsing, then she ran out.

Jagger shut the door after her.

Georgiana turned in his arms and started burrowing.

Then her body hitched when she started crying.

He held her closer.

"*Mwrr?*" Murtagh asked from their feet.

"No, boy, she's not okay," Dutch answered.

Georgie hiccupped with a sob.

Murtagh collapsed on his side at Georgie's ankle.

"When'd Dutch get a cat?" Roscoe asked.

"It's Georgie's," Jagger told him.

"Right," Roscoe muttered.

"You guys need food?" Jagger called.

"Gather the men for a meet," Dutch ordered. "I want to talk to them about what we can do about Carlyle's dad."

Jagger's expression opened up huge, this accompanying the grin that spread on his mouth.

There it was.

Georgie was right.

Dutch needed his family.

And his family needed him.

"I got her," Dutch finished.

"I want a breakfast toaster from Sonic," Georgie snuffled in his neck.

Dutch couldn't stop his smile.

That was his girl.

Take a hit.

Bounce right back.

"I could eat a toaster," Roscoe decreed.

"Three a' those for us, brothers," Dutch told Jagger and Roscoe. "And some Cinnasnacks."

"I want Cinnasnacks too," Georgie blubbered.

"On it," Jagger said, sounding amused. "And by the way, sweet robe, Georgie."

Dutch looked to the ceiling.

"Shut up, Jagger," Georgie said to his neck.

Dutch turned his eyes back to his brother just in time to catch Jag's usual congenial-asshole grin.

"Yo, I'm Roscoe," Roscoe called.

"Nice t'meet you, Roscoe," Georgie sniveled into his neck, taking an arm from around him to reach it behind her and wave a hand at Roscoe.

Now Dutch was finding it hard not to bust a gut laughing.

"Brother, that ass," Roscoe declared in the tone you used to say, *Niiiiice.*

"Fuck off and get us food, Coe," Dutch ordered.

He got a jerk of a chin from Roscoe, another grin from Jagger, and they took off.

Dutch gave her a minute and then he leaned back a bit and forced her to face him with a hand gentle on her jaw.

Christ, she was even gorgeous with red eyes and crying face.

"You gonna be okay?" he asked.

"That was off-the-hook bad," she answered.

"Yeah," he agreed.

"Like, I could think of a lot of ways that would go, all of them ranging from bad to baddest of bad, and that was worse than all of them…*by far.*"

"Yup," he said.

"But maybe it'll be what she needs to get better," she suggested.

He doubted it.

That was extreme, but addicts usually had to fall a lot farther than that before they sorted their shit.

"Maybe," he allowed.

"And bright side, your biker brother digs my ass."

Dutch didn't consider that a bright side, but for her, he'd roll with it.

"Yeah."

Her gaze moved over his face before she rested her cheekbone on his chest and her weight into his body.

He gave her more than a minute to do that.

Then he said, "Babe, I wanna be there for you, but we got a day to tackle. And I think that'll help you get your mind off shit. So, since you got a thing about mascara and foundation, and I absolutely do not, except I dig what you do with it, you get the shower first."

He heard and felt her draw in breath, then her cheek slid on his chest when she nodded.

She gave him a squeeze.

He gave her one back and let her go.

"Come on, Murtagh, time to shower," she called to the cat, and kept talking as she started walking. "Warning, Dutch, he's a bathroom cat in all the incarnations of that."

Dutch had already discovered this fact.

"So noted," he said, moving to the kitchen, and his phone to see if anyone reported in about Carlyle.

But he stopped when Georgie cried, "There it is! You've stolen my cat!"

He looked to her, then down to the floor where Murtagh was entering the kitchen behind him.

"He's a bathroom cat and he knows I'm going there and he's sticking by you," Georgie said.

He looked to her. "Babe, grab a shower."

"I can't believe you stole my cat," she snapped.

"Georgie, get in the shower."

"This is unacceptable," she decreed.

"You can get in the shower or I'll carry you there and take one with you, which means we'll be fuckin' in there when Jagger and Roscoe show, and they won't knock on the door before they come in my house. So they'll hear me fuckin' you because you make noise, gorgeous. And I like it. And I bet the boys will like it too because they'll have it as fodder to give you shit about until the day you die."

That got her.

Though she glared at him before she whirled and flounced down his hall.

But when she did, he learned she was right.

Because, even when Dutch went to the bedroom to rescue his coffee, then came back to the kitchen, Murtagh stuck by him the whole way.

So he'd stolen her cat.

He wasn't too cut up about it.

And he suspected, neither was she.

Chapter Eight

Gone to the Loss

Dutch

"Before we vote, we need to talk a minute about Dutch goin' to fuckin' Nightingale before he brought this to his brothers," Arlo declared, interrupting what Dutch was saying in order to do it.

"There aren't enough words in the English language to describe what a massive waste of time that would be," Shy replied.

"There are less of them to describe how little I care," Chill added.

"Are we even gonna waste time voting? I mean, this kid is out there looking for his dad's killer and he might have a target on his back," Boz stated.

"My vote is in," Hop said.

"Same," High grunted.

"Totally," Dog said.

"Dutch hasn't even told us what he wants from us," Rush pointed out.

Dog looked to Dutch and asked, "You want us wadin' in? Sortin' out this fucked-up mess for this kid?"

He hadn't quite gotten to that part, but to put a point on it in order to get a move on, he answered, "Yeah."

Dog turned back to Rush. "Again, in."

"I'm in," Snap added.

"Me too." That was Roscoe.

"Obviously." And that was Jag.

"Dad, you wanna get off your phone?" Rush suggested to the man sitting at his left.

"Son, I'm texting Slim. Want him to get his hands on the casefile," Tack replied.

Slim, also known as Brock Lucas, one of Tack's best friends, even if he was a cop.

That meant Tack was in.

This coming from Tack—one of the originals, *the* original, who took the Club off the trajectory to hell they were riding and brought them back from the deep, which meant he'd been in the trenches with the others all along the way—Dutch dropped his head and looked at his lap.

"Hound?" Rush called.

"Boy, you gotta even look at me?" Hound asked from his usual place when they sat the table, that being not sitting, but holding up the back wall with his wide shoulders.

"That means in," Jagger translated.

"No shit?" Hop sounded entertained.

"Arlo, you over your tantrum?" Rush asked.

"Fuck you and yes," Arlo answered. "I'm in."

"Joker, Shy, Chill?" Rush prompted.

"In." Joke.

"In." Shy.

"In." Chill.

"Do I even have to ask you, Pete?" Rush queried.

"Nope. But I'll say it anyway. In," Pete replied.

A gavel landed.

Then a number of fists pounded.

When that subsided, Rush asked, "Dutch, you wanna coordinate this or what?"

He looked up.

The room grew still when he did.

And feeling that, he wondered how he could ever think this was just his.

He took a second and looked into the eyes of every man in that room.

He lingered on Jag. On Hound. And on Tack, his father's best friend.

Then he said, "I'll tell you what we got so far, and we can decide how it's gonna go from there."

Rush nodded.

Dutch rolled his chair closer to the table and launched in.

* * * *

He was in the lead an hour later when they all walked out.

So he was the first to see her.

But he was far from the only one.

And what he saw, sitting at the bar in the common room where he left her, in front of a laptop, was Georgie swiveling around when she heard them coming.

But now, clustered around her and a bunch of laptops, were his ma, Tyra, Elvira and Tabby.

Georgie jumped off her stool, and he stopped dead, as did every man behind him, when his woman skipped…

Actually *skipped*…

Through the Chaos Motorcycle Club Compound.

Her face was beaming.

Good that she appeared to be over that scene with her sister.

But…

Skipping?

"Ohmigod, ohmigod, ohmigod," she chanted on her way, "you won't believe what we found."

She stopped in front of him, slapping both hands on his chest.

Then she leaned to the side, looked beyond him and called, "Hey, guys."

Hey, guys?

He heard some chuckles. A few "Yos." A, "Hey, darlin'" from Big Petey. And Arlo asking, "*This* is Dutch's new tail? Jesus, is she an ex-cheerleader like Carrie?" To which High replied, "Who cares, Arlo."

"Did they vote yes?" Georgie asked him, either oblivious or wisely deciding to ignore the byplay.

"Yes," he answered.

"Told you," she singsonged, beaming even brighter.

So much, he was blinded.

"Anyway, come and look." She grabbed his hand and dragged

him toward the bar, all the way babbling. "So, I had my laptop, as you know. And Tyra came in and asked what I was doing, so I told her, and hers was in the office at the garage, so she grabbed it. Then your mom showed, and they live close, as you also know, so she popped back home to get hers. And finally, Elvira and Tabby showed, and Vira had hers in her car, so she went out and got it. And I showed them how to Google up a storm, even though Vira knew how to Google even better than me, and we got a lot. But you gotta look at some of it."

She stopped at the stool she'd left and looked up at him.

"Do you want to sit or…?" she asked.

"You sit," he grunted.

She nodded, slid up on it, but did it being bossy.

"But you gotta look, so get close."

He got close all right.

He came up to her back and leaned into it as well as both of his hands in the bar, trapping her between his arms and putting his jaw to the side of her hair.

After he did this, all the women gave each other looks.

Georgie didn't miss a beat.

"So, last night, before Jackson got handsy—"

Dutch growled.

She twisted her neck to look at him. "It wasn't fun, but it's over, honey."

"We still haven't talked about that."

"I know, we'll debrief, sometime later, but now, *listen*."

He felt the men come up behind him as he nodded go to Georgie.

She looked back to her laptop.

"So, okay, before Jackson proved he was a total dick, he told me the neighbor's name, which I think Eddie and Hank kept from us because I acted like a lunatic and I think they feared for her life."

This was not an incorrect assumption.

"And?" he prompted.

"So, yeah, we got busy on Google and Facebook and *we found her*."

He was not certain what the excitement was about.

"And this is good because…?"

She turned to look at him again, her eyes dancing. "Because she has friends."

"Babe, not sure black-market bad guys have Facebook pages."

"How about we check," she suggested. "We've compiled pictures of all her male friends. Then we collected *other* info about her Facebook friends so we'd be ready to roll if this dude is one of them. I'll click through and you let me know if any of them are the ones you saw Carlyle with at that bar."

It was worth a go, so he lifted his chin.

She turned back to her laptop.

He leaned deeper into her and gave the screen his attention.

She clicked.

"No," he said.

Another click.

"No."

This went on for fifteen fucking clicks, he was getting over it when shit had to get done, and she hit her mousepad and the guy showed up on her screen.

"Fuck, that's him."

"Ohmigod," Georgie breathed.

"Name," Elvira demanded.

"Gary Bronson," Georgiana told her.

"He's one I looked up," his fucking *mother* said. "What do you want? Address? Car he drives? What?"

Before anyone could answer, one of a cluster of cells sitting on the bar started sounding.

Since the screen said Kraken Calling, he knew it was Georgiana's.

She snatched it up, engaged, put it to her ear, and his head dropped once again that day, this time in disbelief at what he heard and the no-nonsense tone in which it was said from his cute, sweet, skipping Georgie.

"Talk to me, bro," Georgie demanded.

Honest to fuck, he had no idea if he wanted to laugh or shout.

"Can someone tell me what the fuck is happening?" Boz asked.

"*Really?*" Georgie squealed.

At that, Dutch lifted his head, put his hands on her hips and whirled her around to face him.

She was back to beaming.

"Where? Now? We'll be there as soon as we can! Thanks! I owe you one! Text the address and we're on our way! See you soon!" She hung up and cried, "They have Carlyle!"

Dutch put both hands to her thighs, got close to her face, and sucked in a massive breath.

"Okay, did we just spend an hour sitting around the table talking about doing what our women were sitting at the bar *actually doing*?" High sounded harassed.

"Seems like it," Hop answered.

"Who's Kraken?" Tack asked.

Tack didn't miss much, and he was close, so he didn't miss that.

"A street tough Georgie knows," Dutch answered, staring up close in Georgie's eyes.

"The chick that skips knows street toughs?" Arlo queried low.

"Brother, clearly she's an all-rounder. You should see the woman in a robe. I'm gonna dream about that until the day I die," Roscoe put in.

Dutch would not be surprised if his body started buzzing since the noise in his head was so goddamned loud.

"Am I in some kind of biker's babe trouble?" she asked quietly.

"I'm not sure how to answer that," he told her.

"That means I'm in some kind of biker's babe trouble," she surmised.

"I would tell you to be less you, but that would suck, because I like all that's you. But I do not need Roscoe dreamin' of you in your sweet robe."

"I didn't *ask* my sister to come to your place and throw a tantrum," she pointed out. "And I didn't ask Roscoe to be there to witness it. But since she arrived in full-bore drama, I couldn't exactly take a sec and get dressed before I saved you from it."

Dutch sighed.

"Are we gonna go get Carlyle?" she demanded.

He straightened from her but did it grabbing her hand and pulling her off the stool.

He then turned to the men. "Hound, Jag, with me and Georgie. We're gonna need a safe house for Carlyle. Who's on that?"

"He can stay up the mountain with Red and me," Tack said. "Distance means more safety. And we got room. But if he's as big as you say, we'll need two, three guys on hand to lock him down if needed."

"I'm up," High said.

"I'm there too," Shy added.

"And me," Joker finished it.

"Right. We're covered," Tack decreed to Dutch.

"How big is he?" Tyra asked.

"Probably six nine, three hundred pounds," Dutch told her.

"I better get to the grocery store," she mumbled.

"I'm in," Elvira said.

"Me too," Tabby said.

"And me," Keely put in.

"I'm on Gary Bronson and I want Snap, Chill and Dog with me," Rush declared. "Keely, give us everything you got."

Rush moved toward his mom.

"As discussed at the table, Pete, Boz, Arlo, you men are on the neighbor," Tack reminded them. "We need to know everywhere the woman goes, get shots of anyone in and out of her house, anyone she meets with, anyone she even gives eyes to. Yeah?"

"Who's got her info?" Boz asked.

"Got you, boo," Elvira said.

When Dutch returned his attention to Georgie, she was giving him a happy *See?* look.

He kissed her quick, looked at his dad and brother, jerked his chin up at them, then pulled his girl out to his truck.

* * * *

The scene they rolled into at the flophouse address Kraken gave Georgie was not what they expected.

Mostly because they walked in not to see Banga and Kraken guarding a probably pissed-as-shit Carlyle.

But instead, they walked in to three guns aimed at them.

Dutch was first in, even if he had to shove Georgie physically behind him to go first, which meant Georgie was right behind him.

"Christ," he bit out.

"Heard of knocking?" Luke Stark, Lee Nightingale's right-hand man, bit back before he holstered his weapon.

Vance and Roam were both holstering theirs as well.

"Ohmigod, what in heaven's name?" Georgie cried, coming around him.

It was a good question, since not only was Carlyle trussed up on the floor…

So were two men Dutch suspected were Banga and Kraken.

"I don't know who to let loose first," she snapped.

"That would be me," the man Dutch knew by hearing his voice over speakerphone was Kraken said.

"It would be me," by process of elimination, he knew it was Banga who said that.

"This fuckin' shit is fuckin' kidnapping," Carlyle said.

"Do not cut Carlyle free," Dutch warned, handing Georgie his knife so she could saw through the zip ties.

Georgiana took the knife, gave him a nod and headed toward Banga and Kraken.

"Shizlayaya, we did not sign up for this shizla," Banga told her. "You didn't tell us the Nightingale mofos were on the case. Shufa!"

"They didn't believe we had this brother for you," Kraken shared. "And I can tell you *truth*, I coulda lived my whole motherfuckin' life without the experience of Luke Goddamned-Fuckin' Stark subduing me. Have you been tased?" he asked Georgie.

"No," she answered.

"I highly recommend avoiding it," Kraken shared.

"I'm so sorry," Georgie told them, going for Kraken first.

"You owe us big, Shizlayaya, for this shizla," Banga shared.

On that, Dutch entered the conversation.

"She had nothing to do with your takedown, so get that out of your head."

"We're not gonna ask her to open up a crackhouse with us, cracker, shizzleazza *owt*," Kraken replied.

"Okay…" Jag said slowly. "The fuck these guys talkin' 'bout?"

"They have their own language," Georgie shared.

Finishing up with Kraken, who was pulling his big, lanky, Black frame topped with its massive Afro with a pick comb stuck in it up from the floor, she was turning to Banga.

"No shit, darlin'? I got that part," Jag returned.

"Shizla means 'shit.' Shizzleazza means 'chill,'" she educated. "Shufa is the F-word."

"Your name from them has the word shit in it?" Dutch growled.

"Also 'yaya,' honky," Banga snapped. Now also free, he was hauling his short, stocky Black body topped with a high, electric-blue mohawk Afro from the floor. "Which means hot mama. Put together it means a hot mama who's the shit."

"Well, that makes perfect sense," Luke Stark drawled.

"I order brownies," Kraken declared Georgie's way.

"The big cookies with the cinnamon," Banga put in.

"Snickerdoodles," Georgie corrected.

"Shizlayaya, I do not say words as stupid as the word 'snickerdoodles,'" Banga retorted.

To that, Hound snorted.

Banga *and* Kraken's eyes narrowed on Hound.

Dutch stepped in.

"Okay, men, thank you for what you did and we're sorry shit got confused but you're off the case."

Dutch tensed when Kraken got close to Georgie and stabbed a finger in her face. "Brownies."

He then stared when she threw her arms around his neck, gave him a hug and promised, "Give me a couple days. I have a new boyfriend and he's keeping me busy." She let go and finished, "But I'll text you after I make them."

"Gotcha, sister, stay shizzleazza," Kraken replied.

Then, fuck him, they did a complicated handshake with a dizzying variety of moves that spanned them from waists to over Georgie's head before they finished it.

Dutch glanced at Jag and Hound to see both of them staring at his woman with huge motherfucking grins on their faces.

Christ.

Banga moved in next, got his hug, handshake and promise of cookies.

Then Kraken bellied up to Dutch before they took off, noting, "I would share, you fuck her over, I'll fuck you up, but then I'd have Chaos all over my ass, and I ain't sheerashaka dumb. So hear me, shanakaka, you fuck her over, know you're just the stupidest shanakaka out there. Ya dig?"

Dutch kinda did, he kinda did not.

However, since he had absolutely no intention of fucking Georgie over, he jerked up his chin.

Banga just stared him down and spat, "Sharashena," before he left.

The door closed.

All eyes turned to Georgiana.

"'Shanakaka' means 'asshole.' The rest of it, I have no clue. And I bribe them for their help with baked goods because I have a talent in that area. It used to work with Jackson too, but that bridge has been irretrievably burned," she explained.

Dutch already was not real thrilled with this Jackson sitch he knew about, but also didn't.

That made him less so.

Though, he was intrigued about her talent with baked goods.

"I'd find this farce amusing, if *I* wasn't still tied up on the goddamned floor," Carlyle stated.

Dutch moved to him where he was still sitting on his ass on the floor and crouched.

"I gotta share you're gonna stay that way until we get you safe, unless you promise you're gonna be cool."

"Fuck you, let me go," Carlyle returned.

"I know what you're doing, Carlyle, and it doesn't seem like it now, but everyone in this room is here to help," Dutch told him.

"You don't know dick and I don't need your help," Carlyle retorted.

"He saw you, didn't he? The guy who shot your dad."

Carlyle's eyes told the truth even as the kid himself shut up.

Georgiana crouched beside him.

"Hi, Carlyle, I'm Georgie."

"Don't give a shit who you are," Carlyle replied.

"I can imagine," she murmured. "But you know, uh, so we can get this situation taken care of as fast as possible, we have pictures we want you to look at so you can let us know if one of them is the guy you saw that night."

That caught his attention. "What pictures?"

"From Jessica, your neighbor's Facebook."

"Bitch, you think I didn't look there first?" he sniped.

Okay, the line was far for Dutch that Carlyle couldn't cross.

But he'd just leaped over it.

"You don't know me," Dutch said low. "And I get you don't wanna know me. But know this, you do not call my woman a bitch. Are you feelin' me right now?"

Carlyle's eyes shot to Dutch, and he didn't even look at the men who had gathered at Dutch's back at hearing his tone.

The kid he really was, the kid his father raised, came out and he looked wrecked for a beat before he hid it.

But Dutch zeroed in.

"That's your father's son, do not lose what you've got left of him by losing hold on that."

"You don't know dick about my father," Carlyle spat.

"You're very wrong. A few seconds ago, I was looking him right in the eye."

Carlyle's entire big body shuddered before he closed his eyes tight and turned his head away.

Dutch knew that feeling.

He'd felt it just that morning.

And his father had been dead for twenty-three years.

"Now, we're pickin' up Gary Bronson, and we're gonna be talkin' to him," Dutch shared, and Carlyle looked back, too young, or too broken, to be able to hide his shock. "And we've got men on Jessica, and we're gonna be watchin' every move she makes. And we know where the warehouse is, and we're gonna be on that too. You got more for us, we'll be all over that. In the meantime, we got a safe place for you to stay with a roof, a bed, food to eat and good people who'll look out for you. And if you'll let me, I'll go to your ma and share you're good, you're safe, and I can bring her and your sister to you so we can prove that to her. But she'll be safe the way I do it. And then you leave this to me, to my brothers, to the men who've waded into this, because we got you."

"I got there before he was down."

It came out beyond his control.

Shit, shit, shit, shit, *shit.*

"Cut him free," Georgie whispered urgently.

Carlyle's eyes were locked to Dutch.

"I saw him take it in the neck."

Roam was behind his back, working fast.

"Give it to me, man," Dutch urged.

"I saw it. I saw him take it in the neck."

Dutch shuffled closer, muttering, not to Carlyle, "Get her back."

Georgie disappeared.

"He went down. He's a big guy like me."

"Give it to me."

"Made a big noise when he hit. Bitch screamed. Loud. So loud. All of that. Seemed louder than the gunshot."

"I can see that," Dutch told him when he stopped talking.

"'Not the kid,' she said, then shoved the guy out the door," Carlyle continued.

At least she did that.

"Dad was down, but his arms were moving, he was looking at me, motioning me to get out of there. I didn't do what he told me to do. I went to him."

After that, Carlyle jerked suddenly, slammed his large fists into the floor beside him, then curled instantly into a ball, his hands one over the other on the back of his head.

"He went down. Never got up. Never got up. Never gonna get up," he said to his thighs.

"Do I need to call Jules?" Vance asked quietly.

"No," Dutch answered.

He didn't touch him. Dutch didn't move.

Carlyle started rocking.

It didn't last long.

Carlyle's hands slid away. They fell to the floor like they weren't flesh he could control, but useless appendages made of nothing.

He lifted his head and eyes filled with everything Dutch had felt all his life, all at once, caught on Dutch's.

Dutch heard Jagger suck in breath and knew Jagger recognized it, just like Dutch.

"I gotta find him, for my dad."

"We'll find him for you, man," Dutch promised.

"It's gotta be me," Carlyle said.

"You gotta stay safe, because there is one thing I know in this world above all other, your mom's gonna need you. Do you understand me?"

Carlyle swallowed hard.

"Do you understand me, Carlyle?" Dutch pushed.

Carlyle just stared at him, gone. Gone to the pain. Gone to the memories.

Gone to the loss.

"Do you understand me?" Dutch demanded.

He sounded like a little kid when he answered, "Yeah."

"Will you come with us?" Dutch asked.

Carlyle nodded.

Dutch didn't waste a second.

He straightened from his crouch and held out his hand.

Carlyle studied it.

And then…

He took it.

Chapter Nine

Meanwhile

Meanwhile…

As Dutch was talking to Carlyle Stephens in Tack and Tyra's living room with a bevy of Chaos brothers and Nightingale men around him …

Georgiana stood out in the chill air on the deck of Kane and Tyra Allen's house.

She was not the least surprised when Keely Ironside joined her.

She didn't look at Dutch's mom when she asked, "He okay?"

"Kid's been through the wringer but think he's tough."

She gave Keely her attention at that.

"I wasn't talking about Carlyle."

Keely's eyes fell on her.

"Do you know what's going on with my son?" she asked.

"Yes," Georgiana answered.

"You're not going to tell me, are you?" she asked.

"No," Georgie answered.

"Can I trust you have him?" she asked.

"Absolutely," Georgie answered.

Keely Black Ironside stared at Georgiana Suzanne Traylor.

Then she said, "He's always been very serious."

"Please don't share with me things Dutch would want to tell me himself."

"What I'm saying is, I wanted him to be free longer so maybe he'd have a little fun."

Georgie cocked her head.

"What makes you think I'm not fun?"

Keely stared at her again.

"I'm loads of fun," Georgie assured her.

"I hope so," Keely whispered.

"Thank you for him," Georgie said to her.

Keely's head jerked.

"He's pretty freaking amazing," Georgiana told her something she knew.

The way Keely was looking at her now was entirely different.

"Yes, he is."

"We should go inside. He's got things on his mind and he doesn't need to worry about his new babe talking to his beloved mother."

"Right," Keely murmured.

They turned as one, and neither of them missed that Dutch's eyes were aimed through the window.

At Georgiana.

"I haven't seen that look in twenty-three years," Keely whispered.

"It's beautiful, isn't it?" Georgie asked.

Keely slid her arm through Georgie's and moved her toward the door, saying…

"Gorgeous."

Chapter Ten

This

Dutch

They went through his side door, Georgie carrying her backpack and laptop bag, Dutch juggling a pizza and a six pack.

She dumped her stuff first, on the counter by the washer and dryer, took off her coat, hung it on a hook, then nabbed the stuff from Dutch.

He locked the door, shrugged off his cut and hung it on a hook.

By the time he'd turned, she was in the living room, cooing to Murtagh.

Dutch followed her.

She was heading to the kitchen.

He moved around turning on lamps.

When he got to the kitchen, she had two beers popped and her head bent to her phone.

She sensed him there, though, because she said, "I'm so wiped, I just want to eat the pizza over the box, down a beer and pass out."

Not even close to the plans he had for them that night.

He didn't get into that, or share another good part of living in the biker world: the fact it was almost a moral imperative not to put your pizza on a plate, but instead, eat it over the box at the same time sucking back a beer.

He also didn't remind her of what he'd already told her. That he'd called, and the restaurant was booked for the next night, but they had a reservation for Sunday, so they had something to look forward to.

On the way from the pizza joint, she'd been giving her phone a lot of attention and not sharing why.

So he got into that.

"Something up?" he asked, leaning a hip against the counter and flipping the pizza box open.

Her gaze came to him.

"Well, my mom has been texting all day, which is no surprise, considering Carolyn has probably been buzzing in her ear."

"Yeah?" he said. "And?" he asked because he knew that wasn't it.

"Now my dad has called twice, and that's unusual, because he kinda figured things out a while ago, at least with the designer stuff Carolyn's always sporting, and since she often went to him for a handout, he cut her off. This caused a big blowup, as I'm sure you can imagine. She hasn't spoken to him in a couple of years."

"So you need to call your dad," he surmised.

"Yes."

He nodded. "I need to call Rush to get briefed on Gary Bronson. You make your call, I'll make mine. And we'll eat over the box. Nab some paper towels, babe."

"You need cloth napkins," she said, even as she moved to the paper towel holder.

"What?" he asked.

She tore some off. "Cloth napkins."

"Bikers don't do cloth napkins," he teased, though he did it telling her the God's honest truth.

She smiled at him as she came over and handed him his paper towel. "Do bikers like riding roads on this planet we call earth?"

"So your bid to save the planet is to use cloth napkins and not paper towels?"

She shrugged. "Every little bit helps."

He shook his head, and since she'd stopped close, he dipped down to give her a lip touch, then he pulled out his phone.

"Call," he ordered. "Soon's we're done with this shit, it can be just us for maybe ten minutes."

She lifted a hand, pressed it into his chest, then made her call.

He made his.

Rush answered straight away.

"The guy giving anything up?" Dutch asked before taking a huge bite of a slice while Georgie murmured and munched close to him.

"Jessica Browbridge launders counterfeit cash the black market operation produces. She does it through that restaurant she manages," Rush told him.

Well then.

He gave something up.

"Though, that shit has stopped since other shit got hot for her after her neighbor was shot dead in her bedroom," Rush went on.

Dutch swallowed his pizza and asked, "Anything on that?"

"That was a harder pull, but yeah. She likes to get laid. Though the guy couldn't pinpoint who was there, since she spread her love around, which Bronson figures might have been the problem. One of them got jealous, came over and got up in her shit, things escalated to a fight. She was fishing too much in a stinking pond, messing with men who don't like to be messed with and have no problem sharing that in ugly ways, even with a woman. Khalon Stephens didn't like the sound of it. And we are where we're at."

"He give you names?"

"He had trouble narrowing it down."

"Jesus," Dutch muttered, taking another bite.

"But it doesn't matter. This racket is highly organized," Rush said. "You're in, you deal with what you deal with. This situation was big, and she's flashy, so she was known, and when that went down, word got around. But Bronson isn't part of the counterfeit cash gig. He's on distribution of Cialis and Viagra that comes in from Canada and Mexico. So for the most part, he doesn't know names, just faces. Until I told him her name, he didn't know it. Just knew what happened with her, and that she was out, and all were told not to associate with her."

"You believe him?"

"He was pretty tweaked he'd been hauled in by Chaos. Can't say he spilled right away, but eventually he was cooperative and absolutely not at one with her shit landing on him, or their racket, in any way. So, yeah."

Fuck.

"You cut him loose?" Dutch asked.

"Pretty certain we got all we could from him, so again, yeah."

"Right."

"The kid?" Rush asked.

"You line ten thousand men up that all meet the same description, he'd pick the fucker out in five seconds flat."

"So we need to be all over that warehouse when you said we can't be all over that warehouse."

"Nightingale is on that. Vance, Luke and Roam met the kid, witnessed his break, and not surprisingly, man hours loosened up. They're all in. They're setting up surveillance equipment as we speak."

"Fuckin' great," Rush said.

"Yeah."

"Between us on her and Nightingale on that warehouse, we'll get him, Dutch," Rush said.

He hoped so.

"Yeah."

"Catch some sleep. Wanna meet with you tomorrow, set a schedule of who's on her, who's on security for Carlyle and his mom and sister."

"Time?"

"Whenever. Your call."

Dutch studied Georgie, who was off the phone and concentrating on eating and not falling over.

He got that.

You could run a marathon, and if you're fit, probably paint your bedroom after.

But emotion will suck it all out of you every time.

"I'll text you in the morning," Dutch told him.

"Right. Cool. Later."

"Later, Rush."

He disconnected, tossed his phone on the counter and asked, "Well?"

She looked up to him and watched him take another huge bite before she spoke.

"Well, taking nothing away from the fact that I think Carolyn genuinely does probably love your brother, and that was part of why this morning was off-the-hook, it's clear another part of it is that she's in some financial trouble and Jagger was her bid to freedom from that. With him out of the picture, she went to our mother, who shot her down, and was desperate enough to break the silence with Dad, who's now entirely freaked out."

"Did he shoot her down?"

"He asked her to come and talk to him. Something she did. And since he hasn't seen her in a while, and she's lost some weight, and was tweaking, he asked pertinent questions he knew the answers to. She lied. He cottoned onto that too. So, yes. He shot her down for money to buy coke or whatever else is at issue. But he offered to pay for rehab. She refused."

"Shit, baby," Dutch whispered.

She looked to the pizza and grabbed another slice, saying, "And now Dad's mad at me because I admitted I knew there was a problem and I didn't let him in on it."

Uh…

No.

"Fuck that, Georgiana," Dutch clipped.

She again gave him her eyes. "I know. He's just worried. He'll get over it."

"The last time you ate her shit happened this morning, baby," he warned her.

"Okay, Dutch, but what if her financial situation involves owing money to a dealer?"

Dutch drew in breath through his nose.

The reason why dope was zero tolerated by Chaos was not solely because that shit was fucked up and they wanted no part of it.

It started back when Tack's sister overdosed.

The Club dealt.

His sister dead, Tack went on a mission and he recruited brothers to that mission, and this mission was to get that shit, and all the other, out of the lives of Chaos.

The final battle sparked when Tabby's best friend, who was a junkie, got in over her head and the Club intervened to get her out of a very bad situation.

Carlyle, they were on board.

Carolyn, they would let swing.

And not just because of the dope.

Because she'd played a brother.

Even knowing this, Dutch offered, "You want me to ask around, darlin'?"

"I don't want you eating shit because of this either," she mumbled irately, and took a bite of pizza.

"And I don't want you worried," he returned.

She chewed, swallowed and refocused on him.

"I'm going to have a conversation and share this with her. Share that this is what she's saddling me with. Mother with. Dad with. This gnawing worry. And I'm going to tell her this one time, I'll intervene with Mother, Dad, and pitch in myself if she promises to get her shit straight. But if she can't, we're done. At least I am. I'll be out. For good. I can't let this infect my life like that. Of course, there is no way I can just switch off the love and worry I have for my sister. But she doesn't need to know that."

"That's a very mature response," he told her.

"It's big words," she replied. "I'm totally going to go back on it."

Dutch started laughing and hooked her with an arm to pull her to him.

He could finish eating with her tucked close.

So could she.

"So…Carolyn down," she put a line under it, sharing succinctly she was done talking about her sister. "What do you have?"

He ran down what Rush told him.

When he was done, she asked, "Do you think we should hand this over to the police? Because, Dutch, pictures Chaos or Nightingale Investigations takes are not admissible."

"We just want Carlyle to identify his father's killer. The cops can deal with black market shit. That isn't the mission here. The mission is justice for Khalon Stephens. The end."

She nodded.

"So we get a picture, and hope to God a name, of the man Carlyle saw that night, then the cops can run with it," he finished.

"Okay," she said, then took another bite.

"Sorry about our date," he said before taking his own bite.

"I don't know if you noticed this, but we're kinda on the longest, most drawn-out date in history," she remarked. "Though, it'd be nice for part of it to be at a fancy restaurant, because if you liked the black dress, you're *really* gonna like the dress I picked for our date."

He pulled her closer and dipped his head her way. "Yeah?"

"Oh yeah," she whispered, that got-your-cock look catching the attention of his cock.

He tossed his half-eaten slice in the box and wrapped his other arm around her.

She followed suit and her arms were around his neck.

They made out and it was righteous, not only because he fucking loved kissing Georgie, but because nothing interrupted it.

However, eventually, Dutch did.

For Georgie.

He pulled away, murmuring, "Finish pizza. Beer. Then I need to give my girl some shut-eye."

"Are you serious?"

At her tone, and the look on her face, he'd been serious, now he wasn't sure.

"Babe, you're dead on your feet."

"I thought we were gonna get busy tonight."

He grinned at her. "We were. But you're wiped. I'm wiped. Today was full of a lot of everyone else's shit, and the first time I'm inside you, I want it all about us."

"Okay, I can be down with that. So payback-for-this-morning blowjob."

Dutch blinked.

His dick jumped.

And his mouth said, "What?"

"Though, caveat, if you're feeling the need to return the favor in any way you might wish to do that, I'm open. You can be stingy with taking your orgasms. I'm all in whenever you feel like doling one out."

It took a beat.

And then Dutch busted out laughing.

When he was done, he realized Georgie had not joined him.

He knew why when she asked, "Do I get to go down on you?"

He hauled her tighter to his frame, and with no humor whatsoever, he growled, "Abso-fucking-lutely."

She smiled.

Then she kissed him.

He let her.

He broke it, broke their clinch entirely, stepped back far enough to come forward bent low, and he hefted her up on his shoulder.

She made that squeal he liked so much and then wrapped her arms around his middle from the back, saying, "Holy wow, you can pick me up."

She was not a lightweight, but he didn't work out, and hard, since he was fourteen not to be able to haul his old lady around when he got one.

Since he'd done what she said, he didn't feel a response was necessary, so he didn't make one.

He just dumped her on his bed when they got there.

Dutch twisted to the lamp and turned it on.

Georgiana scrambled up on her knees.

He lifted his hands to behind his neck and yanked off his Henley.

Georgie went after his belt.

She tugged so hard, his hips jerked.

"Whoa, baby, I'm not going anywhere," he murmured on a grin.

Her head tipped back. "Carolyn is a mess. There's a murderer on the loose. And Murtagh was unusually quiet when we got home so he might interrupt at any time. Not to mention, you have, like, *a bazillion* brothers who all seem very together, but who knows? Couples fight. Kids throw tantrums. A brother might need the soothing goodness of Dutch Black and probably would not hesitate to knock on your door to get it. So shut up. I'm gonna suck you off while I've got a clear shot."

Never in his life would he think anytime, but especially with Georgie, that he'd be laughing when a woman got his zip lowered, yanked his jeans down, freeing his hard cock, and then bent over and went in.

But he was.

He wasn't laughing when she drew him deep.

Fucking *fuck*.

That mouth.

Beautiful.

He cupped the back of her head and whispered, "Baby."

She braced herself on the bed in one hand, took hold of his hip with the other, and she blew him.

Christ.

He knew the minute she had his tongue, this would be what he got, but *fuck* if it didn't feel way fucking better around his cock.

She took him there and he had no choice but to warn, "Gotta fuck your face, Georgie."

She stilled to give her permission.

Dutch took over.

God.

Fuck.

God.

Fuck.

"You swallow?" he grunted.

She wrapped both hands around his ass and dug her nails in.

She swallowed.

Then she sucked, he fucked, and finally he blew down her throat, arching into his orgasm, his head falling back, goddamned fucking *amazing.*

He was barely over it before he hauled his jeans up, tucked his dick in, liking the scrape against his sensitive flesh and the wet of her mouth still there, and ordered a hoarse, "C'mere."

She pushed up to straight and he took control of the fly on her cords.

"Dutch," she whispered.

"Shut it," he muttered, got the zip down, wrapped an arm around her to pull her to him, shoved a hand down her pants and took her mouth.

She was wet, she was ready, she got off on that blowjob, not as much as he did, but enough it didn't take him long to get her there, so he fingered her to orgasm.

She'd swallowed his cum.

He swallowed her whimper.

He ended it like he did that morning, with two fingers deep inside her, but as she recovered, he didn't slide them out.

Dutch trailed his lips to her ear and whispered, "This pussy feels sweet."

"I hope you like it when you finally take it," she whispered back.

He grinned and sucked her lobe in his mouth.

She shivered.

He stroked her inside.

"Dutch," she breathed.

"Love the way you say my name," he told her.

She glided her fingers in his hair.

"Love your ass."

She pressed closer.

"Love how fuckin' crazy you are about a goddamned cat."

She stroked his hair at the bottom, which meant at the same time she stroked the back of his neck.

"Love how you go gung-ho for a kid you've never met. Love how you're gentle with my mom because you know she's dealing with some shit with me. Love how big your tits are. And I know I'm gonna love sinking into this pussy."

He pushed his fingers deeper.

She gasped.

He slid his fingers out and pulled his head back enough she could watch when he slipped them in his mouth to suck them clean.

She watched and she did it on a low, hot moan.

It was Dutch who got the real goodness, though, because she tasted as fantastic as all things Georgie.

Another gasp came when he finished doing that and he caught her hard on either side of her head where it met her neck.

And then he got close.

"Do you know how unbelievably fuckin' amazing you are, Georgiana?"

Tears filled her eyes.

"Honey," she whispered.

"I was lost, and I've not known you a week, and I might not have it together, but I'm on the road to bein' found and that loosens somethin' in me that's been so tight for so long, jackin' me up so bad, I thought it was going to kill an important part of me."

"Dutch—"

"You give great fuckin' head, baby. I love it too that you know when to give over to me. And I love how wet you get doin' it and how quick you come for me. But serious, with all we got, when I slide inside you, it's gonna be all about you for me and me for you. I don't care if I have to take us to Siberia to make that happen."

"I hear Siberia is cold," she said softly.

"I'll keep you warm."

"I've noticed you're good at that," she muttered.

"Babe."

Her focus became hyper-alert.

"Dutch, I'll exist on blowjobs and finger fucking as long as you need to keep it at that to give you what you need to take us where you need us to be when that happens between us. I'll take anything from you. I'll even give you my cat. Because you're that man who deserves it. And you're that man to me."

Her words made something in his chest explode, busting apart, vaporizing.

Because of that, he took her mouth and kissed her tough.

And his Georgie, she took that.

But as the emotion he was feeling faded, he gentled it, she was with him on that too, until finally, he ended it.

"Now, we need some sleep," he said quietly.

"Yeah, Dutch," she replied.

"You get the bathroom first," he said, and for some reason, that made her smile. So he asked, "What?"

"Well, I don't know, that was pretty intense. And all of this is happening fast. And with what's happening, I don't think it comes as a surprise to either of us as to why. But if you ever get to wondering why some woman started falling for you, hard and swift, just remember, you always gave her the bathroom first."

The first part made hella sense.

The last did not.

And he told her that by saying, "Babe."

"Dutch, I first met you when you were doing a favor for your brother. You put others above yourself a lot. A *whole* lot. You gave me stuff about giving you the security code to my building when you know you're not going to be that creepy jerk if things go wrong with us—"

"Things aren't gonna go wrong with us."

"You get my point."

"Georgie—"

She slid her fingers into his hair on either side of his head and gave it a gentle jerk.

"You're just that guy, Dutch. *That* guy. And I'm just *really* glad I met you." She pulled him to her for a quick kiss, before she moved away and got off the bed. "Now we both need sleep. Because who flipping knows what's gonna happen tomorrow."

And she disappeared in the bathroom.

"Mwrr?" Murtagh asked from the door.

Dutch looked at the cat. "Yeah, we're done."

"Mwrrrrr," Murtagh said, strolled in, jumped on the bed, did a yoga pose, and started licking his foot.

In fifteen minutes, he'd double-checked his house was locked down, the pizza box was in the fridge, the lights out, and Dutch was on his back in bed with Georgie tucked down his side, her cheek on his pec, Murtagh settled in on his abs.

Dutch was staring at the shadowed ceiling.

He knew by her breathing that Georgie was staring at his chest.

"What'd my ma talk to you about?" he asked.

"She's worried about you," she answered.

"What'd you say?"

"I told her I got you."

He had his arm around her, and at that, he pulled her closer.

Because she had that right.

She had him.

Time passed.

Georgiana didn't slide into sleep.

Neither did Dutch.

She knew that, which was why she relayed, "Just so you know, if you ever want my avid attention when you've got something really sexy and sweet and awesome to say, feel free to do it with two fingers inside me."

Dutch started chuckling.

"Though, I will warn you, my attention was scattered seeing as that was hotter than you taking over my blowjob," she continued.

He kept chuckling but spoke through it this time.

"Baby, you give fantastic head. I had to fuck that mouth."

"Feel free to do that too. Whenever the spirit moves you."

Murtagh flew off, protesting with an irate, "*Merow!*" when Dutch shifted to his side so he could pull Georgie in his arms, full frontal.

"You're not supposed to move when Murtagh's settled in, Dutch," she educated.

"He'll settle in again."

"Yes, on *you*," she mumbled. "Because you're a cat thief."

"Georgie, baby?"

"Yeah."

"Be quiet, please, and go to sleep."

"Okay, honey," she whispered, and nestled closer.

That must have been what she needed, Dutch needing her to go to sleep, because within five minutes, she was gone.

Dutch was not.

He couldn't get used to the new feeling in his chest, something he'd never felt.

It was weird.

Warm.

It wasn't empty.

But it wasn't tight.

He just didn't know what was filling it.

He felt Murtagh settle in at the back of his head on his pillow.

The cat purred for a while.

Then that stopped and Dutch knew he, too, was asleep.

And it was then, Dutch got it.

All of it.

Everything.

His whole life.

His dads' life.

Both of his dads.

And he lay in that bed with Georgie in his arms and what had become their cat on his pillow, and he knew what he'd been looking for.

He knew what his path was.

He knew what his life was about.

He thought it was big.

He thought it was dramatic.

Being a soldier in a war.

A man on a mission.

A brother with a purpose.

But it was simple.

It was just…

This.

Your house dark and quiet.

And your woman in your arms.

Happy and safe.

Chapter Eleven

Chaos Strikes Again

Dutch

"You have got to be…fucking…*kidding me*," Dutch groused when his phone ringing woke them both the next morning, him on his stomach, Georgie again curled into his back.

"Gluh," she mumbled, pressing closer as Dutch reached for the phone.

He saw on his bedside clock it was late morning, they'd slept way in, it was after ten.

They should have set an alarm.

He grabbed his cell and didn't know what to think when he saw it said Eddie Calling.

"Shit," he muttered.

"What?" she asked.

He twisted. She shifted.

He caught her sleep-cute eyes.

"Eddie."

"Oh boy," she said.

He took the call with a, "Yo."

"I don't even know what to say," Eddie replied.

"You woke me up in bed with my woman," Dutch told him.

"Then whatever it is, I best get to sayin' it." Eddie Chavez sounded amused.

"I'd be obliged," Dutch returned, moving more, so he was up in bed, back to the headboard, Georgie moving too, to stick close.

"Jessica Browbridge, I'm thinkin' you know who I'm talkin' about, strolled in bright and early this morning, tweaked as *all fuck*, falling all over herself with apologies, doing her best to impress on us just how very upset she was at the time she falsely reported to police officers she was in the middle of an attempted rape when her assailant became a killer and shot Khalon Stephens. She shared effusively how much she liked her neighbors. They were nice. The wife gave her Christmas cookies. The husband fixed her sink and switched out her smoke detectors when one started acting up. The kids were always nice and respectful."

The more Eddie said about how the Stephenses had looked after that woman, the more Dutch thought he was going to be sick.

"Instead," Eddie continued, "she shares she was having one helluva tiff with her boyfriend who'd found out she was sleepin' with some other guy. Stephens shows when this guy is in the throes of bein' seriously fuckin' pissed his piece is steppin' out on him, so much so, he's jackin' her up and brandishing a weapon. Since he is, as she put it, 'not himself,' he lost it when Stephens arrives. So Stephens takes a bullet."

"Holy shit," Dutch whispered.

"Yeah." Eddie did not whisper.

Georgie pressed closer.

He gave her his eyes.

When he did, she read them and hers got big.

"She gave us a name," Eddie carried on. "And incidentally, Hank and me are close when this is goin' down, but Hank's on the phone with Lee, talkin' about Lee and Indy lookin' after his and Roxie's kids so Roxie and him can hit Breckenridge to do some skiing, 'cause they got whacked with a huge early snowfall last night, and they're feelin' some slope time and then some alone time. I overhear Browbridge. Hank overhears her. Lee has already filled both of us in that he and his boys are on the job and they know where Carlyle Stephens is and what he saw. The detectives get a name. Unsurprisingly there's a mugshot. Hank texts that to Tack, and a judge is called out of his bed early on a Saturday morning for a warrant."

His heart racing, Dutch curled his hand around the back of Georgie's neck and brought her closer.

Eddie kept talking.

"Browbridge is now a font of information and can share where he is. And as such, James 'Jimmy D' Dooenck was picked up five minutes before I phoned you. He's been charged with murder. And as cooperative as she was, the minute the man was cuffed, she was charged with false reporting and accessory."

"Fucking A," Dutch pushed out.

"Chaos strikes again," Eddie said.

When he did, Dutch stared unseeing at Georgie.

"Now, as a cop, there is no way in fuck I'd advise a citizen to charge into an uncertain situation. As a man, and the man I am, I get it, and so does every cop I know. And I'll tell you what, this case has been stickin' in all of our throats. So you got our gratitude. And the officers on this case are gonna push hard neither of them get a deal. No matter that woman finally did the right thing, she's been lying for three months. And no matter what else they're involved in, and I suspect you know what I'm talkin' about with that too. But I'm gonna warn you, and I'll do it advising you warn Carlyle Stephens and his family, if they got good shit to stop bad shit floating around the streets of Denver, they'll probably both swing deals."

"Right," Dutch grunted.

"Good work, Dutch," Eddie said.

"Yeah."

"Later, man."

"Later."

Eddie disconnected.

Dutch dropped his phone hand.

"What?" Georgie asked.

"Jessica came clean. They picked up Khalon's killer this morning."

"*What?*" she cried, bouncing up to her knees, a smile spreading on her face.

Seeing that, he started grinning.

"How did that happen so fast?" she asked.

"I don't know. But I suspect it's about something Vance said to me."

"What's that?"

"Vance said people like this, the shit they're tied up in, don't like mess or distractions. She made a mess. Chaos picked up

Bronson and he probably reported that to his superiors. It's been a while since we've been in the game, but we've proved, repeatedly, we get the job done and we don't fuck around. Eddie said she came in and she was tweaked. So my guess, they served her up to serve up the killer, and in the meantime, they probably packed up that warehouse and are currently setting up in Pueblo or something."

"Well, whatever, has Carlyle confirmed this is the guy?"

Dutch nodded.

She threw herself at him to give him a hug.

He lifted and rolled as he returned it but did it so he ended it with him on her and Georgie on her back.

"This is amazing, Dutch," she said, beaming up at him.

"Yeah, it is."

"Does Carlyle know?"

She asked that as his phone rang.

Since it was still in his hand which was at the end of his arm that was around her, he pulled his arm from under her and looked at it.

It said Tack Calling.

"I'm about to find out."

He kissed her quick and took the call.

"Yo," he greeted.

"Yo, Dutch. Listen, Carlyle wants to see his mom and sister. If you want in on that, you best get your ass up here with them because Red and me don't think he should wait. I also wanna make sure all is copacetic before we expose him. So Chaos needs to roll out with an escort."

"I'm in. Does he know the guy's been arrested?"

"Eddie was talkin' to you while Hank was talkin' to me."

"How is he?"

A beat of silence then, "There's relief, brother. But with this obstacle out of the way, nothin' left to hold back grief. Get his mother here."

"On it," Dutch said.

"See you soon. Later."

They disconnected and he looked to his girl.

"We gotta go. Carlyle wants his mom and sister."

She shoved him off before he could roll off and he got a view of her ass as she scrambled out of bed while he pushed up on an elbow.

She did this bossing.

"This time, I'm on coffee and cat food. You in the bathroom first. I'll sort travel mugs. You just pour the coffee in while I get ready. Then we're outta here!"

The last two sentences were shouted from the hallway.

He only had a second to stare at the door.

But he took that second to let it settle in his woman was safe and happy.

And the man who took Khalon Stephens from this world was going to pay for it.

Then Dutch got out of bed.

* * * *

"They're right, Shizlayaya is the shizla."

Dutch looked from Georgiana—who, along with Carlyle's little sister, Christian, was trying on about seventeen pairs of Tyra's shoes—to Carlyle.

"Yup."

Carlyle turned into him, and the way he did, his back was to the room and Dutch was hidden.

"Man—" he started.

"You don't have to say it," Dutch told him quick and low.

Carlyle looked to his shoes.

Then back to Dutch. "You didn't mess around."

Dutch looked around him to Georgie, muttering, "I had help. A lot of it."

"Did they find yours? The guy that—"

Dutch again caught his gaze. "Yes."

Carlyle aimed his eyes over Dutch's head.

Dutch made a decision.

"Listen, Carlyle," the kid looked back to him, "I wish I could say this is closure and one step closer in a process to bein' able to lock up the feelings that grip you so fuckin' tight, you think they're gonna choke the life right outta you. But there is no process. This is just another day in a life without him."

Carlyle looked back to his shoes.

"You steer clear of your mother and sister because he saw

you?" Dutch asked.

"Yeah," Carlyle grunted.

"Okay then, that seals it."

Carlyle lifted his head. "Seals what?"

"He's not lost because you're here. You're gonna look after your mother and sister. You're gonna become the man he made you. Him. In his image. He carries on because he made a good kid who's gonna become a good man like he was."

"That's not enough." His face froze. He cleared his throat. And then he said, "I want him back."

Dutch clapped him on the shoulder and held on, tight.

"You don't get that, brother. But what you earned in this mess is me. I know how this feels. And when those feelings creep out of that box you put them in and grip you tight, you call me, and we'll figure out some way to get you past them."

Dutch dropped his hand.

And Carlyle asked, "Why you doin' this?"

"Because I'm the man my father made me."

It hit him then and Dutch didn't look away when the wet shone bright in his eyes. He kept hold on Carlyle's gaze when the first one silently fell. And the next. And the ones after.

They stood that way, Carlyle's back to the room, Dutch giving him his attention, until Carlyle sniffed. He lifted his hands and rubbed his face with the heels of his palms.

Then he took them away.

"I'da've liked to've known your dad," he said quietly.

"And I'd have liked to have known yours," Dutch replied.

"Carlyle, Georgie's gonna take me shopping!" Christian shouted.

Carlyle sniffed again, muttered, "Definitely the shizla," lifted his chin to Dutch and turned. "Girl, you don't need more shoes."

"A girl always needs more shoes," Christian retorted.

"This is the God's honest truth," Tyra decreed.

"Jesus," Tack grunted.

Georgie was smiling at Dutch, so as Carlyle headed his sister's way, he started hers.

He felt something and looked right, to see Tamira Stephens studying him.

Seeing that look on her face, a look that he'd seen carved into his mother's face way too many fucking times his entire life, he gave Carlyle's mom a tight smile.

She closed her eyes slowly.

Opened them.

And returned it.

* * * *

"I told you, a couple of days. I'm on vacation. Tomorrow's my man's day. It's brownie baking and snickerdoodle-rama Monday," Georgie said on the phone to Kraken as they made their way down the mountain.

It was early evening and they were headed home.

Georgie had been sharing they got the bad guy.

She was now listening.

Dutch kept driving.

She again started talking.

"I don't know what getting tased by Luke Stark buys you. I make a really good cheesecake with this kinda sour cream-like layer on the top. It doesn't sound good, but it cuts the sweet of the cheesecake *amazingly*." Pause then, "Listen, just come over for dinner."

Dutch choked on his own breath.

He felt her eyes on him when he did.

"We'll see. I'll talk to Dutch. Maybe Tuesday or Wednesday," she said. "I'll be in touch." Pause then, "Yeah. Yalola back at cha."

Out of the sides of his eyes, he saw her phone hand drop.

"Before you ask, 'yalola' means 'catch you later,' and I have no idea how that came about," she shared.

"Tell me you did not invite those two men to your place for dinner."

"They're harmless."

"They found, captured and tied up a six foot nine, three-hundred-pound seventeen-year-old."

"They live on the streets so they know how to get by on the streets," she returned. "But Kraken is a graffiti artist, and a really good one. Even at twenty years old, or maybe because he's that young, Banga is a master of spoken verse, and his poetry is honest and sometimes hard to take, but it's unbelievably good. They're

African American men who are members of yet another generation that has been let down by the system, so they don't acknowledge the system in any way. Even dedicated non-conformists would think, 'Yeesh, these two need to get a job.' But I hope they never do. Because Kraken might become the next Banksy. And there is no one like Banga. He's so committed to what he does and how he does it, I don't think he's ever written down a word of what he creates. But if someone listens, writes it down and shares it, I think his words could change the world. We might not understand everything they say when they come over for dinner, because they hate the system so much, they've made up a language so they don't have to speak white man's English. But they'll be a fun night in."

One thing to be said about that, he couldn't argue it.

"What article were you writing when you met them?" he asked.

"It was about disenfranchised minority youth," she told him. "That was a tough one. But I met those two through it, so it's one of my favorites."

"Hand," he ordered.

She gave it.

He threaded his fingers through hers and put them to his thigh.

Then he said, "Right, now it's time to share what went down with that Jackson fuck."

Her fingers spasmed in his.

"Dutch—"

"Babe, even if he was a total asshole, I'll only rough him up a little bit."

Another spasm and a horrified, "What?"

He started grinning.

She yanked her hand from his so she could swat his arm.

And then she caught his hand again when she was done.

"So?" he prompted.

"So…what?"

"What'd that Jackson fuck do?"

"Well, I will preface this by saying, I do not take any responsibility for him being a lech. However, I may not have played that as I should, and it was all your fault."

The fuck?

"*My* fault?"

"You're gorgeous and you had my cat and I wanted to get to

your house. So I started in asking him for information that we didn't get from Eddie and Hank without buttering him up. He gave a little, then said something total *eww* like 'you gotta pay to play' and grabbed my breast *right at the dinner table.* So I told him I didn't have to do anything of the sort, and if he didn't want me to punch him in the throat, he could slide out of the booth where he'd pinned me. I must have looked pretty ticked, because he didn't argue. He got out and I took off."

Dutch said nothing.

"So you see, it wasn't that bad. It was just gross."

Dutch still said nothing.

"Dutch."

"Maybe I'll rough him up a lot."

"Dutch!" she snapped.

"That's the kind of hardcore Chaos is too," he informed her.

"Ohmigod, I shouldn't have told you."

She was right.

She shouldn't have told him.

"Are you being serious right now?" she demanded.

"No, baby." He gave her fingers a squeeze while he totally lied, "I'd never do something like that."

"You're totally lying, aren't you?"

He decided not to field that one.

"Dutch!" she snapped.

"What would you do if some woman I didn't want to touch my junk, touched my junk?" he asked.

"I wouldn't rough her up," she answered.

"Babe," he said low.

He'd seen her go after her sister for doing a lot less just the day before.

So she couldn't stick with that.

And she didn't.

"Okay, if I witnessed it, I'd probably lose my mind and I would like to say I could hold my temper without it getting physical, but your junk is *your* junk and that is *so* not okay. But I'd also like to think that, given time, cooler heads would prevail."

"And?"

"And what?"

"And you know where to find this woman and you know what

she did. That'd be it?"

She was silent.

"Georgie."

She remained silent.

"Georgiana."

His girl did not lie.

So she burst out, "Okay, Dutch! My retaliation would be more cerebral and longer lasting, and there would be retaliation. But it wouldn't be *roughing her up*."

That was a good idea.

Retaliation that was more cerebral and longer lasting.

He'd have to think on that.

"Jackson's totally going to lose his job or similar soon, isn't he?" she inquired.

Dutch couldn't believe what he was hearing.

"You're gonna stick up for this guy?"

"No. A reporter is asking for information and you don't want to give it, just say no. So yeah, we were playing a game and I was giving him my time to get something in return, but that doesn't give him carte blanche to grab my breast. But this is cruddy. He's a jerk. We've had a really good day, finally, and we shouldn't be discussing jerks. And I don't want you to have to get involved."

Except that last part, he couldn't argue the rest, so he ignored the last part and just said, "Okay, darlin', we'll stop talking about him."

"Thanks," she rapped out. Then asked, "Are we gonna have sex tonight?"

"No."

"Are we gonna have sex tomorrow night?"

"Yes."

She huffed out air.

Then asked, "Am I gonna blow you tonight?"

"I don't know. I know I'm gonna eat you, and I'm not gonna do it sixty-nine. You're too good with your mouth. It'll fuck with my concentration when I'm goin' down on you. So after I make you go, if you're up to give some head, I'll be all in."

"Then we have a plan," she said curtly.

"Sounds like it," he said amusedly. "Though, we gotta get some food first. You wanna roll through a drive thru, order some Chinese, what?"

"We have more than half a pizza left, since we got busy last night and didn't eat it. We can have that."

He was disgusted.

And he sounded it when he asked, "Leftovers?"

"You don't like leftovers?"

"You eat leftover pizza for breakfast when you're hungover. You heat it and eat it for lunch when you're in a bind. You don't feed it to your woman on night three of the longest date in history."

She now sounded amused when she asked, "Are those hard and fast rules?"

"Emphatically."

Georgie busted out laughing.

He tucked her hand into the bend of his hip and smiled at the windshield thinking he really loved the sound of Georgie laughing.

"Chinese," she said when she was done.

"You got it, baby," he replied.

"Dutch?"

"Yeah?"

"You okay?"

He lifted her hand to his mouth, touched her fingers to his lips, then tucked it back in his hip.

"Yeah, Georgie."

"Okay."

They fell silent and neither broke it the rest of the way to his place.

He let them in and Murtagh came right to them and shared how he felt about being left alone all day.

In other words, the cat was ticked.

Dutch locked the door, but when he turned to shrug off his cut, Georgie was there, and she hadn't yet taken off her coat.

"Did you want to go out and get Chinese?" he asked.

She didn't answer.

She put her hand to his chest, but she did it watching her hand, not him.

She then traced her fingernail through the bottom, outside edge of his Chaos patch in a weird way like she was copying a line.

Still, he thought he read what she was doing so he assured quietly, "I'm past what you said about bikers too, Georgie."

She tipped her head back.

"Your dad made this scratch."

Dutch stilled, and asked, "What?"

"This scratch." She looked down and traced it again, then back to him. "It happened when your dad had this jacket."

He stared at her.

She gave him a small smile that was a little wobbly.

"I asked your mom about it the other night. I didn't think she'd remember it, seeing as it's a tiny little thing, and she probably wasn't even around when it happened. Maybe didn't even notice it. But she did. She said she couldn't share precisely how it happened, but it happened when your dad took it off and tossed it aside when, uh…you know, they were—".

"Yeah," he grunted.

"He saw it and he was upset that the patch was damaged. She checked it out and assured him it'd be okay. It was worse on the leather, but he buffed it out so it didn't look that bad and you can barely notice it, unless you're looking."

He'd noticed it.

But he'd been looking.

He didn't think to ask about it.

But Georgiana Traylor, Ace Reporter did.

And now he knew.

Now he knew.

He wore that cut every day, he wore his father *every day*, and now he knew what made part of that cut.

"Jag got his bike," he shared, his voice strange, hollow, far away.

"Yeah?" she asked, shifting closer, probably because of his voice.

"We had to pick between us, who got his cut, who got his bike. We couldn't. Hound helped us. We both wanted the cut."

"I can see that."

"But then, before Ma handed them over, she kissed Dad's bike with red lipstick. She told us she'd said goodbye and we could come get our dad's stuff. We went right over. We both saw that mark, like, at the exact same time. Like it spoke to us. I don't think either of us said anything for about five minutes. We didn't move. We couldn't tear our eyes off that kiss. Once we pulled our shit together, I swear to fuck, Jag protected that mark with everything that was him until he could get it sealed under a clearcoat. And when I got the cut, I felt kinda guilty I got it, since I knew Jag wanted it, and I had more of Dad than he did, even if it wasn't a lot. But when Ma did what she did, I wanted the bike because, with her mark on it, it was both of them. You know?"

She nodded. "Yeah. I know."

"I couldn't say anything. Talk about a switch. The decision had been made. But he's my little brother. He barely remembers him. I do. I have that. He doesn't. I feel that for him because Dad was such *a Dad.* I remember he'd make us peanut butter and chocolate chip pancakes every Sunday. I remember how long his legs seemed, like they went on for miles, when he lay in bed beside me, reading me a book before I went to sleep. I remember how he'd stare at Ma's legs when she walked around the kitchen in shorts with this smile on his mouth I didn't get, because I was a little kid, but it made me feel safe and it made me know how much he loved her. I have all that. Jag doesn't. And I feel that. I *feel* it. So I couldn't say anything."

"Yeah, honey," she said softly. "I totally get that."

"It's weird, a five-year-old remembering all that."

"Very fortunately, not many five-year-olds lose their dad at that age. But grief seals memories hermetically, I suspect, even for five-year-olds."

Dutch didn't suspect shit.

He knew she was right.

"She talked about him to you?" he asked.

Her expression grew concerned. "She doesn't with you?"

"We avoid it. Losing him broke her. Bad."

"You need to talk to her about him, honey. You need it. And she needs to give him to you."

"Yeah," he muttered.

She smiled, small and sweet, pushed up to kiss him under his jaw, then she whispered, "I'll order Chinese. What do you like?"

"Sesame chicken. Orange chicken. Kung pao chicken. Cashew chicken."

"So something chicken."

"And egg rolls and pot stickers. Fried, not steamed."

She smiled again and then…

Fuck…

She kissed his Chaos patch where the scratch was.

Then she turned and walked out, scooping up Murtagh along the way.

He wasn't thinking clearly, but still, he could swear that cat was looking over her shoulder at Dutch, his eyes screaming, "You! Come get me!"

So he was sorta smiling when he shrugged off his cut.

But he wasn't smiling when he ran the pad of his thumb over that scratch.

Now, in his way, he had them both too.

"Hope I did you proud today, Dad," he whispered.

Then he cleared his throat.

Turned.

And shouted into the living room. "If you pay for that on your credit card, no sex tomorrow night either!"

To which he got, "Dutch!"

So he entered his living room grinning.

Chapter Twelve

Cerebral and Long-Lasting

Dutch

Dutch did a double take when Georgie walked into his kitchen the next morning.

And that wasn't about the fact he left her in his bed and told her to keep her ass there, he was going to bring the coffee.

It was about the fact she was wearing glasses.

"You wear glasses?" he asked.

"Normally, I wear contacts." She fit herself front-to-front to his frame, arms curved around his waist, looked up at him and murmured, "We're having a lazy day so I'm not going to bother with them until you take me out to wine and dine me tonight, even though I'm *oh-so-totally* a sure thing."

He grinned down at her and slid a hand along her jaw into her hair.

"You're supposed to stay in bed," he reminded her.

"You were taking too long."

"Babe, I'm about to fill the cups. You had to wait two more minutes."

"Okay then, you don't want to know why I came out."

"Yes, I do."

"No, you don't."

"Georgie."

"Dutch."

They went into staredown.

His woman talked so he knew he'd win.

And he did.

"It's gushy, but," she pushed closer, "you were too far away."

He buried his hand in the back of her hair, the curls wrapping around his fingers like they were holding him there, and he dropped his face close to hers.

And then he said, "You are so fuckin' into me."

She rolled her eyes and replied, "Duh."

He bent further and kissed her.

When he broke it, he said, "You look cute in glasses."

"I have it on good authority I'm cute a lot of the time."

"Yeah? Whose authority is that?"

"He's a badass biker. You don't want to cross him."

Dutch was chuckling at the same time totally not caring if his caffeine fix came ten days from then, he liked Georgie in his kitchen, being cute, almost more than he liked her fifteen minutes ago, on her back, letting him eat her out.

Regrettably, on this thought, there was a knock on the door.

Georgie grabbed onto his biceps, crying, "Quick! Hide!"

"Babe," he replied, that word shaking because he was laughing.

He let her go.

She sighed.

He headed to the door.

Murtagh followed him.

He opened it to Carolyn.

He immediately started to close it making a mental note to get a goddamned peephole, even if he hadn't gotten one up until then because he didn't want it fucking with the look of his door.

She threw out a hand to catch it and begged, "Please, Dutch. I'm not here to cause problems. I'm here to talk to Georgie."

"That's not gonna happen," he informed her.

"Serious. I'm not gonna be a bitch. I promise."

She said this putting her other hand on the door, and all her weight into both.

"Stop pushing on the door, Carolyn."

Her gaze went beyond him, and she exclaimed, "Georgie! Please. I was out of line and I'm sorry. Totally. But I need to talk to you."

He felt Georgie's hand on the skin at the small of his back because he was again only in his sleep shorts before Georgiana said softly, "Dutch."

Fuck.

He opened the door.

Carolyn came in.

He shut the door, then moved to stand in front of Georgie so he was to the side, in order she could see her sister, but he was still out front.

And he started it by laying his one ground rule.

"Any shit comes outta your mouth to your sister that I do not like, I swear to fuck, Carolyn, I'll put you out."

She stared at him, a weird longing on her face that started to make him feel nauseous, until he got it.

It wasn't about him.

It was about what she lost in Jagger.

"Carolyn," Georgie called her attention.

Carolyn looked beyond him to her sister.

"I'm in a bind," she said.

Dutch crossed his arms on his chest.

"I get it," she continued. "It's not your problem. It's not anyone's problem. But mine. But I'm going to be evicted, like, tomorrow if I don't give them at least three months' rent."

She stopped talking and Georgie didn't start.

"Georgie," she pleaded.

"I want to help you," Georgie said in a quiet voice.

Shit.

She said she'd back down on her declaration and there it was.

"But I can't help you," Georgie went on.

Thank fuck.

She was standing strong.

Georgie kept going.

"Because if I give you money…and three months' rent, Carolyn, just saying, that will put *me* in a bind…still, I can't know you won't buy drugs with it."

"I need a roof over my head more than cocaine."

"You say that now—"

"It's not the problem you think it is."

"How am I supposed to trust that?"

"Because I'm telling you."

"Can you put yourself in my shoes with me having your history, and I was saying these things to you, would you risk your nest egg that isn't much, but it's at least a little peace of mind, on me?"

"What am I supposed to do?" Carolyn asked. "I can't live on the streets."

"Move in with Mother."

"She said no go."

"Move in with Dad."

"No way," Carolyn spat.

Since he knew where this was heading, Dutch had to intervene.

And he did it to say a warning, "Georgie."

Georgie was silent.

Carolyn looked between them, back and forth and again and again, fast.

Then her hands flew out and she cried, "You've known each other…what? *Days*? And you're picking him over me?"

"You can't live with me. I have a roommate," Georgie pointed out.

"She's not there. She's in Somalia or whatever."

"She's paying for that space and not for you to stay there."

"I cannot believe my ears," Carolyn spat, her tone and the twist in her face saying she was losing it.

And that shit was not happening again.

"Chill the fuck out," Dutch bit.

Carolyn glared at him then sucked in a breath.

When she got a lock on it, she said, "I'll sell some stuff. I have good stuff. Consignment won't take long. I'll take extra shifts. They're always asking for extra shifts and I get time and a half. It'll be a month. Most, two."

"No, Carolyn."

Carolyn tossed a hand Dutch's way. "Okay, seems like you're gonna be here most of the time, I can stay in your space."

"Carolyn, I cannot imagine how scary it would be to be evicted," Georgie began. "But if it's taken them three months to do it, you've had plenty of time to sort this out before the final hour. You have to have at least twenty, maybe it's even thirty thousand dollars of stuff in your closet. That's nearly two years' rent. This is not my problem. It isn't Mother's problem. It isn't Dad's. It's yours.

You're ticked at Dad he wouldn't give you money to overspend and whatnot. But I'd bet he'd give you a room in his house while you sorted out your life."

"Guilt money and he owes me and you too," Carolyn declared.

"I don't know how you figure that."

"He left us with *her*, that's how I figure *that*. Why do you think I bump?" she asked snidely. "I mean, Jesus, Georgie, we can't all be you. You never gave a shit about anything anyone thought. You just went along, being Georgie. Mom rides your ass to lose weight, you're like, 'Whatever,' and off you go to Bonnie Brae Ice Cream with your girl squad."

"She's ridiculous, Carolyn. She rode your ass about your weight too, and you've always been thin."

"Right, because I took diet pills, mainlined Red Bull, and when I could get my hands on it, snorted coke."

Dutch heard Georgie's hissed-in breath.

This right before she asked, "That's why you do coke?"

"I don't do it all the time because I can't afford it. But I'm not Mom. I don't have the will-power to starve myself my whole life so I don't commit the unforgivable sin of being over a size six."

"Yes, but you started hiding you were using," Georgie pointed out.

"Yeah, because you gave me so much shit about it," Carolyn shot back.

"Okay, but seriously. Nobody gives a crap about weight anymore," Georgie stated.

"*Wrong*, girl. *You* don't give a crap. Do you think I'd snag half the guys I snag if I let myself look like you?"

Dutch reentered the conversation.

"Yes."

Carolyn's body jerked and she looked at him.

"Some guys like thin girls. Some guys like curvy girls. Some guys like girls who don't give a fuck what anyone thinks, are smart, hilarious, gorgeous and have weird obsessions with their cats. Jagger wasn't into you because you're skinny. In fact, you're not his type for that reason. He was into you because you knew how to have fun. But the point is, mostly guys like girls who have it together and aren't headcases about stupid shit like that."

Carolyn said not a word, just stared at him.

So Dutch kept at it.

"But the bottom line in any scenario, if you're with anyone, man or woman, who your body size matters more than who the person you are is, it's you who should think they're not worth it and scrape them off," Dutch advised, and finished, "Including if that person's your mother."

Now Carolyn stared at him, her mouth hanging open.

They had a day, just them, if they could get shot of this woman, so Dutch moved to end it.

"Now you're blaming your mother. You're a grown-ass woman, Carolyn. Take some fuckin' responsibility. Call your father. Consign your shit. Stop doin' coke, for fuck's sake, to stay skinny. And introduce yourself to yourself. I've been around you a lot. All this shit aside, you're worth knowin'."

When Carolyn didn't reply, Georgie came to Dutch's side, leaned into it, he slid an arm around her shoulders, she slid both hers around his middle, and she said to her sister, "Talk to Dad. He's going to help. If he doesn't, you can't stay at my place. I won't give you any money. But I'll ask around. I'm pretty sure I can find you someplace to crash for a few weeks. But in that time, you have to unload some of your designer stuff and get yourself ahead."

"What'll I do with my furniture?" Carolyn asked.

"I don't know. I'll intervene with Dad. Maybe he can put it in his basement or something."

Carolyn shook her head, looked away.

When she looked back, she said, "I'll talk to Dad."

Thank Christ.

"I love you and I hate this is happening to you just as I'm glad it is because I want you to get beyond this," Georgie told her. "It worries me to death. Dad's freaked out. And Mother is Mother, but I bet she's freaked too. Enough. For you *and* for us."

Carolyn stared at her sister a beat, before she pushed out, "I've been a bitch."

"Stop bein' that, sort your shit, and it's all gonna be good," Dutch told her.

Her eyes hit him and lit.

"Do you think Jag—?"

He shook his head and ended that before she started it.

"You two are done. There's no goin' back. It's not about a

grudge. It's about trust. And shitting on family. You broke the first, and worse, committed the cardinal sin of doin' the last. He's gone for you."

"He's a good guy," Carolyn said softly.

"Yeah," Dutch agreed to the obvious.

"Like you," she murmured, pulled in another big breath, her eyes shifting between them again, before she settled on Georgie and something else hit her face, something he'd never seen.

But it was the something Georgiana knew was there, buried until then, but not gone.

Carolyn's life was in the toilet.

But she knew her sister was happy.

So she was happy for her sister.

Carolyn again spoke.

"I'll call Dad. I'll let you know if he's not being cool. Then I'll call you."

"Call me anytime, Caro, don't forget the part about me loving you. We'll do lunch or dinner, and for that, I'll buy."

One side of Carolyn's lips went up and she said, "You're such a bitch because you've always been so cool."

Hearing that, Dutch was about to lose it when Georgie replied, "You're such a bitch because you've always been such a free spirit. It's annoying."

"You're annoying."

"Your face is annoying."

"Your face is obsessed with a cat."

"Your face needs an ice cream sundae."

"Got that right, sister."

After Carolyn said that, they both started cackling.

Jesus Christ.

Were they serious?

"Come here," Georgie bid, breaking from Dutch to go to her sister.

They were serious.

They hugged.

And didn't let go.

He heard Georgie whisper, "Dad's gonna take you in."

"I know, but *bluh*, he watches so much football and Michelle fusses."

"She wants us to like her."

"She's been around two decades, we like her already, geez."

"Just be cool."

"*You* be cool."

"I'm always cool."

"Annoying."

Fortunately, this sister shit didn't go on a lot longer, and after Carolyn apologized again for the day before, and interrupting them that morning, Georgiana got her out the door.

And as Dutch watched this, he thanked fuck he had two brothers.

When Georgiana shut the door on her sister and turned to him, he asked, "You all right?"

She took one skipping-running step to him, another, then she body-slammed him and curved her arms around.

He did the same with his arms around her.

"She's gonna be okay," she said, smiling brightly up at him.

"Yeah," he murmured, taking that in, feeling it filling his chest, knowing that was all he needed to get through this day.

Hell, probably the next week.

"It's gonna suck for her huge, though, because Dad is the consummate NFL junkie and Michelle *totally* fusses."

"You're gorgeous, you know," he decreed.

She blinked, her chin jerking back, before she asked, "What?"

"You're gorgeous. Beautiful. Great face. Great hair. Great body. Perfect skin. You know that, don't you?"

She melted into him and said, "I feel I must inform you, Dutch Black, that although you have a body carved by God himself, so beautiful it makes me salivate, my down-with-the-patriarchy days, which, mind you, are not over, include me being *not* down with the patriarchy-led gazillion-dollar diet and workout industry. Which I will allow, some of them actually strive toward offering humans an avenue to a healthy lifestyle. But especially with the diet industry, it feeds on insecurity and the media's utterly impossible-to-achieve version of beauty, making fat white cats big bucks. So since I was about twelve, I considered my curves a badge of honor."

"Good."

"Though, it's sweet of you to say."

"Pointing out, God carved your body too."

Another blink and chin jerk and then a smile and a soft, "Yeah."

"Do you need coffee?"

"I'm only about to die without it."

Shit.

Georgie and her quick mouth.

Fuck, he dug this woman.

To share that, he brushed a kiss on her lips, let her go, and finally went and poured them both some joe.

* * * *

Dutch drove them home from the fancy-dinner part of their marathon date mildly pissed.

And since he was, he got into that.

"You did that on purpose."

"Mm," she hummed.

"Mm?" he asked.

"I *did* tell you," she reminded him.

"No man likes a tease."

She let out a giggle he'd never heard before, it was feminine and hot, and he became less mildly pissed and more just straight-up pissed.

"It's not about the tease," she educated. "It's delayed gratification which I'll remind you *again* was *your* idea."

"That right there," he stated. "Retaliation."

She said nothing.

He remembered their conversation of the night before.

"Cerebral and long-lasting," he grunted.

She giggled again and he got why he felt that in his dick.

Because it was the auditory sound of her got-your-cock look.

She slid a hand on his thigh, stopping way too close to his cock, and told him, "We're almost home. So your torture is almost over. And so is mine."

Torture was a good word for it.

Her.

In that red dress.

Short, mid-thigh, fitted skirt. Sleeves that came down to just under her elbow.

All that relatively modest.

It was the cleavage.

A scalloped, semi-wide v-line that went all the way down to her midriff.

You could see a lot full-on, but if you caught a view from the side.

Fuck.

Which meant her gorgeous tits had been in his face all night.

He didn't even taste his steak.

And if it wasn't for her dark hair tumbling down her back and all over her shoulders, lush with curls. The red lip she gave him that reminded him how those felt wrapped around his dick. Her heavily made-up eyes that made her look sultry—because it was the classy, glamorous kind, not the trashy, overdone kind—he wouldn't have looked at anything else.

And he barely thought of anything else but how many ways he was going to fuck her that night.

If asked, he would have called it that he would hook up with a woman in the life. Like Snap did with Rosalie. Rosie's dad was a biker, she knew their world and didn't want to leave it.

He did not suspect he'd find someone like Tack found with Tyra or Hop found with Lanie, or even Joke found with Carissa.

He got his own version of that.

Rosalie could get dolled up and it'd be hot, in an objective way from Dutch's point of view.

But she wouldn't be caught dead in a dress that hinted at professional, was demure in almost every way, but in truth, was designed to drive a man out of his mind.

"If *I* had to endure the torture *for days*, you can do it for one dinner," she declared.

"Babe, since we started to get busy, you've had five orgasms, sucked me off three times and got me off with a hand job. You've hardly gone wanting."

"Mm," she hummed again, squeezing his thigh.

He realized talking about this shit wasn't helping.

He caught her hand when it shifted dangerously, and when he did, she said, "You give good date, Dutch Black."

"I don't know how you can think that. You turned me into that loser who can't stop staring at a woman's tits."

"Honey."

At her tone, horrified and remorseful, he glanced at her.

Which instantly turned him the latter.

"Babe, it wasn't that bad," he somewhat lied.

"I think you need to know something," she told him.

"What?"

"That's the best date I've ever been on."

This, "What?" was surprised.

"You know, I've got a mirror, so I know conventionally, with the symmetry of my face and the thickness of my hair and whatnot, I'm considered attractive."

Suddenly, at her detached and impartial assessment of her own looks, he wanted to laugh.

He didn't and she kept going.

"That said, every girl who goes on a date with a guy she really, *really*," she squeezed his hand, "likes, wants that guy to stare at her through the date like he can barely control himself from pouncing on her. Not only is it sexy as hell, it feels unbelievably nice."

"Glad you enjoyed yourself," he muttered.

"Sorry you didn't," she said. "That sucks."

Well, shit.

"Georgiana."

"Yes?"

"I'll remember you sitting across from me in that red dress and how proud I felt that you were right there, with me, and you'd end the night in my bed and I'd end it in you, for the rest of my life."

"Dutch," she whispered.

"So don't listen to my bullshit. I'm just impatient to get you home."

"Then hurry," she urged.

He was not about to get in a wreck that would end a fantastic day in blood and trauma, so he did not hurry.

He didn't go slow either.

And outside Carolyn showing, and maybe even partially because of Carolyn showing and how that eased the mental load for Georgie, it had been a fantastic day.

They'd fooled around in bed all day, whispering to each other and dozing between times, getting out of it only to grab food and when it came time to get ready to go out to dinner.

Georgiana told him about her mother, who was definitely a *mother.* A woman who sounded dedicated to nothing but striving to mold her girls into physical perfection that would attract a man in a way he would not get shot of her.

Not surprisingly, that meant they had a strained relationship that included what amounted to duty visits and texts only, with the occasional dinner thrown in and the obligatory rotation of holidays between her and Georgie's dad.

Dutch told her how Hound was his dad without being his dad, this not about blood, but about not hooking up with his mom until a few years ago.

She told him she was uncertain about the crime beat, because it required a fair amount of aggression and legwork, and she wanted something that was more about face-to-face interaction and research.

He admitted working in the shop wasn't so bad, but there had been something about doing what he did for Carlyle that meant something to him and he'd have to think about that and what it meant because Chaos wasn't about that. Not anymore. Every brother either worked the shop or worked in the garage. But Dutch was not into builds, or cars, though he was into bikes but only in the sense of riding them and knowing what he had to know to keep his running.

They'd also had the necessary conversation about birth control.

She told him she was on the Pill, hadn't been "active" in a while, but she didn't take anyone ungloved when she was. And he shared he never went in ungloved. When she learned that, she told him when they got there that night, she wanted nothing in between.

That was the obvious choice for him too, but he pushed the discussion so he could make certain she was totally on board with that.

She was.

He still was uncertain.

Until she said, "It's a matter of trust, Dutch."

That said it all.

She trusted him.

He trusted her.

And that ended that particular discussion.

It was easy, their flow. Even when he got into the difficult shit, like where he was going in his life, it was effortless to give her that. Look in her eyes, their limbs entwined, no judgment, Georgie not jumping in to suggest shit or say things to make him process it when he wasn't ready.

So yeah.

It had been a fantastic day, discovering time with Georgie was that good when there wasn't drama swirling with Georgiana proving she wasn't only gorgeous, but good in a crisis, had a crazy-awesome head on her shoulders and a spectacular sense of humor.

And on these thoughts, it was not a surprise to him that he could no longer see her in that dress with her beside him in his truck, her coat on, but still, when he pulled in his drive beside her Subaru, he had his door open before he had the ignition shut off.

Georgie wasn't fucking around either. When he met her at the hood of his truck, she practically ran on her gold stilettos beside him, holding his hand, to get to his side door.

He knew Murtagh was well and truly his boy when the cat came to the doorway to the mudroom, let out a truncated, "Mur—?" but at one look at them, he turned around and moseyed off.

When their coats were on hooks and Georgie had thrown her gold bag to the counter, their knuckles slammed together as each sought the other's hand.

He shot her a grin.

She returned it.

He enfolded her fingers in his, and even if she was jogging behind him to keep up with his long strides, he did not adjust those strides as he pulled her to his bedroom.

No way he was having her fully for the first time without being able to see, so he wasted the time it took to hit the light.

When he turned to her, she had her hands at the back of her neck to undo her zipper.

"You take off that dress, you wait until tomorrow for my dick," he growled.

Her arms instantly dropped.

Yeah.

She knew when to give over.

And that scored right through his cock.

"Turn around," he ordered.

She didn't delay.

He moved in behind her and put his hands to her hips.

"Pull your hair aside," he demanded.

She didn't delay with that either.

He went in and kissed the exposed side of her neck.

Just with that, she shivered.

"Dutch."

His name trembled.

That went through his cock too.

All of it did.

Working the area under her ear with his lips, teeth and tongue, he took his time moving one hand up her back to the zip.

He also took his time sliding it down.

"*Dutch*."

That was a plea.

Inside her dress, he ran his hands up her skin on either side until he got to her shoulders.

He shoved the dress off and she instantly shimmied it down until it hit the floor.

Dutch turned her then and looked at her.

Open shoulders, gorgeous clavicle, ample tits, nipples aimed high, rounded belly, wide hips, shapely thighs, pretty ankles now with thin gold straps around them.

And little, black lace panties.

"Lose the panties," he instructed.

She didn't waste time shimmying those off too.

Trimmed, dark bush he'd already seen, and knew he loved, she'd left enough there it was all woman.

So he went there first, diving in, fingers slipping through her wet.

"You weren't the only one ready for it all through dinner," she whispered.

He stared into her eyes.

His Georgiana.

He slid his hand away, caught her by the waist, threw her on the bed…

And joined her there.

Dutch knew it'd go like it went. It was what he wanted for the both of them.

This being *wild*.

This bringing *fire.*

She almost tore his shirt getting it off him. He knew he lost a button or two.

In fact, she was so lost in it, one of his boots didn't hit the floor, it hit the wall, she threw it so hard.

It was a tussle, who could get the most the fastest in every way imaginable. Lips and tongues and teeth and hands and fingers and arms and legs, even toes.

And he knew when she was done, ready for it, also she wanted up top so she could see him as she took him.

But that shit was not happening.

And Dutch had no issue with using his superior strength to roll her to her back and power-twisting his hips until they fell between her legs.

"Dutch," she protested.

"Shut it," he replied.

"Dutch!" she snapped.

He caught her under her jaw, gentle but firm, and she stilled under him.

Then she started panting, the pink in her cheeks rising, as he shifted his hips to find her, both of them staring in each other's eyes.

"Dutch," she breathed, the word heavy with want, need, hope, yeah, Christ yeah, it was there.

Right there.

Love.

He didn't respond verbally, because he found her, pressed in with the tip, and she lifted her knees, pulling in the whole head.

"Baby," he murmured, because just that was beautiful.

She ran her hands up either side of his spine, then drifted her nails, feather light, down the length of it.

When she curled her arms around his back, pressed her thighs against his hips, slowly, he slid in to the root.

She released a *huh* of sweet breath, clutched his sides in two ways, and Dutch closed his eyes and dropped his forehead to hers.

He'd been right.

Heaven.

He opened his eyes and hers were right there, warm and tender and hot and sexy and open and giving and Georgie.

"It's done, you know that, yeah?" he asked quietly.

"Yeah."

"It's done, Georgie," he repeated.

"Yeah, honey," she replied.

He got that from her, so he kissed her and only then did he start moving.

The road to that point was a tussle.

The act was slow and deliberate, every stroke feeling like a minor miracle, but that wasn't who they were and that wasn't how it ended.

The same time Dutch needed more was the time Georgie caught his ass in her hands and they had to stop kissing because Georgie was gasping, Dutch was grunting, he went in hard, and she rocked with him, encouraging him to go at her harder.

He caught a fist full of her hair against the bed and she scraped her nails up his ass, his back, and then curled her arms so she could hold on to his shoulders, the better to take his fucking.

Phenomenally her pussy squeezed and released with each thrust, and he knew when she lost control of that, and the tips of the gold heels she still had on dug deep into the backs of his thighs, that she was gone before she cried out his name, then whimpered, arching her body, her neck…

And he held on long enough to watch that, file it away, then he let go and shoved his face in her neck, her perfume filling his nose, the rest of her controlling his senses.

He shut his eyes tight, his body tautened, he drove deep and shot hard.

His frame shuddered as he kept coming, and she finished hers and held on tight as he kept coming more.

He felt fluid when it was done and he settled into her, like he'd ooze all over her, when his orgasm let go of him.

And he nuzzled her neck with his nose, drifted a hand over the skin of her side, hip and thigh and held his weight in his other forearm for a long time after.

Finally, he lifted his head and knew by the soft, dazed, affectionate look on her face the answer before he asked, "Worth the wait?"

And Dutch started laughing, still buried to the hilt inside her when she answered…

"Totes."

* * * *

Dutch switched off the light to the bathroom as he entered the bedroom after he'd cleaned Georgiana up after their third go, and he saw her there, in his bed, on her belly, her hair everywhere, the sheet up, barely covering her ass where he'd tossed it after he'd taken care of her, and she looked asleep even though she was awake.

Hottest thing he'd ever seen, Georgie worn out after Dutch put a fair amount of effort into making her that way.

Murtagh was curled in at her waist.

Dutch turned his head and looked to the bottom of the wall under which his boot rested.

This meant he walked to the bed, knowing he was smirking,

He arranged her how he wanted her, their cat arranged himself how he wanted to be (tucked in at the bend of her body, since they were spooning) before he twisted and turned off the light.

He went back to Georgie, tugging her closer.

"Babe, you put a dent in the wall, throwing my boot," he said into her hair.

"Shut up, Dutch," she mumbled in reply.

He grinned in her hair.

She settled her ass further into his groin.

"Best quit doin' that, darlin', or you're gonna take my cock again," he warned.

"I cannot believe I'm going to say this, but you're a machine. I cannot take anymore. I need at least…" she gave it a beat, two, then decided, "half an hour to recover."

Dutch started chuckling.

"How many positions did you do me in that last time?" she asked.

"Just so you know, you wearin' that dress and dinner lasting two fucking hours because you were eating so goddamned slow, I had plenty of time to think about all the ways I wanted to fuck you."

"Did you have to do them all in one night?"

"Yeah. You complaining?"

"No."

"I didn't think so," he murmured.

"Do you want a rundown of my favorites?"

"Favorite what?"

"Positions?"

He was surprised she had favorites.

And intrigued.

"You got favorites?"

"Right now, at the top is you fucking me into the bed on my stomach, which, as you know, was the end of the last session. I will note, however, and importantly, that I reserve the right to change that opinion considering the list rearranges itself depending on how you're doing me."

He was chuckling again when he said, "So noted."

"Do you have favorites?"

"Drillin' into you leapfrog while I got two handfuls of your ass when you're down up front, but on your knees. Sittin' up with you bouncin' on my lap, your tits in my face. Watchin' you take it with your ankles on my shoulders. You on your side with your leg wrapped around my hip so I can get serious leverage and still look you in the eye. When—"

She cut him off to remark, "So essentially every way you fucked me is your favorite."

"Yup."

"Leapfrog?"

"Yup."

"There's an actual name for that position, or did you just make that up?"

"You told me today you like to do research, but now I see you clearly haven't been doing the right kind."

She started laughing softly, drowsily.

Dutch could stay up all night and banter with her about anything, especially fucking her, until she'd recovered enough for them to do it again.

But his girl was sleepy.

"Go to sleep, baby," he murmured, tucking her closer.

"Okay," she replied.

He felt her relax against him, her breath evening out, and that content sensation had started invading his chest, when she called, "Dutch?"

"Not goin' anywhere, Georgie."

"Thank you for picking me up at the airport."

He shoved his face in her curls.

So it was there he said, "You're welcome, gorgeous."

On that, she fell asleep.

Which tripped the switch that sat deep inside the man who was Dutch Black that he could do the same.

So he did.

Epilogue

Camellia

Dutch

"So what'd you decide?"

Dutch asked this question sitting on his ass on a folded-over throw, one of two Georgie had put in his truck for this purpose. A throw that was covering a layer of snow.

And he asked it with his eyes aimed at the weathered bottle of tequila that lay at the base of his father's gravestone.

That bottle was mostly full, and it had been there for years.

Dutch had no idea how it lasted that long without being nabbed by some vagrant or asshole kid.

Maybe it was the ghost of his dad that protected it, seeing as his mom put it there.

Maybe it was just obvious this was a biker's grave, it had the Chaos insignia etched into it, and the specter of their Club protected it.

Whatever reason, it hadn't moved for six years.

"Stanford," Carlyle said, sitting on a throw at his side. "It's closer to home than Massachusetts."

Dutch got that.

And Stanford was far from a bad choice.

"You come here a lot?" Carlyle asked.

"No. But often enough he knows I haven't forgotten him," Dutch answered.

Carlyle didn't say anything.

Dutch didn't fill the silence.

They both stared at the black marble tombstone.

Carlyle broke the silence and he did it using a voice so quiet, Dutch barely heard him.

Since Dutch was listening hard, though, he heard.

"Do you think he's around somehow to know?"

"Yeah," Dutch said.

Carlyle had nothing to say to that.

"Though, doesn't matter," Dutch went on. "I don't forget him. And I make a point to make sure he knows I don't forget him, if he's out there somewhere to see, or not. But the bottom line is, his son is a man who makes that effort. And he does because his father was a man who deserves it. And that's all that matters."

It took a few beats, then Carlyle muttered, "Yeah." He cleared his throat and said, "I haven't been back. To Dad's grave. Since the funeral. Mom and Christian go. I don't."

It was Dutch's turn to say nothing.

Carlyle was back to muttering when he said, "I should go."

"You should do what you feel is right for you. What I do is what I do. You'll figure out what you gotta do and it'll be right for you."

"I see it in my dreams," he blurted. "The hit. The blood. Him going down. The look on his face when I was pressin' on the wound, thinking I could stop the bleeding. Him sayin' in that raspy voice that wasn't how he normally talked, 'Get outta here, son.'"

Dutch said nothing. Didn't move.

His heart hurt, but he didn't move.

He stared at a grave and listened.

"But his last words were, 'Your momma…' then he was just gone." Carlyle whispered. "And it's whacked because I think there's something right about that. How I was there with him, but his last thoughts were of my mom. And I think what he was going to say was that he wanted me to take care of my mom."

With that, Dutch clapped him on the back, but that was all he did before he returned his wrist to his bent knee, murmured, "That is far from whacked," and went on listening.

"Mom knows I'm having bad dreams but I'm lying to her and tellin' her I'm not because I don't want her to worry," Carlyle shared.

"Stop doing that, Car," Dutch advised. "She needs you and you need her, and you all need to share this shit. Only balm she's got right now is you and your sister. She's got a piece of him right there through both of you. Trust me, that means everything. You gotta let her take care of you. It'll help her. Like it helps you to take care of her. I didn't know him, but 'spect your dad would want that. You all lookin' out for each other."

It took a beat, but then he said, "You're right. He'd want that."

"You tell her your dad's last words?"

It was forced when Carlyle said, "No."

"You need to find a time to do that, man. She should know."

"Yeah," Carlyle said low.

They were silent another while before Carlyle again cleared his throat and stated, "You know, we got friends. Family. But when I go off to college—"

Dutch didn't make him finish.

"I'll look after them."

He wasn't looking at the guy, but he still felt him relax.

"I think, uh…the first time I go, you know, if I, um, lose it or something, I should, uh…without them…"

He felt Carlyle's eyes, so he turned his head to look at him.

"Will you take me to his grave?" he asked.

"You wanna go now?" Dutch asked in return.

"Yeah, if you—"

Dutch pushed up to his feet, saying, "Let's go."

Carlyle pushed up too, but he did it with his eyes to Graham Black's grave. "Do you want a minute to say goodbye?"

Dutch looked down at the tombstone and said, "Later, Dad."

A burst of quick, deep laughter came from Carlyle and Dutch returned his attention to the kid.

"Just like that?" he asked.

"Sure," Dutch said. "My dad was a seriously laidback guy."

Carlyle was grinning as he bent to grab his throw.

Dutch nabbed his.

They were walking to Dutch's truck when Carlyle queried, "You think your dad would like me?"

He told him the truth.

"My dad liked everybody." Dutch lifted his hand and squeezed the back of Carlyle's neck and left it there before he finished, "But he'd *really* fuckin' like you."

Carlyle did the same to Dutch's neck and replied, "My dad

would dig you too."

They held on that way for a bit, until they both felt it was weird, then they let go and finished walking to the truck.

They got in.

And Dutch drove Carlyle to go visit his dad.

* * * *

"Babe," he growled into the phone.

And he'd become accustomed to the growling gig considering Georgiana was now a fixture in his life, and proof was that night they were celebrating their one-month anniversary, or what Georgiana had declared was their one-month anniversary. That being one month from when he picked her up from the airport.

She'd made them a reservation at the Palace Arms.

He'd set Tyra and Elvira on a mission.

Which was where he was heading to discover the results, with his phone to his ear, listening to his woman say shit that did not make him happy.

"Dutch," was her only response.

"I thought this decision was made," he said, and pointed out, "by *you.*"

"She's sold so much stuff, it's insane. I've seen the receipts. And she's working so many shifts, she's bleary-eyed. The only good part about that is she's not at Dad's much, because if she hears another football game droning in the background, she might bomb NFL headquarters. And if she wakes up to Michelle making her breakfast to order again, she might throw herself off a cliff."

"Dutch!"

He stopped on his way from the shop, across the forecourt, heading to Tyra's office at the garage, when he heard Rush's call.

He looked toward the Compound, saw Rush jogging his way, and jerked up his chin to the brother.

"And she's going to pay rent," Georgie finished in his ear.

"How 'bout you give her more time to prove herself," he suggested.

"Is this another conversation?" she asked.

And her tone was one he didn't like.

"What kind of conversation?" he asked back.

Rush stopped in front of him and Dutch gave him a one-minute finger.

"Maybe I made an assumption," she muttered.

"What assumption?" he pushed.

"I haven't left your house since I entered it, I mean, in that way. Half my clothes are at your place, you gave me three drawers, and you only have six. All my toiletries…"

Yup.

They were That Couple.

Met. Didn't hit it off with a bang. Hit it off with a bigger bang. Now inseparable.

He sensed his mother was moderately worried, though only moderately.

For his part, Dutch would probably tie Georgie to his bed if she tried to spend the night alone at her place.

"…I thought since I wasn't using it, and Carolyn's going to pay rent, since I was—"

"You're moved in, Georgie, maybe not officially, but only because we've been busy. Let Carolyn crash at your pad. We'll discuss how and when we'll make our sitch official when we have time."

She sounded dubious, and a little freaked, when she asked, "You sure?"

He gave Rush a look, and Rush turned his attention elsewhere as Dutch gave the man his shoulder and said, "This isn't about us. We're solid. You slept anywhere but beside me, even if we're fightin', I'd lose my mind. It's about her. She did my brother dirty. Fucked with your head. You might be there with her, but I'm not. Not yet. But it's not my pad. You're okay with it, then I'm okay with it. But the minute she jacks you over for rent, we'll have another discussion. Deal?"

"Yeah, Dutch."

"See you tonight?"

"Of course."

"Rush wants a word, I gotta go."

"All right. Later, honey. Love you."

Dutch stilled.

"Dutch?"

She was over it, she sounded casual now, calling out to him

because he hadn't said his final goodbye.

But she'd just told him she loved him.

He knew it was going there, for both of them.

Hell, he knew it was already there for him….and her.

But neither of them had said it.

"Later, baby. Love you too," he replied.

"Cute," she said and hung up.

He swallowed the lump in his throat and turned his attention to his brother.

"What's up?" he asked.

"You got a second?"

He had all of them that day that didn't involve time with Georgie.

He nodded.

"Right, well, I got a situation," Rush declared.

Dutch tensed. "What kind of situation?"

"The thing, with your boy, Carlyle…"

Dutch tensed even more.

"…it's made it clear the brothers are restless."

That wasn't what he expected.

"Sorry, Rush, don't get what you're sayin'," he told him when the man said no more.

Rush put his hands on his hips and stated, "Brother, we had decades where we were men with a mission. Now we got a few years under our belts where things are copacetic. Situation is, the men are not men who are good with managing an auto supply store and building rides for customers, the majority of whom are assholes who got money with the occasional joe who knows cool."

Dutch just stood there, staring at the president of his MC, knowing he had not once thought he might be the only brother in his Club who felt adrift.

But maybe he wasn't the only brother who felt adrift.

"They jumped in for you, for Carlyle, and I know that," Rush carried on. "But it was not lost on me they *jumped in.* Chompin' at the fuckin' bit to have something righteous to turn their minds to."

"I still don't get what you're sayin'," Dutch told him, though he thought he did.

He felt it in his gut.

A heat.

The good kind.

"Chaos needs a righteous cause and I have no idea what that is and how to give it to them, but I have a feeling you can help me," Rush replied.

"Fortunately, there are not many Carlyles in this world," Dutch pointed out.

"Yeah. So I suggest you and me go talk to Beck."

Dutch blinked in shock. "Say what?"

Beck was the president of Resurrection, another Denver area MC.

And Resurrection was to Chaos what Nightingale Investigations was to the Denver Police Department.

For the most part, the causes they took on were just, but their route to resolving them was seriously direct, nebulously legal, and in Resurrection's case, if need be, brutal.

"The brothers who want something to sink their teeth into, they'll get it. The brothers who want to kick back and enjoy life without that shit can do that," Rush told him.

"You know all the brothers will kick in," Dutch said.

Rush shrugged.

Then grinned.

After that, he got down to business.

"It's not once, but a number of times Beck has come to me to ask if we'd wade into shit they got goin' on."

"I know. You bring that to the table. And it's always voted down."

"We weren't ready. I think now we're ready."

After their own dance on the dark side, Resurrection had leapt so far to the good, they were on the other edge of the dark.

It was understandable. They had all, but mostly Beck, lost hold on their decency.

A man with something to prove was a man to keep an eye on.

A biker with something to prove was a man you didn't take your eyes from.

An entire fucking MC with that was a force of nature.

Chaos knew that all too well.

The last situation Rush had brought to the table from Resurrection had been about a woman whose husband had cleaned her out—every dime in their accounts, every stick of furniture—left her with a mortgage, a toddler, a baby in her belly, but not one thing else, and disappeared.

Dutch hadn't paid much attention, because he knew in the end how the vote would eventually go, but discussion had been intense around the Chaos table before that was voted down.

Though he had been one of three—him, Jagger and Hound—who had voted "in."

Word was, the guy was found.

And when Dutch heard, he'd thought distractedly, because it wasn't in his sphere, that he wished he knew how it did, and he wouldn't have minded being a part of that.

"We'd be assist," Rush said. "Not up to our necks, but enough to give the men something to feed that need. And I think you'd be a good go-between. Know what we'd want, bring it to the table, even know if Resurrection passes on somethin' we'd pick up."

"Rush, you were totally against this vigilante shit the entire time we were doin' this vigilante shit," Dutch reminded him.

"That was then, this is now, and this is entirely different."

"How do you reckon?"

"We'll have control of what we get involved in and we won't get involved in anything that will get our women kidnapped, for one."

There was that.

"For another, this won't be about attacks on the Club we gotta defend against. We won't be on our back foot. *Ever.* We can go in knowing what we're facing, discuss it and decide."

And there was that.

"And last, this isn't us going out and possibly buying trouble in an effort to keep our patch clean. Risks will be measured and discussed. And we can cut loose if shit goes somewhere we don't wanna follow."

And yeah, there was that.

Rush studied him acutely. "You're not into this idea."

"I'm one hundred percent into this idea."

And he was.

He was no cop and no private investigator.

What he was, was Graham Black and Shepherd Ironside's son.

And he'd been thinking it was either go to Jules and see if he could work with other kids on a volunteer basis or suck it up and enjoy building things with Georgie while he sold fan belts.

This was better.

Way fucking better.

"I'm glad you said that. Because what I haven't told you yet is that Lee has also been in touch. They got so much business, it's comin' out their ears. In that, there's a steady stream of people who need him, approach him, but when they find out his rates, they gotta take a hike because they cannot afford him. He told me he does a shit-ton of pro bono work, but he needs a good place to punt. What you did with Carlyle, he reached out and asked if we wanted to be a receiving team. I said I'd take it to the table."

Dutch was back to staring at his brother.

It didn't take long before he started smiling, slow.

It took even less time for Rush to return it.

And his was fast.

"I'll call a meet," Rush finished it.

"And I'll be there. But just sayin', I got as far as I got with Carlyle's case mostly because of Georgie."

"Is she going anywhere?" Rush asked.

"Fuck no," Dutch answered.

Rush smiled again and this one was bigger.

And Dutch returned it.

They clasped forearms, Rush turned and jogged back to the Compound, and Dutch finished making his way to Cherry's office.

He barely entered it when Elvira declared, "I love your girlfriend, and me gettin' to do this isn't the only reason why."

With that, she slapped a little black shopping bag against his chest that had white writing on it and a pretty flower stuck to it.

"Now, I gotta get back to the commandos," she said and walked right out.

Dutch looked to Cherry behind her desk.

"I think Georgie will really like them. But if she doesn't, she can take them back and get what she wants. Don't open the box and look, though, honey. They tie it up really pretty and she'll want to undo it," Tyra said.

He nodded and said, "Thanks."

"Anytime. *Seriously*," she replied.

He lifted his chin to her, walked out to the steps that led up to her office and looked into the bag.

At the bottom was a little black box tied up with white fabric ribbon and it had another of those flowers stuck on top.

Such total class, even if Georgie didn't dig what was inside, she'd like the packaging.

He'd stowed the bag and was back behind the counter of Ride, shooting the shit with Chill and a prospect they called Hugger (and they called him that because the dude hated to be touched) when his phone rang.

And he saw from what was on his screen, if it was what he thought it was, that day was going to be a very good day.

"Yo," he greeted Eddie.

"Thanks for the heads-up, man. Dropped a few lines in a few ears, people started opening their eyes and watchin', then a coupla supervisors called in a few female employees, and Jackson Stamper has been creepin' on them somethin' sick. They didn't want to say anything because they thought they were bein' too sensitive and it was only them he was gettin' too close to, pushin' for dates, and findin' ways to rub up against them that couldn't exactly be called sexual harassment, even when it totally was. He was let go this morning, and so they didn't do that ugly, he was warned not to ask for a reference, and told, in a nice government HR way, he could go fuck himself for severance."

All right then.

Dutch didn't know if that was cerebral.

But he hoped like fuck it'd be long-lasting.

"Right."

"We got any other issues we don't know about that you do that you can help us solve?" Eddie joked.

"Not right now," Dutch told him.

"You know my phone number when you do. Later, Dutch."

"Later, Eddie."

Dutch tucked his phone in his back pocket.

"Why you grinnin' like that?" Hugger asked.

The kid was surly. Big. Beefy. According to Carissa, he was "teddy-bear good-looking."

But he was a teddy bear to teddy bears like Chucky was to dolls.

None of the brothers knew what was under his skin.

Except maybe Rush.

Rush had put him forward and Rush read—and the man had done nothing since they took him on five months ago to contradict it—that the core of Hugger was decent, solid.

So he wasn't lovable.

Hound had hidden he was that for two decades.

Catch the man with his mother, or Wilder, for two seconds, you'd know where he was at.

"It's just a good day," Dutch answered.

"Yeah, I'd have a good day every day, I woke up next to your tail," Roscoe declared while strolling up to them, giving Dutch his usual shit about Georgie.

Dutch opened his mouth, but Hugger got there first.

"You wanna taste your gonads in your throat after I punch them up there, you keep talkin' 'bout his woman like that."

And there was the solid.

"Relax, mountain man, I'm just givin' him shit," Roscoe said good-naturedly, "mountain man" being what Roscoe called him since Hugger was blond, with a massive, bushy light-and-dark beard, like Grizzly Adams.

"Find somethin' else to give him shit about, leave his woman out of it," Hugger warned.

And Dutch had to hand it to the guy, he was prospect, and he didn't hide he wanted the patch and was willing to work for it, but he was not backing down from a patched-in brother.

Roscoe was assessing him, unoffended, but with interest.

Then Coe looked to Dutch. "You good?"

"Yup," Dutch answered.

"Excuse me, do you carry WD-40?" a woman asked.

They all looked to her.

She was pretty.

And she was stacked.

"Let me lead the way," Roscoe offered magnanimously.

They took off.

Dutch turned his attention to Hugger. "It's his way of tellin' me he digs I got a good woman, man. If he didn't like Georgie, he'd keep his trap shut on all accounts. So appreciate the backup, but you can chill."

Hugger looked him right in the eye.

"You don't talk about women like that."

And there it was.

What Rush read in Harlan "Hugger" McCain.

"You're heard," Dutch muttered.

Hugger grunted.

Chill gave Dutch a look.

Dutch shook his head.

And a man came up to the register with three five-quart jugs of motor oil, a gallon of wiper fluid and a spray bottle of Armor All, so Hugger went to the register to grunt his greeting, scan his shit with bad humor and grunt his "I'm done with you, get the fuck out of here."

All of this being precisely what Hugger did.

So the customer left, looking confused about why he'd just paid money to have someone be ambiguously rude to him.

And that meant that, after the doors swooshed closed behind him, Dutch started laughing.

* * * *

Dutch lay on his back, staring at his woman who was sitting on his still-hard cock.

Uncontrollably laughing.

He loved her laugh.

He loved she was doing it wearing nothing but the earrings in her ears that were interlocking CCs with dangly bits coming down that had little pearls on them. Earrings she'd barely looked at before she was pulling the ones she had in her ears out to switch them with the ones in box.

He loved that they'd had a great dinner where he got to stare at her looking gorgeous and happy while they cuddled together in one side of a booth, neither of them giving that first shit what anyone thought about them being that far into each other.

And he loved that he'd just watched her ride him until she came, then kept watching her ride him until he did.

What he didn't love was, after she gave them that, she'd leaned down while he was still thrusting the last jets into her, and said in his ear, "My new source in the DPD said Jackson got canned today for sexual harassment. You wouldn't have had anything to do with that, would you, honey?"

Which of course made him clamp her on either side of the head, force her to look at him, and the only thing he could manage in that moment was to force out, "Georgie, the fuck?"

Which took them to now.

Georgie having pushed up and she was sitting on his dick, busting a gut.

Her laughter dwindled and he waited until she was simply smiling down at him.

Hugely.

"You done?" he asked irritably.

Then it came over her.

With a new look on her face, she bent slightly toward him and ran her fingers along his cheekbone, down his jaw, along his throat, and ended this journey with her palm pressed over his heart.

He waited.

He waited for her to say what was shining in her face.

He waited for her to repeat what she'd said earlier that day.

So he could repeat it.

And they could stamp it clear, right there, in their bed, between them.

Forever.

And she did say it.

Absolutely.

She just didn't use the usual words.

Instead, she whispered…

"Cute."

And right on cue, after she said that, Murtagh jumped on the bed.

"*Mwrrrow*," he called his "are you done?"

Dutch framed Georgie's face in his hands, her hair pressed against his flesh, and he smiled up at his girl.

She smiled back.

And it was stamped clear, right there, in their bed.

Forever.

Georgie slid him out and then melted into his side.

Dutch wrapped an arm around her and reached the other out to their cat.

Murtagh settled in, ass to bed, body draped over Dutch's side, resting into his paws on Dutch's abs, Dutch scratching his booty, Georgie scratching his head.

And all was right in the world.

* * * *

Meanwhile

Meanwhile…
As Dutch slept with Murtagh on his pillow…

Georgiana slid carefully out of bed.

She went to the bathroom, grabbed her robe off the hook on the back of the door and shrugged it on.

She then moved out of the room and down the hall to the mudroom.

They'd had their minds on other things, so they'd put their anniversary gifts on the counter in the mudroom to deal with later.

She went to them now.

She ignored the Chanel bag that held the box and ribbon and camellia flower with her discarded pair of non-Chanel earrings.

And she threw open the top of the box that Dutch had opened at dinner.

What he'd discovered inside caused him to instigate a makeout session that she had to admit might have bordered on obscene.

But from where she was sitting, it was all kinds of awesome.

She nabbed what was inside and walked back to the bedroom.

She set it up on the nightstand on Dutch's side of the bed.

Then she went back to the bathroom, took off her robe, put on her nightie, and moved back to the bed.

She should have known.

She should have known she couldn't leave him without his knowing.

And he knew.

All of it.

He demonstrated this by gathering her in his arms, front-to-front, and murmuring, "You couldn't even wait the night."

"Is it okay?" she asked, a little worried.

He bent and kissed the tip of her nose in the dark.

"It's perfect, baby. Absolutely perfect."

She settled into him.

She then settled into sleep.

Eventually, he rolled to his belly like he always did.

And she woke enough to adjust to fitting herself to his back.

But this time, catching it in her periphery, she woke a little more.

And in the moonlight, on his nightstand, she saw the double frame.

The left side contained the picture of Graham Black tossing his beloved firstborn son up in the air, the toddler beaming down at him.

The right side held a photo of Shepherd Ironside and Dutch Black both leaning into beers over the bar in the Chaos Compound, their heads turned right, their eyes aimed at Georgiana, who stood at the end of the bar holding her phone trained on them.

Georgiana loved both those pictures, but she had to admit, she liked the one on the right the best.

Because Dutch had a particular look on his face in that photo.

And it was *beautiful*.

* * * *

Dutch

"Stupid snow," Georgie groused to the side window of his truck.

"Babe," he replied, amused.

"At this rate, I'm not gonna ride on the back of your bike with you for maybe, I don't know, *forever*."

He loved she wanted on the back of his bike.

He was not a fan of the fact it had been either cold, or snowing, since they met so he could not put her ass there.

Mostly, he loved how this had become an obsession of hers after he told her how his father had never put another woman's ass on his bike except his mother's.

Graham Black waited until he found the right one. And when he found her, she was the only one who rode there.

And Dutch could not tell Georgie he'd never had a woman on the back of his bike, because he did not know this story until after he'd done that.

But since he'd learned it, he'd ridden solo.

Though he told her, the minute that option was open, her ass was there.

And the obsession began.

Through these thoughts, he laughed then he said, "I think you're being dramatic."

"Whatever," she muttered.

"It's Christmas Eve. We're gonna have a white Christmas."

"*Whatever.*"

"And Wilder loves snow."

She made a *huh* noise.

She adored his baby brother.

So he knew that'd get her.

And it did, since she quit bitching.

Her adoration for his brother was further proved when he parked next to Jag's truck in his ma and Hound's driveway.

And she wasted no time grabbing one of the bags of their presents (they had three, two of them filled with shit for Wilder, and that was enough proof right there, but it didn't end there), this as well as the bag stacked with three tins of Christmas cookies she made.

And she hightailed her sweet ass to the front door.

It was open before they got there.

By Jag.

"Please, fuck, tell me you brought some of those butter cookies," he said as greeting.

"Jagger Black!" his mother could be heard shouting from inside. "Watch your mouth around your little brother."

Grinning unrepentantly, Jagger stepped aside to let them in, divesting Georgie of all she was carrying, even if she tried to protest. Though, one of the tins held her butter cookies, because she knew how much Jag liked them, and Jagger probably knew that.

Jag getting her hands free was a good call.

"*Georgie!*" Wilder squealed as he raced into the room.

He hit her so hard, if Dutch didn't put a hand to the small of her back, she'd have gone down.

"Yo, bro," she greeted, her hands smoothing back his messy dark blond hair.

He tipped his head back. "*It's Christmas Eve! Santa's coming!*"

"He sure is," Georgie agreed.

And he sure was, because there was another bag of presents,

not only for Wilder, in the truck. Presents Dutch had been forced to promise he wouldn't bring in that he was going to go back out and get when the time came.

Presents that were from "Santa."

He'd informed her the adults knew there was no Santa Claus.

She'd replied, "Santa only dies if you let him, and file this away, bad boy, I am *never, ever* gonna let Santa die."

Since she was so cute saying that, Dutch didn't push it any further, not even to tease her.

"C'mon." Wilder grunted as he pulled at her hand. "Daddy and me are wrappin' Momma's gift and you gotta help 'cause Daddy *sucks at it*."

"Boy," Hound warned from the mouth of the hall.

"You do. You suck at it, Daddy," Wilder declared.

"You're right, son, I do," Hound agreed. "I'm not talkin' about that. I'm talkin' about the words you're usin'."

"Well, how do you say someone sucks at something when they really, *really* suck at it?" Wilder demanded to know…loudly.

"If you two don't give me granddaughters…I…will lose…my effing…*mind*," Keely, standing in the door to the kitchen, declared Georgie and Dutch's way.

"Momma said *effing*!" Wilder screamed with glee.

His baby brother was his usual hilarious.

But Dutch was thrown.

It wasn't that Keely had not accepted Georgie. She had. From that first night.

It was that she'd been holding back.

Maybe because of how Carolyn did Jag dirty.

Maybe because she sensed Dutch was going through some shit.

Maybe it was just a Ma Thing.

But this was the first indication she'd given that she was all in.

"I hate to tell you this, Wilder, but I'm not too hot at wrapping presents either," Georgie admitted.

"I bet you're better at it than Daddy," Wilder shot back.

Probably couldn't argue that.

And Georgie didn't.

Giving Dutch a look, she let herself be led away.

And it was not lost on Dutch that Wilder, who used to worship him, hadn't even looked at him.

So she did that with Dutch saying, "I stole your cat, you stole my brother. This is not even."

Which made her smile.

Massive.

But it also made Wilder stop dead.

"Where's Murtagh?" he demanded.

"He's at home, little bro," Georgie told him.

Wilder finally looked to his oldest brother.

And he did that to order, "Go get him."

"We got enough going on without a cat in the mix," Hound declared.

Wilder looked up to his father. "But Daddy! Murtagh can't be alone on *Christmas*! He's *family*!"

Hound looked at his son.

Then at his other son.

That being Dutch.

And he did what he always did if it was within his power to do it.

He gave them what they wanted.

"You mind gettin' him, Dutch?" Hound asked.

Dutch dumped the bags he was carrying and said, "Be right back."

This bought him an even bigger smile from Georgiana before she took off to help his brother wrap a present, and Dutch took off to go get their boy.

It was much later, Wilder was finally down in a way he'd stay down (they hoped), and they were all sitting around, the men drinking whiskies, the women drinking wine, when Hound got up from the couch after a quick kiss for his wife, and loped off.

Dutch didn't think much of it, figuring he was going to the can.

Instead, he was thinking he was glad he and Georgie got the guest bedroom, which meant Jag had to take the couch, because Wilder would probably be up in about four hours, and the first person who would get his wakeup call would be the one who was on the couch.

He was also thinking that he felt no guilt about the fact Georgie wasn't super close to her family, so he and his family got her for

Christmas.

Sure, the next day, they were heading to her dad's house for a drink and to give him, Michelle and Carolyn some time, but Georgie promised that would last an hour, at most two (her mother was on a cruise, something she did every year—a rare bonus from that broad, who Dutch had now met twice, and he couldn't dilute it, she was such a haughty, disapproving bitch, this aimed at him, but mostly at Georgie, he detested her).

And Georgie had let Dutch promise Keely they'd be at her Christmas dinner table, so he knew she was serious about that.

These were his thoughts when he got early warning that Hound didn't hit the head when he came back too soon, and Dutch felt Georgie tense against him as he did.

Then Hound stood in his own living room carrying what looked like a very thick scrapbook for only a second before he announced, "It was Georgie's idea and I was down with helpin' her because what she said was right. This shit's gotta stop. If you're doin' it for me, or whatever reason you're doin' it, it's just gotta stop."

He then dropped the scrapbook on the coffee table with a loud *thud* and the nearly decimated plate of Georgiana's cookies jumped when he did.

So did everyone in the room, including Dutch.

"Now, me and Georgie are gonna hang out outside by the firepit and give you time. Take it," Hound finished.

Then he reached a hand Georgie's way.

Jag was staring at the scrapbook like it was going to form a mouth and bite him.

Dutch was staring at his mother.

She was glaring at Hound.

But before Georgie could catch Hound's hand, Keely snapped, "If that book is what I think it is, don't you take one single step out of this room, Hound Ironside." Her eyes swung to Georgie. "You either, Georgiana."

"Woman, this needs to be Black's," Hound returned.

Dutch felt his throat close and his arm around Georgie, who was nestled into him in a cuddle chair, tightened.

"Okay, it wasn't my place—" Georgie started.

"It is absolutely our place. And you were right, it's high time and was about twenty years ago," Keely decreed, reached for the book, opened it and lifted her gaze to Hound. "The brothers help with this?"

"Yeah," he grunted.

She looked down at the opened scrapbook.

And her face got soft.

"Seriously, your father was one good-lookin' man," she whispered.

Dutch's attention shot to Hound.

But he just said, "That brother got all the good pussy."

"He sure did," Keely agreed.

Georgie giggled, somewhat nervously, mostly with humor.

"Someone, kill me," Jagger said. "I mean it. Right now. Kill me dead."

"Shut up, Jagger, and come sit by your momma," Keely cooed, flipping through the pages.

"She's talkin' to me like I'm Wilder's age, so, seriously," Jag was staring at Dutch, "*kill me.*"

It was then it struck Dutch for the first time that his baby brother was at the age Dutch was when he'd lost his dad.

But Wilder was asleep in his bed, and outside in his living room was a mom and a dad, two brothers, a sister, a ridiculously social cat, and so many presents waiting for him to open up the next morning, it was more than a little insane.

And that was when it occurred to him that God took his dad away so they could have Hound, Wilder and all of this.

Dutch did not know if he'd trade it to have his dad back. He did not know, if his dad knew this was what would happen, if he'd welcome that blade at his throat to give them the precious things that would come to their lives after he was gone.

He just knew his father loved Keely, Dutch, Jagger, Hound, he'd adore Georgie because he'd know Dutch did, as well as Wilder.

So in the end, it didn't matter.

This was what they had.

And it was beautiful.

And Graham Black would think the same thing.

He pushed Georgie up in front of him then took her hand and guided her down on his lap as he sat beside his mother who had shifted to the middle of the couch.

She didn't stay seated for long.

Hound pulled her up, sat in her place, then yanked her down on his lap.

Jagger took the other side.

Keely got right down to it, flipping back to the front.

"Okay, this one, I can't believe it, who remembered this? It had to be Millie. Maybe Rush got it from Naomi, which makes this is the *only* thing I'd ever thank that woman for, but this is us at the first Chaos hog roast I attended. I met your dad that night."

On her words, Dutch zeroed in on the first picture in that scrapbook that was just a photo of the two of them standing together. His dad was smiling down at his mom, but in hearing what she said, he could see the flirty way she was standing, and the relaxed, confident line of his father's frame.

"I played hard-to-get for, oh, I don't know, all of about two seconds," she went on.

Dutch tore his eyes from the photo and looked across at Jagger to see Jagger already looking at him.

What he was feeling was in his brother's eyes.

They had something precious now, in that room, in that house…

And in a scrapbook.

Jag dipped his chin.

Dutch did the same.

"God, you look so much like him, honey. Every time I see it, I think it's so cool," Georgie breathed.

It was.

So cool.

His hold on her tightened.

Then he looked again at the book and Dutch settled back, leaning into Hound.

His woman settled, leaning into him.

And his mother kept talking.

He looked and listened.

When Hound came to them, *really* came to them, and made them a whole family again, Christmases got good again.

It wasn't that his mom didn't give good holiday, she did.

It was just that Hound made it a whole lot better.

When they got Wilder, especially when he got old enough to get into it, it got off-the-charts better.

But that Christmas…

Right there…

Before the actual day even got there…

It was the best Dutch could remember.

"Murtagh, don't eat that ribbon," Georgie ordered.

"Mwrr."

"Murtagh, don't make me come over there," Georgie snapped.

"*Mwrr!*" Murtagh fired back, then flounced away from the tree and jumped into Jag's lap.

"Yeah, it sucks, but we don't need that comin' out the other end, dude," Jag told him, curling him in his arms.

"Murr-ow," Murtagh replied.

Jag started stroking.

Murtagh started purring.

"Okay, this was the night Boz got so tossed, he challenged every brother to an arm wrestling contest," his mother said, and Dutch looked down to a photo of his father sitting in a chair, his mom draped over his back with both her arms around him, both of them looking at the same thing, laughing. "He lost. To everyone but Chew. We should have known about Chew right then, shouldn't we have, baby?" she asked Hound.

Hound grunted.

Keely turned a page.

* * * *

Meanwhile

Meanwhile…

Two weeks later, in a heat snap that was not unknown during Denver winters, the first time Dutch could take his Georgie on his bike…

Georgiana was surprised, when Dutch went for his wallet to pay, the big, frightening-looking barista said, "That's on me, brother."

They exchanged a look.

More surprising, Dutch didn't fight it and took his hand from his pocket.

Five minutes later, she took a sip of the best coffee she'd ever tasted.

Apparently, it was true what everyone said: the coffee at Fortnum's Used Books was the best in Denver.

Dutch got his and took her hand to walk her back into the stacks, but he exchanged another glance with the biker-looking guy who was behind the book desk.

She didn't ask.

If Dutch wanted her to know, he'd tell her.

Though, from what she could read, it seemed the thing that was being communicated was that something was all good.

Georgiana and Dutch spent the next two hours in the stacks, twenty minutes of it making their selections, the rest of it curled up together in a big chair in the way back, sipping coffee and reading.

They walked out to buy their books when Dutch heard Georgie's stomach growling.

He took her out to dinner and then he took her home and right to bed.

It would be the next day, Sunday, when Georgie won a round and talked Dutch into letting her be the one to get up and get them coffee.

And while it was brewing, she went and grabbed the books from the mudroom and stowed them on one of Dutch's many shelves.

By the picture of his dad.

She reached out a finger and touched the miniscule Chaos patch on the man's jacket.

Then she whispered, "Thank you."

After that, she poured herself and her man some coffee.

And went back to bed.

The End

* * * *

Also from 1001 Dark Nights and Kristen Ashley, discover Dream Bites Cookbook, Quiet Man, Rough Ride, Rock Chick Reawakening, Wild Wind, and Gossamer in the Darkness.

Discover More Kristen Ashley

Gossamer in the Darkness
A Fantasyland Novella
Coming April 19, 2022

Their engagement was set when they were children. Loren Copeland, the rich and handsome Marquess of Remington, would marry Maxine Dawes, the stunning daughter of the Count of Derryman. It's a power match. The perfect alliance for each house.

However, the Count has been keeping secret a childhood injury that means Maxine can never marry. He's done this as he searches for a miracle so this marriage can take place. He needs the influence such an alliance would give him, and he'll stop at nothing to have it.

The time has come. There could be no more excuses. No more delays. The marriage has to happen, or the contract will be broken.

When all seems lost, the Count finds his miracle: There's a parallel universe where his daughter has a twin. He must find her, bring her to his world and force her to make the Marquess fall in love with her.

And this, he does.

* * * *

Wild Wind
A Chaos Novella

When he was sixteen years old, Jagger Black laid eyes on the girl who was his. At a cemetery. During her mother's funeral.

For years, their lives cross, they feel the pull of their connection, but then they go their separate ways.

But when Jagger sees that girl chasing someone down the street, he doesn't think twice before he wades right in. And when he gets a full-on dose of the woman she's become, he knows he finally has to decide if he's all in or if it's time to cut her loose.

She's ready to be cut loose.

But Jagger is all in.

* * * *

Dream Bites Cookbook
Cooking with the Commandos
Short stories by Kristen Ashley
Recipes from Suzanne M. Johnson

See what's cooking!

You're invited to Denver and into the kitchens of Hawk Delgado's commandos: Daniel "Mag" Magnusson, Boone Sadler, Axl Pantera and Augustus "Auggie" Hero as they share with you some of the goodness they whip up for their women.

Not only will you get to spend time with the commandos, the Dream Team makes an appearance with their men, *and* there are a number of special guest stars. It doesn't end there, you'll also find some bonus recipes from a surprise source who doesn't like to be left out.

So strap in for a trip to Denver, a few short stories, some reminiscing and a lot of great food.

Welcome to Dream Bites, Cooking with the Commandos!

(Half of the proceeds of this cookbook go to the Rock Chick Nation Charities)

* * * *

Quiet Man
A Dream Man Novella

Charlotte "Lottie" McAlister is in the zone. She's ready to take on the next chapter of her life, and since she doesn't have a man, she'll do what she's done all along. She'll take care of business on her own. Even if that business means starting a family.

The problem is, Lottie has a stalker. The really bad kind. The kind that means she needs a bodyguard.

Enter Mo Morrison.

Enormous. Scary.

Quiet.

Mo doesn't say much, and Lottie's used to getting attention. And she wants Mo's attention. Badly.

But Mo has a strict rule. If he's guarding your body, that's all he's doing with it.

However, the longer Mo has to keep Lottie safe, the faster he falls for the beautiful blonde who has it so together, she might even be able to tackle the demons he's got in his head that just won't die.

But in the end, Lottie and Mo don't only have to find some way to keep hands off until the threat is over, they have to negotiate the overprotective Hot Bunch, Lottie's crazy stepdad, Tex, Mo's crew of frat-boy commandos, not to mention his nutty sisters.

All before Lottie finally gets her Dream Man.

And Mo can lay claim to his Dream Girl.

* * * *

Rough Ride

A Chaos Novella

Rosalie Holloway put it all on the line for the Chaos Motorcycle Club.

Informing to Chaos on their rival club—her man's club, Bounty—Rosalie knows the stakes. And she pays them when her man, who she was hoping to scare straight, finds out she's betrayed him and he delivers her to his brothers to mete out their form of justice.

But really, Rosie has long been denying that, as she drifted away from her Bounty, she's been falling in love with Everett "Snapper" Kavanagh, a Chaos brother. Snap is the biker-boy-next door with the snowy blue eyes, quiet confidence and sweet disposition who was supposed to keep her safe…and fell down on that job.

For Snapper, it's always been Rosalie, from the first time he saw her at the Chaos Compound. He's just been waiting for a clear shot. But he didn't want to get it after his Rosie was left bleeding, beat down and broken by Bounty on a cement warehouse floor.

With Rosalie a casualty of an ongoing war, Snapper has to guide her to trust him, take a shot with him, build a them…

And fold his woman firmly in the family that is Chaos.

* * * *

Rock Chick Reawakening
A Rock Chick Novella

From *New York Times* bestselling author, Kristen Ashley, comes the long-awaited story of Daisy and Marcus, *Rock Chick Reawakening*. A prequel to Kristen's *Rock Chick* series, *Rock Chick Reawakening* shares the tale of the devastating event that nearly broke Daisy, an event that set Marcus Sloane—one of Denver's most respected businessmen and one of the Denver underground's most feared crime bosses—into finally making his move to win the heart of the woman who stole his.

About Kristen Ashley

Kristen Ashley is the *New York Times* bestselling author of over seventy romance novels including the *Rock Chick*, *Colorado Mountain, Dream Man, Chaos, Unfinished Heroes, The 'Burg, Magdalene, Fantasyland, The Three*, *Ghost and Reincarnation, Moonlight and Motor Oil, Dream Team* and *Honey* series along with several standalone novels. She's a hybrid author, publishing titles both independently and traditionally, her books have been translated in fourteen languages and she's sold over three million books.

Kristen's novel, *Law Man*, won the *RT Book Reviews* Reviewer's Choice Award for best Romantic Suspense. Her independently published title *Hold On* was nominated for *RT Book Reviews* best Independent Contemporary Romance and her traditionally published title *Breathe* was nominated for best Contemporary Romance. Kristen's titles *Motorcycle Man*, *The Will*, *Ride Steady* (which won the Reader's Choice award from *Romance Reviews*) and *The Hookup* all made the final rounds for Goodreads Choice Awards in the Romance category.

Kristen, born in Gary and raised in Brownsburg, Indiana, was a fourth-generation graduate of Purdue University. Since, she has lived in Denver, the West Country of England, and now she resides in Phoenix. She worked as a charity executive for eighteen years prior to beginning her independent publishing career. She currently writes full-time.

Although romance is her genre, the prevailing themes running through all of Kristen's novels are friendship, family and a strong sisterhood. To this end, and as a way to thank her readers for their support, Kristen has created the Rock Chick Nation, a series of programs that are designed to give back to her readers and promote a strong female community.

The mission of the Rock Chick Nation is to live your best life, be true to your true self, recognize your beauty and take your sister's back whether they're friends and family or if they're thousands of miles away and you don't know who they are. The programs of the RC Nation include: Rock Chick Rendezvous, weekends Kristen organizes full of parties and get-togethers to bring the sisterhood together; Rock Chick Recharges, evenings Kristen arranges for women who have been nominated to receive a special night; and Rock Chick Rewards, an ongoing program that raises funds for nonprofit women's organizations Kristen's readers nominate. Kristen's Rock Chick Rewards have donated nearly $145,000 to charity and this number continues to rise.

You can read more about Kristen, her titles and the Rock Chick Nation at KristenAshley.net.

Also From Kristen Ashley

Rock Chick Series:
Rock Chick
Rock Chick Rescue
Rock Chick Redemption
Rock Chick Renegade
Rock Chick Revenge
Rock Chick Reckoning
Rock Chick Regret
Rock Chick Revolution
Rock Chick Reawakening, a 1001 Dark Nights Novella
Rock Chick Reborn

The 'Burg Series:
For You
At Peace
Golden Trail
Games of the Heart
The Promise
Hold On

The Chaos Series:
Own the Wind
Fire Inside
Ride Steady
Walk Through Fire
Rough Ride, a 1001 Dark Nights Novella
Wild Like the Wind
Free

The Colorado Mountain Series:
The Gamble
Sweet Dreams
Lady Luck
Breathe
Jagged

Kaleidoscope
Bounty

Dream Man Series:
Mystery Man
Wild Man
Law Man
Motorcycle Man

Dream Team Series:
Dream Maker
Dream Chaser

The Honey Series:
The Deep End
The Farthest Edge
The Greatest Risk

The Fantasyland Series:
Wildest Dreams
The Golden Dynasty
Fantastical
Broken Dove
Midnight Soul

The Magdalene Series:
The Will
Soaring
The Time in Between

The Mathilda Series:
Mathilda SuperWitch
Mathilda SuperWitch, The Rise of the Dark Lord

Moonlight and Motor Oil Series:
The Hookup
The Slow Burn

The Three Series:

Until the Sun Falls from the Sky
With Everything I Am
Wild and Free

The Unfinished Hero Series:

Knight
Creed
Raid
Deacon
Sebring

Other Titles by Kristen Ashley:

Complicated
Fairytale Come Alive
Heaven and Hell
Lacybourne Manor
Lucky Stars

Penmort Castle
Play It Safe
Sommersgate House
Three Wishes
Loose Ends, Vol. 1

Sign up for the 1001 Dark Nights Newsletter
and be entered to win a Tiffany Key necklace.

There's a contest every month!

Go to www.1001DarkNights.com to subscribe.

**As a bonus, all subscribers can download
FIVE FREE exclusive books!**

Discover 1001 Dark Nights Collection Eight

DRAGON REVEALED by Donna Grant
A Dragon Kings Novella

CAPTURED IN INK by Carrie Ann Ryan
A Montgomery Ink: Boulder Novella

SECURING JANE by Susan Stoker
A SEAL of Protection: Legacy Series Novella

WILD WIND by Kristen Ashley
A Chaos Novella

DARE TO TEASE by Carly Phillips
A Dare Nation Novella

VAMPIRE by Rebecca Zanetti
A Dark Protectors/Rebels Novella

MAFIA KING by Rachel Van Dyken
A Mafia Royals Novella

THE GRAVEDIGGER'S SON by Darynda Jones
A Charley Davidson Novella

FINALE by Skye Warren
A North Security Novella

MEMORIES OF YOU by J. Kenner
A Stark Securities Novella

SLAYED BY DARKNESS by Alexandra Ivy
A Guardians of Eternity Novella

TREASURED by Lexi Blake
A Masters and Mercenaries Novella

THE DAREDEVIL by Dylan Allen
A Rivers Wilde Novella

BOND OF DESTINY by Larissa Ione
A Demonica Novella

THE CLOSE-UP by Kennedy Ryan
A Hollywood Renaissance Novella

MORE THAN POSSESS YOU by Shayla Black
A More Than Words Novella

HAUNTED HOUSE by Heather Graham
A Krewe of Hunters Novella

MAN FOR ME by Laurelin Paige
A Man In Charge Novella

THE RHYTHM METHOD by Kylie Scott
A Stage Dive Novella

JONAH BENNETT by Tijan
A Bennett Mafia Novella

CHANGE WITH ME by Kristen Proby
A With Me In Seattle Novella

THE DARKEST DESTINY by Gena Showalter
A Lords of the Underworld Novella

Also from Blue Box Press

THE LAST TIARA by M.J. Rose

THE CROWN OF GILDED BONES by Jennifer L. Armentrout
A Blood and Ash Novel

THE MISSING SISTER by Lucinda Riley

THE END OF FOREVER by Steve Berry and M.J. Rose
A Cassiopeia Vitt Adventure

THE STEAL by C. W. Gortner and M.J. Rose

CHASING SERENITY by Kristen Ashley
A River Rain Novel

A SHADOW IN THE EMBER by Jennifer L. Armentrout
A Flesh and Fire Novel

Discover 1001 Dark Nights

COLLECTION ONE
FOREVER WICKED by Shayla Black ~ CRIMSON TWILIGHT by Heather Graham ~ CAPTURED IN SURRENDER by Liliana Hart ~ SILENT BITE: A SCANGUARDS WEDDING by Tina Folsom ~ DUNGEON GAMES by Lexi Blake ~ AZAGOTH by Larissa Ione ~ NEED YOU NOW by Lisa Renee Jones ~ SHOW ME, BABY by Cherise Sinclair~ ROPED IN by Lorelei James ~ TEMPTED BY MIDNIGHT by Lara Adrian ~ THE FLAME by Christopher Rice ~ CARESS OF DARKNESS by Julie Kenner

COLLECTION TWO
WICKED WOLF by Carrie Ann Ryan ~ WHEN IRISH EYES ARE HAUNTING by Heather Graham ~ EASY WITH YOU by Kristen Proby ~ MASTER OF FREEDOM by Cherise Sinclair ~ CARESS OF PLEASURE by Julie Kenner ~ ADORED by Lexi Blake ~ HADES by Larissa Ione ~ RAVAGED by Elisabeth Naughton ~ DREAM OF YOU by Jennifer L. Armentrout ~ STRIPPED DOWN by Lorelei James ~ RAGE/KILLIAN by Alexandra Ivy/Laura Wright ~ DRAGON KING by Donna Grant ~ PURE WICKED by Shayla Black ~ HARD AS STEEL by Laura Kaye ~ STROKE OF MIDNIGHT by Lara Adrian ~ ALL HALLOWS EVE by Heather Graham ~ KISS THE FLAME by Christopher Rice~ DARING HER LOVE by Melissa Foster ~ TEASED by Rebecca Zanetti ~ THE PROMISE OF SURRENDER by Liliana Hart

COLLECTION THREE
HIDDEN INK by Carrie Ann Ryan ~ BLOOD ON THE BAYOU by Heather Graham ~ SEARCHING FOR MINE by Jennifer Probst ~ DANCE OF DESIRE by Christopher Rice ~ ROUGH RHYTHM by Tessa Bailey ~ DEVOTED by Lexi Blake ~ Z by Larissa Ione ~ FALLING UNDER YOU by Laurelin Paige ~ EASY FOR KEEPS by Kristen Proby ~ UNCHAINED by Elisabeth Naughton ~ HARD TO SERVE by Laura Kaye ~ DRAGON FEVER by Donna Grant ~ KAYDEN/SIMON by Alexandra Ivy/Laura Wright ~ STRUNG UP by Lorelei James ~ MIDNIGHT UNTAMED by Lara Adrian ~ TRICKED by Rebecca Zanetti ~ DIRTY WICKED by Shayla Black

~ THE ONLY ONE by Lauren Blakely ~ SWEET SURRENDER by Liliana Hart

COLLECTION FOUR

ROCK CHICK REAWAKENING by Kristen Ashley ~ ADORING INK by Carrie Ann Ryan ~ SWEET RIVALRY by K. Bromberg ~ SHADE'S LADY by Joanna Wylde ~ RAZR by Larissa Ione ~ ARRANGED by Lexi Blake ~ TANGLED by Rebecca Zanetti ~ HOLD ME by J. Kenner ~ SOMEHOW, SOME WAY by Jennifer Probst ~ TOO CLOSE TO CALL by Tessa Bailey ~ HUNTED by Elisabeth Naughton ~ EYES ON YOU by Laura Kaye ~ BLADE by Alexandra Ivy/Laura Wright ~ DRAGON BURN by Donna Grant ~ TRIPPED OUT by Lorelei James ~ STUD FINDER by Lauren Blakely ~ MIDNIGHT UNLEASHED by Lara Adrian ~ HALLOW BE THE HAUNT by Heather Graham ~ DIRTY FILTHY FIX by Laurelin Paige ~ THE BED MATE by Kendall Ryan ~ NIGHT GAMES by CD Reiss ~ NO RESERVATIONS by Kristen Proby ~ DAWN OF SURRENDER by Liliana Hart

COLLECTION FIVE

BLAZE ERUPTING by Rebecca Zanetti ~ ROUGH RIDE by Kristen Ashley ~ HAWKYN by Larissa Ione ~ RIDE DIRTY by Laura Kaye ~ ROME'S CHANCE by Joanna Wylde ~ THE MARRIAGE ARRANGEMENT by Jennifer Probst ~ SURRENDER by Elisabeth Naughton ~ INKED NIGHTS by Carrie Ann Ryan ~ ENVY by Rachel Van Dyken ~ PROTECTED by Lexi Blake ~ THE PRINCE by Jennifer L. Armentrout ~ PLEASE ME by J. Kenner ~ WOUND TIGHT by Lorelei James ~ STRONG by Kylie Scott ~ DRAGON NIGHT by Donna Grant ~ TEMPTING BROOKE by Kristen Proby ~ HAUNTED BE THE HOLIDAYS by Heather Graham ~ CONTROL by K. Bromberg ~ HUNKY HEARTBREAKER by Kendall Ryan ~ THE DARKEST CAPTIVE by Gena Showalter

COLLECTION SIX

DRAGON CLAIMED by Donna Grant ~ ASHES TO INK by Carrie Ann Ryan ~ ENSNARED by Elisabeth Naughton ~ EVERMORE by Corinne Michaels ~ VENGEANCE by Rebecca Zanetti ~ ELI'S TRIUMPH by Joanna Wylde ~ CIPHER by Larissa

Ione ~ RESCUING MACIE by Susan Stoker ~ ENCHANTED by Lexi Blake ~ TAKE THE BRIDE by Carly Phillips ~ INDULGE ME by J. Kenner ~ THE KING by Jennifer L. Armentrout ~ QUIET MAN by Kristen Ashley ~ ABANDON by Rachel Van Dyken ~ THE OPEN DOOR by Laurelin Paige ~ CLOSER by Kylie Scott ~ SOMETHING JUST LIKE THIS by Jennifer Probst ~ BLOOD NIGHT by Heather Graham ~ TWIST OF FATE by Jill Shalvis ~ MORE THAN PLEASURE YOU by Shayla Black ~ WONDER WITH ME by Kristen Proby ~ THE DARKEST ASSASSIN by Gena Showalter

COLLECTION SEVEN

THE BISHOP by Skye Warren ~ TAKEN WITH YOU by Carrie Ann Ryan ~ DRAGON LOST by Donna Grant ~ SEXY LOVE by Carly Phillips ~ PROVOKE by Rachel Van Dyken ~ RAFE by Sawyer Bennett ~ THE NAUGHTY PRINCESS by Claire Contreras ~ THE GRAVEYARD SHIFT by Darynda Jones ~ CHARMED by Lexi Blake ~ SACRIFICE OF DARKNESS by Alexandra Ivy ~ THE QUEEN by Jen Armentrout ~ BEGIN AGAIN by Jennifer Probst ~ VIXEN by Rebecca Zanetti ~ SLASH by Laurelin Paige ~ THE DEAD HEAT OF SUMMER by Heather Graham ~ WILD FIRE by Kristen Ashley ~ MORE THAN PROTECT YOU by Shayla Black ~ LOVE SONG by Kylie Scott ~ CHERISH ME by J. Kenner ~ SHINE WITH ME by Kristen Proby

Discover Blue Box Press

TAME ME by J. Kenner ~ TEMPT ME by J. Kenner ~ DAMIEN by J. Kenner ~ TEASE ME by J. Kenner ~ REAPER by Larissa Ione ~ THE SURRENDER GATE by Christopher Rice ~ SERVICING THE TARGET by Cherise Sinclair ~ THE LAKE OF LEARNING by Steve Berry and M.J. Rose ~ THE MUSEUM OF MYSTERIES by Steve Berry and M.J. Rose ~ TEASE ME by J. Kenner ~ FROM BLOOD AND ASH by Jennifer L. Armentrout ~ QUEEN MOVE by Kennedy Ryan ~ THE HOUSE OF LONG AGO by Steve Berry and M.J. Rose ~ THE BUTTERFLY ROOM by Lucinda Riley ~ A KINGDOM OF FLESH AND FIRE by Jennifer L. Armentrout

On Behalf of 1001 Dark Nights,

Liz Berry, M.J. Rose, and Jillian Stein would like to thank ~

Steve Berry
Doug Scofield
Benjamin Stein
Kim Guidroz
Social Butterfly PR
Ashley Wells
Asha Hossain
Chris Graham
Chelle Olson
Kasi Alexander
Jessica Johns
Dylan Stockton
Kate Boggs
Richard Blake
and Simon Lipskar

Made in the USA
Las Vegas, NV
07 January 2022